TELL ME YOUR SECRET

DOROTHY KOOMSON

TELL ME YOUR SECRET

REVIEW

First published in 2019 by Headline Review
An imprint of HEADLINE PUBLISHING GROUP

2

Cataloguing in Publication Data is available from the British Library

Hardback ISBN 978 1 4722 6037 6
Trade paperback ISBN 978 1 4722 6038 3

Typeset in Times LT Std 11.25/15 pt by Jouve (UK), Milton Keynes

Printed and bound in Great Britain by Clays Ltd, Elcograf S.p.A.

Headline's policy is to use papers that are natural, renewable and recyclable
products and made from wood grown in well-managed forests and other
controlled sources. The logging and manufacturing processes are expected
to conform to the environmental regulations of the country of origin.

HEADLINE PUBLISHING GROUP
An Hachette UK Company
Carmelite House
50 Victoria Embankment
London EC4Y 0DZ

www.headline.co.uk
www.hachette.co.uk

For our Alex.
A dab hand with the Romulan Ale.
Miss you mate.

Prologue

'If you want to survive this weekend . . . there is only one thing you must do – keep your eyes closed . . . For forty-eight hours you must not open your eyes. If you do open your eyes, I will end you.

'No matter what you feel or hear, you must not open your eyes, not even for the briefest of seconds . . . If you do as I ask, I will release you and you can go back to your ordinary little life . . . It's really that simple. Do you understand?

'I'm going to take off this blindfold in a few moments, but before I do, nod if you understand . . . Come on, just a little nod to show you know what I'm talking about. A nod . . . That's it, that's right. Thank you. Now our weekend together can begin.'

Part 1

Pieta

Monday, 10 June

Keys, bag, coffee cup, tape recorder, notebook.

Pens. Mustn't forget the pens. I open my bag and peer inside. All present and correct.

Right, time to go.

Inhaler, car keys, memory stick, painkillers.

I open my bag for the third time. Definitely all there. I can go.

Purse? Security pass? Spare pair of armwarmers?

Gosh, I'm being slow today. I open my bag, *again*, and check everything is in there. Great. All there. Now it's time to go. Properly go.

At the front door, I turn to the woman and boy who have been standing in the corridor, waiting for me to leave. I grab my laptop in one hand and my reusable coffee cup and car keys with the other.

'Thanks so much for coming over early, Sazz,' I say to the childminder. 'I really couldn't have made this breakfast meeting without you.'

'No problem, Pi-R,' she says with a smile. She's known me many years and has shortened my name (Pieta Rawlings) like this pretty much since day one. She wraps a protective arm around my son and affectionately draws him to her. 'Me and the Kobster, we'll have a great time getting ready.'

No one else – not even his beloved grandparents – would get away with calling my boy that. Kobi is very serious about his name – except when it comes to Sazz (real name Sarah Sazzleoj). Sazz can pretty much do anything she likes without consequences. Me? I'm regularly treated to a combination of 'the look' and a tone of voice that scorches every letter as it leaves his mouth for the smallest of indiscretions.

I have to put down all the things in my hands to reach for my son. I wrap my arms around him, pull him close, kiss his head. I linger over our goodbyes, I always do. It'll only be a few hours till we see each other again, but I get so few of these moments with him in life, I want to enjoy and savour every second of every one.

'Have a good day. I love you,' I say. 'Eat your breakfast. Behave for Sazz.' I let go before he pushes me off and begin to gather my stuff up again. 'And enjoy yourself tonight with Miles and Austin.'

'It's Sam and Oscar, actually,' my son informs me.

'What?' I pause. 'It's Miles and Austin tonight. That's what you told me. That's what I wrote down, that's what's been arranged.'

My son shakes his head. 'Nope. Sam and Oscar.'

'But that means . . .' I plonk down my coffee cup, dump my keys, open up my light-red, suedette bag and start to fish around for my mobile. 'I'll have to message Karen to double-check she's let the school know that Sazz has to pick up Oscar and Sam. And then I'll have to text Allie to make sure she knows that it's not tonight . . . and I put rice for dinner beca—'

Sazz steps forward, picks up my coffee cup and keys, the latter jangling as she moves them across the gap between us. She forces them into my hands, then jams in my laptop bag, too. 'I'll sort it Pi-R. All of it. I'll call both sets of parents, let the school know, then pick them up and bring them home. No worries whatsoever.'

She's hustling me out of the door, trying to get rid of me because I'm stopping their fun. I'm never quite sure what they get up to when I'm not there, but they regularly make me feel like I am excess to requirements.

'OK, if you can't get hold of Allie, then call Mike,' I say. 'Baycroft, they're Baycroft.'

'Allie, then Mike, got it,' she says, still manoeuvring me towards the door.

'And it's Karen and Julian Newby for—'

'I know, I know,' she says with that big grin of hers. Her smile – open and friendly – was one of the first things I noticed about her. The second thing was that, out of all the nannies and childminders I'd interviewed (eight of them) she was the only one who asked to see the baby. 'I've dealt with them all before. I'll sort it.'

'Bye, Mum,' Kobi calls approvingly when Sazz reaches around me and opens the door.

'See you, Pi-R.'

'Oh, just one more thing—' I say.

'You have the best of days, OK?' she says. 'I'll be rooting for you.'

Involuntarily, I step backwards onto the path outside my house.

'Bye,' Kobi calls before the door is shut in my face.

'It's always lovely to know you're superfluous to your life,' I reply to my black front door. 'Always.'

7

Jody

Monday, 10 June

I'm not sure about other detectives, other officers, but this never ever feels real to me.

Not straight away, I mean.

Not until I actually see the person, and then it's brought into sharp relief, a big dose of reality forced into my face. But until then, when I am approaching a crime scene, when there are area cars and blue-and-white tape and uniforms, high-vis jackets and tents and people dressed in white overclothes, it all looks like something off the telly.

My heart feels like it is in my throat right now, but if you look close enough, you'll be able to see it hammering away in the middle of my chest, as though it's trying to escape. Because I know this is going to be number six. I desperately don't want her to be, I want her to be someone different, someone who isn't dead because of me.

I've been dropped off at a place called Preston Park in Brighton. When I'd asked for a PC to drive me there because I didn't really know Brighton beyond the seafront and the flat I'm staying in, I'd been expecting the same type of park as the one near where I live in London. Nice and green, trees, paths and benches, a slight incline here and there, but essentially you can see the other side wherever you stand. If a body had been found in that park, you'd have no trouble finding out where you needed to be. 'Which part of Preston Park?' the driver asked as we strapped ourselves in.

'No idea. The parkiest bit?' I replied.

'It's quite a big park, Inspector,' he stated.

'To be honest, it's seven thirty in the morning. I came in early to set up my incident room, I wasn't really expecting to be called out, I haven't got my bearings or anything. Can you take me there and we'll have to look for where the incident is.' That wasn't totally true. I *had* been expecting to be called out but at the same time, I had been hoping I was wrong about the pattern that had been playing out for the last seven months. I'd been rather successfully pretending to myself that I was wrong about what would happen on this particular day because it was the sixth Monday.

The officer who was driving me had kept his face neutral as he nodded in agreement. When we arrived at the park and I realised what he meant about it being 'quite big', I was impressed that he had managed to hide his irritation so well. To be fair, though, it didn't take that long to find the incident. He'd asked if I wanted him to wait for me, but I'd said no. I didn't know how long I would be there and I didn't want to keep him hanging around.

As I approach the garland of blue-and-white police tape that links the trees and protects the area from prying eyes, I realise I'm holding my breath because this has an added dimension.

It's not a simple case of the horror of finding a dead body, the confirmation that people can do terrible things to other people, this is a reminder, like I said to you before, that another woman is dead because of me; that this is all my fault.

Surprisingly, there are no media vans or cars, no reporters desperate for a story but I'm not sure if this has been called in yet. I know the last three – found in Queen's Park, Hollingbury Park and Hangleton Park – were reported as suspicious deaths, which kind of gave the impression that they had been deaths as the result of misadventure (i.e. drugs or drink or both). Very little information had been given out because very little had been known. It was only when I linked them with the ones in London that I was allowed to come to Brighton to assess the bodies, and was allowed to call them the work of a serial killer. More than three means the work of a serial, after all.

The press down here haven't caught on, yet.

'What have we got?' I ask the PC who stands guarding this outer part of the cordoned-off area.

She tips her head back slightly to look at me because her too-big helmet sits below her eyebrows. I should probably pull her up on that – remind her of the importance of looking neat, especially when you're out here where the public can see you. In the grand scheme of things, it isn't important, though.

'Ma'am?' she replies. What she means is, *Who are you?*

I flash my warrant card and say, 'I'm down from London on secondment.' *Kind of.* 'I received a call asking me to attend this scene.'

'Ma'am.'

'What have we got?' I repeat when it's obvious she's not intending to say anything else.

It's likely she won't know, which is why she isn't speaking, but

I want to give myself a moment before I find out if this one is one of *them*. If this one is body number six. She will be, they wouldn't have called me if she wasn't, but I can hope, can't I?

'Dog walker found her,' the officer says, realising that I want something, no matter how inane. 'Up near the centre.'

Never get a dog, my friend Sharon used to say. *You'll either get murdered while walking it or find a dead body.* It's quite disturbing how right she was. (I often wonder if that's why she named her dog Lucky.)

'I don't know much else,' she admits. She doesn't know much, I'd bet, because she is incurious. She won't have asked, she won't have looked, she will have been told to stand here and so she is going to stand here and do nothing beyond that. She's the perfect PC for this job, really, because no one – press or member of the public – will be able to pry, bribe or trick any information out of her. Hopefully the other officers stationed at different points will keep a better eye on who is watching us, who is taking a keen interest in what is going on, who is – potentially – the killer sticking around to watch his handiwork be uncovered.

I take another look around at the park, its shapes and nuances, its colours and its shades coming slowly alive, into fuller focus, as the light arrives with the continued rise of the sun. *What a place to meet your end*, I think. *What a place to have this happen to you.*

'Thank you,' I say to the PC, as I negotiate my way under the tape.

I hate this. I hate the 'off the telly' feeling, but the 'about to be real' moment really gets to me, churns me up like a plough through soil. It never gets easier, it only ever gets worse. Statistics tell me that someday, it'll be someone I know. Possibly someone I love. Someone I can't bear to be without.

I've been in Brighton three days. It's unusual for someone who doesn't know the terrain to be assigned as Senior Investigating Officer (SIO) on multiple murders, but after I'd linked the London and Brighton murders, after I campaigned hard at every level to not allow them to dismiss this as simply 'drug related', after I persuaded and cajoled, showing all the evidence I'd amassed on my own, I think they gave me the assignment just to get rid of me. I could not let this go. Could not let anyone else take charge of this. Not when I had been there at the very beginning.

I shake my head to stop that line of thought. I'm here now, I'm doing this. I will make things right.

The path has obviously been cleared from the outer cordon through to the tent where the body is. In other words, the ground had been searched for evidence before the small metal footplates had been laid down for us all to step on to get to the murder site.

'What have we got?' I ask the plain-clothes officer who is approaching me via the footplates with the speed of someone who is desperate to cut off an intruder into their realm, and certainly before I make it into the inner cordoned-off area.

'And you are?' he asks.

'Detective Inspector Jody Foster,' I say.

He double-takes either at my name or my position, or maybe both. 'Jody Foster?' he asks, questioning the name over the position.

'She spells her name differently and you need to get over it, really quickly,' I say. I pull out my warrant card and his back stiffens, his demeanour formalises. 'What have we got?'

My eyes focus on his face – jowly, sagging, sallow. He's done his time, but he isn't ready to wind things down yet. He is small, wiry, his hair white and black at the same time. I'm studying him because I do not want to look over at the people in white overalls, I do not want this to be real. If I focus on this man, maybe I can delay the inevitability of what is coming just that bit longer, so that when we reach the time when I have to look, maybe, just maybe, I'll be able to cope.

'Black woman. Mid-to-late thirties. They're guessing strangulation right now, but no one's hanging their career on that because the bruising hasn't appeared yet. Not sure if she's been sexually assaulted. Looking likely.'

'Any unusual marks?' I ask as casually as I can.

He nods. 'I'll say.'

My heartbeat quickens. It still might not be. It could be some other sicko. 'What is it?' I ask.

'It'll be easier if I show you,' he replies.

Easier for who? Not for me, certainly.

We cross the distance to the white forensics tent and I pull on the white overclothes, tuck my hair inside the hood, and then snap the face mask into place. Once I am suitably attired, we walk towards the inner cordon with him in front. I have to force myself to keep eyes forward, to not show any weakness or fear, to not give in to the little white creature of terror that sits hunched on my shoulder, dribbling its *'this is all your fault'* poison into my ear.

Will this one have been deliberately placed, like the others, laid face down, displayed so we'll instantly know? So I'll *instantly know.* It does feel personal. It feels like all of this is being done to get at me, to remind me how fallible I am.

13

The sergeant crouches down, and I watch his rubber-covered fingers reach for the edge of the sheet, slip it back over the shape of her body. He does this more respectfully than I've seen others in his position do.

Definitely placed; absolutely displayed.

And there it is. That mark, that brand.

Breathe, Jody. Breathe.

Pretend, Jody. Pretend.

You are a police officer. An inspector. You are hardened and wise, experienced and knowing. You do this day in, day out, you've seen so many bodies, so many permutations of people being dead that it doesn't touch the sides. It's the crime that bothers you, the audacity of those who think they can get away with it.

Come on, Jody, I cajole myself. *This shouldn't bother you. You shouldn't be standing here, hoping she was unconscious when it happened. No, when it was done to her. You shouldn't be allowing yourself to slip into the vortex by imagining the hell of the pain she went through first time around and then the terror she went through again right before the end.*

I stare at the woman, knowing she should be full of life.

She should be walking, running around, reclining on a sofa scrolling through her phone, running a bath, washing up, cleaning her toilet, or not tidying up her living room. She should be doing a million other inconsequential and more vitally important things than lying here.

Stop it, Jody. Stop this! I tell myself fiercely. *You can't be a SIO if you're going to do this, be like this. Focus, concentrate, be a police officer and take down the particulars of this scene.*

Around this woman's head is a blindfold. Silk, expensive,

stretched over her eyes and tied with a single knot at the back of her head.

Her body is doughy, like she didn't work out but kept herself slim. Her back is bare and the skin is a soft, chestnut brown that is blemish-free and clear down to where it disappears under the sheet. Her back. It was a perfect, untouched canvas. Until the weekend that changed her life. Until his calling card was cruelly pressed into her back.

I want to tear my eyes away. I want to stop imagining the agony, the fear, the horror. But I can't. *Won't.* This is part of the job. This is part of the process of stepping out of the surreal into the reality. This is my life.

And this is him.

What I am looking at right now is him.

The Blindfolder. This is all him.

Pieta

Monday, 10 June

Well, that was a bit of a disaster.

That could be me catastrophising – making something huge out of something not so huge – but it's put a dent in my morning, which will impact what time I can leave work. And that is a bit of a disaster as far as I'm concerned.

Lillian, my boss and the editor of *BN Sussex*, the weekly news and lifestyle magazine and part of the Brighton newspaper group I work for, has (probably unintentionally) stitched me up this morning.

I'd got Sazz over early so I could drive the twenty minutes out to Stanmer Park for the breakfast launch of a new beauty product that was going to revolutionise skin care and put Brighton on the map (I thought Brighton was already on the map but clearly, according to the press release, I was wrong).

I'd approached the stately home and noticed the lack of cars, the paucity of people milling around, and the absence of attendants with clipboards. The launch, as it turned out, had been cancelled at the end of last week and Lillian, who controlled all launches with the iron grip of a woman whose whole existence seemed to be one long stream of Fear of Missing Out, had neglected to tell me. I wasn't sure if she'd genuinely forgotten or had seized on another opportunity to bawl me out on a Monday morning.

It'd taken twenty minutes – *twenty* – to find someone who knew vaguely what planet we were living on and what day it was, to find someone *else* who could find out whether the launch was going to be later than billed or had been cancelled. The person who sent the press release and invite obviously didn't bother to answer their phone and there was no answer at the offices of the beauty company.

At one point, I'd stood in the plush café area of Stanmer Park House, and wondered if some elaborate joke was being played on me.

And now, the post-punchline punchline, is being stuck in traffic around Preston Park as I try to get back to work.

I stare powerlessly at the line of cars waiting to get around the park; they stretch out in front of me like multi-coloured beads on a necklace.

Preston Park is shaped like a segment of pie, with a little corner eaten out of the widest bit at the top. Earlier, when I'd driven past, there'd been something going on near that nibbled bit by Surrenden Avenue – I'd seen blue flashing lights, flickering like Christmas tree lights, and I thought . . . maybe a mugging? Car jacking? Actually, I hadn't even really thought that. I'd seen the lights, noted them, and driven on, keen to get to where I was meant to be.

Now it's impacting traffic, pushing all of us to a standstill, I'm paying more attention. Even from where I am, not quite at that bit of the pie, I can see the police cars are still there, but there are a few more of them now. Vans, too. There are more people as well – some in high-vis jackets, others in white jumpsuits, most of them congregated just out of sight. Police tape, which I didn't notice before, is wound around trees near the area, and flutters like bunting in the breeze.

This isn't a small crime, something that will barely make it on to the pages of our newspaper or will fill out a few lines on our website. This is something serious. Something big.

Every single one of my journalistic nerves has been stroked to attention. This is what I loved when I lived and worked in London. I used to thrive on getting the first hints of a story, would be gagging to be in the early scramble to gather as much information as possible; to be *RIGHT THERE* as the tale unfolded and I got to know the people involved and had the chance to relay their story.

That was also what made me a rubbish journalist in the end. I was always far more interested in the people behind the crime than the *actual* crime. I always focused on what the crime did to the victim's lives and the lives of those around them, instead of trying to explain how the crime was going to damage, shape or influence society. 'Society' being the lives of the readers, of course. Eventually, after one too many stories where I explained the victim's personal devastation, I was 'promoted' – to the editing department. In other words, I was taken away from the news and put somewhere I could inject the human element into the harder-edged stories, but wouldn't sully anything important with talk of emotions.

I watch another couple of people, I assume plain-clothes

police officers, head towards the line of tape, lift it to go under and then move towards the area that is just out of sight.

Murder. It'll be a murder, of course. A body found in Preston Park. Probably alone, definitely ended. My stomach falls away.

That could have been me. The thought bolts across my mind before I can stop it. *That could have been me being looked at, wondered about, examined for clues. That almost was me: a dead body left in a park, alone, ended.*

I hit the button on my car stereo to take it off mute and bring the music, summon the noise – something that will take my mind away from there.

The discordant, siren-like notes and the heavy beat of 'Opps' rise up from the speakers and instantly fill the car. *Don't go there,* I warn myself as the music starts to throb through me. *Just don't go there.*

I watch the police move around their cordoned-off area, observe members of the public pausing to see if they can get a glimpse of what is going on. Some have mobile phones up, others stand and stare. Everything is slowing down, winding down into slow motion. Slow-motion world, slow-motion life, slow-motion slide back into the past.

I am still here.

I am still here.

I am still here.

I am still here.

I remind myself of that all the time.

I am still here.

My fingers grope for the stereo knob and I turn it up, try to connect with the beat, try to hook myself into the present. These thoughts about what could have been, they lurk around my head, wanting to be thought through; desperate to be explored. And I need to stop it.

A person in a white jumpsuit moves back away from the site. He carries a camera, and he pauses at the top of the slight rise, lifts the camera to his face and starts to take pictures.

That was almost me.

I wrench the volume as high as I can get it. It's too loud, pounding at the nerves in my ears, smacking the cells in my brain, but fighting off the flashes of my memory, too.

That was almost me.

That was almost me.

That was almost me.

Jody

Monday, 10 June

Have you ever done anything really bad?

You, yes, you, reading this. I'm talking to you because there is no one else I can share stuff with. I'm not using you, I simply need someone to listen who won't go and blab and probably won't judge me as harshly as people in my real life.

Have you ever done anything really bad?

Not mean, or snarky, or even unpleasant, I mean, *really* heinous? The type of thing that you could technically be locked up for? I have.

Like most people, when I did it, I didn't actually realise how terrible it was. It was an act born of frustration and irritation and . . . oh, I don't know, of not wanting to be the responsible one for once in my life. And then . . . *argh*. I didn't know. I simply didn't know. I didn't realise I was going to end up here.

I'm standing in front of a large board of smiling faces. All of them have had their lives extinguished because of me. Because of this terrible, actually *evil* thing I did. I'm not trying to keep you in the dark, it's just really very difficult to talk about it. To even think about it.

This investigation has been given a room right at the back of Central Brighton Police Station. We've only got a room and not that many bodies because of budget cuts and because it started in London and the victims have, so far, it seems, been from London and brought down here after they were killed, so nobody's really sure when I'll be heading back there. Not any time soon, since this morning.

There are desks in here, telephones, computers, and at the end, a small glass-walled office for me. I've been SIO on murder investigations before, but never officially on a serial killer. And never on my own. There have always been people overseeing me. This is all a little irregular and I'm sure the usual Brighton CID/MIT (Murder Investigation Team) will have their noses put slightly out of joint. Officially, they are in charge of this investigation, unofficially, I am because of my connection to the London cases.

I'd wanted to get into the office earlier, to get the place properly straight, to pin up the pictures of the women we would be talking about, before everyone arrived. Unfortunately, the latest face for the board had changed that. Her photo will be magicked up from somewhere soon and tacked next to the others.

I stare at the photos of the other five again.

The five of them have been killed over the last seven months. One every sixth Monday.

They all look so real, so vital, so *alive*. It ignites a dull ache inside to see them. Seeing victims like this always does.

How can you not exist any more? I ask them as I stare at their photos.

Each of them has a smile, one that says she was part of the world. That she had a place, that she fit and that there is a shape missing from the world now that she is not there. Harlow Gravett: cute, bantu knots, liked to watch television and read books. She wrote real letters and drank tea made in one of the many teapots she collected. Shania Devenish: cropped, straightened hair, liked to dance. She loved clubbing and started her own dance troupe for the non-waif-like women she knew. Freya Occhino: cheek-length twists, was into cars. She was fixing up a classic Mini, replacing its worn parts piece by piece. She liked shoes, and owned so many they had their own wardrobe. Gisele Monte-Brown: long, long dreadlocks, loved the earth. She grew her own vegetables in her allotment, and herbs in her window boxes, she visited her family almost every weekend. Bess Straker: pretty, short, halo-like Afro, didn't do much. She went to work, she saw friends, she liked the odd cigarette and drink, but she did nothing remarkable.

I stare at their photos, their smiles, their eyes, their uniqueness that has been deliberately snuffed out. They weren't just killed in one go, either – from what I knew of what The Blindfolder did, these were the ones who'd survived their first encounter with him; who'd managed to do what he'd demanded of them and had got out of there alive. And after the devastation, after what he did, they rebuilt their lives. They managed to get themselves as close to whole as they could get. They got their smiles back, their lives back, their *themness* back . . . and then this happened.

I shouldn't look too long. Every time my eyes linger on them as they were, and my mind pauses on their stories, I well up, my heart starts to skydive through space, my hands tremble and quake, as I slide into becoming too involved.

I blink away the emotion that is clouding my mind. The irony, of course, is that most people think I don't care. I've heard the whispers, listened to me being described as a bit of a cold fish, an unemotional puppet; more barren than the Serengeti. And here I am, practically weeping for the cut-short lives of some women I didn't really know.

Get a grip, Jody, I tell myself harshly. *Get a grip on yourself. Falling apart, crying, showing any type of emotion to the rest of the relief won't help these women. It won't help to save all those others out there, either.*

I hear the muted, thick flumph of the door opening. *And so it begins*, I think as I blink faster, harder, trying to get rid of any residual vestige of my silliness.

I'm doing it for them: the vibrant women who are pictured up there on the boards, not the bodies found face down, with blindfolds tied around their faces and their backs bare to highlight their markings. I'm doing it for the women they were before, the people with the smiles, the outwardly happy eyes, who grinned at a camera, never dreaming of what could go wrong.

And I'm doing it for the others who are out there and need to be found and protected before the sixth Monday rolls around.

I'm doing it for her, too, the one I let down. The one who I should have tried so much harder to rescue.

Pieta

Monday, 10 June

The lift doors swish open on the tenth floor and I step out onto the floor of *BN Sussex*, the lifestyle magazine I work for, and I have to take a deep breath before I contemplate heading for the double glass doors into our office.

This building, in the redeveloped area behind Brighton train station, is swish and shiny; glass and steel and architectural excellence combined. It houses, on its top four floors, the biggest local newspaper network on the south coast. There've been rumblings, though, over the last couple of years, as profits have fallen and people have been getting their news from the internet, that we're going to have to move from this building. Probably to somewhere in the back of beyond where rents are cheaper.

BN Sussex (an 'interesting' pun that plays on saying Be iN Sussex as well as playing on the BN that prefixes Brighton postcodes) is a weekly magazine that comes inside *The New Sussex Times*. We are always, according to Lillian, under threat of closure. We don't pull in enough ad revenue, she tells us, we don't have enough of the major stories that will put us back on the media map in a significant way, we don't coast along enough (we do sometimes get the big stories) to be invisible to those in charge. At the Monday morning editorial meeting, we are all reminded how close to folding we are, how close to being 'out there' in the wilderness that is journalism with publications going under all around us as more and more people rely on social media and the web to keep up to date.

I'll have missed the Monday meeting now, which is not good for anyone. I take another deep breath, press my security card against the white security panel, wait for the beep and push open the doors.

The meeting is always held at this end of the office, nearest to the exit and, as I expected, it's over so everyone is on their feet, chairs in front of them, ready to wheel them back to their desks.

Lillian looks pointedly at the clock and then back at me with her perfectly shaped right eyebrow hoiked up into an arch of disdain. 'Nice of you to join us, *Pi-eta*,' Lillian says. (She often says my name wrong, not 'Peter' like the boy's name, when she's especially annoyed.)

'I had the launch for the new Sea Me, Sea You Beauties cosmetics line?' I reply. 'Over in Stanmer Park, remember?'

'That was cancelled last week,' Lillian snaps. 'They emailed and said someone had been called away suddenly so they were going to reschedule . . .' Lillian's voice peters out as she realises that she didn't pass on the message. And, not only that, she's obliquely admitted she didn't pass on the message – in front of others. In this situation, there's only one thing she can do – make it my fault.

'You should have called to let me know where you were going,' she says. 'I would have reminded you then it was cancelled.'

I smile at Lillian, raise my sustainable bamboo 'Mama Needs Coffee' cup to my mouth, slot my lips over the little oval hole in the lid and take a sip in lieu of a deep, irritated breath. *Kobi's school fees*, I think as I take another unwanted but necessary sip of coffee. *Eating. Electricity. Living in the warm. Running water. Clothes.* I think of these things and I sip my coffee.

Because I have silenced myself, Lillian sweeps her gaze around at the others who are still standing there in the meeting area. *What are you hanging around for?* she asks silently. *Don't you have work to do?*

The other members of staff scuttle away, wheeling their chairs and carrying their pens, pads and their flatplans of the magazine with them.

'My office, *now*,' Lillian says to me.

'Do you want me to come as well?' Tiffany asks. She's the senior features writer and columnist to my position as deputy editor.

'No, I need to talk to Pieta alone.'

In her glass-walled office, Lillian sits behind her desk, kicks off her spaghetti-thin heels and leans back in her chair. I sit on the edge of the seat of the left-hand chair on the other side of the desk. She doesn't speak for long seconds, instead she looks down her nose at me, appraising me, it seems, with her green-hazel eyes. It feels like she is trying to peel back the layers of who I appear to be in an attempt to find out who I truly am. Five years we've worked together and she has only recently started doing this. And it almost always precedes her saying one of two things.

Either it's: *'We need a win, Pieta'* coupled with a templing of her hands; or it's: 'What on *Earth* are you wearing?' Which is today's opening gambit.

I resist the – very strong – temptation to say 'clothes' and instead look down at myself. I've still got my red jacket on, and peeping out from its sleeves are the edges of my rainbow-striped armwarmers, the holes of which are hooked over my thumbs to keep them in place. I've also gone for a white top, navy-blue denim skirt and rainbow-striped leggings. I'm quite tame today.

'What do you mean?' I ask her.

'You look like you're auditioning to be on children's television! Do you really expect anyone to take you seriously dressed like that?'

I say nothing because Lillian will never comprehend how colour helps me get through the day. I may seem ridiculous, I may not dress my age, but without colour, everything would be a struggle. When I brought colour into my life in a significant way, everything became better. She won't understand that. And anyway, if I stay silent long enough, she will get to the point, eventually.

Predictably, she temples her hands and I notice her nails are manicured a dusky pink that matches her lipstick, just before she says: 'We need a win, Pieta. *You* need a big win, Pieta.'

I relax then. Now she's said it, I edge myself back in the seat and almost collapse against the back.

'I don't mind telling you that things are looking bleak for you at the moment,' she adds.

There are shelves lining the walls behind Lillian's desk, and these are the shelves where physical evidence of previous 'wins', past glories, are displayed. Gold statuettes, glass trophies, framed certificates. All of them denoting excellence and achievement, more than half of them displaying my name as the winner of said award, be it for beauty writing, political comment, or lifestyle insight. I am an award-winning journalist whose trophies reside in her editor's office because they are, as she says, the result of a team effort. 'Wins' always are. Losses, yeah, well they're all mine to carry alone.

Deborah used to be Lillian's deputy editor. And she used to be the person being treated like this. As the newspaper's, and therefore *BN Sussex*'s, fortunes took a dive, Deborah's life got worse and worse. She couldn't do anything right; everything she commissioned, wrote and edited was ripped apart at an almost microscopic level to find something wrong with it. Every. Single. Thing. We all saw, we all cringed, we some of us even tried to intervene. But when Deborah left, we all knew it could be any of us next. The art director, Jacob, didn't hang around to find out if he'd be next in the firing line: he decided to pursue his life-long dream of becoming a coffee shop owner and handed in his notice on Deborah's last day.

Lillian did well for almost nine months. The loss of two such senior people seemed to shock her back to her normal self. But then she decided someone in her office *was* to blame for the general state of the magazine industry. And that person turned out to be me, the idiot who'd accepted promotion to deputy editor.

'Do you want me to resign?' I ask Lillian.

Yes, I have a son, bills, responsibilities but this dance has got to its death throes now. We've been circling each other for months,

29

doing this dance where she becomes more and more intolerable. I need to kick-start this conversation and get it over with.

'What are you talking about?' she replies with utter disgust on her face and in her tone.

'You've been treating me as if I'm not good enough for months now, Lillian. I haven't had a "win" as you keep reminding me, but I wrote most of the stories in the last three issues. You said yourself at last Monday's editorial meeting that advertising around those stories went up significantly in those last six weeks, but you still act as if I'm not good enough, I'm not cutting it and I need to buck up my ideas. It's fine, I get it, you want rid of me. I'm costing you money, you can't really see the gains – despite me doing the best I can—'

'You are being ridiculous,' she says. Gaslighting. She is great at that. Gaslighting, rewriting history. 'Stop being ridiculous.' She sits forward in her seat. 'A big news story is about to break,' she continues as though I haven't broached the unspoken stand-off we've been having. 'It's a local woman – well, local as in she's from Sussex, and she is willing to sell her story to which-ever publication will give her the best deal.'

'Won't *BN Sussex* be up against the nationals?'

'She's from Sussex, so we have the home-field advantage. And she doesn't want to talk to the papers, she wants to talk to a news magazine so they can do a bigger story on her. So, yes, she will also be meeting journalists from the national newspaper mags, but, like I just said, home-field advantage.'

'She seems to have an unusual amount of say and control in this,' I reply. 'Doesn't that mean she has a huge story that we can't afford to pay the kind of cash the nationals will have?'

'For goodness' sake, Pieta, how many times do I have to say

"home-field advantage"? She has set her fee at a level that every-one can afford. She says it's not about the money, it's more about the story getting out there as soon as possible and protecting other women from what she went through.'

'Right. So who was she having an affair with?' I ask. This woman may not be charging the Earth for her story, but it will cost us thousands in solicitor fees getting it checked and checked and rechecked to remove any legally contentious material.

'No one,' Lillian states.

And anyway . . . 'Are you asking me to pitch for this?'

'Yes.'

'Really? Are you sure you want me?' I say. 'Wouldn't you pre-fer Tiffany to do it? You said it yourself that she's got a wonderful fresh new voice and she really speaks to the readers with her writing style. Wouldn't Tiffany be better for this story?'

In response, my boss's eyes bore into me like a drill pushing its determined way through concrete. Lillian doesn't like being reminded of the time she came to the pub and told all of us how wonderful Tiffany was and how inadequate the rest of us were. *You could learn a thing or two from her*, a drunk Lillian had told me. *She is so talented, the future of journalism, you just churn out stories.*

I return her gaze unabashed. It's not often I can look people in the eye, I often avoid eye contact as much as I can, but not today, not at this point. She can't have it both ways – either Tiffany is the second coming of journalism or I am good at my job.

'We both know that Tiffany is not up to this,' Lillian says quietly. 'She wouldn't even know where to begin with the inter-view, let alone with writing it up.'

'But I thought—'

'I know you don't just edit her work before it comes to me, I know you completely rewrite it,' Lillian hisses. 'We both know that Tiffany is not experienced enough for this.'

That cost her, admitting that. And that admission makes me sit up straighter in my seat. It wasn't a resounding 'you're amazing' but it wasn't 'get the girl half your age to teach you your job, you amateur', which is as close as Lillian gets to compliments these days.

'I'll come to the budget in a minute, but when you go in there, go in hard. Chuck as much value added as you can get. Offer her a serial if you think that will appeal to her. Let her know teaser pieces will appear in *The New Sussex Times* in the week leading up to publication, and they'll probably be picked up by the nationals, all the while keeping her exclusive with us. Look, suggest that if the story goes down well, you're willing to work with her on writing a book about her experiences.'

'Am I willing to do that?'

'We need this story, Pieta. If she could write it herself she would, so if she thinks she'll get someone to ghostwrite her life story and make money from a book, she might go for us over the nationals.'

'Right.'

'But we'll have to box clever. She'll be talking to lots of journalists, so even if we sign an exclusivity contract, we can't stop them talking about the story. You'll have to work fast. I've found the right photographer, who I said would go along to meet her with you. He seems to know what I'm looking for and so if she turns out to be large or ugly, he'll be able to tell me how we can improve on her looks.'

'I didn't hear you say that, Lillian,' I reply. In all my years of journalism, nothing has really changed. We still want the most hideous stories from the prettiest people – anyone else has to be camouflaged.

'I want this story, Pieta,' my boss says, ignoring me. 'I really want this story.'

'Yeah, I'm getting that,' I say. 'What is her story?'

Lillian actually shudders in response. 'It's horrible. Really nasty and scary. But the basics she's told anyone so far is that a few months ago, she was smoking outside a club when someone kidnapped her. She was taken somewhere and kept prisoner for two days – a weekend, it seems. That isn't even the worst part. She says that the man who kept her said that she wasn't allowed to open her eyes for the whole weekend. No matter what he did to her, she had to keep her eyes closed. And if she did open her eyes, he would kill her.'

Lillian is a blur. Before my eyes the image of her has disintegrated into fuzz, everything around me is opaque, the light merging with colours and shadows, the edges blunting themselves until everything is out of focus.

'She's convinced he's done it before, and had killed others. So basically, she's the living victim of a serial killer. I'm pretty sure the police are actively hunting him if she wants to tell all. And we have the chance to be right in the middle of it. That's why I want her story, Pieta.'

I have to keep my eyes open.

I can't let my eyes relax for even a second to blink.

I must not shut my eyes.

My eyes are open but he is here – creeping into the unexpected places.

I feel the cold, sharp point of the knife tracing a pattern over my skin, I have the weight of silk being removed from my face, I have the smell of him crawling up my nose, I have the echo of his voice thrumming through my nerves.

'If you want to survive this weekend, there is only one thing you must do – keep your eyes closed . . . If you do open your eyes, I will end you.'

Jody

Monday, 10 June

'For those of you who don't know, my name is Detective Inspector Jody Foster.' I wait for the titters, the amused looks, the frowns from those who think I'm taking the mick.

'As I say to everyone who hears my name, you're going to have to get over it. She had it first and mine's spelt with a y.'

There are twenty people in this room, some of them from regular CID, others who will be working with me just on this. I managed to get five people, full-time, a miracle by anyone's reckoning.

I have to get every single person in this room onside – and quickly. They don't know me, they don't know what I can do, who I am, or why I'm here. They only know that I'm in charge of this side investigation that everyone should be working on and that I'm not one of them. I'm a Londoner and I may well have Londoner airs and graces.

'Assistant Chief Constable Floyd couldn't be here to address you all as he was called away at the last minute.' I am stating his name and rank quite clearly so they know that I'm not just some-one who's decided it might be a bit of a laugh to play at running a serial killer investigation. I'm here because I know what I'm doing, and I know this man, The Blindfolder, better than anyone. 'If ACC Floyd was here, he would be telling you that I'm on secondment from London to oversee the running of this side investigation. That's not because Detective Chief Inspector Nugent and the other people in CID aren't capable or don't know what is going on, it's that I know this case better than anyone. I've been working on it for nearly thirteen years.'

That gets their attention, throws up frowns, sparks whispers amongst themselves. As far as they're aware, this has only been going on for seven months. Not years.

I move towards the clear board displaying the women's pictures. She's in the middle, simply because she was the middle one to be found, but it's good for me. Good for this bit.

'This is going to be a different type of investigation,' I state as I come to a standstill in front of the board. A lot of the information on it has been compiled by the CID people running this investigation. Late last night and this morning, I've added more. Things that I knew that they didn't, stuff we found out in the London operation, stuff I found out from when I first started looking into all of this. 'I'm going to be a part of all of it. I know it's really irritating when someone new comes in and thinks they know it all, won't leave you be to do your job, keeps asking annoying questions that they should know the answer to, but like the thing with my name, you're going to have to get over it.'

I reach up and tug down her picture. The smiling one. Not the other one. The other one can stay where it is.

'This investigation is personal.' I hold up her photo. She has her head to one side, and her eyes are sparkling as she grins out at us. 'This is Harlow Gravett. Take a really good look at her picture. I . . . I . . .' No! No! My voice is failing, cracking up, betraying me. 'This is personal,' I manage. *Do not do this to me*, I order myself. *If you want them to go above and beyond on this investigation, it has to be because they respect me, they understand where I'm coming from, not because they think I'm going to cry every two seconds.* 'Thirteen years ago, Harlow Gravett walked into a police station and told a young PC her story. It was such a fantastical story about being kidnapped for a weekend and not being allowed to open her eyes for forty-eight hours, that very few people believed her.

'She eventually gave a statement but declined a physical examination. She came to us even though she'd been warned by the man who hurt her that if she went to the police she would be murdered. On the fourth of February this year, Harlow Gravett was murdered and her body was dumped in an Islington Park in London.' I show her picture again. 'I was the PC who she told her story to. I was the one who told her that now she'd told everything to the police she would be OK, that nothing else would happen to her. I was the one who, it turns out, lied to her. This is very, *very* personal. Harlow, like the other women, trusted us to keep her safe. She trusted *me* to keep her safe and alive. I failed. I can't bring her back to life, but I can do my best to help you lot find him. Cos I know you can do that.'

That's better. I've hit that point, I can hear it in my voice that I'm in charge. It's clicked into reality, it's stopped feeling like I'm on the telly and none of this is real, I've landed at that moment where I can finally start being the person I pretend to be most of the time so I don't get found out.

'The files on this man and what he does are easily available, so I will only be telling you about this investigation and giving you a brief history of the case so far.'

I clear my throat. 'This man has killed five other women in the last seven months. He seems to be looking for his past victims. Since 12th November 2018, he has killed one every sixth Monday, and left their body in a park. Why parks? No one knows yet. Why every sixth Monday? No one knows that either.

'Originally, he was kidnapping women from the street. Usually nightclubs or late-night drinking bars, sometimes just from the street in dodgy areas where druggies and prostitutes hang out. Sometimes from areas which are quite busy and are considered "nice" and "safe". He was holding them for forty-eight hours and ordering them not to open their eyes otherwise they'd be killed. During that time he assaults and tortures them. He doesn't appear to be doing that this time around.

'Harlow was one of the few live victims we have on record who was still willing to talk about it years later.

'In 2007, a woman called Carrie Baxter walked into Lewisham Police Station to report that someone calling himself The Blindfolder had kidnapped her and held her for a weekend. Problem was, Carrie Baxter had a history of petty crimes to her name. She was examined and they found, apart from his last act of torture, there was no forensic evidence on her at all. I doubt anyone believed her and certainly no one gave her the impression they would properly investigate it or encouraged her to keep in touch. Ioana Halliday walked into Tottenham Court Road Police Station in early 2008 and told them a story that no one believed. Ioana was a known prostitute and drug user, again she was examined and apart from the way she had been scarred, no evidence was found. Again someone took her statement, but didn't chase it up nor try to link it to any previous crimes. If they had done, they would have matched her story to two other reports, and this man who calls himself The Blindfolder would probably have been identified as a serial all the way back when. In 2009 a prostitute called Tonya Runnde told a police officer in Ealing a fantastical story about being held for a weekend but, again, there were no DNA or forensic clues of any kind found on her.

'And again, this report wasn't taken seriously. Basically, we – the police – messed up on this case. We allowed the sketchy pasts of the victims, the places they were likely to be hanging out, to cloud how we policed this case. We're not going to let that happen this time. We are going to run down every lead, read statements again, treat *every* victim equally. It doesn't matter what they look like, what it says on their records, what they may have done in the past, we are going to treat every one of them as though they matter. Because they do.

'And the clock is *literally* ticking on this. We have a lot to do and we need to get a breakthrough before Monday 22nd July in six weeks.'

The soft fump of the door at the back of the room opening causes me to pause. The civilian receptionist who was sitting at the front desk earlier sticks her head around the door. She looks like someone who is used to smiling, but doesn't dare do it too much at work in case it's not appreciated. She nods her head and raises her eyebrows at me, a non-verbal way of telling me my visitor has arrived. I nod my understanding and gratitude.

'As I said, this is going to be a different type of investigation.

To that end, I haven't got a second in command as such. Detect-ive Sergeant Noi is officially going to be filling that role, but he will have other CID cases to work on and won't be here full time. One of you who *is* here full time will probably get that role as things progress. Having said that, when I'm not here, DS Noi will be just down the corridor so everything is to be officially fil-tered through him. He's up to speed on the case and he'll talk you through it when he arrives back from the current crime scene.'

An unsettled murmur goes up in the room. I'm surprised they don't know this.

'I assumed you knew. For those who didn't, another woman was found this morning. Same MO, same victim profile: blind-folded and then left in a park lying on her front. Preston Park it was. I had to come back to introduce myself to you all, but this is the sixth past victim of The Blindfolder who has been found on the sixth Monday. If I had a giant clock, I would set the timer for forty-two days' time so we never forget another woman is being lined up to be murdered. And that is assuming he sticks to his pattern and doesn't move things forward now he seems to have a taste for killing. You'll have to excuse me now, I have another problem I need to deal with.'

'What sort of problem?' a woman sitting near the front asks. Contempt. All I get from her is contempt. She doesn't like the idea that I'm going to be meddling in her stuff and wants me to know from the off how irritating it is to have someone do that. Clearly she's decided to ignore my advice about getting over it.

'They're dead, not much of a problem apart from the obvious,' she adds.

The way she says 'dead' spikes me at the centre of my being.

They were once alive. They are people, we shouldn't ever forget that. I do not like this woman, I decide. She has no respect for me, she has no interest in the victims, she is, basically, someone who is going to cause problems if I let her.

This is one of those situations where what I say, how I respond, will inform the way they think of me from now on. My reply will be the basis for the way they filter information to me, how they speak to me, draw me into their circle, shun me.

'What's your name?' I ask her.

'Karin Logan. Detective Constable.'

'And you do?'

'Mainly Disclosure,' she says. 'You know, I compile all the material we gather along the way that goes to defence as part of disclosure for trial,' she adds helpfully. She was trying to patronise me by explaining what she does but it's actually helpful because it shows that it's not just about me meddling, it's about her being ambitious and being pissed off that I am an inspector when she is a constable; I've got the job she clearly thinks she should have by now.

I'm not like the other people she's behaved like this to, though. I'm not going to shrink away and I'm not going to give her the satisfaction of seeming to add some validity to the 'aggressive black woman' stereotype. I've been here before – many times – and I know exactly what to do. I know how to put her in her place, make sure she only questions me when she has legitimate reasons, and also show everyone in this room who I really am.

I smile at her. 'Oh, that's fantastic, since you get to see everything, that means you are perfectly placed to do something else that needs sorting.'

She draws back, as does everyone else. They are already over-burdened, have far too much work to do, an overwhelming amount to cram in to the few hours of the day they are at work; the last thing they want is to have more stuff to fit in.

I widen my smile; I can look really sweet when I need to. Sweet, with a supersized side order of 'mess with me and you'll end up screwed'.

'You can coordinate the TIE . . . you know, the Trace/Interview/Eliminate and marry that with being a coordinating FLO, you know, being the coordinator for the Family Liaison Officers for the five – soon to be six – women. That'll work perfectly with the disclosure stuff. I've always thought one person should do these jobs, you know, straddle them all so we get a good coordinated effort and one person – apart from me – who sees everything.'

'I haven't had any FLO training,' she protests desperately, seeing all her time disappearing before her eyes. We've had strict instructions: there is no overtime, so there is only her own time. This will teach her – everyone – not to fuck with me.

'I'm sure you can learn on the job. I have utter faith in you, Karin Logan. Detective Constable. Utter faith.' Gently, I place Harlow's picture back on the board, give her a small smile. I turn back. 'I really do have to go and deal with this new problem now.' I search the faces for someone who can help me. One woman catches my eye. She has blonde hair cut into a shoulder-length bob, she keeps stealing glances at the board and biting her lip. I need someone like her.

'What's your name?' I ask, pointing at her.

She points to herself. I nod.

'Laura Whittaker,' she says.

'OK, Laura, come with me, you're going to help me with this problem.'

'I am?'

'You are.'

As we walk down the corridor to where my visitor is waiting, Laura says, 'At the risk of getting more work, what exactly is this problem?'

'You're not going to get any more work for asking a question, Laura. Karin Logan. Detective Constable. Was begging for more work, you could just tell.'

Laura smirks.

'You have to keep this to yourself for now,' I tell her. 'The latest victim of The Blindfolder has come to us for help again. She was taken and held about ten months ago, she reported it last September, just before he started killing his previous victims. She's here now to talk again.'

'I don't understand, how is that a problem?'

'It's how she wants that help that's the problem.'

Pieta

Friday, 24 April, 2009

'Why are you doing this, Jason?' I asked in a frustrated whisper.

It was late and I wasn't as drunk as I'd planned to be by that point of the night. I was working on *The Weekend View*, a newspaper magazine over in Tower Hill, and a few of us had been there late, putting the magazine to bed. Late night meant late drinks at a nightclub. Only Erena, the beauty editor, was dressed for a club (because that's how she always dressed) so she'd managed to talk us into the place. But I hadn't had a chance to drink much or dance much or even relax because Jason kept calling me. This was his sixth call in an hour. Sixth!

'It's like you can't let me go out and enjoy myself without you,' I continued in a whisper because I was standing right next to the smoking area and didn't want anyone to overhear. 'You're driving me crazy.'

'Mmmmphhhhh,' he replied. I couldn't hear him above the sound of people talking as they dragged on their cigarettes, and the waves of music flooding out of the propped-open doors. I stared longingly at those doors. Inside, in the darkened bar, I had a drink waiting for me, I had friends who were shouting at each other over the noise and others who were dancing. I had all the ingredients for a good time right there and Jason was stopping me from indulging in it.

I took my phone away from my ear and held it up towards the door of The Evangelicals for a few seconds, before returning it to my ear. 'Do you hear that?' I asked him. 'That is the sound of the good time I'm not having because I'm standing out here, talking to you.'

He said nothing. I waited for him to speak, but his silence continued; it was potent and uncomfortable, and it stretched and expanded so rapidly it threatened to dampen out even the noise spilling out from the club.

The worst part of all of this was that he wasn't even my boyfriend.

We'd met through work nearly a year ago. I'd been the stand-in magazine staffer on a shoot that the picture editor hadn't been able to attend. Jason owned the warehouse where we had set up. He'd made a beeline for me, I realised later, and proceeded to explain that he not only owned this warehouse, he ran a company that collated and managed photo-shoot and filming locations. I'd listened politely, and nodded just as politely when he declared: 'I live upstairs.'

When he'd then asked for my number, everyone in the room had stopped and stared at him. Embarrassed, he'd quickly mumbled something about wanting to forge better links with our magazine. When we'd eventually met for a drink, he'd made it clear that he only wanted casual sex. *Fine by me*, I thought. It wasn't as if I had any time away from work to start a relationship.

It wasn't like I'd had anything nearing a romance in over a year. It wasn't like he was hideous-looking and unpleasant. It wasn't like I didn't like sex and didn't miss it during fallow periods such as the one I was having.

Eight months later and I was being treated to this sort of behaviour.

'Look, Jason, I'm going to go. It's for the best,' I said when the silence felt like a muffler thrown over the night.

'I love you,' he said suddenly.

I heard that, all right. Above the din and my irritation, those words came through loud and clear.

No you don't, I wanted to scoff. Of course he didn't. How could he? We barely spent any time together before or after sex. If 'I love you' meant 'I like having sex with you' then yes, he did. If it meant anything else, then no, he most certainly didn't. I had to tell him that.

'Hold on,' I said. I couldn't tell him all these things with an audience and limited volume, so I walked away from the building, down the well-lit alleyway that led to the street. At the entrance to it, a thick, red rope was slung across and a doorman stood with his back to the alleyway to make sure no one tried to duck in that way.

'Excuse me,' I said to this solid form. Slowly, the doorman turned to look at me. Look down at me, actually, because he was huge. He was twice as tall as he was wide, and I gulped when I realised just how gigantic he was.

'If you leave you can't come back in,' he informed me.

I raised my hand, showed the angel stamped on the back.

He shrugged. 'That only applies if you leave through the front of the club.'

'How are they going to know if I left through the front or the back?' I replied.

He shrugged. 'Dunno.'

'OK,' I replied because I wasn't going to argue with someone who clearly was making things up as he went along. I looked at the phone in my hand – no, I didn't argue with them, I just slept with them, it seemed. 'Can I go out and I'll take my chances with trying to get in again?'

'It's your funeral,' he said as he unhooked the rope and stepped aside. I was surprised the ground didn't shake every time he moved.

As I stepped out onto the street, I looked right at the entrance to the club. *Great.* There was a queue of people waiting to come in now. Thankfully I'd taken my bag with me, because it was very likely I wouldn't get in again, whether the Goliath doorman was telling the truth or not. I returned my phone to my ear, now extra pissed off with Jason. Why the hell was he doing this? What did he think he'd gain by being like this? I began to walk towards the end of the road, in the opposite direction to the queue.

'What's this all about, Jason?' I said as I passed the shut-up shop fronts along that stretch of the road. 'Why are you saying things like that?'

'Because . . .' I could hear him now, and he sounded nervous, like he hadn't planned on saying what he'd said and was wondering if he could take it back. 'Because . . .'

'That's it? "Because"?'

'Pieta . . . This is really hard for me. I don't think you understand that. It's utterly confusing. I wasn't looking for anything like this at all. I thought we'd have fun, knock about together for a while. I didn't expect to want to be your boyfriend, for it to go further. To want to talk to you every minute of the day. I mean, jeez, I know how irritating it is that I call and text so much. I'm not stupid. I've had loads of women do it to me. I just never understood it until now.'

'But I'm not your type,' I said. 'You've all but said that a million times. We're only a good fit in bed.'

Silence was his reply. Blessed as he usually was with the gift of the gab, it was disconcerting. I turned back and looked at the queue to get into the club. It snaked back, almost to the corner of the road. There was no way I was getting back in there tonight – stamp or no stamp.

I rolled my eyes at myself. Why didn't I just ignore his calls? Why did I think, 'If I talk to him it'll make him go away'?

'All I know is that I love you,' Jason eventually said.

'OK,' I replied with a sigh shoring up the word. 'This probably isn't the conversation to have when I'm half cut and standing in the street getting colder by the second.' My jacket! Erena had convinced me to put it in the cloakroom. Great. I'd now have to queue to get it back. Thanks again, Jason. 'I'll call you tomorrow.'

'Will you? Will you really?' That was it. His neediness was the final straw. I had to finish this 'thing' for good.

'Actually, I'll come over,' I replied.

'What if I come to yours instead?' he replied. 'Save you the journey.'

There was no way he was coming to my flat. If he came to mine, he'd never leave if I dumped him. 'No, I've got some stuff to do first, so I'll come over afterwards, OK?'

'OK,' he said sulkily.

Yeah, that's going to endear you to me, I thought. 'Got to go, Jason. See you tomorrow.'

'See you tomorrow,' he grumbled.

I hung up and sighed, utterly frustrated.

I bashed my mobile gently on my forehead. *Stupid. Stupid. Stupid.*

I *knew* I shouldn't have got involved with him. It was there, in neon letters, when I was handing him my business card. *Don't do it, don't do it, don't do it*. And I'd ignored my instincts. Had instead—

A hand clamped around my mouth, an arm fastened around my waist. A sudden motion and I was jerked backwards off my feet.

Quick, sudden, unexpected.

I heard a crack as my mobile hit the pavement, and suddenly my heart was in my throat, the sound of my blood racing through my veins was rushing into my ears, my eyes were wide with shock.

No. No. This was not going to happen to me. This was not going to be it.

I screamed but it was swallowed by the hand around my mouth, the heart plugging up my throat.

Move. Struggle. Fight. Don't let this happen. Don't let this be it.

Another jerk, tightening around my body.

No, no, no, no! This wasn't going to happen. Not to me. Not to me. This wasn't going to happen. *Fight*. I knew how to fight. I knew how to—

The pain in my neck was sharp, precise, like a needle going in.

My head swirled, the world upended. I couldn't feel my body

any more, I couldn't move a single muscle. The world was floating and I—

Monday, 10 June

I make it to the toilets and throw myself into a cubicle. I think I'm going to be sick. I think all the breakfast I haven't eaten is about to come spewing out of me. Bent double over the white (thankfully clean) toilet bowl, I heave a few times, my body jerking uselessly to try to expel everything that isn't inside me.

Slowly, I stand upright and just as slowly run my hands over my head.

Lillian had wittered on, but she was a blur, her image fuzzy and ill-defined; her mouth a thin, dusky pink, curved line that moved together and apart; her voice a fog of sounds instead of words. I forced, cajoled, coerced myself to hold it together. Eventually she stopped talking and I got up, walked out of her office. I marched past all the desks in the office to the corridor outside and then had to run the last bit to make it.

I need music, I need something loud and distracting like earlier to bash this out of my head.

Mostly, I don't think about it. I don't dwell, don't wallow, don't even think about it as anything other than ancient, forgotten, buried history.

Mostly, I play loud music, wear bright colours, and pretend my life has always been about living in Brighton, being a mother, working on *BN Sussex* and generally travelling from today to tomorrow without troubling the universe too much.

Occasionally, I step outside of myself and I look for others like me – victims who survived too. I use my journalistic abilities and I research as much as I can, seeking and searching. In ten years, nothing. I'd heard other things, had seen the pictures of other women who'd been murdered and hurt and disappeared but nothing like the man I encountered.

Occasionally, I step outside of my fears and I try to remember anything that might tell me who he was. I will question myself: what did he smell like? What did he sound like? What did he feel like? What did he say? How did he say it? Why did he say it? In ten years, nothing new has come to me. I remember it all, but nothing new has surfaced in my mind.

Sometimes it hits me, what happened, and I all but collapse into myself as I have to ask myself again and again how I survived.

Friday, 24 April, 2009

My head. It was pounding, every part of it throbbing in an agony that was crushing my skull.

I groaned and that sound was like two cymbals crashing in my mind; the inside of my mouth was dry, almost cracked it was so parched but I couldn't produce enough saliva to begin to wet it.

What did I drink last night? And how did I get home? I asked myself, too scared to move in case it caused more pain. *What the hell did I do?*

'Ah, you're awake.'

The voice made me jump. It wasn't familiar and I didn't do one-night stands or falling asleep next to random men.

Panic rose through my body, dragging in its wake the violence of being grabbed. The hand over my mouth, the arm around my waist, the falling away of the pavement as I was lifted in the air, the smell of my fear, the pain in my neck before the blackness took over.

I couldn't move.

There was a heavy weight around both of my wrists, and my arms were above my head spread out and held. My ankles had a similar weight around them, and I couldn't move them either. And there was something on my face, soft but heavy, covering my eyes. I could barely feel it through the agony in my head, but it was there.

I couldn't move anyway, I realised. The weights were tying me down, but even without them, I couldn't move, couldn't use my body because I felt disconnected from it.

'The drugs haven't completely worn off yet, Pi-eta,' the voice said. 'When they do, you'll be able to move.'

The sound of my blood was rushing in my ears again, my breath kept catching in my chest.

'Don't be alarmed, Pi-eta.' The voice was low. Calm. Almost soothing. Almost. 'They call me The Blindfolder.'

That was why there was that weight on my face, a tightness around my head that I couldn't reach up and move away.

'We are going to spend the weekend together, Pi-eta. For the next forty-eight hours, we are going to get to know each other very well.'

I gasped as the tingling started in my legs.

'Ah, there, you see, the feeling is coming back, like I promised it would.'

The prickling sensation began in my arms, too, tiny sparkles as the feeling crept back into my body.

'I am not going to kill you, Pi-eta. I very much want to keep you alive. But if you want to survive this weekend, there is only one thing you must do – keep your eyes closed . . . For forty-eight hours you must not open your eyes. If you do, I will end you.'

My torso had come back to life and I could feel the breath stuttering in my chest.

'No matter what you feel or hear, you must not open your eyes, not even for the briefest of seconds.'

The tingling in my fingers hurt, the sparkles like little knives digging into my flesh.

'If you do as I ask, I will release you. I will put you back where I found you. And then you can go back to your ordinary little life. It's really that simple. Do you understand?'

The pain in my head was intensifying, it felt like it was being crushed.

'I'm going to take off this blindfold in a few moments, but before I do, I want you to nod if you understand . . .'

No, I didn't understand. I didn't understand any of it. Couldn't work it through my brain. I didn't know why it was happening, why I was here. Where I was. Why he chose me. And how he knew my name but wasn't saying it properly, like the boy's name, but was instead separating it after the 'I'. None of this made any sense, so, no, I didn't understand.

'Just a little nod to show you know what I'm talking about. A nod to let me know you're going to do as I say, that you understand.'

I didn't understand and I didn't want to nod.

But I did want to live.

More than anything, I wanted to live.

'Come on, Pi-eta, nod for me.'

More than anything, I wanted to live.

'That's it, that's right. Thank you, Pi-eta. Now our weekend together can begin.'

Monday, 10 June

Everyone's going to find out.

The thought lands with a thud in my mind like the arrival of a heavy parcel. I'm washing my hands, watching the white soap suds slip and slide over my fingers, while simultaneously pulling myself together so I can go back into the office and get on with my job, when the thought is delivered.

Because there is someone else now, someone who is going to tell everyone about him and what he does, everyone is going to find out about me. That I was one of them, that he did that to me.

This is like the time when I was twelve and I took one of my mother's favourite ornamental plates out of the sideboard in the living room. I'd just wanted to look at it, because I'd been obsessed with the painting of the sea on it. I wanted to see it up close and touch the paint, which was so glossy it looked wet, to see if it was still tacky or if it was that way because of how the light fell on it.

Somehow, I wasn't ever sure how, it slipped out of my hands and fell. It cracked in several places, before breaking completely into three. I'd stared at it, horrified. We weren't allowed to look too long at my mum's plates, let alone touch them. And look, I hadn't just touched it, I'd broken it.

Working on fear, I'd glued it back together with superglue before replacing it in the cupboard. I told no one, not even my sister, what I'd done. I just put it back and pretended nothing had happened.

I hadn't fixed it, of course. The cracks were there if you were looking, but who actually looks at something they've seen every day for years? Who actually looks at anything closely when they're used to it just being there? *I* knew it was there, cracked, broken, badly fixed, but I could live with that secret, I could pretend away what I had done.

This feels like that. I know something is broken, I know I attempted to fix it, but it's always there, damaged and imperfect; waiting to be discovered, unmasked, held up to scrutiny in its disfigured, damaged state.

Everyone is going to find out.

The thought of that, the idea that everyone will find out this secret I've harboured and carried for ten years, sends me back to the toilet to spew out pale green, coffee-tinged slime.

Tuesday, 28 April, 2009

BANG! BANG! BANG!

The banging on the door wouldn't stop.

It'd started as a knocking sound, hammering through the fug. *Knock-knock-knocking* to be let in. It went on for a while, getting louder, more insistent, as if the person knew I was in but wasn't coming to the door.

Tuesday. It was Tuesday. I was pretty sure it was Tuesday. Did Tuesday mean banging, hammering at the door? Is that what Tuesdays were about?

I edged it open, scared suddenly of who was on the other side.

What if he'd meant it? He now knew where I lived, like he'd known my name, and what if he was back to finish the job? I hadn't gone to the police. I hadn't gone anywhere. But what if that wasn't enough? I'd *thought* about going to the police, telling them everything, showing them . . . I'd only thought about it, but what if he knew I'd thought about it?

I realised that I shouldn't be opening this door, but by then, it was too late, I'd broken the seal, I'd let the outside in.

'I knew you were in there,' he said. 'I knew you were in there and you were trying to avoid me.'

His face was familiar, it was a blur – everything was – but it was known to me. And his voice, though the edges of it were fuzzed; I knew it, too. Everything was hazy, confused. I closed my eyes, tried to reset, tried to start again.

Jason.

This man was Jason. I'd spoken to him in The Before.

I knew him in The Before.

This was how my life was going to be carved now, I realised. Before. After. The Before. The After. The During.

'Jason,' I said carefully.

I brought my hand up to tug together the top of my red towelling dressing gown, to hide the skin at the top of my chest, obscure the flesh at my throat.

'You didn't come over and you haven't answered your phone all weekend,' he said. His words were accusatory. I remember in The Before, we'd made plans. I was going to see him, I was going to finish it with him, whatever it was that we had. Love. He'd thought what we had had bled out into love, I'd thought it was time to call it a day.

'I'm sorry,' I said to him. 'Something came up.'

I watched his eyes, a dirty green-blue, fringed by light-brown eyelashes, look me over. From my scraped-back hair to my slipperless feet. 'What have you been doing all weekend?'

I shook my head, I couldn't speak about it. Not now, not to him.

'Have you been shooting up or something?' he asked when I didn't speak. 'You look like you've been on the biggest bender of all time. And I've had the police at my door.'

I tugged the top of my dressing gown even closer together. 'Jason, this isn't the best time.' Words were hard. Difficult, gruelling, rough enough to stick in my throat. I remember in The During, words were all I had. Talking, speaking, saying whatever was needed to get . . . It was a struggle now, to form them, to deliver them, to be able to see what the effect is of having them heard.

'Right. Not the best time. I tell you I love you and you decide it's not the best time. Is he here?'

'Who?'

Jason craned his neck, trying to see past me into my flat. 'Whoever he is. The one you spent the weekend with. The one who you got into this state with. Is he here?'

I shook my head. It was not just the words, it was the lining of my throat. Sore, rough, scratched. My head thumped, a vice-like pulse that threatened to macerate my skull. *I do not want to have this conversation. I don't want to have any conversation ever again.* The sound of my voice was like thunder in my mind, lightning incinerating my nerve endings.

'Right. Great. So you admit it? You spent the weekend with someone. I told you I loved you and the first thing you do is find someone else. Or has it been going on for a while?'

'You don't love me, Jason,' I managed to say.

'You don't know how I feel,' he replied. 'Don't tell me how I feel.'

My mind was scattered. Thoughts about anything other than The During were even more difficult than words. I knew that this man did not love me. How could anyone love me? Even if he had loved me in The Before, there was no way he could love me in the now, The After, with all that had happened, all that had been done, all that I had done.

He took a step forward and my whole being reared up. No, I did not want him near me. I did not want him any closer. I needed space, I needed a boundary.

'What the hell?' he said, disgusted and hurt in equal measure as he stepped back and away. 'I'm not going to hurt you. You're acting like I'd ever hurt you. What the hell is going on, Pieta?'

I shook my head. 'Jason, I can't do this right now. You don't love me. You don't even know me.'

You don't know that I woke up outside The Evangelicals, the club I was in on Friday night, with all my stuff, except my driving licence. You don't know that I had to beg a taxi driver to take me home because I live south of the river and black cabs will still avoid coming down this way, no matter what the law says they have to do. You don't know I've been sitting here for hours, unsure what to do, how to go back to normal life. You don't know that I thought I'd felt pain before, but I am in so much agony right now, I think I'm going to pass out. 'You don't know me at all.'

'Just tell me who he is and how long it's been going on for and I will leave.'

'I don't know what to say to you,' I reply. 'I don't want you to love me. I don't want to see you any more. I want "us" to be over. I want this conversation to be finished.'

Even through the fug and clouds, I could see the truth finally hit home – I didn't want him and no amount of pressure was going to change that. Jason looked crestfallen; hurt and humiliated. I didn't even do anything to him, it was his ego that had finally heard the words I was saying and it was his ego that was smarting. The rest of him would be fine, the rational part of him would not only accept but would embrace the end of 'us'. It was just that his ego, which had been used to having whoever it wanted, to being satisfied and sated on a regular basis, had 'lost' this time and that hurt him.

'I . . . Bye, Pieta,' he eventually said.

'Bye, Jason.'

I shut the door and tried to walk. Tried to move. But I couldn't. That had taken all my energy. Being normal had zapped every last bit of strength I had. My knees buckled.

The sound of my body hitting the ground was loud, violent. I lay in my corridor, unable to do anything except stay very still and wait for the ability to do anything to come back to me.

Monday, 10 June

'All right, who wants a cup of tea and who wants a coffee, and who wants to tell me quick before I change my mind?' I say when I return to the features desk.

Our office is divided into what I like to think of as zones. Nearest the frosted glass, security protected doors, is the zone with the four people in our online team. They are pushed up against the back wall where they work on the *BN Sussex* website, uploading stories, sending out social media updates, constantly trying to stoke interest in the magazine and newspaper.

Next are the four women who work at the fashion and beauty desks. All of them are impossibly well turned-out; I rarely see any of them having a bad-looks day, even if I know they're going through a personal crisis. Lippy and make-up seem to hide many, many things. Their desks face each other and are situated opposite the beauty and fashion cupboard where they store the dresses and outfits they are sent for cover photo-shoots, fashion stories and beauty features. The cupboard is also unofficially known as Lillian's personal boutique. As more people have left and new ones arrived, Lillian has got less and less bothered about hiding the fact she 'borrows' the designer outfits sent in for shoots and misappropriates the expensive products that are sent in for review. Nowadays, she walks into the small room at the side of our office demanding service like she is on Bond Street in London. It got so bad at one point – where we had to delay shoots because key pieces had disappeared – I told the team to hide stuff. If it was important, I advised, don't let it be there for Lillian to find.

The next bank of desks belongs to the art department; they shape and define the look of the magazine to the tiniest detail – design the pages, arrange the photo-shoots and illustrations, decide the fonts, the size of headlines and the placement of text. Opposite them is the flatplan of the magazine. The pages we need to fill are printed out as portrait rectangles and tacked up on the side of the fashion cupboard so they can instantly see what they've done and what they've still got to do.

Beside them are the subs. The sub-editors, the people who

check the spellings, write the headlines, write the big quotes, the intros, and check every fact to within an inch of its life. I started there, at *BN Sussex*. I'd been writing freelance articles for the magazine for nearly two years when Lillian called me in a crisis asking if I knew anyone who could sub-edit as all her subs had been struck down by the same illness on the same day. I told her that I'd been a chief sub-editor back in London and she asked me to come in and do a few shifts. Sazz had been all too happy to look after Kobi a few more days a week, so I'd come in. Fresh-faced and eager to help out, to maybe get a full-time job. Obviously Lillian neglected to tell me her subs desk had all con-tracted Lillianitis and had all individually decided they couldn't put up with her a moment longer.

At the other end of the office is Lillian's desk, and outside her glass walls is the features department, where I sit. Now that I'm the deputy editor, I sit at the desk closest to her office and I have to angle my screen so she can't look out and see what I'm up to. I'm not given to doing much of anything but work in work hours, but I still don't like the idea of Lillian watching me so I do what I can to keep my computer private. Across the way from the features desk, nestled in the little cove made by the end of the fashion cupboard and the back wall, is the lifestyle desk. They cover homes and health, as well as the travel that the features department don't deal with. There's a lot of crossover and unspoken rivalry between the features and lifestyle desks and I've wanted, more than once, to suggest we merge them to stop it, but I'm leaving that conversation for a day when Lillian doesn't come into work wearing her 'just try me' face. It's been eighteen months and counting waiting for that day.

'Skinny latte with soya milk,' Tiffany says without raising her head.

'Café mocha with almond milk,' Avril chimes in.

'Organic, hand-roasted beans with steamed milk and half a teaspoon of agave syrup for me,' Connie adds.

'So, that's coffee from the jar in the kitchen all round, is it?' I say to them.

'Yeah,' they all reply.

I grab my reusable bamboo 'Mama Needs Coffee' cup that Kobi bought me in the great plastic cull of 2018. He'd been mortified when my eyes filled with tears and I covered his face in kisses saying thank you. I embarrass my son at least ten times a day just by being me.

I walk the length of the office, smiling at my colleagues, at the chaos of their desks, the plans for the next issue, the propped-open door to the cupboard, the pile of filing that sits on top of the filing cabinets. I belong here. I fit in, I enjoy myself and, despite certain Lillian moments, I wouldn't want this to end. But something has become quite clear since I heard about that woman – I can't interview her. I can't sit in the same room as another survivor. Not when I know that it could be my fault because I didn't tell the police what had happened. And definitely not when it could lead to everyone knowing I was there, too.

Yes, I want to find out if it really is the same guy that I've lightly investigated over the years, but at the same time, I can't. I simply can't.

I love this job, but I'm going to have to resign. That's all there is to it. I can't speak to that woman so I have to leave.

Thursday, 30 April, 2009

It's Thursday.
 Knocking at the door means it's Thursday.
 Knock, knock, knock. Again.

It couldn't be Jason. I was sure he wouldn't come back. The phone had been ringing and the answer machine was full. *Ring, ring, ring.* Now *knock, knock, knock.*

My door didn't have a peephole so I was answering the door without knowing who would be on the other side.

The who on the other side were two police officers. One male, one female.

'Hello,' the female officer said. 'Are you Pi-eta Rawlings?'

'It's pronounced "Peter" like the boy's name. But yes, that's me.'

'Can we come in, Miss Rawlings?'

'Why, what's happened?'

'Nothing, now that we've found you,' she said.

'Was I missing?' I replied. I knew I was missing, but did anyone else?

She smiled. 'Can we come in?'

I'd rather they didn't. I didn't know who was watching, but I couldn't say that to the police. I stepped back and the two police officers crossed the threshold. They were about my age, but suddenly, with their uniforms and boots, and radios, truncheons and handcuffs, I felt like I was nine years old. I don't know why nine and not ten, or eight, but there it was. I felt young, immature and small in their presence.

We stepped into the living area and I immediately pulled my

cardigan around myself. I'd got dressed. Wednesday. Wednesday was getting dressed day. And Thursday. I got dressed on Thursday too. Although Thursday was knocking at the door day as well.

'We had a report that you were missing,' the police officer stated.

I stared at her. *Is he watching? Would this count as going to the police even though I didn't call them? Would he know that, though? If he's watching me, all he would know is they arrived here.*

'I'm PC Jerrand,' the male police officer said. 'This is PC Koit.'

'Yes, sorry, I'm PC Koit. I'm a bit surprised, really, you're the first person I've found so easily.'

'Who told you I was missing?' I asked.

'Can we sit down?' was PC Jerrand's reply.

The living room was quite dark since I'd kept the blinds down. I craved the light, wanted my eyes to have lots of it flooding in, but I wasn't sure if he was out there watching me. If he was, I didn't want him to see me any more. He'd watched me for the whole time he had me. I didn't want his eyes on me any more.

I indicated to the sofa and to the seats, set in a formation that meant you could see the television from wherever you sat. While they settled themselves, I went to the low, circular coffee table, picked up the black remote and snapped off the television. I hadn't really been watching it, more staring through it.

This was better than when Jason had arrived, I realised. I wasn't so scattered, disassembled. I could do this now – I could speak to people, answer questions.

'Who said I was missing?' I asked for the third time.

'Your mother reported you missing on Saturday evening,' PC Koit replied. She and her colleague kept looking around as though searching for something, while wondering what I had to hide by having the blinds down on such a glorious day.

'My mother.'

Mum worried about me. I was single and I lived alone and if I didn't speak to her every other day, she immediately thought I'd fallen and I was lying in my single person's house unable to reach the phone to call for help. She would ring and ring and ring. Then she would send my dad to get the two buses and a train to come over to double-check I was still breathing.

I was still breathing.

Despite everything, I was still breathing.

Both police officers peered at me in the gloom, waiting for me to say something else. I thought it was easier than speaking to Jason, but it was not. It was harder, so much harder in completely different ways. I had to focus now. I had to appear normal and as though I had nothing to hide.

'My mum does this. If I don't answer the phone she sends my dad over. This is the first time she's actually called the police, though.'

'Is that because this is the first time you've not been here when your father has called round?' PC Koit replied. 'It wasn't that you just didn't answer your phone – your mobile was handed into a police station late Friday night, early Saturday morning in East London. Did you know that?'

'My mobile?' I was on my mobile just before it happened. 'OK.'

'When your mother reported you missing, we spoke to the

most frequently called numbers on your phone and we spoke to a man called Jason Breechner? Your partner?'

'He's not my partner,' I said. 'He was barely a boyfriend.'

'He said you were meant to come over to his flat on Saturday but you didn't show up. Didn't answer your phone, when you always do. Can we ask where you were?'

'I thought someone had to be missing forty-eight hours before the police would get involved?' I said to stall for time. I couldn't tell them, of course I couldn't tell them.

'That's not actually true,' PC Jerrand said. 'It's a common misconception. We get involved if someone does something completely out of the ordinary with no real explanation. For example, if a woman who always answers her phone and lets people know when she's going away suddenly disappears, we would get involved if no one knows where she is. Especially when she's lost her mobile and doesn't seem to have noticed and tried calling it to find it.'

I studied him for a moment. A moment was all I needed, though. He was a tall man. He was muscular. He had no discernable scent. His voice sounded normal. It could be him. *He* was tall. *He* was muscular. *He* seemed to have a normal voice that he disguised by husking it while he spoke. It could be *him*, sitting on my sofa, telling me why they knew I was missing. This could be it. The test. The reason he decided to come after me again. *He* told me he would know if I went to the police and said he would be back if I did.

I stopped surveying the police officer, tugged my cardigan tighter across my body.

It could be him.

66

'Where were you?' PC Koit asked gently.

'I, erm, kind of . . . I went on a bit of a bender.' Jason had said I looked like I'd been on one, and that would explain away a lot.

My knee started to jiggle, though, the lies making it move. I got to my feet to hide it, even though they wouldn't know that this was a giveaway because they didn't know me. 'I didn't offer you tea. Would you like one?'

They both shook their heads. 'If we get this sorted out, we can get out of your hair and allow you to move on with your day.'

I tugged my cardigan more tightly around myself, folded my arms more firmly across my chest and braced myself to lie again. 'I went on a bender.'

'What sort of bender?' PC Jerrand asked.

'You know, the bender kind.' *Smile. Smile and act normal, Pieta.* 'I'm not sure that telling the police what I got up to on a bender is the wisest thing.'

'We're all adults, and we're not going to arrest you for doing something adults do,' PC Koit said.

'Just tell us,' he insisted.

It could be him.

'All right. Erm, it was drink, mainly. Some drugs. Sitting up late most nights and talking absolute shite. And, of course, eating terrible takeaways.'

'Why didn't you go to work?' the male officer asked.

'What do you mean?'

'That was why we took it seriously,' he explained. 'We were told you haven't been to work all week. Haven't called in sick. In fact, we came here to search for a clue as to where you were. We weren't expecting you to be here.'

'I, erm, well . . . I work in the media. On a magazine. It's really obvious to my editor – my boss – which people are on a comedown. I did not want my reputation as a good girl to be tarnished.'

My words, burdened as they were with lies, fell flat. We could all hear the echo of mendacity, but they couldn't argue with it.

It could be him, I thought again. All the muscles in my body contracted, causing a flare of pain to ignite through me, especially on my back where . . .

'Miss Rawlings—' the policeman began.

'Ewan, give us a minute, would you?' PC Koit cut in.

Frowning, he turned to her. She jerked her head to the door, telling him to leave.

'Thank you, Miss Rawlings,' he said as he got to his feet. Standing, I could see all of his height and it ricocheted more terror through me. I instinctively stepped back to make sure I was out of easy reach. 'I'm glad you're home.'

I nodded at him but didn't dare look in his direction as he vacated my space.

The woman PC didn't say anything, but I could feel her light-coloured eyes on me, openly studying me, until my front door clicked shut behind her partner. *Are they in it together?* I wondered. *Is this where the other part of the test begins? It could have been him, but it could be her with him, too.*

'*I'll know if you talk to the police,*' he'd said. '*I'll know and I'll come for you.*'

'Are you all right, Miss Rawlings?' the PC asked gently once we were alone.

'Yes, of course, why?'

She stood up and came towards me. 'Did something happen to you this weekend?' she asked, just as carefully.

Alarmed, I took a couple of steps back to keep the same distance between us. I didn't want her any closer, and I didn't want to answer her question. *Is this her trying to draw me out? Is she working with him, trying to see if I will tell someone everything the first chance I get? Or did I give myself away? Was I not pretending hard enough?* I had to pull myself together. If a stranger could tell, then everyone else would. And that would mean . . .

'I . . . erm . . . I don't understand.' I injected as much confusion and normality into my voice as I could. 'I told you I was on a bender.'

'Forgive me if I seem to be overstepping the line a little, but you're showing several signs of being in post-traumatic distress. Did something happen to you this weekend? Were you assaulted or similar?'

No.

I wasn't assaulted or similar.

I was taken.

I was held.

I was strapped down.

I was . . .

I shook my head, slowly at first, then faster, more firmly.

No, actually, that didn't happen to me. I was not going to have let that happen to me. None of it. Not to me. And I had to act that out. I had to show this person that it didn't happen to me. If I could convince her, I could convince other people. I could maybe even convince myself.

'I'm fine,' I stated. 'I told you, I'm the good girl, everyone knows it. Always have been. Drugs aren't my usual thing. I'm, erm, I'm sorry I wasted your time. And worried everyone. I have a lot of making up to do.'

She bobbed her head up and down, openly unconvinced by what I was saying.

'So much for "just say no" to drugs, eh?' I joked with a smile. 'If I'd stuck to that, like I have since I was in school, we wouldn't be here now and you wouldn't have wasted your precious resources on me.'

PC Koit looked for a moment as though she was going to say something more, try to coax whatever I was telling her wasn't there out of me. Instead, she reached into her uniform pocket. 'This is my business card. Call me if you want to talk. You don't have to report anything, explain anything, just come in for a chat. Or just to let me know how you're getting on.'

'How I'm getting on? What do you mean?'

'Just take my card.' She smiled at me. 'I can always pop back to talk to you, if you'd rather not come to the station in the first instance.'

Smile, I ordered myself. *Smile*. Take the card. My fingers groped the distance between us until I gripped the small white rectangle. She hung on to it for the smallest fraction of a moment, connecting us, allowing her the type of access I didn't want to give any more.

Our gazes connected in that fraction of a moment, and I knew she could see. And I knew why *he* had done it. Shut off that part of me for a weekend.

In someone's eyes you can see everything, you can see their perfections, their flaws; their joys, their pain; their truths, their lies.

And they can see yours.

That was why *he* had taken away my sight for the weekend – he didn't want me to see him for who he really was.

She could see it all. This policewoman, in that moment, could see everything from the weekend. But she couldn't decipher it. Who could decipher that without being there?

'Thank you,' I replied when she finally let the card go. 'I don't need it, but thank you for caring. It's not often you get a stranger taking an interest in you to this degree. I wish my magazine did more of the human interest pieces I like to write, you'd be a great subject.'

'Even if you've got nothing to talk about, it'd be good to hear from you, Miss Rawlings,' she said, determined not to be swayed from what she was trying to say to me.

'Thank you,' I repeated. *Thank you, but I don't have the words. Thank you, but I don't know that you're not in on it. Thank you, but I want to pretend none of this happened.*

The male police officer was standing outside my door, facing the other way, as though he'd been tasked with guarding the place, preventing anyone from coming in. Thankfully the corridor outside my flat was empty, and there were no direct windows in from the street so no one outside would see.

'Oh, you should arrange to come and collect your mobile phone,' she said. 'The screen is cracked from where it was dropped, but it still works.'

'Oh, yes, yes, I'll do that. Thank you. Bye.'

My legs wanted to collapse after they'd gone. They wobbled, they struggled, but I resisted. I had phone calls to make. I had to stop this happening again by calling people, proving I was alive, lying that I was well. If I did that, maybe they would leave me alone for a little while longer.

I turned away from the door, heading for the telephone. I needed to listen to messages, return calls, answer emails, see if I still had a job, integrate myself back into the world. My legs shuddered again, shook, staggered, collapsed.

It was Thursday.

Thursday was all about sitting behind the front door, trying to pull myself together.

Monday, 10 June

'Pieta, do you have a minute?'

Reggie, the art director, is waiting for me outside the office. I've got three full coffee mugs and my cup balanced between my hands in a precarious way and I'm going to have to do a gymnastic lift of my hip to hit my pass against the flat white security panel to allow me into the office.

'Not really, Reggie.'

'Oh. I just really need to talk to you.'

'And I'd really like to listen to you, but I've got a delicate balance of cups with hot liquid going on here and I'm not sure how much longer I'll be able to keep hold of them.'

'Oh, sorry, I'll wait here for you to go put them down,' he says and stands to one side.

'Or, you could, possibly, take a couple off me and we can talk now? Just a thought.'

'Oh, sorry, sorry,' he says, relieving me of two of the cups.

'See? This is how much she's got into my head, that didn't even occur to me.'

Reggie asked me out once. Three years ago, not long after he started, we'd got talking and discovered not only were our parents from the same country in Africa, but they actually lived near each other in London. Whenever a group of us would go out for drinks or for Christmas meals or leaving dos, Reggie and I would end up chatting alone. We talked and laughed and discovered we had a lot of the same interests – particularly sci-fi movies and pottery. One day, out of the blue, or maybe not if you thought about it, he asked me if I wanted to go to dinner with him. Just him. We'd been in the queue at the coffee shop around the corner and he'd just asked.

He'd stared at me as he waited for an answer. I'd stared into the mid-distance, completely blindsided. What did someone funny and entertaining and good-looking want with me? *Me!* I wasn't in any position to go out one-on-one with a man. I wasn't in any situation to even think about kissing a man, and the idea of being naked with anyone, when my body was so *damaged . . .* I couldn't do it. I just couldn't. He'd obviously seen the panic on my face and had asked if he'd read the signals wrong, was I seeing someone? 'Kind of,' I'd said because I didn't know how to explain that I'd love to go out with him but there was no way I could. 'OK, sorry,' he'd replied. I stopped going out for drinks as much, and a few months later he clearly got over me by dating Susie in the syndication department, who was extremely pretty and had a reputation for being just the nicest woman.

Since then, it's been a little awkward between us (mainly because I was monumentally jealous) and we've kept it professional.

'It's Lillian.' His voice sounds like it has been sharpened on flint and I can tell he's nearly at the precipice of no return. I'd seen so many people on this ledge over the years. When things got too much and work was near intolerable, people would find themselves at this point. Right now, Reggie was standing near the edge, glancing behind him at Lillian and the things she did and then gazing ahead at the hundred-foot drop that is walking out of a job with nothing to go to. We all know it's hard out there, magazine jobs outside of London are extremely rare, and even the London ones, at his level particularly, come up very infrequently. But did that mean staying? Being treated like dirt?

'What's happened?' I ask gently.

'She's just called me in for another "chat" about how the design is so bland and uninspiring it's not only not increasing sales figures or advertising but it's actively harming them.'

Oh Lillian, I sigh internally.

Reggie is good. Actually, he's fantastic. He's talented and has a real eye for design (and I'm not just saying that because I fancied him once upon a time ago). He can read a story, find the pictures and put them together in a way that always makes you stop and read the article. He has brought the magazine right up to date and made it fresh, exciting and innovative. Lillian knows this, but she's Lillian so she has to find someone to blame for anything that is going wrong.

She doesn't realise that Reggie will walk, though. He isn't like the others who put up with it for over a year before they get out;

he will walk straight away and he will sue her. He's said that before: 'I won't be putting up with that crap. She starts on me she will regret it right down to the constructive dismissal lawsuit.'

Apart from anything, I don't want that for Reggie. He doesn't need a lawsuit on his record, and everyone else in the office doesn't need to bear the brunt of her indignation at someone standing up to her.

'I'll talk to her,' I say to him. 'I'll get her to back off.'

'What are you going to say?'

'Oh, I don't know, either, "Oi, Lillian, cut it out, now." Or, "Oh, Lillian, Lillian, please pick on me instead of anyone else, I really enjoy being targeted by you." I'll decide which one I go for once I start talking to her,' I reply. It has the desired effect and makes him laugh. I love the way his face creases up when he laughs, the way his smile lights up his eyes and face.

'I can stand up to her,' he explains.

'I know.'

'I just know I'll be painted as the aggressive black man if I say anything, and I'm not sure anyone in the office is ready for what would go down.'

'I'll sort it, don't worry.'

This is one of the reasons why leaving isn't such an easy choice – I kind of feel responsible for the other people who work here. Being deputy editor means running interference between Lillian and the rest of the staff. I soothe their savaged feathers, remind her that she's going too far, and try as hard as I can to make the place pleasant and fun. No one told me that the role of deputy editor was about this, but I realised a few days after taking the job that that was exactly what it was about – Deborah, who had the job before me, had done it for us, now I had to do it for them.

'Thanks, Pieta.' Our eyes meet for a moment. I rarely make eye contact with people, hardly ever give them enough of me to do that. But it's an accidental collision with Reggie and I don't mind at all if he sees me, smiles at me exactly as he's doing now. 'We should grab that drink we talked about sometime, you know, just you and me.'

'What about Susie? Can't she come along?'

He grimaces. 'We split up a couple of months back,' he explains. 'She moved out last month. All good, no harm, no foul, so yes, she could technically come along as we're still friends, but it might cramp our style a bit.'

'I see.'

'I've been meaning to try out that pottery café in Brighton where you can make your own stuff and bring your own wine for while you make it? Care to join me?'

I'd love that: I love making pottery and I'd love to go out with Reggie.

'I'd . . .' I begin. *'We are going to spend the weekend together, Pi-eta,'* cuts through my brain like a sharp knife through soft flesh. *'For the next forty-eight hours, we are going to get to know each other very well.'*

I can't date Reggie. I can't date anyone. Why would I even consider it?

'I'd, erm, I'd better get these coffees back to the features team before they go cold,' I say.

'Oh, right,' Reggie says, surprised and disappointed at my sudden change of gear. I'd been about to say yes, and he could

76

tell I'd been about to say yes, but now I've stopped and he's confused.

'I'll sort out that thing we talked about,' I reassure him while he settles two of the mugs on my desk.

'Thanks,' he mumbles and walks away without looking in my direction again.

Jody

Monday, 10 June

Callie Beckman sits in the soft interview room and tells us her story again.

I read the original statement she filed in London nine months ago and I watched her original video. It was another report I came across as part of my own investigation, because nothing had come of it when she'd originally come in. There was nothing to come of it: she had left it weeks to report, she'd got rid of the clothes she was wearing at the time and nothing new had come to her beyond what had happened that weekend.

We listen to her story again with the camera running, but this isn't the reason why she is sitting here today. She had called the original police station she reported it to and asked for help. They'd passed her on to my London station, who had passed her on to me here. When I spoke to her on the phone yesterday (Sunday) and said I was in Brighton but would come to see her, she'd said no, she would come to me.

I'd been planning, once I had set up my incident room down here, to go back to London to speak to Callie. I wanted to hear her story first-hand and I'd wanted to gently warn her about personal safety. I didn't want to terrify her with the fact that The Blindfolder's past victims were being killed, but I did want to put her on alert. Maybe ask her to stay elsewhere for a few weeks, switch up her routine, stop being predictable to make it harder for him to track her.

But she'd pre-empted this by getting in touch, and now she's blown all my intentions of being gentle with her out of the water by telling me what she is planning.

After telling us her story, she has repeated what her plan is: tell her story to the newspapers and the media.

This would be a disaster.

Laura, who I was right to ask to come with me, has tried to explain why she shouldn't do it. I have tried to explain to her why she shouldn't do it. And she will not listen.

Callie doesn't realise that she is different from the other women who we know of, the ones whose bodies we have found.

She's white and, so far, all the women we've encountered have been black. Coupled with our very sparse amount of forensic evidence, it means this has thrown off everything we've gleaned so far. We can draw up psychological profiles, we can plot dump sites and original disappearances on geographical maps, we can guess and speculate, but without forensic evidence, we are guessing into the void. And now Callie presents another direction, another way to look at this that we hadn't considered.

How many other white women has he taken? How many Asian women? How many mixed-race women? How many other types of women? Has he just decided to start with killing the black ones? Will he then go after the white ones? The Asian ones? The mixed-race ones? Or do they happen to be the ones he's found first?

Callie has opened up a whole new avenue of investigation. That is why she is so important. And why I do not want her to mess this up by doing something like talking to the press.

'Callie . . . can I call you Callie?' I have to try again to get through to her.

'Yes,' she replies. In her hands she holds a tissue that she twists and twists into an ever-tighter spiral. It's one of the outward showings of her anxiety.

'Callie, this is for your own protection as well, you know? Dealing with the press can be brutal. They take no prisoners and will get into every detail of your life.'

'I've got nothing to hide,' she replies.

Yeah, course not. If I had a penny for every person who has said that . . . 'We all think that, until the people who spend their time searching things out turn their attention on us.'

'Detective, I'm trying to help other women. Do you really think I care about them finding out I once shagged a boy under a pile of coats at Jimmy Crawford's seventeenth birthday party? That I used to sometimes go out without wearing knickers? That I sometimes don't recycle? I don't care, not when people are dying!'

Everything stops.

I sit up straight, lower the notepad and pen in my hands.

'How do you know people are dying?' Laura and I ask at the same time. We look at each other, a little delighted that we've done that when we've only just met, then we both turn back to Callie with grim looks on our faces.

She stares at us both. Her navy-green eyes dart from me to Laura, back to me. She twists the tissue so hard it snaps. Laura and I wait for an answer; she sits and trembles.

'It's not what you think,' she eventually whispers. 'It's not at all what you think.'

'We're not sure what to think,' I eventually say.

Her eyes suddenly, unexpectedly, fill with tears. 'He . . . told me.'

'He *what*?' Laura and I say at the same time.

She brings her hands up to her face and cringes back against the sofa to protect herself from our promised onslaught.

'You know who he is?' I ask, bracing myself for the answer.

She shakes her head quickly, vigorously. This is the first time she's shown real emotion beyond the anger and bravado, the first time she's displayed anything that isn't a blatant attempt to avoid accepting what happened to her. 'No. No! If I knew him, I would tell you. He . . . he sent me a letter, telling me what he had done. With a picture of . . . With a picture of the woman he'd . . . It was hideous.' She clutches herself tighter and shudders.

I look over Callie Beckman again. She is thirty-eight. She has mousy-blonde hair that she wears scraped back into a ponytail, her face is well-proportioned, dainty, uncomplicatedly beautiful. She is also fierce. That is what has come through in all of this: she is fierce and single-minded and determined. And, I thought, help-ful. She wanted this man caught as much as we did. But maybe not. Because why would you not tell us about this before now?

'Why didn't you tell us this?' I ask as gently as my shock will allow.

'I was scared!' she wails. 'Really scared! I thought it was a warning. I thought he was going to come after me because I'd been to the police. He said he would come for me if I go to the police. And then there was this picture of . . . I couldn't tell you that.'

'Do you still have it?' Laura asks. Her voice is exactly like mine – incredulous and angry at the same time.

Another vigorous head shake. 'No, no. I couldn't keep it. I couldn't have that around me. I shredded it then I burnt it.' She wrings the two pieces of tissue together. 'I just wanted to get rid of it completely. Putting it in the bin wasn't enough. I had to completely destroy it. You don't understand, it was so horrible, seeing her like that. I couldn't . . . I couldn't sleep while it was around me. I could hardly breathe. So I had to get rid of it. Totally. Completely.' She's trembling, her voice an erratic symphony of fear and her eyes lose focus for a few moments as she relives the letter, the photo.

'You say he sent it to you. When and where?' I ask.

'He sent it to my home address in London. I didn't understand how he knew where I was at first, then I remembered, he took my driving licence. Remember, I told you that? So he had my address. I don't know, I didn't think he'd use it. But he sent it to me. Which is why I left my house and came to Brighton. You do understand, don't you?'

I don't understand keeping that kind of information back, no. I honestly don't. And this is the sort of thing people with 'nothing to hide' always have lurking in the corners of their lives, just waiting there to be discovered and exposed. I've never met a person yet who truly has nothing to hide. We all have something we'd rather keep hidden, it's what makes us human.

Something else has occurred to me, though. And it allows me to avoid telling her I understand. 'When did you move to Brighton?' I ask.

Laura is stupefied; horrified that this woman would do

something so counterproductive. I can see she's itching to shout at her. But that's not going to help any of us, especially not with persuading Callie not to go to the papers.

'A few months ago. I was too scared to stay in my flat in London, so I moved down here because I grew up near here. Got an Airbnb then found a room in a shared flat.'

'When exactly is a few months ago?'

'February.'

February. Also known as three murders ago. Well, four murders now. This is what we couldn't understand: why he killed these women (all of whom are from London) in London and moved them down here. Now it's clear he's chasing Callie.

'Who did you tell you were moving down here?'

'I didn't put it on social media, if that's what you mean. I don't have social media any more. I told you that. Ever since . . . ever since I was hurt, I don't have social media on my phone.'

'Did you tell anybody in real life?'

'Only my brother and my mother. But they wouldn't tell anyone. I had to resign from my job. I loved my job. And I was just getting myself back together and then that postcard and photo came and then that's it, BOOM everything's gone.'

'We're going to have to take you into protective custody,' I tell her. 'I mean, witness protection.'

That changes her again, she grows very still and stares right at me. 'Why?' she eventually manages, even though she barely moves her lips.

I sigh. 'He knows you're down here and has been leaving his past victims in different parks around Brighton.'

'No. No, no, no.' She shakes her head. 'He's found me?' She

crushes the tissue in her hand. 'This is why I need to do the interviews,' she says suddenly, desperation soaking each word. 'I need the world to hear. I need those other women to hear so they'll come forward and tell you their stories. The more stories you hear, the more likely you'll get something that will help you find him, won't you?'

'In a way,' I reply reluctantly. She does have a point. Just a general appeal should do it, but I understand human nature too. More people will respond if there is a face, a pretty one especially, saying what happened. I sigh again. 'I will have Laura here and another officer accompany you to get your stuff and we'll find somewhere for you to stay. After that, we'll talk about the media thing. I'll ask around and see if there are any trusted journos you can tal—oh, what now? Why have you got that look on your face?'

'I . . . I already sent out an embargoed press notification. I let people know that I'll meet them on Wednesday. The location will be kept secret until a couple of hours before so they'll respect the embargo. I was specific enough to get their interest but vague enough not to give too much away.'

'You've already sent it?' Laura asks. She sounds more incredulous than I feel.

'Yes. I worked in public relations, I know how to get the press interested. I had to do something to protect myself. And you said it yourself' – she's pointing at me – 'we need as many people to come forward as possible to keep me alive.' I didn't say that, but she's extrapolating and embellishing to suit her point.

'At what point were you going to tell us you'd done this?' I ask.

'I'm here now, aren't I?' She crushes the tissue in her hand. 'Look, I am not a victim who is going to wait around to be picked off like that other woman I got the picture of. That is *not* me. I have to do something.'

I can understand that. *I* am that. It's just disconcerting when someone screws up your work by doing that something.

'All right,' I say tiredly. 'Go get your stuff. I'll find you somewhere to stay where you can meet the journalists who respond. We'll have to move you afterwards.'

I was saying this, but wasn't sure how I was going to get budget approval for it. We were already piggy-backing off the CID budget. This was not on the cards. I knew Callie existed, had read her statement, but I didn't think The Blindfolder would be so focused on her that he would be doing this.

'I'm sorry I didn't tell you everything straight away,' she says, looking completely remorseful. 'I was just scared and I had to protect myself. I'm so sorry.'

I find a smile, one that convinces her that it will all be OK. Laura isn't able to do that. She is absolutely appalled by all of this. I am too, but I've had more experience at pretending the absolutely outrageous is absolutely fine.

'It's hard to know what to do sometimes,' I say. 'But please, don't do anything else without asking us first. It really is in your best interest to let us take charge of everything from here on in.'

She nods, looking shamefaced. 'I will. I absolutely will.'

And if I believe that, I really don't deserve the title of detective inspector.

Pieta

**Monday, 10 June

I still don't know what I'm going to do.

I don't want to meet this woman, I am sure of that. Yes, on many levels I do want to meet her, but really, how will I listen to her tell me her version of my story and not give myself away? Not break down?

But the only way out of this would be to call in sick tomorrow or Wednesday and not go back to work because if I do not get Lillian that interview, my life will be unbearable.

The thoughts about what to do are still whizzing around my mind like racing cars on a track when I arrive home. Nothing seems easy or simple.

I climb the steps to my large, split-level flat in a Victorian villa in Hove, knowing I have to shed all of this. One of the promises I made myself when I had Kobi was to make sure, *absolutely sure*, that I brought nothing home from work. I wanted his life to be unburdened by the things that stalked the world; uncomplicated by me; unblemished by the adults that seemed determined to make life hard and brutal.

Stay there. Stay there. Stay there, I repeat as I climb the steps. *I'm not going back there, and there isn't coming here.*

My keys feel rubbery, light and unreal as I raise the silver Yale one to slot into the lock. When I first thought about moving here, settling by the sea, I assumed I'd end up in Brighton. And then I came here and realised very quickly that Brighton was too much for me. I was escaping London, I was escaping chaos, I didn't need to simply downsize it. Brighton was vibrant, buzzing, always moving; like the sinewy body of a person so comfortable with themselves they didn't care what anyone thought and, in fact, didn't stop to even notice that they didn't care. Brighton was frenetic and I needed calm. I ended up buying this split-level place in the other half of the city – Hove – a bit further along the seafront. It's right near George Street, the sort-of high street in Hove, and the train station. It was ideal for the time when I'd be OK to commute up to London for work and it was only one block away from the sea. It was the perfect place and I knew from the moment I walked in I would be able to live here, heal here, be whoever I needed to be now that I was in The After.

The me I was before *him* was gone. I needed to be away from London and who I was in The Before. And I promised Kobi, even before he had his name and he was outside of me and alive, that I wouldn't allow the difficult bits of The After to infect him.

The flat oozes with happiness and contentment when I open the door, it rushes to greet me like a happy dog relieved and excited that its owner is home. Sazz does that. She and Kobi have a relationship that is solid and fun; he wouldn't dream of trying to scam her out of doing homework, brushing his teeth, staying up after lights out. He saves all of that for me.

I kick off my shoes, head for the toilet by the door, pump a couple of squirts of lavender liquid soap into the well of my palms then wash my hands in the small sink. 'I'm home!' I call while I dry my hands. No answer.

In the living room, Kobi sits on our low, brown leather sofa beside Sam, one of his best friends from school. They each have a games controller in their hands and they are fixated on the twenty-two computer-generated football figures that run around a green pitch. 'Hello, Sam,' I say, because clearly my son isn't going to acknowledge my existence while he is in the middle of football glory.

'Hello,' he says and takes his eyes off the screen for a moment to at least look and smile at me.

'How are you?' I ask. 'How was school?'

Horrified that I might want to talk to him when he has a footie game to finish, he mumbles, 'Fine' and returns to the screen.

'Hello, sweet child of mine,' I say to my son. 'How was school?'

'*Mum!*' Kobi hisses through his teeth.

'Sorry I asked,' I reply.

I go to him and press a kiss on the top of his head. *Love you*, I whisper inside my mind. Because he can tell when I'm doing that, even when I say it silently.

'Hello, Pi-R,' Sazz says as she enters the room. From the kitchen I can smell the dinner she's made – Bolognese – and I can hear the CD of musicals she's been playing. Sazz likes to sing when she cooks, and I've caught her dancing between stirs before.

'Hey. Where's Oscar?' I ask. Even though Oscar is the year

above Sam and Kobi, he always comes over whenever the younger two arrange to get together.

'He's upstairs, doing his homework.' She directs her voice to the other two. 'He wanted to get it done before dinner. You know, sensible, like.'

In unison Kobi and Sam look at Sazz, double-checking she isn't telling them to go and do their homework now, because they would. No arguments, no fuss, if Sazz was decreeing something, they would scramble to do it.

She winks at them, they grin at her. Clearly I'm not needed here.

Upstairs, I pop my head around the door of my office. Oscar sits at my desk with his head down as he writes something on the large, A2 sheet of paper in front of him.

'Hi, Oscar,' I say.

He lifts his head and looks at me, a bit surprised, then perplexed. Clearly I have interrupted him at a crucial moment and he's having trouble returning to this world from wherever he was while he was homeworking.

'Hello,' he eventually says.

'How was your day?' I ask.

'Fine.'

'Good, I'm glad. I'm sure Sazz will let you know when it's dinner time.' I'm talking for the sake of it, now. Those poor boys. It's really not fair on them to have me trying to start a conversation when they're clearly busy, but I can't help myself.

'Thank you,' he responds, itching to get back to what he was doing before he loses his train of thought.

'OK. Well, see you soon. At dinner.'

He nods and I back out of the room, feeling foolish. This is clearly why Kobi only invites people over when Sazz is doing pick-up – he can't risk having me put his friends through this every time.

Thursday, 15 September, 2011

She was smiling, like the universe was chock-full of wonderful things and she had a trillion and one things to grin about.

'Hello, I'm Sarah Sazzleoj, most people call me Sazzle or Sazz,' she said at the front door. 'I'm fine with any of them, but I'm so used to Sazz now that I don't really answer to Sarah first time.'

I stepped back to let her into the flat. Immediately I felt the warmth from her, she was naturally at ease with the world and her place in it. She was younger than me, but seemed to have everything sorted.

I didn't hold out much hope for Sazz. On paper she seemed ideal – but so had the other seven I'd interviewed. They'd all been highly praised by the agency, had a battery of credentials and experience and each of them had left me cold.

When Sazz had arrived, I was still reeling from the last woman who'd just left. She had been twenty-four, lived on the outskirts of London/Croydon so couldn't be expected to get here before 10 a.m. She didn't smoke but asked me if it would be a problem if she needed to nip out for a cigarette break every now and again; she suggested I brush up on my French if I wanted to be able to communicate with her properly, and then told me she didn't think children needed much stimulation so spending hours in their cots was perfectly fine. She'd been the best one.

Kobi was precious to me. I'd had him eighteen months and every day – *every day* – I woke up terrified he'd be taken away from me. By someone who thought I couldn't cope, by someone who thought I wasn't looking after him properly, by someone who saw the terror in my eyes at making a mistake with him and decided to relieve me of that burden.

Whoever was going to look after my son had to be as close to perfect as I could get. Selling my flat in London had given me enough money to live on for a while, and the bits of freelance I managed to crowbar in around Kobi's naps kept us afloat, but I needed a proper plan. I needed someone who could look after him in the flat so I could keep an eye on them while I worked. I couldn't keep asking my mum to come down from London. It wasn't fair on her, and after two days we were both ready to throttle each other.

'Can I see him?' Sazz asked in the corridor. 'The agency said you had a boy, can I see him?' She kicked off her shoes without being asked.

'OK.' I was confused for a moment. None of the others had even mentioned seeing Kobi, they'd come for an interview and that was that.

We climbed the stairs to the bedrooms and I quietly opened the door to his room. He was fast asleep, flat on his back, eyes tightly shut, dreaming his way through the evening.

'Hello, buddy,' she whispered before stepping back to let me close the door. 'He looks like a proper little character,' she said as we descended the stairs.

'He is,' I replied.

Sazz was disarming. Her dark brown skin was flawless, her

nearly black eyes sparkled with curiosity and excitement, and a grin was never far away from her mouth.

'So, what is it you're looking for?' she asked as she settled herself right in the middle of my sofa.

'Sorry?'

'Do you want someone to play with him? Or do you want me to read with him, teach him stuff? Take him to playgroups or nursery? Take him to swimming lessons and the like? Clean up his stuff when he's asleep or not here?'

'A bit of all of that, I guess.'

'No problem. How often?'

'Erm . . . a couple of days first of all, maybe more, maybe less depending on my work.'

'No problem. You tell me the days you need and we can sort it out. That's if I get the job. Mustn't get ahead of myself there. I'm often doing that, I say stuff then realise I'm making some huge assumptions.' She flicked one of her shiny black plaits that had fallen over her shoulder away. 'Sorry about my hair, when I'm working, it's always up and out of the way. I wear comfy clothes so I can chase after the kids. I'm not the best cook, but I can get by and I will make sure he eats healthy food as often as possible.'

'If I was to go ahead, when could you start?'

'Whenever you want me to.'

'Don't you have another job? I saw that you're training to be a doctor?'

'I'm not training any more, I've finished. Passed with flying colours. Just call me Dr Sazz. Actually, don't. That sounds rubbish.'

'And you're doing this job? Don't you have debts?'

'I do, some of them are huge, but I work for about six families – no one needs me all the time – so I manage my schedule really carefully. I earn enough to do this, get by and start to pay off my debts.'

'Don't you want to be a doctor?'

She shrugged happily. 'My mum and dad – typical African parents – always said to have a second career in case my first one didn't work out.'

'Being a doctor is your second career?'

'Yes. I've always loved looking after children.'

'Oh, right. What about being a paediatrician?'

'This is more fun.'

I nodded.

'Shall I go away and you can think about it, check my references and then let me know? I can come and meet him, see if he likes me. But if you decide against me that's totally cool. It's been great meeting you.'

Her grin was back, fastened over her energy that fizzed with happiness. I needed that around Kobi. I needed him to be safe from my fears and worries. I kept them in check every day, reminded myself to be grateful to be alive, to be here to be his mother, but sometimes I would falter – the memory of The During would snare me in its barbed fingers and I would be stuck. I would have no way out. That wasn't good for Kobi. We were on our own down here, having someone like Sazz around him could only be good.

'Let's arrange for you to come and meet Kobi next week,' I said to her at the door.

'Sure thing, Pi-R,' she replied with a wide grin. She immediately grimaced. 'You don't mind if I call you Pi-R, do you? Can't help myself sometimes.'

I shook my head. 'No, I don't mind at all.'

Monday, 10 June

Sazz has gone by the time the boys' parents come to pick them up. 'Thank you so much,' Karen, Sam and Oscar's mum, says at the door. 'Just let us know if you want us to have Kobi over. Any time.'

'Any time,' echoes Julian, the boys' dad.

'I didn't actually do anything, it was Sazz who picked them up, made them dinner and then supervised homework. I just came home and embarrassed my son by talking to his friends.'

'*Mum!*' Kobi hisses, mortified all over again.

'See?' I say as my son stomps off down the hall to the stairs and then climbs them. 'Eternal embarrassment.'

The Newbys laugh (the adults, anyway) and then wave as they leave me to the wrath of my first and only born.

'I love you, Kobi!' I shout up the stairs.

The righteous silence of my son is my reply.

'I love you, Kobi,' I whisper. 'And that's what makes this decision so hard, because I don't know what will happen to you if everyone finds out what happened to me. I don't know what will happen to all of our family if that ever comes out.'

Jody

Monday, 10 June

I've only been here three days, so I'm not used to the flat or Brighton yet. This place is not far from the sea and it's down on a nice mews-type road. There are two flats downstairs, two on the middle floor and then this one on its own on the top floor. Lots of slanted ceilings but not oppressive, and nicely furnished.

When I open the door to the flat there is music, warmth, the smell of home-cooked food. Winston, my fiancé, isn't meant to be here, but I'm glad he is.

'Hellooooo,' I call. The door clunks shut behind me and my shoulders fall, my body relaxes, my mind attempts to unwind.

My reply is a large glass of white wine peeking out of the kitchen doorway. 'You are the perfect man,' I say, kicking off my shoes.

Winston and I have been together ten years. He was a professional footballer (some people still recognise him in the street and ask for selfies) but he moved into property development and has been successful at it ever since. This flat is one of his properties.

In the kitchen, the table is set with candles and linen napkins.

The lights under the wall units are on, casting the kitchen in a soft, yellow-orange glow. The music surrounds me, as does the smell of plantain, gari and red stew with chicken – my favourites.

'What have I done to deserve this?' I ask as I pull up a chair.

'Nothing. I just want us to connect again. We haven't been doing that.'

I lower the glass from my lips and look at my fiancé. He's gorgeous. Truly. I love the way he shaves a line on the right side of his closely cut hair, the curve of his forehead, the shape of his chin, the succulence of his lips, the rich darkness of his eyes. He is tall and he is solid and he is fit. He is also mine.

'Are you going to dump me?' I ask.

Neither of us wanted children back when we met. Then, like we all do, we changed, we decided that we did want children. And then found we couldn't. *I* couldn't. Turns out it wasn't simply heavy, crippling period pain I had every month. It was fibroids, it was polycystic ovaries . . . It was several operations, changes in lifestyle, change of diet, acupuncture, yoga, reflexology, herbs, drugs and test after test after test, and soul-destroying I V F until it was clear: no baby. Was that too much for him to take? Was this the end of the road for him?

He's frowning when he abandons his stirring to ask me, 'What?'

'You've cooked, you've opened nice wine and got the good cutlery out. This is big stuff. It either means you're going to dump me or propose. And seeing as we're already engaged . . .'

'Or how about I'm doing something that means I get to sit

96

with my partner and eat a meal and talk to her without distractions?'

Yes, how about that, Jody.

'Right you are,' I mumble into my glass. I forget, sometimes, that not everyone does things to get something in return.

She's sitting at my kitchen table, a whole tea service in rainbow colours is laid out in front of her. She sits patiently, her hands folded in her lap, waiting for me to arrive. When I come in, I'm a whirl of activity, ready to grab a couple of slices of bread to slot into the white toaster before I go to shower and change to head back to the office.

'Sit with me a moment,' she says and smiles.

I need to get going, get detecting, but I do as she asks since she's asked so politely. She was like that, though, polite. Calm. Even though her body must have been raging, ravaged as it was with pain, she was calm and polite, gentle.

'What I find really hard to accept, Jody, is that you knew, didn't you?'

She pours me tea as she condemns me.

'You knew. You could have stopped this. All of this, couldn't you?'

I can't look at her, so pretty as she is. I can't stand to see the quiet suffering in her eyes.

'You could have stopped this a while ago, couldn't you?' Bess says. She is sitting beside Shania. She's not calm. She's visibly angry. 'There was no need for this to have happened to me, was there?'

'And me, there was no need for me to die, either,' says Freya.

'You knew, didn't you, Jody? You knew and you didn't stop it,'
Harlow says, sipping her tea.

My eyes fly open and I wake up, gulping air. Trying to swallow,
trying not to suffocate.

The light from the TV casts images over the dark room, its
sound is on mute so there are no words or music to go with the
flickering. Winston is working on his laptop, white headphones
snake from his ears to the computer.

I struggle upright, pushing myself away from the dream, desperately trying to integrate myself into the waking world again.

Winston pulls his headphones from his ears. 'You just sparked
out. So much for spending the evening together,' he teases. He
sets aside his computer and pulls me into a hug.

The last thing I want right now is a hug, an interlude, a tender
moment when I can forget for even a moment the mistake I made
fifteen years ago. The mistake I made that has meant so many
women have suffered.

'You clearly needed that sleep, though,' Winston says, lovingly running his fingers through my hair. 'You've got the cutest
snore.'

I don't deserve this. I don't deserve an adoring fiancé, a comfortable home, an unburdened life. I don't deserve any nice thing
to happen to me.

I'm sorry. Every day I want to say that. To all of them. All of
them who came afterwards, all of them who are dying now, I'm
sorry. I'm so very, very, very sorry.

'Hey,' Winston says as I squeeze him tight, hold him close, try to show him how sorry I am. 'It's all right, you know? Everything's going to be all right.'

It's not going to be all right.

Six women are dead because of me.

Six.

Seven, if you count my twin sister, Jovie.

Part 2

Pieta

Tuesday, 11 June

I pick up Kobi from school on Tuesdays, Wednesdays and Fridays, Sazz does Mondays and Thursdays, but it's only on Tuesdays that I have to get there for 4:15 p.m. I love Tuesdays.

On the other days, I have to pick him up at the back gate from his after-school classes, but on Tuesdays I get to do the school gates. I get to experience the special 'I'm a mother' joy of watching him leave the building. He'll have his green rucksack hefted on one shoulder while his black sports bag, covered with mud, will trail behind him. His hat will be on askew, his tie will be spirit-level straight, a triangle of shirt will be hanging out of the waistband of his trousers like an overgrown tooth.

Today the air is chilled even though the sun is out. I watch my son make his way across the playground towards me. He's flanked by his two friends, Miles and Austin, and I just know that I'm in some kind of trouble. It often feels that I am in trouble with my boy. This will be about yesterday's playdate mix-up, about me not organising it properly, even though I did.

'Mum, I'm going to have a cooking birthday party,' Kobi says to me when they arrive in front of me.

My eyes flick from Miles to Austin, both of whom look very serious. Austin is two years below Kobi and Miles at school, but is almost as tall as his brother and my son.

'Pardon?' I reply. I'd braced myself for a telling off, not for this proclamation.

'My mum will run it,' Miles tells me.

'Yeah, our mum will do it,' Austin says.

The three of them are looking over my right shoulder as well as talking to me. I follow their line of sight and notice for the first time their mum, Allie. I didn't see her when I got here because I was still in another world, trying to decide what to do about the meeting tomorrow.

'What will I do?' she asks cautiously.

'A cooking party, apparently,' I reply. I turn back to my son and his friends. 'You hate cooking,' I remind Kobi.

'No, I don't,' he replies.

'Yes, you do. Every time I try to get you to help me make dinner it's like I've asked you to go down the mines – you practically accuse me of exploitation and refuse to do it.'

'No, I don't.'

'Yes, you do.'

'I cook with Sazz all the time,' he says with a shrug. He hands me his sports bag and rucksack. 'And Miles and Austin's mum would hold a great party. Other people have had parties at her kitchens and they say it's really good. Fun.'

'It's true, they are,' says Mike, Miles and Austin's dad, while pushing his glasses back on his face.

'But it's not your birthday for another eight months,' I remind him.

'Me and Miles and Austin talked about it at last break, we could have a joint party. And we could have it at their mum's kitchens.'

'But your birthdays are months apart.'

All three of them shrug at the same time and 'Doesn't matter,' they say in unison.

I look to Allie again and she's curled her lips into her mouth, trying to keep in her laughter.

'And who's paying for this?' I ask my son.

He squeezes up his face as though I'm being ridiculous. 'You, of course. It's my party.' He sheds his blazer and shoves it in my arms. Miles and Austin do the same to their parents.

'Of course,' I say.

'That's you well and truly told,' Mike says with a laugh.

'Right, you, piano lesson and then home for dinner.' I've decided to take charge of this ridiculous situation. 'You can help me make it since you're such a dab hand at cooking you're planning a party eight months in advance.'

'Erm, Mum,' he says carefully, as though speaking to someone who needs careful handling. 'Allie is a professional cooking teacher, you're not. She's good at making things fun, you're—'

'Don't finish that sentence. If you want to eat in our house ever again, do not finish that sentence.'

'Good on you for deciding what you want and sticking to it, Kobi mate,' Mike says and sticks out his hand for a high five. My child slaps his hand as we go past.

'Let me know when you want me to book in that party,' Allie calls with a laugh.

'Yeah, thanks, Baycroft . . . Baycrofts,' I add, extending it to Mike who is chuckling to himself, too.

'Do you really want to have a cooking party with Miles and Austin?' I ask Kobi on the way home from his piano lesson.

'Yeah,' he says tiredly.

'Even though their birthdays are quite far away from yours?'

'Yes,' he replies. 'You see the thing is, Mum, sometimes you have to do things that are good for everyone, not just yourself. Miles and Austin want to have a cooking party with me and I want to have one with them because we're a team.'

'You're a team.'

'Yeah. And sometimes you have to do things that are for the good of the team. That's not being selfish.'

My eyes go to him in the rear-view mirror. He sits tall on his booster seat, his tightly curly black hair is almost shaved on the sides and neatly squared on top. His face, which he *hates* being called cute, is open and wise despite his age. Kobi does this more times than I think possible for a young boy – he seems to know the right thing to say at the time I need it.

I've been vacillating about what to do about meeting the so-called Miss X all night and all day. (Lillian had shown me the press notification and that's what they were calling her, 'Miss X'.) And I was no nearer to making a decision. I could only see what it would cost me if I couldn't control myself, if I let anyone know what happened to me. But then, could I really let everyone down?

I'd all but decided to call in sick tomorrow and then plan to leave as soon as possible, but that would be selfish, as Kobi has just verbalised.

If *BN Sussex* got this, it could change everything. It could put us in the big leagues, help to comfortably set up the paper and magazine, as well as the people who work there, for a long time.

The people who work there are my team; we fall out, we have disagreements, we get on each other's nerves, but that's all part of it. They were, and continue to be, an integral part of rebuilding my life in The After. Without them, my life wouldn't be as balanced as it mostly is. Not going to this interview, not doing my best to get it, that would be selfish.

'Mum,' Kobi says.

'Yes, light of my life?'

'We're the A team, though,' he says.

'What do you mean?'

'You know, like at school? In the matches? You have the A team and B team and C team. Me and you, we're the A team.'

I grin to myself as my heart feels like it's going to burst with the rush of love I have for him. He does this. He makes me feel like everything is going to be OK. That I can handle anything the world throws at me because him and me, we're together for ever.

Jody

Tuesday, 2 February, 1988

'You don't see it, do you, Jodes?' Jovie said. 'You can't see how they make you dance to their tune.'

I rolled my eyes at my sister because she was the eternal conspiracy theorist. We were thirteen and she was always railing against 'The Man' and wanted me to do it, too. 'I don't dance to anyone's tune,' I replied.

There was a bit of a gap between our beds, big enough to fit a bedside table. She had the top drawer and I had the bottom one. Nothing much fit in there and it certainly wasn't big enough for our secrets.

'I wish you'd open your eyes, Jody. I wish you would see what's going on around you.'

'Just because you've read a couple of "right on" political books, doesn't mean the world is a rotten place.'

'I don't think the world is a rotten place. I just think there are a lot of rotten people with power in it.'

I couldn't argue with that. I was trying to read by the light from the corridor and Jovie wouldn't stop talking. Theorising, trying to get me to see things the way she saw them. Jovie was always in trouble. She was my twin, my other half, but we could not be more different. Mummy and Daddy were always down at the school because she was in hot water for this or that. I just kept my head down and got on with my schoolwork.

'When was the last time you got an A in English, Jody?'

I didn't have to think about it, I hadn't had one all year. Last year I got them all the time, this year I couldn't seem to manage it, no matter how hard I worked. 'None this year.'

'But you still like English, right?'

'Not really, no.'

'Why not?'

'I don't know, I just don't any more.'

'Could it be you've been told in so many subtle ways that you're not good enough at it any more, or there's something going on with the teacher? I mean, you read more than anyone I know. You're always scrawling away in your notebooks, but never anything more than a B. Reckon there might be something going on with Mrs Binchcliffe?'

'No! I'm not like you, I don't get in trouble with the teachers over every little thing.'

'I'm fine with my Cs cos I know I put in no effort. But are you OK with your Bs when you've slogged your guts out?'

'Maybe she doesn't think my work is up to it,' I said. This was the problem with Jovie – she knew how to get under my skin. What she was saying sounded so true, but Mrs Binchcliffe was just the nicest woman, the loveliest teacher. She was always singing my praises, using my work as an example, telling my parents how super I was.

'All right, Jody. How come blonde Caitlin is always getting As but Mrs Binchcliffe *never* uses her work as an example to the class for how it should be done? Not ever. Whose work does she use . . .? Oh, that's right, *yours*. Even in my class she puts up your work. Not A-student Caitlin's.'

'What are you saying?'

'I'm saying you have to work a hundred times harder than people like Caitlin to get a lower mark than her. And you can't argue with it because people like Mrs Binchcliffe are ever so nice.'

'Why are you telling me this, Jovie? I can't do anything about it, it just makes me down. Makes me not want to bother.'

'You need to open your eyes, Jody. You can't let them win by giving up, by letting people like Binchcliffe stop you liking English, but you can't close your eyes to them, either. You need to see them for who they are. Then you can beat them at their own game.'

I tossed my book onto the bedside table, I couldn't read now. What Jovie was saying was wafting around my mind like the fumes that hooked into your clothes whenever you stood near someone smoking a cigarette. I loved English, reading, writing, but I hadn't enjoyed it as much this year. Mrs Binchcliffe was, it often felt, looking for reasons to mark me down. The slightest thing and she took off a mark. It all made sense when you looked at it the way Jovie explained it. But would it make just as much sense if I tried really, really hard to find another way to explain it?

Jovie was always forcing me to think about things. I wasn't ever allowed to ignore stuff, try to pretend away the injustice and hurt. And sometimes, I just wanted to. Sometimes I just wanted to keep my head down, to believe all the nice people around me who were at pains to tell me that the prejudice and injustice and racism I was seeing just wasn't there; that I was mistaken and wrong and just a bit hypersensitive. I wanted to do that because everything would be so much easier if I didn't have to deal with the truths of my life.

When my twin wasn't getting into trouble, she was trying to make me open my eyes to the world when, sometimes, I just wanted to lie very still with my eyes shut.

'I feel utterly depressed now, thanks, Jovie.'

'Don't feel depressed,' she said. 'Like I said, just open your eyes.'

'What if I don't want to open my eyes?' I replied. 'What if I want to keep them shut.'

'Well, that's fine, just make sure you do it properly!' she said with a laugh and lobbed her pillow right at my head.

Monday, 12 July, 1993

'So this is your graduation?' Mummy said to Jovie. 'This is the day we have all come together to celebrate your achievements.'

We were sitting in the waiting area outside the courtroom, waiting to go in to hear her case. There was dark wood everywhere and the dark, royal-blue soft furnishings were all worn in several places. I didn't feel like we belonged here, surrounded by criminals; sitting among people in badly fitting suits, looking as if they'd give vital body parts to be allowed to smoke in here.

Jovie was wearing a suit because Mum had made her. She'd been all for wearing her jeans and trainers and 'Fight the power'

T-shirt to appear in front of the court after being caught smoking weed in a park. She had, apparently, shrugged when the police officer accused her of it, saying, 'Yeah, what of it?'

I could totally imagine it, the defiance that would have shaded her face, the contempt that would have coloured her eyes. She'd only started taking the whole thing seriously when Mum told her that she'd be living on the streets if she didn't show the court some respect by wearing one of the suits she had for interviews.

My twin and I had continued on different paths. I loved her – fiercely – but the things she did . . . not only did they upset our parents, they made me sad and mad in equal measure. Why couldn't she just play the game? Keep her head down, try to get on?

'Why should I?' she'd replied when I asked her that one time. 'I have just as much right to be whoever I want to be as those middle-class white kids out there.'

'I know but . . .'

'But what, Jodes? I can be anything I want, isn't that what living in a democracy like ours is all about?'

'I suppose.'

'Aren't I allowed as many youthful indiscretions that people will turn a blind eye to when I want to get a job as the next person?'

'Yes, but—'

'Am I not a human being with all the same flaws and complications and reasons for doing what I do as the people we're always being asked to give understanding and sympathy to?'

'Yes.'

'Well then, why should I spend my time kowtowing to people

who mean me harm? Why should I keep my head down, try to get on without letting them know I'm a different, darker shade to them? Why can't I live just like everyone else?'

I had no answer. She was right. Why did I always assume that my way, the 'don't let them notice you' way, was best? Why didn't I just speak out instead of quietly working to prove people wrong? I had no idea. I just didn't.

The court clerk came out and I locked eyes with him just before he said, 'Jovena Foster.' It bothered me that we were here. That my sister had broken the law and that she was right in that she should be able to do that just like everyone else did and have the opportunity to turn her life around.

It bothered me more than anything that she was right. That the world didn't work like that, no matter what I liked to pretend. That, no matter what people tried to tell me, not all petty criminals were created equal.

Friday, 17 March, 2000

'You can't keep doing this to me,' I told her. 'You can't keep getting into trouble and then calling me to come and sort it out.'

'Holy fuck,' the charming man with dirty blond hair, clammy skin and mud-coloured eyes said as he visually, unpleasantly, devoured me. 'She really is the good angel version of you.'

I was standing in the middle of a squat. It wasn't an official squat, in that it had a proper front door and doorbell, but everything else about the place would have it pegged as one. The windows were covered with sheets and blankets, casting a dank, fusty atmosphere over what was probably once a nice living room. There were papers all over the floor, the furniture was frayed, the carpet ripped and torn, the surfaces covered with dirty plates. I hated standing there for so many reasons. Not just because I was in uniform, having come here on refs, but because I hated watching where Jovie's life was leading.

It was another slip down the spiral, her descent to rock bottom. There'd been so many times in the last seven years, so many times since that day at the court when she'd called and I came. She'd rung me today, her voice slurring out the panicked words that said she needed to see me, needed my help.

'I told you,' she said to the man she cuddled up with on the sofa. 'I told you she's like the good angel to my bad devil.' She was incredibly thin, the skin hanging off her bones like clothes hung off her body. Her skin was a grey-brown, her eyes underscored by dark circles, her lips dry and cracked. We looked nothing alike now. We used to, back when we used to think and act differently, when it was only our attitudes and beliefs that separated us. But now, she looked nothing like me.

'What is it you want?' I asked sternly.

'You know how it is, Sis,' she said. 'I just need a few sheets.'

'Money?'

She shrugged an emaciated shoulder at me.

I rubbed my hands over my face, trying to calm my body down. 'My partner is outside, it's his refs too. And it's bad enough that I've dragged him here, but he's sitting in an area car. Do you know how much trouble I could get in just being here with you, with all this evidence of drug-taking? He and I could both get royally screwed. This isn't on, Jovie.'

The man, who was starting to piss me off in ways he couldn't imagine, started laughing. 'You're called Jovie?' He made his voice posh to say her name. 'I thought you were cool "Vee" not "Jovie".'

'Shut it, you!' I said, my patience finally leaving me.

He smirked. 'Yes, officer.'

'Did you really call me here because you want cash, Jovie?'

'We just need to pay back a couple of people. It can't wait. They are not nice people. I just need to borrow a few sheets and then they'll be off my back.'

This was not what Jovie was meant to be for. This was not the life she was meant to live. She was so bright, so funny and astute. She was always that bit sharper than me, more clever, more brilliant. She was incandescent. She could see things that I couldn't, she had worked out how the world really worked a long time ago. And, I knew, this was where that insight – those hideous, painful truths – had led her.

I'd asked my partner to stop at the cashpoint on the way here because I knew what she wanted. It was what she always wanted these days. Money.

'This is all I've got,' I said to her. I reached into my pocket and pulled out the bundle of twenties. 'Two hundred.'

She tore herself away from the scumbag next to her and held out her hand. *This isn't my sister*, I thought. *This isn't my twin. This is a condition that she may never recover from.* 'Once you take this, don't call me again,' I said. 'Take this cash and know that I won't come next time. No matter what you say.'

She hesitated at that. Our eyes locked across the distance in the oppressive gloom, and she realised I was serious. This was the last time I would do this. It wasn't about my job, it wasn't about her taking drugs and living in this squalor, it was about not being able to stand this any more. There was always some awful guy, some dodgy place, some sign that my sister wasn't going to make it. I simply couldn't watch it happen any more.

If she didn't take this money, if she showed me that she might find another path, I would stick around.

Her fingers clasped around the 'sheets' and she took them from me.

I left without saying goodbye.

Thursday, 27 June, 2002

'Well look at my sister, working for "The Man" and thriving on it.'

I came down the steps of Raynes Park Police Station to find Jovie standing a little to the side, waiting for me. I hadn't seen her in two years, not since I'd given her £200 and told her not to call me again. She had, of course, but I'd stuck to my word, followed through on my proclamation and hadn't gone to her. No matter how desperate she sounded.

I had to protect myself, and her. Me giving her money was not helping her. Yes, I probably just told myself that to make myself feel better about what I was doing. It wasn't easy, it wasn't simple, but it was what I'd decided to do and I was sticking with it.

She looked like my twin again. Her body had filled out, her skin was back to its usual tone, her eyes were bright and quick, and she had such a smile on her. I liked her camel-coloured coat that buttoned up on her left shoulder across her front, and her legs were back to a normal thickness in her jeans. I grinned at her. She was back. I knew she could do it.

I waved to my two colleagues that I'd see them tomorrow.

'Got time for a coffee? Fairtrade, of course,' Jovie said.

'Eurgh! Why do I have to drink crap coffee because you're a socialist?' I replied.

She hooked her arm through mine. 'That's just the way of the world, baby.'

'You look really good,' I said to her. The coffee wasn't crap, it was actually nicer than my usual stuff.

'Looks aren't everything,' she said.

'Why? What's wrong, are you ill?'

'No,' she scoffed. 'I mean, we live in a looks-obsessed world. Looks aren't everything. Sometimes beauty isn't even skin deep.'

'Are you all right?' I asked, scared of the answer. What if she'd changed back too late?

'I am fine, Sis, I'm fine. I got a job. I got somewhere to live. I've even found a therapist who is helping me deal with a lot of issues.'

'Really?'

'Yep. It's been enlightening. I feel better for a lot of it.'

'Not all of it?'

'Therapy isn't easy. Therapy is bloody hard work. But I can handle it.' She sipped her coffee and smiled at me. 'Had to see you. Missed you so much. Did you miss me at all?'

'Every day, *every* day.'

'Do you feel old? I feel old. I feel like I've lived a hundred lifetimes and I haven't even scratched the surface of growing up.'

'I know what you mean,' I said.

'So, what you been up to, apart from the police officering? Any new men? New house? New normal stuff?'

'No new men. Well, not really. Unless you count . . .'

'Unless you count?'

'Ah, you don't want to hear about that.'

'Oh I do, I do, I absolutely do.'

'All right then. Unless you count this guy I met at this club the other week.'

Jovie sat back and listened to me talk, just like we used to when we were young and proper sisters.

Pieta

Wednesday, 12 June

You can do this, I remind myself.

I've been pep-talking myself all morning, all last night. I've decided to do this, to see this woman who may be another survivor of the man I encountered.

Oh stop it, Pieta, I tell myself sternly as I arrive on the *BN Sussex* floor. *Stop thinking about it in euphemisms; in polite, friendly terms.*

You didn't 'encounter' anyone. You were kidnapped, you were held, you were . . . My mind veers off at that point. It always does. I can only confront so much at any given moment, even in the privacy of my own head.

My pass bleeps the entrance pad from red to green and admits me into the hollow of our office. Most people are already there, working away, creating a comforting, familiar buzz with their phone calls, computer clicks, typing, chair rolling, chatting. From the entrance I can see that Lillian has someone in her office – most likely the photographer who'll accompany me to meet this potential interviewee. We don't usually engage a photographer before we know we have a story, but Lillian thinks showing that we're ready to go will mean Miss X takes us more seriously.

You can do this, I remind myself. *This is like the moment of Mum's cracked plate being discovered – it was always going to happen, but unlike the plate you can manage it. You can handle it. You can shut off everything you need to and get through this.*

'Pieta!' Lillian calls from her office before I've even settled my coffee cup on my desk or unhooked my bag. She waves her hand for me to come into her office.

I shed my raincoat and other 'coming to work' items and straighten the jacket and then the skirt of my charcoal-grey suit. This suit gives me fortitude, it makes me feel more powerful than I am and I need all the strength I can get. I've left most of my colour at home and have opted for a red, long-sleeved top under this grey suit.

'Perfect timing,' Lillian says with the most charming smile on her face. She clearly fancies the man in front of her – only an attractive man can make her behave. 'This is Ned Wellst, photographer extraordinaire. Ned, this is Pieta Rawlings, one of the journalists here.'

Ned gets up from his seat and holds out his hand for me to shake. 'Pleased to meet you,' he says pleasantly.

I shake his hand and generate a smile to match his.

We've met before. We've met many, many times before. The fact that he is here, and he is the one doing this means that something I've long suspected is obviously true: someone 'out there' really, *really* likes to mess with me.

*

We're heading for the White Tern over in Arundel, the country-side to Brighton's bright lights, big city. Ned has suggested he drives us over there since he'd have to move his car from where it was parked soon, anyway. Through one of her smiles, Lillian had told me not to come back if I didn't secure the interview. Ned had laughed, clearly not realising that she had meant it.

He has a large, family-sized car, but no type of child car seat in the back, no normal child debris anywhere in sight, which makes me think that he probably doesn't have children. The blast of music that had greeted us when he'd turned on the engine was the same *Black Panther* soundtrack I keep in my car to turn up when I need to drown out my thoughts. He'd immediately hit the mute button because of the language coming out of the speakers and when I glanced sideways at him, I noticed that he had flushed an embarrassed red.

'So this story is something, huh?' Ned says as we head up towards Dyke Road to join the A27 towards Worthing.

'Yup,' I reply.

I keep stealing looks at him from the corner of my eye, just double-checking, I suppose, that it is him. If he really is the person from my past.

'She must be very brave to talk about it like this.'

'Yeah,' I reply.

Silence between us again.

'Anyway, we've got forty minutes or so until we get there, and we're hopefully going to be working together after this if you get the nod for this interview, so do you want to tell me about yourself? Where are you from?'

I consider his question for a few minutes, the hum of the

engine counting out the hush like the ticks of a clock. 'You really don't remember me, do you?' I eventually say.

I notice his body sag and then his fingers tighten on the black, padded steering wheel, as he exhales. 'What did I do?' he asks tiredly.

'What makes you think you did anything, if you don't remember me?'

'No one ever starts a conversation with "You don't remember me, do you?" if the other person has been good to them. If it was positive, you'd have said, "OMG! It's so amazing to see you again!" So, what did I do?'

'Just for the record, I don't say things like "OMG". And certainly not in that voice you just did.'

'Look, I was a bit of a dick when I was younger. Actually, I was a lot of dick. I slept around, a lot. And I didn't behave very well towards the people I bedded. I'm sorry I didn't call you. It really wasn't you, it was all me and my general arsehole behaviour.'

My giggles, small and discreet, start in my chest, but they move rapidly and fluidly through my whole body until I'm clutching my stomach as I convulse with laughter.

'What are you laughing at?' he asks. 'It wasn't that bad of an apology, was it? I meant it, but maybe it sounded a bit rubbish. I'm sorry . . . What? What *are* you laughing at?'

'I'm just laughing at the idea of me and you together,' I say through the gaps in my mirth. 'You and I *did not* sleep together. I can't actually think of anything that would be further from the—' I smirk, ready to collapse into giggles again. 'Nothing could be further from the reality of how we know each other.'

'I don't understand.'

'We went to school together. St Leonard's Middle School? Actually, we went to Westegate Primary together first from nursery. Then St Leonard's. Then we went off to different high schools. And then we ended up at the same university in Leeds.'

'Really?' His eyes are frantically searching through time, ransacking his memory for a point when he remembers me. I clearly never really featured in his consciousness after the first year of university, when he was done with me. 'We were linked in so many ways and I don't remember you?'

'Ahh, it's no big deal. I wasn't that important to you, but maybe you'll remember the nicknames you made up for me? Pig-eta?'

'Oh . . . *bloody hell*,' he breathes as his body draws still while his face and hands drain of colour. I think for a moment he's going to take his hands off the wheel and I'll have to grab it to keep us on the road. 'Oh . . . *bloody hell*.'

'Or how about, Roly-Poly Rawlings?'

'Oh . . . *bloody hell*,' he whispers.

'The Ultimate Lights-Out, Eyes-Closed Shag?'

'Oh . . . *bloody hell*.'

'Yup, that's me.'

I turn my body to face the formation of cars all moving in the same direction as us, trying to get from here to there with as little trouble as possible.

Tuesday, 18 September, 1984

'Do you know what?' said Ned Wellst, my best friend from primary school, as he came running up to me in the playground. I was standing against the wall, waiting for Dana Bradley to come back from the toilet so we could do double-Dutch skipping again.

Ned was quite a bit taller than me now. His family had gone to stay in Spain for six weeks and I hadn't seen him at all. And when I had seen him at school, he'd barely looked at me, let alone spoken to me. I'd run up to him in the playground a week ago to say hello and ask if he wanted to play with me like we used to and he'd just stared at me. I thought I had snot on my face or something, because he looked at me like I was the yucky stuff left in the toilet when it wouldn't flush properly, and then he turned away.

He didn't want to be friends any more. That made me a little sad, but I had other friends, girls who would play adventurers and skipping with me, and he would, I suppose, go and play with the boys. He'd always liked football and now he had other boys to play it with.

'What?' I asked him.

'Your name should have a "g" in it. Then you'd be "Pig-eta" cos that's what you are! A pig!'

I stared at him. It was like he was talking a different language. I didn't understand why he said that and what he meant by it. He had been my best friend and now he was calling me names. Why?

'Pig-eta the Pig!' he shouted and then ran away to a group of boys who were all snickering and then started chanting, 'Pig-eta, Pig-eta.'

I didn't understand. I just didn't understand.

Saturday, 17 March, 1990

'Oh, God, I bet you she only started working here because of me.' Ned Wellst. He was sitting in my section of the café where

I had a Saturday and holiday job. He did this almost every week-end. I'd had three years free of him through high school and then six weeks ago, he had walked in with a girl he was clearly on a date with. My heart had sunk when I saw him walking through the door and I'd been praying, hoping, that he wouldn't remember me. That he'd moved on from his campaign to destroy me. I never worked out in middle school what I'd done to provoke him, why he chose me, why he and the boys wouldn't stop, not even after a teacher had a word with them.

When I went over to ask what he and his date would like, he'd clocked me and I had hoped for a second he would, at the very least, pretend to not know me.

'Hello and welcome. My name is Pieta, what can I get you today?' I asked.

'She'll have a cola and I'll have a pint of whatever's on draught,' he said. He was obviously trying to play the big man in front of his girlfriend, but I couldn't get him a beer.

'I'm sorry, I'm not able to serve you alcohol, can I get you anything else?' I said.

Anger flared in his eyes, on his face. 'Why can't you serve me alcohol?' he demanded. I could tell by the tone of his voice that he was giving me a chance to not embarrass him, not let on that he was only sixteen and couldn't buy or drink booze.

'I'm not old enough to serve it. And you're not old enough to buy it,' I said.

His face hardened. He'd given me a chance and I hadn't taken it.

'Is there anything else I can get you?' I asked.

'Two cokes,' he mumbled.

I noted it down on my pad and turned away.

'You know, when we were in school, they used to call her Pig-eta and Roly-Poly Rawlings,' he said loudly as I walked away. 'It was hilarious, because, well, look at her.'

The girl he was with laughed, loudly. I walked away with their laughter scraping away at the insides of my ears.

And he kept coming back. Kept bringing pretty young women with him who would laugh at what he said to please him, to keep in with him. No matter how much it hurt me, demeaned me, these girls giggled and simpered and, sometimes, joined in.

'You really think she started working here because of you?' asked one of the girls squeezed into his booth. His latest entourage was made up of four pretty blondes, all of them perfect size tens with flawless make-up.

I was cleaning up next to them, taking away plates and wiping down the table and the vinyl seats.

'Oh yeah,' he said loudly. 'I mean, we used to call her Pig-eta at school. I thought it was funny at the time, I think it's absolutely genius now. If you saw how she spelt her name, you'd know what I meant.'

'Oh, I thought you called her that because she looks like a pig,' one of his blondes smirked.

'Oh, don't,' Ned said. ' "She's got a heart of gold," people used to say. The teachers kept telling me and my friends that. "She'd do anything for you, she's got a heart of gold that one." '

'She'd have to under all those rolls of fat.' At least that blonde had the good grace to lower her voice for that, but they all laughed at a volume that shuddered through me.

'You're evil,' Ned said to his companions. 'But not lying. She really is the ultimate lights-out, eyes-closed shag.'

I picked up the tray of plates and half-full drinks and moved towards the kitchen, ready to go and hide away. Then changed my mind and instead went in the direction of his table. He was sixteen and he was not allowed to do this. I was sixteen and I didn't have to put up with this. I'd had enough of it in middle school, I didn't deserve it now. We were older, we shouldn't be stuck in this pattern.

I made it look good; made a huge performance out of tripping over my feet and the tray flying out of my hands, the contents landing almost exclusively on Ned Wellst.

'You stupid cow!' he said, as the dribbles from four different drinks dripped down all over him. 'You'll pay for this.'

The other girls at his table just stared at him, then at me.

'I'm so sorry,' I said, my voice a monotone as I moved slowly to pick everything up. 'I don't know what happened.'

The girls fell over themselves trying to clean him up. Ned and I made eye contact in the midst of the flurry of activity. And my look said very plainly: Screw you.

July, 1990

He didn't stop. Even after I dropped a tray on him, he carried on coming to the café with his female acolytes, sniggering at me and making piggy sounds whenever I was in earshot. I ignored them mostly, but sometimes I would glare at them until they looked away. On the outside – to them – I wasn't bothered, but inside every comment and laugh and sound was a laceration on my soul. I rose above it to them, I almost drowned in it to me. Their scorn would scorch me, their ridicule would wound me.

I still didn't understand. I just never understood what I'd done to provoke Ned; what it was about me that meant he targeted me.

Saturday, 24 October, 1992

I was at university in Leeds and so was Ned Wellst. I'd seen him on our first day and my heart had stopped. He'd looked at me like he knew me, as if he remembered, but he hadn't said anything. He had, for the most part, acted like I was a total irrelevant to his life. Which was fine by me.

I still held my breath whenever I saw him, still felt the explosion of fear as my defences went up and I braced myself for what he might say, but these past few weeks had been fine. He stayed away from me and I him.

'What can I get you?' I asked Ned and the blonde woman beside him.

I had a job in a cocktail bar right in the centre of Leeds. It was by the station and was in an old observatory, with a retractable roof and fully working telescope up in the eaves. After-hours we would regularly climb up there, pick our way through all the dusty boxes and relics that had been unceremoniously shoved up there, and look out at the night sky through the lens.

I liked working there, not just for the money, but I got to talk to people, make new friends, learn how to mix cocktails.

'Nice to see you, Pig-eta, I mean, Pieta,' Ned said with a sly grin.

My stomach turned. He was obviously going to do this to play the big man to his date. Great. And there was nothing I could do to retaliate because I did not want to get sacked. I simply looked at him and the woman beside him, waiting for their order.

'What the hell was that, Ned Wellst?' his companion practically shouted to be heard above the thumping music.

'What do you mean?' he asked, confused.

'You just insulted that woman, called her names and then stood there smiling about it. How dare you! Who do you think you are?'

I blinked at her, as surprised as Ned was shocked.

'Apologise to her.'

'What?' he asked again.

'Apologise.'

'What?'

'*A-pol-o-gise*,' she said slowly so he could understand. 'Or I go home. Alone.'

He was blinking at her, totally stumped. He hadn't been expecting that. To be fair to him, neither had I.

Swallowing, he turned to me. 'I'm sorry. I shouldn't have said what I said.' He glanced back at his companion and she raised an eyebrow at him, indicating it wasn't enough. 'It was rude,' he started up again. 'And I apologise. Unreservedly.'

I wanted to tell him where to shove his apology (it was somewhere the sun didn't shine) but instead I moved my gaze to his companion. 'What can I get you?'

'I'll have a piña colada, please,' she said. 'And whatever you're having yourself.'

'Are you sure?' I said, with my head on one side.

'Oh absolutely. Get yourself whatever you want.' She pointed. 'He's paying.'

We both glanced at Ned, who was hanging his head, completely mortified at how this evening had played out.

After that night, he never did it again. I stopped existing for him, it seemed. Even when he split up with the woman from the bar he stopped harassing and bullying me and we spent the next three years at university passing each other like the unconnected strangers we were.

Wednesday, 12 June

Ned pulls into the car park of the White Tern. It's well known as having nice pub lunches, an ideal setting for weddings and lovely quaint rooms to stay in should you come to a wedding or just fancy a night in a country pub.

I've kept my bag on my lap during the drive so I could regularly reach in to make sure I have my tape recorder, my notebook and my ID. We were told, categorically, that if we didn't have at least two up-to-date forms of conventional ID, we wouldn't be admitted to the 'bidding chamber'.

'Pieta . . .' Ned begins and then stops.

'That's my name,' I reply to his sudden muteness.

'This is beyond awkward. I feel terrible. And I'm sorry.'

'OK,' I reply.

'Didn't we used to be friends?' he asks, genuinely puzzled. 'I don't understand why we fell out and why all that stuff came afterwards.'

I grin first of all, then start to giggle. Maybe someone 'out there' isn't messing with me after all. Maybe they knew that what I needed at this time was Ned Wellst, comedian extraordinaire.

Why did we fall out? The man was an absolute joker. As if there was ever anything equal in what he did to me. 'You're really funny,' I tell him. 'Really, really hilarious.' I open the car door and let myself out.

'What did I say that was funny?' he asks when he has uncurled himself from the car, too.

'That's the most amusing part, you don't even know why you're so funny.' I giggle some more. 'It's genius.'

I wait for him to grab his portfolio from the back seat, and then side by side we enter the hotel/pub. As with most places of this age, the change in light and atmosphere is immediate and brutal as soon as we cross the threshold. The dark beams are oppressive, they seem to be holding the gloom in instead of keeping the building up. The dark carpets speak of an old, worn opulence; its flock wallpaper is expensive but feels too eager to suck up light from the space.

A receptionist meets us as soon as we come over the doorstep. 'We're closed for a private event,' she states coolly.

Her tone seems to have triggered some sort of silent alarm because suddenly a uniformed policeman is standing just a little behind her. Both Ned and I focus on him, shocked by his quick appearance.

'Yes, we're on the list,' I say with a smile. 'Pieta Rawlings and Ned Wellst.' I hand over my driving licence and latest gas bill. 'And here are our two forms of up-to-date ID.' Ned hands over his passport and a bank statement. *New passport*, I say in my head. *I need to renew my passport – and Kobi's.* I scrawl the words on the chalkboard in my mind so I don't forget.

'Of course,' she says, suddenly all smiles. 'Can I ask you each to read through and sign these legally binding non-disclosure agreements, while I go and photocopy your identification documents.' She indicates to a seating area where we can perch while we read through the contract. 'Officer Perry will wait with you.' She hands me her clipboard and scuttles out of sight.

Officer Perry stands like one of the Queen's foot guards outside Buckingham Palace, his feet turned slightly out, his hands by his sides, his face set, his eyes staring straight ahead, but I know he can see us and he would physically tackle us if we tried to get past him.

Ned leans down close to my ear and I shudder, flinch away, I can't stand people doing that to me – it makes me feel physically sick. 'What did I say back there that was so funny?' he asks.

'Oh, stop, Ned, you'll make me laugh out loud in front of this nice policeman.'

Ned straightens up, still perplexed. I read and sign the agreement – which basically says I personally, as well as my publication, will be sued if we disclose any part of the story before the blanket media embargo has been lifted – and then hand the clipboard to Ned for him to sign the copy below.

The receptionist relieves me of the red clipboard and pen, checks both of our contracts, matches our signatures at the end to the signatures on our ID. This is serious stuff. Obviously we both pass the test. 'If you could leave your mobile phones and any recording devices in this box,' she says, holding up a plastic container. Once we comply, she hands us a ticket with a number to get our phones back. 'Can I remind you that there are to be absolutely no photos and no note-taking. Thank you. If you don't mind following Officer Perry, he will take you to where you need to be.'

I glance over my shoulder at the gash the doorway makes in the gloomy interior. It's an escape route. A way out of here before I put myself through this.

I think of Kobi's words about selfishness. I think about Lillian's words about not coming back if I don't get the interview.

I think of my mother's face when she hears that her daughter spent the weekend with a murderer and didn't report it to the police.

You can do this. You can do this. You can do this.

Jody

Wednesday, 12 June

I put Callie on notice.

I told her what she can and can't talk about. How she should listen more than talk. What she has to keep back.

I warned her in no uncertain terms that she would be putting her life in danger if she revealed too much. I threatened to end the interviews and make it impossible for any publication to publish a word of her story if she wasn't careful.

'You want to do this to feel safe,' I reminded her. 'Don't mess it up.'

'I won't,' she promised. 'I won't.'

Inside, I'd rolled my eyes at her and myself. We both knew the second this audition process started she'd abandon everything we discussed and I'd be powerless to stop her. Callie is desperate to be heard, to have her story out there to protect herself. I understand her thought process: once this secret is told, other women will join her. She will not be alone, she will not be the sole focus of The Blindfolder, she might stand a chance of escaping from this alive. I also understand that the way she does things is going to get us all into trouble.

The last two journalists of the morning are about to arrive. There has been a steady stream of them, all of them displaying different levels of curiosity, and they have all been, to a certain degree, understanding that this is a big story, that their cooperation is likely to net them it, and that – non-disclosure agreement or not – all bets will be off once they don't get picked as her mouthpiece.

Pieta Rawlings and Ned Wellst from *BN Sussex* enter this plush meeting room out in this place called Arundel. I chose here because it is a pain to get to and we can move back to Brighton a lot easier after being here.

I barely look up as they enter the room. They don't need to engage with me, they only need to know I'm there – that the police are taking this seriously, which means they should as well.

'I'm Callie,' she says when the pair take a comfy seat each across from her. I roll my eyes inside again. So much for 'Miss X'. So much for anonymity until the publication has been chosen – this is the twentieth time she's told people her real name. I'm surprised she doesn't give them her surname and be done with it.

'The woman at the back is a police officer. Detective Inspector Foster. She's supervising the interviews. She's basically making sure that I don't do anything naughty.'

She's putting them at ease by being a bit ditzy. This is what everyone has encountered so far. She comes across as friendly, a little flighty then . . .

I settle down in my chair at the back, ready to listen to Callie once again break all the rules I set; prepare myself to listen for any new clues in her tale once I hear it another time.

Pieta

Wednesday, 12 June

I'm not sure what I was expecting.

Up until now we haven't been told her real name – she's just been known as Miss X because they don't want us to do any background checks on her and put her in jeopardy.

I've never done this before, and I've never been so closely monitored and controlled by the police before. And, of course, I've never met anyone who went through what I experienced.

I watch her watch me while I tell her my name, Ned's name and a little about our magazine.

She's blonde and pretty, too, although she plays that down. She has not one scrap of make-up on. Her skin is a light-buttermilk colour, she has dark circles under her eyes. Her lips are pale, and I get the impression from the way she doesn't reach up to push it back, she wears her shoulder-length hair in loose waves to hide her face. She has navy-green eyes that fix on you while you're talking, watching your mouth, observing your expressions, studying for mendacity in everything you do.

She wears a dark grey skirt suit with a white shirt buttoned up to just at her breasts, while her suit jacket is buttoned up, too.

She has on matt-black heels with toothpick-thin spikes that I'd never be able to stand on, let alone walk in. She's dressed for a job interview, even though she's the one vetting suitable candidates. Once I stop talking, she moves in her comfy pink velvet seat to look at Ned. *And you are?* her expression says.

'As you probably heard, my name is Ned Wellst,' he says. 'I'm a photographer. I've come along because if you like my photographs, and you choose to be interviewed by my colleague, here, I will be the one photographing you. I'll do a formal shoot if you prefer, but I think candid shots as you talk to Pieta will work best, will show you as you are, capture your emotions as you talk about your story.' He hands over the large, black, leather-bound portfolio. 'These are some of the photos I've taken. They're of different things but it'll give you an idea of what I can do.'

Methodically, she flicks through, pausing every now and again to stare at particular photos. I continue to study her as if she is under a microscope. I want to know how she's coping, how she's carrying on. I couldn't have done this. Not at ten months. I was scared, jumpy, afraid to look anyone in the eye.

And even now, it only takes a sound, a smell, a sensation to snap me back to that place. It can be a voice, a phrase, a snippet of something I hear in the crowd and I am returned to those hours and the agony of being unnaturally restrained.

It can be the scent of someone's aftershave, a couple of woodsy notes wafting through to me as we pass on the street, and I am back there in that room, fighting the unrelenting urge to scream.

It can be the touch of silk, smooth and cool and luxurious, against my skin and I am transported to that place where I am agreeing to something I know I won't be able to do.

'Do you want to hear a basic outline of my story?' she asks.

I nod. Force myself to say yes. Ned does the same.

She visibly braces herself as she begins to talk. I brace myself as I prepare to listen . . .

'I'm not likeable,' she says suddenly. I hadn't realised I had slipped away, climbed so far into somewhere else while she was talking that I needed lassoing and bringing back to the present.

Her dark-green eyes are focused on me. 'If you were to write my story, you'd have to understand that I'm not likeable. I'm not a proper victim, you see. I'm not dressed like one.' She puts her hands over her neat breasts, unintentionally displaying her unmanicured, severely bitten nails. 'My chest is on show, you can see my skin.' She drops her hands. 'I've had sex. A lot of sex. And I drink and I smoke. Well, I used to. I can't smoke now. I used to swear, too. In fact, I still do. Bollocks. Fuck. Shit. See?' She slumps back in her chair. 'Half the people who were here earlier were salivating at the thought of my story in their news-papers or magazines. Do you want to know why?'

I can't speak. For some reason, this has stalled me, stopped me from being able to engage.

'Why?' Ned asks in my place.

'Because I'm pretty, because I'm thin. I could see the relief on their faces that I'm not eighteen stone with bad skin, a pram face and an address from the wrong side of town. Cos they'd never get their readers to care then, would they?'

I can't say anything to that because I know Lillian will be relieved that she is attractive, there's no point pretending otherwise. And

Ned, well, I learnt first-hand how he feels about fat girls and ugly girls a long time ago.

'I'm not a proper victim, am I?' she says to me. 'That's why you're sitting there, looking at me like that.'

'I'm not looking at you like anything,' I reply.

Her face creases into a bitter smile; the edge of it could slice through metal. 'You . . . you're like all those other people out there. You look at me and judge me because I'm not being how you think victims should be.'

Her eyes dart to Ned and then return to me. Her smile develops another edge so sharp it could slice air. 'Do you have any idea who I was before all this? I was someone who was in control of my life. I could do what I wanted.' Her hands tremble as they go to her throat, as if trying to hold air in her body. 'I got a double-first at Oxford, I did a little modelling, I had a brilliant job, I had an amazing social life . . . and all of that was ripped away by that . . . by that *animal*.'

Her hands tremble, her leg jiggles. She looks exactly how I feel. 'So, yes, I don't dress all in black, I don't shy away from eye contact, I don't care if you can see my cleavage. None of what happened was my fault. Nothing I wore or said or did could stop what happened. And I refuse . . . *refuse* . . . to be a quiet little victim because that's what people expect, that's what makes them comfortable. Women like me are being killed.'

'What?' Ned and I say at the same time.

'That's why I've come forward. That's why I want to tell the world my story – other women, women who went through what I did with The Blindfolder, are getting killed. He said he'd come back for me if I told anyone, and all this time later he's following up on his promise.'

I look over her shoulder at the policewoman sitting in the corner. She has been watching us all this time, now she seems very focused on the ground, on the blue carpet in front of her. Her face is furious, though. I don't think Callie was meant to tell us that. Which means it's true.

Deep breath. Deep breath. I remember, when Kobi temporarily needed an inhaler, I would put the spacer over his nose and mouth, and say, 'Deep breath.' After a few days, the second I picked up the yellow-tipped plastic tube, he'd say, 'Deep breath. Deep breath.' I can hear his three-year-old voice in my head now: *Deep breath. Deep breath.* My head is swimming. *Deep breath. Deep breath.* I can't get air in.

'I don't want publicity and fame,' she snarls. 'I'm trying to save myself, and all the other victims out there. He's coming after us. The police have proved they can't save us, so I want to warn the others out there.'

'How do you know there are others out there?' I ask. I may need to deep breathe, I may need to force myself to stop shaking but I can still be a journalist. I can still do my job and ask questions.

'You *still* don't believe me, do you? I can see he does, but you don't,' she says. '*Still.*'

'It doesn't matter if I believe you or—'

She is suddenly on her feet, she rips her suit jacket off and doesn't seem to care where it falls. Then she is untucking her crisp white shirt, tugging it out of the waistband of her grey skirt. Her eyes are fixed on me as her slender fingers with their chewed nails reach for the top button of her shirt.

The policewoman is on her feet, too, and stepping forward. 'I don't think this is a good idea,' the policewoman says. 'I warned you about this, I warned you not to do this—'

Callie's fingers close around the last button.

'Callie, please do *not* do this,' the policewoman says.

Callie doesn't seem to care that Ned is sitting right next to me. That he is seeing her body, her demure white bra. She slips the shirt over her shoulders and stands there in front of us, glaring at me.

'How do I know there are others?' she snarls.

She turns, faces the police officer and shows us her back.

There it is. Proof that it is the same person – the same method, the same name. The same mark.

It sits there on the lower left side of her back. The skin is a vicious, mottled red; seared and scarred; burnt and scorched. The edges of it are sharply defined, perfectly branded into her skin. It is large – almost the size of my hand – and it is prominent.

No matter what she does, what she wears, where she goes, she will always carry this with her. She will always be this number. *His* number.

'I know there are others,' she says, 'because I'm number 26.'

I knew there were others. I've always known, because, I'm . . . I'm number 25.

Jody

Wednesday, 12 June

Once the journalist and the photographer leave the room, shutting the door behind them, I take my time to move out of my seat.

Slowly, carefully, I get up and walk across the room to stand in front of the door. I take my time in looking over Callie Beckman. I want to shout at her. The number scar branded into his victims' skin is the one thing we were going to keep back from everyone – especially the media. It's the one thing we've managed to suppress and hold back so far in the news stories about the other women – and Callie Beckman has just blown that because she thought the woman was baiting her.

That journalist, Pieta Rawlings, wasn't doing anything of the sort. She was, if anything, displaying all the hallmarks of post-traumatic stress disorder – a rape victim reliving her experience through Callie's story. I see it all the time: women who haven't dealt with what they've been through falling apart when confronted by someone who reminds them of what happened.

'That wasn't brilliant, was it?' I say diplomatically. I'm a police officer but sometimes I feel I have to act like a counsellor – to give the impression of being understanding and empathetic.

Callie is keeping her head lowered and taking an age to tuck her shirt back into her skirt.

'I mean, we weren't going to disclose the nature of your scarring so it could help us distinguish between those who had been held by him and those not. We can't do that now.'

'You saw how she was with me,' Callie protests. 'How they've all been with me. I couldn't take it any more. She was the final straw. Her face, the way she kept looking at me, questioning everything I said with her eyes, and this sneer.'

'She wasn't doing that,' I say gently. Can you hear the calmness in my voice? The way I'm emptying it of all the anger I feel right now. Anger, frustration, fear. I don't know who those people are. The perpetrator could very easily put himself into this investigation. He could very easily muddy the waters, push us in the wrong direction, plant evidence, disappear clues. It was always a risk doing this, but she was so determined and the potential gains of finding another live victim were too great to not let her do it. But the clock is ticking, the days are counting down to the next sixth Monday, and the very strong possibility of another body. 'She honestly wasn't doing that, Callie. I think she has a lot of unresolved stuff to deal with. I think your story brought up a lot of pain for her and, if anything, she felt a lot for you.' You can't tell I'm pissed off, can you? I sound like I understand her and the journalist. Not that I want to scream at her: '*You fucking idiot!*'

'You think?' she says.

I nod. 'I really do.'

'Oh, no.' She runs her fingers through her hair. 'I didn't realise.' She drops heavily into the padded bucket seat she was sitting in. 'About any of it, I mean. I didn't realise they'd be like that.

They just asked me anything, they implied that I might have enjoyed it, that I shouldn't be able to function.' She wipes at the corners of her eyes.

I go to her, lower myself into the chair where the male photographer had sat. 'That's the thing about the press, Callie. You can't control them, you can't play them.' I rub my eyes. 'Look, it's out there now, your story. All you can really do is have a list of things you want to talk about and be as honest as you can.'

'I really shouldn't have done this, should I?' she says, her voice sounding small and scared. She has mostly been running on anger and bravado, it's been obvious. The hurt and fear have been submerged so she can avoid dealing with what happened to her. She's been desperately trying to claw back control since her ordeal. She hasn't been doing that the way people expect 'victims' to, and that's what has made everyone react badly to her. Except possibly that Pieta woman, she understood her. Victim seeing victim.

'Look, I know I wasn't a fan of you doing this, but it's done now. We need to focus on getting this story out there and see if it brings other women to us.'

'What if it gets them killed, though?' she says.

'It won't. That's what my team and I are here for. We're going to protect you and everyone else who he did this to.'

'I hope so.'

'Were there any of the journalists that you felt comfortable with?' She started this merry-go-round, she dragged us all on, and we can't get off so we're going to have to ride it as best we can.

'I'm so sorry, Detective Foster,' she says. 'I'm so sorry for all of this.'

'Call me Jody,' I say to her. 'And you were just doing what you thought was best for you. And that's fine. That's all any of us can do at any given moment.' I stand up. 'Come on, let's go and collect PC Perry outside and head back to Brighton. When we get there you can tell me if there was anyone you might want to talk to. If there isn't that would be fine, too. We can just put out a general appeal.'

She moves like a weight is resting on her shoulders, something that was there is now so heavy she can barely keep herself upright.

Callie has just seen what she's let herself in for. Before, all she could think of was getting her story out there, letting the world know what happened so it wouldn't happen again. Now the weight of what being involved with the media actually entails is dawning on her and it is crushing down on her.

'*This is your fault*,' the devil on my shoulder whispers in case I decide to let anyone else shoulder the blame. '*This is all your fault.*'

145

Pieta

Wednesday, 12 June

My back is throbbing.

At that point where number 25 lives.

It took more than a year for the skin on my back to completely heal. Even then, *even then*, it was agony. I can feel it now, the skin tugging and pulling as my body physically reacts to seeing Callie's number 26. And with that physical tug, comes the memory . . . *the sizzle and sting as the red hot metal touched my body . . . the atrocious, acrid smell of my skin melting . . . the harrowing, relentless sound of my own screams.*

She's number 26, I'm number 25.

So why did he wait nearly ten years?

What has he been doing all this time? Did he go back to a normal life and forget about all of that? Was he hurt and couldn't continue? Had he been in prison?

'That was intense,' Ned says.

We are driving back the way we came, the greenery rushing past the window in a bright, patchy whirl.

It's loud in here. The engine, the buzz of the electrics, his voice, my breathing, the air rushing around. It is so loud in here.

I remember, afterwards, everything – *everything* – was heightened. All of my senses were turned all the way up to 100, and everything was loud, smelly, prickly . . . *overpowering*. It comes back sometimes, like now, when I've been reminded.

'Intense,' escapes my lips. I hadn't meant to speak, but I am fascinated by his use of that word.

He turns briefly to me, nods his head. 'Yeah, really intense.' He makes a small 'puh' sound with his lips. 'Can't even imagine . . .' His voice trails away as his mind takes up what his words started and wanders down that path, trying to put himself in that place.

'She was so strong, though.'

Slowly, I turn my head to face the man propelling us through the countryside back to the city. 'What?'

He glances my way again. 'Callie, she was so incredibly strong. I mean, she'd been through so much and I couldn't imagine how I'd cope with that. But her . . . she was just so strong.'

'OK,' I breathe. I can't really speak to him right now. I return my gaze to the windscreen. When I find I can't do that without him being in my periphery, I have to shift to stare out of the passenger-side window. There, better. No shape of my past to torment me with frippery words and throwaway sentiments. 'Strong.' What does that even mean? Strong? Because she can sit in front of strangers and tell us off for our reactions, does that make her strong? Does me not leaving the house for a week afterwards make me weak? Does my avoiding eye contact and keeping people at arm's length make me pathetic? Does keeping what was done to me locked up inside make me feeble?

Strong. Does any of the way I deal with what happened make me strong or weak? Because I think people would see it as weak. And sometimes weakness is just about finding the best way to cope. And being strong is just another way to avoid the reality of your existence.

'Pieta,' Ned says when the silence has got too much for him. 'I don't remember completely what I did to you. I remember you, now, I remember I was an *utter* bastard. But I don't know the real mechanics of how I made you feel.

'Sadly, you weren't the only person I treated like that. I was a nasty, entitled bastard and I kept getting away with it so I kept doing it. And I can only apologise. Because even though I can't remember it properly, I'm pretty sure that you can't forget it.'

I continue to watch the greenery, wondering what he wants from this. He can't go back in time and undo what he did, I can't tell him it's OK because it isn't.

'I'm sorry,' he says. 'For all of it. For not being a better person back then. For not having the guts to apologise to you in college. I'm sorry, I'm truly sorry.'

When I don't say anything else, he continues: 'I'll completely understand if you ask Lillian to work with someone else. I do have other projects in hand, so I'm not trying to guilt you when I say that. I'm just saying, if you'd rather work with someone else, I won't fight it, and I won't hold it against you. I'd think it totally fair, actually, seeing as I hurt you so badly.'

That makes me smile. 'You don't know Lillian very well, do you?' I say, my face still close to the glass of his left-hand door. 'I can just imagine her face when I say, "Lillian, this photographer you spent ages choosing, well, he was a bully in school and I'd rather not work with him."' I burst out laughing at the idea of it. 'Oh my God, I can just imagine her face! She'd think there was a hidden camera on her or something.' I laugh again; the sound and the act of doing it is a sweet relief.

'You reckon she wouldn't go for it?'

The silent giggles quake my body.

'What if I talk to her? Explain how—'

The giggles explode out of my mouth. 'You're hilarious, you know that?' I can't stop laughing now. 'You should have your own show.'

'I wasn't trying to be funny,' he says.

'I know and, like I said before, that's the best part of it.'

'So, are we good?' he asks once my laughter subsides.

'No! How would we be good? You really think one conversation is going to make us "good". No, it's not. But we're in a place where we can work together if necessary.'

'I suppose that's as good as it's going to get.'

'We won't need to worry about it, anyway, Ned, she'll probably go with one of the bigger publications, much more coverage for her story.'

'No,' he says with such certainty I have to look at him. 'She's going to go with you. I know she is.'

'How do you know that?'

'She showed you her scars. No one shows someone their scars, makes themselves that exposed and then goes and talks to someone else.'

'She probably showed it to everyone.'

'Nope. You saw how the policewoman reacted. Callie hadn't done that before. That scar is something they've kept back.'

'She did it to get a reaction,' I explain.

'Yes, because you stirred something in her.'

He's right about that, at least – my attempt to keep myself stable and 'normal', to hide how all of this was making me feel, was interpreted by her as disbelief. And she had reacted accordingly. 'She's going to go with you, I promise.'

'Maybe,' I mumble and slide myself to looking out of the window again. I'm not sure I want her to go with us. In fact, I definitely don't want her to go with us; I don't think I could sit through something like that again.

'No maybe about it . . . I don't know how you managed to do it, how you guessed that was the way to go, but it worked.'

Jody

Wednesday, 26 May, 2004

When the phone rang at 3 a.m., I knew who it would be.

I'd been working night shift for the last two weeks and this was the first time I hadn't seen the open pores on the cheeks of 3 a.m. in a long time. There was only one person who would call at that time.

I picked up the receiver, put it somewhere near my ear as I grumbled, 'Hello.'

Heavy breathing, a sob, and then, 'Jodes, it's me, I need your help.'

No, I groaned inside. *No, it was all meant to be sorted. It'd been two years. Two years without incident, without any of these phone calls and middle-of-the-night dashes to help. Two years and I thought that was it, we were all right and she was all right and everything would be all right.*

'Jovie, I told you I can't do this any more.'

'I don't want money,' she said, her voice doused with tears. 'I just . . . I just . . .'

'You just what?' I asked irritably.

'Something happened. And I'm not sure if I should go to the police or not.'

Well something was bound to happen. The way she lived her life, the people she hung around with, it was a miracle something hadn't happened before. Or maybe it had and she was too far out of her head to even notice. But I couldn't have her going to the police, talking to my colleagues, letting them see what my sister was like. It was hard enough being a black woman on the force. If they saw that my sister lived up to every wrong stereotype they had, it would make my life a million times more difficult. I knew they were already waiting for me to prove I wasn't really one of them; they were gagging for me to have to choose between what they saw as legitimate policing and what was violating the rights of a black person. I wouldn't put it past some of them to use this against me.

'I'm coming over,' I said.

'Tha–thank you,' she said through her tears. 'Thank you.'

She was shaking when she let me into her flat. The place was immaculate, I couldn't smell any drugs, and I knew she'd given up drinking when she came off drugs four years ago.

She rarely talked about how she detoxed, but she'd been clean all that time and had shown no signs of relapsing. Her home showed no signs of it, either. She was wearing navy tracksuit bottoms and a hooded top. Her hair was hanging around her face, and she looked like she hadn't slept in days. After she let me in, she slowly led the way to the living room where she bundled herself into an armchair and began picking at her nails.

'What's going on?' I asked, when I couldn't stand it any longer. I was so tired because, you know, I had a real job. I had to get up in the morning, go earn money, go do my bit.

'I . . . I was raped,' she said.

'Oh no, Jovie,' I said. Inside, anger exploded. I knew this would happen. 'When? Do you know who it was?'

She shook her head.

'I'm so sorry,' I said to her. And I was sorry. No one deserved that. No matter what, no one deserved that. I dropped into the armchair opposite hers. 'When did it happen?'

I was doing it all wrong. I should be making her feel at ease, asking if she was in pain, if she needed medical attention, if she wanted to talk about it somewhere more comfortable. But I couldn't help it. I had to know what I was dealing with. If it was someone from her old life, or someone from her new, hidden life.

'Over the weekend,' she said. 'The whole weekend.'

'The *whole* weekend?'

She nodded.

'What, did you go back to his house or something?'

She shook her head. 'I was outside a nightclub.'

Scoring. She was outside a nightclub scoring. This guy probably saw an opportunity and took it. Or . . . probably did it in lieu of payment.

'I was outside a nightclub, about to go home. And I was grabbed from behind. Bundled into a van, knocked out. He told me I had to keep my eyes closed for the whole weekend or he'd kill me.' She started to tremble, her voice fragile and small. 'He . . . I can't even talk about it.' Her eyes found mine, beseeching me to help her. 'I don't know what to do.'

I didn't know what to do, either. Her story sounded fantastical. It *was* fantastical. With her history, no one would believe her. I wasn't sure I believed her and I knew her. I knew there was no way she would lie about something like this.

'And he . . . he branded me.'

'Branded?'

She nodded and showed me.

I had to cover my mouth with my hand when I saw her back. The skin was blackened in some places, a raw, pink-red in others, the burnt area was large and distinguishable.

'He did that?'

My sister, the other half of me, nodded as she started to cry again.

The branding, the marking her as belonging to someone, sealed it for me in my mind – it was definitely to do with her past. This is the sort of thing the people she was involved with did to people to teach them a lesson.

'I don't know what to do,' she said.

'We'll do whatever you want,' I said gently. 'Do you want to report it?'

'Yes, I suppose. But I don't want to make trouble for you.'

'It wouldn't make trouble for me,' I said. 'But, Jovie, they will bring up your past. They might think it's someone from those days trying to get back at you. You have to be prepared for that.'

'But I'm not like that any more.'

'I know, and I will tell them that, I just want you to be prepared, that's all.'

'You don't believe me, do you?'

'I do, I absolutely do . . . I just want you to know what people will say. The stuff with the van and the closing your eyes for two days. Those are the things people will struggle with.'

My sister didn't speak for a long time, just sat staring into space. I watched her, wondering what to do. Mum and Dad had been OK again, proud again of their daughter, and this was going to drag us all back to a place where Mum was defending Jovie and doing anything she could to see past her behaviour, and Dad would be wanting to defend her but being too ashamed and guilty to do anything except ignore it all. And I would start to overcompensate. Try to be extra good; try to be enough daughter to make up for the one they couldn't really be proud of.

'I'm going to try to get some sleep,' she eventually said.

'All right. Do you want me to wait here for you, or shall I come back tomorrow when you've had a chance to think about what you want to do?'

She scrubbed at her eyes with the sleeves of her top. 'You might as well go. I think I'm going to take a couple of days to think about it.'

'Are you sure?' I felt bad now. I shouldn't have told her that. I didn't want her to be put off reporting it because no matter who did it or why, they deserved to be arrested, but at the same time, I didn't want her blindsided by what the other officers could say to her. 'Do you want me to put a dressing on the burn?'

Jovie shook her head. 'I'll be fine. I'll be fine.'

'It looks like it still hurts. Do you want me to get you some painkillers?'

She scrubbed at her eyes again. 'I can't . . . since I stopped, I don't take any of those things.'

'But this is different.'

'It's not, Jodes, it really isn't. Drugs are drugs when you are an addict. Look, I'll be fine. I'm off to bed. You can let yourself out.'

I felt utterly wretched. She really was clean and off the drugs.

I hadn't given her the benefit of the doubt, I'd suspected she was outside the club buying drugs.

'I'll call you tomorrow, all right?' I said to her.

'Yes, talk tomorrow.' Jovie conjured up a smile, even though I could see the agony clawing at the edges of it, threatening to take over.

'Jov—'

'Goodnight, Jodes.'

I shouldn't leave her, I kept thinking. *I shouldn't leave her, I shouldn't leave her, I shouldn't leave her.*

'I'm going to leave it,' she said to me three days later. 'Forget about it, move on. It'll be fine. It'll all be fine.'

Sunday, 6 February, 2005

Dear Jody.

Hard to know what to say. At times like this, I want to reach for words that will mean something. I want them to have a lasting effect, after all. I want them to do so much. I want them to inform and comfort and bolster and reassure.

Have you ever noticed that we ask so much from words? Maybe too much? Maybe we should expect less and we will get more?

I have reached the end of this road.

I didn't realise that my stretch of it was going to finish here, but it makes total sense to me now. This is where I hang up my walking shoes and rest.

I can't do it any more. The pretending is too hard. The forgetting is too difficult. I've tried. I've honestly tried. And it doesn't work any more. I can't go back there and I can't carry on like this.

Keep your eyes open, Jodes. See the world for what it is. Its beauty. There is so much beauty and wonder out there, I can hardly stand it sometimes. And see its horror, Jody, its hidden face, the pain it inflicts sometimes every moment of every day.

I don't know which road I'll be on next – if it is a pause rather than a stop, but I hope I see you there, one day. Not too soon, mind. Just at the right time for you.

Miss me, Sis, I deserve it. Oh come on, you know I do.

Take care of Mummy and Daddy like you always have.
Jovie x

She posted the letter to me, I guess to make sure I had no chance to stop her.

I opened it and read it and then I was running. Dashing outside to my car, tearing through the streets, using my spare key to barge through her front door, telling myself that maybe, just maybe, it'd turn out all right.

You know, she'd changed her mind, she'd thought again, she'd picked up the damn phone and spoken to someone. There would be someone out there who would tell her no, who would make her see there was another way. There was another way. There was always another way.

I told myself as I rounded the corner into her bedroom that I would make it all right. I would take her to the police station, explain what had happened, make sure they pursued him, make sure they found him, make sure they would get justice for what he did to my sister.

I told myself so many, many things.

But I'd always been stupid. I'd always been walking around with my eyes half-closed. Why would this time be any different? Why would it turn out the right way, when I'd done so much to make sure it turned out this way?

Pieta

Wednesday, 12 June

Ned is bringing his car around the A27 into Brighton and I have no desire to go back to the office. I can't sit there, not after this.

I can't be who they think I am – deputy, Lillian-whisperer, coffee-maker, temper-soother, ordinary woman. I have to think. Properly think. There is a murderer out there. He is coming after us. The ones who survived. Do I run now? Do I pack up my son and leave? Or do I call the police? Do I tell them what I should have told them all those years ago? Will they protect us like they're keeping Callie safe? Or will they look at me like I am guilty. Like this is my fault because I kept quiet?

'Could you drop me at the corner of North Road and Queen's Gardens, please?' I ask Ned.

'Sorry, I've not lived here for long enough to know where that is.'

'OK, if you head back past the station, I'll direct you from there.'

'Are you not going back to the office?'

'Not straight away.'

'Fancy some retail therapy, huh?'

'Something like that.'

'I don't blame you. I need something to decompress my head, too.'

'Head left from here,' I reply.

Once he has delivered me to the place I need to be right now, he pulls up on double yellows and sticks his hazard lights on. Their loud clicks fill the car, a metronomic sound. My mouth floods with saline suddenly. I always remember the ticking of the clock. It was somewhere, ticking away the time before it would be over. Not the end of those forty-eight hours, but the end of me. I knew almost as instantly as I heard his words that I wouldn't be able to keep my eyes closed for that time.

I couldn't.

I didn't.

I didn't keep my eyes closed for forty-eight hours.

I can't stand ticking clocks, even on a watch, it sparks a tidal wave of nausea. So many inconsequential things, so many triggers.

'I meant what I— Please don't start laughing at me again, I'm being serious. You can tell your boss you can't work with me. I won't protest. In fact, say the word and I'll call her, tell her I can't handle this story and want to pull out. It's up to you. I'll do whatever you want.'

I stare down the street as he talks, watch the busy-ness that carries on when I am usually shuttered up in the office. I don't often think about the world that carries on around me when I am not there to see it.

Right now, more than anything, I want to run. I want to get over to Hove, I want to snatch my son and head for somewhere away from this.

'Tell me what you want me to do, and I'll do it. It's your choice, totally up to you.'

'We talked about this, Ned. Until we know who she chooses, there's nothing really to discuss. OK?' I said. 'I'll see you. Thanks for the lift.'

I escape the car, the man, the relentless clicking. Sometimes it feels that everything is too much. Even though I remind myself to appreciate life, living, it feels too much.

When he drives away, I cross the road to the shop. It's painted in outlandish primary colours that clash and make it stand out on the corner of The Lanes. There's a little bell that tinkles when I enter and the place is busy, with six or seven different people dotted around, paintbrushes in hand, intense concentration on their faces as they paint plates and bowls and mugs and money-boxes and teapots and coasters.

Mirin, the willowy, bespectacled owner, comes out of the back at the sound of the door. She blinks and frowns. 'Pieta!' she exclaims and comes to greet me like we're old friends. Which we are since I've been coming here for about ten years. 'We don't often see you here at this time.'

'Bunking off work,' I say.

'Cool,' she says. And she gives me that knowing look. I used to come here in a panic, barely keeping things together. You could only tell I was trembling if you looked carefully at my hands; you could only tell I was about to scream if you stared intently at my clenched jaw; you could only tell I was falling apart if you examined the tangled threads of my life to date.

'Paint or throw?' she asks.

'Throw,' I reply.

'You know where the aprons are.'

'Thanks, Mirin.' She's one of those people who doesn't ask questions. She's seen enough, I guess, to not force anyone to talk or confront anything they don't want to.

Saturday, 25 April, 2009

'Please,' I whispered.

I could hear my breath, ragged and laboured in my ears as the fear trembled through every nerve in my body. I was cold, freezing, my skin a mass of heightened, painful goosebumps, and I wasn't sure if it was from the temperature or from the way my body was shackled.

I wanted to scream, I wanted to shout and yell and twist and wrench my body out of the things on my wrists and my ankles. I wanted to cry and plead and beg. I wanted to say and do anything through those tears, promise everything, if he'd just let me go.

But I couldn't. I couldn't do any of that.

I had to be *calm*.

I had to *breathe*.

I had to do *this*.

'Please,' I whispered again.

My upper eyelids were too heavy, they felt like lead weights on the lower part of my eyes. My eyelashes were like shards of glass on my skin. I wanted to open my eyes, to relieve the pressure but I couldn't. I knew what he would do if I did.

'Please,' I said a third time, slightly louder. I knew he was there, I could hear him, his breathing was even and normal, like this was nothing out of the ordinary for him; I could feel the way his body displaced the atmosphere somewhere to my left.

'Please.' A bit louder. 'Please.' Louder still.

'What do you want, Pi-eta?' he eventually said.

I tried to hide how I quailed inside at his voice: it drizzled fear over my skin, trickled terror through my veins.

'My name.' I swallowed. I had to do this. I had to try this. 'My name is not Pi-eta. You're meant to say it like the boy's name – Peter. Pieta.'

He said nothing and he did not move. I held my breath, stilled my racing heart as best I could. Would this work? Would he go for it?

'Pieta,' he eventually said. 'Pieta.'

A sob almost escaped, nearly gave me away. It worked. It worked.

'What's . . . what's your name?'

He said nothing, but I could hear him breathing.

'What should I call you?'

His mouth was right near my ear, making me flinch as he said: 'Peter.'

He laughed, the sound a chainsaw hacking at my flesh. 'Call me Peter.' More laughter. More and more laughter.

Wednesday, 12 June

Descending the white-painted stairs at Mirin's Pottery Palace is like lowering yourself into a pale cocoon. The floor is the colour and texture of dried, unfired clay. The walls are a pale, pale pink terracotta, and the shelves, of which there are many, are stripped

163

wood. There are six small, individual potter wheel stations. They have multi-coloured stands, with pedals each side of the long, low base, and a large bowl on top that holds the wheel and water, sponge and tools, including the sharp potter's scalpel and wire garrotte. Around the corner, the room stretches back to hold six tables for other types of pottery-making, two sinks to wash up, with the loos beyond that, and the kiln right at the back of the space, hidden behind locked doors.

It's empty down here at the moment, which is ideal for me. I grab an apron from the shelf under the stairs, replace it with my jacket and bag, then fold up my sleeves before I take my seat in front of the red wheel.

Saturday, 25 April, 2009

'Peter?' My throat was so dry I could barely form words.

I'd been trying to count the ticks, trying to keep time so I could work out how much longer. How much more time. But I got lost, I couldn't keep up, the numbers got jumbled in my head and if I didn't concentrate, I knew I'd open my eyes. The ticks – constant, unchanging, relentless – started to remind me of a bomb. Of a metronome that would never know music. Of the countdown to when I opened my eyes and the end came.

'Peter?' I whispered again. My lips were cracked, sore and split, the tang of blood skittered across my tongue whenever I tried to lick them.

'Peter?' I knew he was there. I could always tell when he was there. He liked to pretend he was gone sometimes, would be still and quiet, would hold his breath for minutes at a time, just to see if I would defy him, if I would open my eyes because I thought I was alone.

I always knew, though. His scent had been around me enough for me to know when he was there, watching, waiting. His shape had been near enough for me to tell when it was close. 'Please? Peter?'

I had to try again. It was my only hope. I had to try again.

He stepped forward, and I could feel him properly, standing over me. He didn't speak, he simply waited.

'My shoulder . . . I had surgery on it last year. It hurts so much like this. Can . . . can you lower it . . . *please*?' I swallowed, the words were like ash in my already parched, scorched throat. But I had to sound normal. I had to speak like he was a normal person, this was a normal situation. 'It just hurts so much. The left one is fine. The right one. You can leave the left one as it is, just the right one, please? Please?'

His footsteps as he left and the shutting of the door were his reply.

My body sagged, the wrench in my right shoulder, firing agony through me. He didn't go for it; he didn't help me. But he didn't hurt me this time, either.

Wednesday, 12 June

The clay is a small, grey heap on the low, red wheel. I slide into the seat behind it, my foot on the pedal, ready to press down, press forward and start the process. The mound, wet and slick, begins to move, spinning round and round as I 'fire up' the wheel with my right foot. I gently press my finger into the top of it, causing the smallest of depressions. I push down a little harder, harder, and the crater begins to appear, the speed and my finger forcing the clay outwards and upwards into walls. I keep going, watching the clay shape itself with only the slightest amount of pressure from me.

My fingers move downwards until it's a centimetre from the bottom, then I take my finger away and add a tiny amount of water from the container sitting beside the wheel to wet it down. Then I bridge the sides of the bowl with my forefinger and thumb, precisely moving each section up and up, pulling, elongating the bowl, strengthening the walls, bringing it to its correct height. Each piece I make has its own height, its own width, its own smoothness or roughness of walls. I remember years ago reading someone saying that they didn't make a sculpture from rock, the art was already there, they just took away the extra pieces. I remember thinking how pretentious they sounded, how ridiculous. I had to eat my own snarkiness when I started making pottery because I finally, *finally* understood what they meant.

When I start a piece I think I know what it's going to be, how it's going to turn out, until my hands are on the clay and they are shaping, working, adjusting the grey stodge to become something approximating the bowl/cup/vase that I started out to make.

This bowl wants to be high-sided with a small bulge around the middle, it wants me to place my forefinger and thumb here, smoothing out the upper edge so it can flute outwards. It wants me to use a sponge to even out the inside so you can't see my nail marks, it wants me to stop pushing the pedal now. It needs me to take the scalpel with its white, paint-splattered handle and small, neat, triangular, razor-sharp blade, and to peel away the top edge of the bowl. It's begging me to use both hands to drench it in water, then to take the garrotte with two corks on either end to slice it away from the stand. Once, twice. And then it's done. My bowl is done.

I move it carefully to the small wooden board and then carry it across the studio to the drying shelves. It's an odd little thing: misshapen around the middle, the top edge uneven, its outside saddled with rings of different textures. This is despite me using the techniques I've used a hundred times before. This is how something can turn out wrong, no matter how hard you try.

Saturday, 25 April, 2009

The left first, then the right. A tug, a tightening, then loosening. My arms flopped down onto the silk pillows, heavy and numb, aching and deadened. I couldn't move them if I tried. *This is a test, a trick to make me open my eyes, a way to end me sooner*, I realised.

First the left, then the right, tied again, clamped again, but this time with my arms down by my sides. Tied on each side, restrained, not enough to move or untie the other, but not like before. Not as painful as before.

'Thank you, Peter. Thank you so much.'

Wednesday, 12 June

My pot is mush.

My hands accidentally crushed it while I was trying to fix it; trying to make it even and much closer to perfect than it had been. I lower the small wooden tray and stare at the caved-in pot, its sides being swallowed up by its centre, its walls cracked like gaping sores.

I have to stop this.

None of this is helping. None of this is going to make going home to Kobi any easier. There is a centre that I can often find. When I am sitting at the pottery wheel, when I am rolling coils of clay, when I am standing at the beach with the sea behind me, when I am watching my son sleep, there is a centre where everything makes sense. Where nothing matters, nothing has happened and everything is at peace. I need to find that centre, that place.

I dump my tray onto the table, this bowl will not make it onto the drying shelf. I can't find that centre right now. I can't seem to do anything but remember. *Urgh*. Maybe that's it. Maybe sometimes I have to give in to the other stuff. I can't be positive, I can't rise above it, I can't find a way to make it all better.

And sometimes, I just have to throw this grey mess that I call life back onto the potter's wheel and start again from scratch.

Jody

Saturday, 11 March, 2006

'PC Foster, you're up,' one of the officers who worked on the front desk said as he stuck his head around the canteen door.

I hated him. He was a PC like me, but was much, much older than me and had been in the job for many years. With it, he was rude and condescending, even though technically we were the same rank. 'Sorry?' I called.

He stepped into the canteen and cocked his head towards the door. 'One of your lot is out there asking to talk to someone.'

'My lot? You mean, a human being?'

'A coloured girl, blathering on about talking to a girl officer.'

'Oh, you mean, a black woman has come in to report a crime and it's probably of a sexual nature and she wants to talk to a woman officer instead of someone who reminds her of the person who abused her? Is that right?' I said. 'Wow, turns out I can speak all sorts of languages, including old-fashioned PC.'

Vanessa, Jacquie and Graham, who I'd been having a coffee with on refs, smirked and the desk PC's lip stiffened.

'Just get on with it PC Politically Correct,' he replied. 'She's in one of the interview rooms. You can go bond together.'

He'd put her in the interview room nearest the main entrance and she was pacing the floor when I arrived, even though each step looked like it was agony. 'Do you want to come with me?' I asked her.

I took her to the soft interview room, where there were comfy sofas and chairs, cushions and rugs. It was more pleasant, and it helped people who were traumatised or scared to relax.

'I'm PC Jody Foster, what's your name?'

Gingerly, she lowered herself onto the grey sofa, picked up the cream cushion beside her and cuddled it on her lap. Comfort and protection at the same time. She looked traumatised; a woman who had been through a lot and was almost ready to talk about it. *Almost* ready. How I responded would probably help her decide what she wanted to do.

'Harlow.'

I didn't get my notebook out yet, that would scare her, and I didn't switch on the video camera because this was just an initial chat. There might not be anything to write down. She might not want to take it forward.

'How can I help you, Harlow?'

'Something happened. Someone . . . I was kidnapped. It sounds ludicrous when I say it out loud, like something that happens to rich kids on American TV shows. But . . . that's what happened to me. I was kidnapped from outside a nightclub . . . He knocked me out with some kind of drug. He said he was called The Blindfolder and he would let me go if I didn't open my eyes for forty-eight hours. He said he would kill me if I did open my eyes in that time. He . . . he hurt me. Really badly. Really . . .' She covered her mouth with her hands, as if to stop the words and therefore stem the memory of the pain of what he did. 'And he, he burnt me. On my back.' She winced as though talking about it mined another level of pain. 'He burnt the number 15. It looks so awful. And it hurts so much.'

I didn't breathe for a moment. Didn't speak, didn't breathe. I felt sick – so queasy I thought for a moment I was going to empty my stomach contents right there on the room's ugly blue and yellow rug.

'That's a horrific story,' I said to her. 'I'm so sorry that happened to you. I'll go and find one of my CID colleagues to take a proper statement.'

She shook her head. 'I don't want to talk to anyone else right now, I like talking to you. Do you believe me?'

I nodded. 'Yes,' I said, even though my voice was quivering, and I was shaking. 'I believe you.'

'I thought no one would believe me,' she whispered, staring at her hands. 'I told my cousin and she didn't believe me. She said things like that don't happen in real life. Even when I showed her my back.'

'They do, I know they do,' I told her.

She closed her eyes and her face contorted with agony as she shifted in her seat.

'Are you in pain?' I asked.

She smiled and she nodded. 'Yes,' she said. 'It's my back . . . I'm in pain all the time.' She exhaled, as though now she could admit that, she could relax a little, unclench a fraction. 'It hurts, so much.'

'Have you seen a doctor?'

'No.'

'Do you want me to get the FME to examine you?'

She looked blankly at me, as though I'd spoken a different language.

'Sorry, I mean the Forensic Medical Examiner, the police surgeon. He or she will look at you. Or I can take you to the hospital?'

She shook her head. 'No. I can't have anyone touch me again. I spent so much time being touched and controlled. I can't do that.'

'OK, OK, I won't ask you to do anything you're not ready for.'

'I want to go home,' she said.

'That should be no problem,' I told her. 'I'll just get my colleagues in CID to talk to you. And then someone should be able to take you home. Or I'll take you.'

She shook her head. 'No, no. I can't talk about it again. I just want to go home. I just want to forget any of this happened.'

'I don't think that's going to be possible,' I said gently.

'I have to try,' she replied. 'I feel better now I've told someone and they've believed me. I can hold on to that. I can hold on to that.'

My sister. My poor, poor sister.

I locked myself in one of the toilet stalls, and pressed myself against the wall, shaking, trying not to cry. Trying not to *howl*.

I didn't believe her. I said I did, I told myself I did, but I didn't, not really, because she wasn't the perfect victim. She was flawed, she'd messed up in the past, she'd been angry, she'd been railing against the system. She wasn't the perfect victim and I hadn't supported her because of it.

I had a picture of the right type of victim in my head and Jovie wasn't it. I screamed at myself in my head. *My poor, poor sister.* She might still be here if I'd taken her in my arms, if I'd done all I could to make sure they focused on the crime not the survivor. This was on me. This was my fault.

I'd comforted myself, appeased my prejudices, by telling myself it was a result of her previous life. I absolved myself of responsibility to just be her sister and allow her to be like everyone else. When we were children, when we were teenagers, when we were adults, she kept trying to make me see, she kept trying to get me to open my eyes and acknowledge that we were created equal, but we were not treated equally by the outside world. And the only people who benefited from trying to make us believe we *were* treated equally and fairly were the ones who benefited from that continued inequality.

I thought I understood, I thought I was so clued up. But look at what I did. Look at what I did to my own sister because she wasn't perfect in every way.

Jovie, Jovie, Jovie. I wanted to wail her name. I wanted to bang my head against the wall, rip the skin off my face. *Jovie, Jovie.* This was all my fault.

I'd been brainwashed, convinced that only certain people deserved compassion, only certain struggles were worthy of support.

I should have hugged her. I should have told her . . .

I should have, I should have, I should have.

'I take it your "friend" was wasting your time, PC Political Correctness?' the desk PC said as we passed in the corridor. He obviously thought he was being so amusing and witty calling me PC Political Correctness. Probably thought it'd needle me while forcing me to laugh along with his 'banter'.

'Pardon?' I replied.

I was tempted to rip his throat out with my bare hands, and that probably showed on my face because his face stiffened and his body drew back a little. 'That girl who was in here earlier. What did she want? Wasting police time, was she?'

'That *woman* was actually very helpful,' I said. 'She helped me to see a lot of things really clearly.'

He wasn't sure if I was being serious or not, didn't have a clue what I was talking about. Worst of all, he didn't get the rise out of me that he wanted. Without saying another word, he walked away.

I wasn't lying. Harlow had been very helpful. I'd realised what I had to do: I had to find The Blindfolder and then, I had to kill him.

Pieta

Wednesday, 12 June

I've made my peace with buying a takeaway coffee in a takeaway cup. I know this cup is recyclable, but my son is an eco-nut and he will give me a stern talking to if he finds out. And I've made my peace with that.

Ashley, the barista who usually fills my cup, raised an eyebrow as I ordered a black Americano without handing over 'Mama Needs Coffee' first. 'At least it's organic,' I said as I handed her a fiver.

'Good luck explaining that to your son,' she'd replied with a laugh.

Deep breath, Pieta, I think as I press my pass against the security square and the door unlocks itself. *Deep breath, shoulders back, head high. Lillian can't possibly know what you did.* The police aren't like the publicity people I've dealt with in the past who would have been straight on the phone complaining about my behaviour. She can't know yet how I upset the interviewee, the surprisingly unmysterious Miss X, and how I've lost this opportunity for *BN Sussex*.

When I enter the office, it falls quiet. Reggie is out of his chair and down the office in seconds. 'Get out of here,' he says, hustling me towards the door. 'She's been ranting and raving in her office ever since she got a phone call and the only thing we've been able to make out is your name. Run for it while you can.'

Before I can take in what he's saying and turn and run for it, Lillian spots me. She throws down the phone in her hand and jumps to her feet.

I turn around and look back the way I came in. I could still make a run for it. Pretend I didn't see her spot me.

But before I can do anything, she is thundering down the office towards me. 'Tell me your secret,' Lillian says as she arrives in front of me.

Startled, I blink at her a couple of times, then look around at the others who are all on the edge of their seats waiting. 'Pardon?' *How could she know? How could anyone know?*

'Tell me your secret, Pieta. I've just had the police on the phone. Miss X has chosen *BN Sussex* as the publication to tell her story to.'

'What?' The air around me is gradually, steadily, closing in.

'I don't know what you said, or did, and I didn't think we'd hear back so soon, but you did it. We have the exclusive story of the year!'

Delighted clapping erupts around me, startling me enough to make me physically jump and almost drop my coffee.

'We have so much planning to do,' Lillian says. 'Call that babysitter of yours and tell her she's going to be working late tonight. Same goes for you, Reggie,' she says while giving him a filthy look. 'I can't believe you managed to do it. I think it was the dishy photographer that gave us the edge, personally, but the most important thing is that you didn't mess it up.'

My jaw is clamped shut to stop me screaming, my fingers are curled to hide the shaking and my eyes are wide open to stop the memories that creep in whenever it's dark.

Part 3

Jody

Wednesday, 12 June

Jovie was number 1.

When she showed me the burn on her back, I'd been able to see quite clearly that the charred flesh, the pink-red rawness, was contained by the very distinct frame of the number 1.

She was the first. He hadn't even called himself The Blindfolder yet, that was how inexperienced he was.

That's why I blame myself for all the women who came afterwards. No serial killer gets it right first time, they get better with practice as they hone and perfect what they do. If I had encouraged her to report it, if I hadn't been such a judgemental bitch, she might be alive right now. The other women might be alive right now. And we would have some forensic evidence.

Are you still wondering about the decision to kill The Blindfolder that I made all those years ago? That was thirteen years ago. Things change over time, don't they? You change, life changes you, and the things that seemed important at that time, the thoughts that fuelled and powered you then, don't always stay the distance.

I mean, in between then and now, there has been a lot of water flowing under the various bridges in my life. Between then and now, I have done a lot of soul-searching, truth-confronting, me-admonishing. *I* did that to my sister. Me, just me. I wasn't there for her when she needed me and I put her off reporting what had been done to violate and hurt her.

And then, she found a way out that meant I could never make it up to her.

I'm staring at the pictures of Harlow, Shania, Bess, Gisele, Freya. And now, Yolande Calverley, the latest woman who was found in Preston Park. I've stuck their pictures on the glass wall opposite my desk so I can look at them. Callie is outside on the main board. In here is for the women who didn't make it, the ones I've let down. That isn't Callie, yet. I haven't given the team the pictures of Carrie, Ioana and Tonya to put up, either. Their names are on the board, their story outlines are up there. But not their photos. It was a judgement call based on the fact I could only find mugshots of the three of them. They seem to have dropped off the face of the Earth and I do not want the team to only see pictures of them in a terrible state and waver for one second in their quest to find this man. If I put up mugshots, they may unintentionally backburner any fervour they may have.

I know I should have Jovie's story and picture up there, but then everyone would know. Everyone would realise because she looks exactly like me. I look exactly like her. I keep Jovie apart, anyway. When the other women come to me, when they sit and smile at me, acting normal, before they remind me that it is my fault they are dead, Jovie never comes.

'Guv',' says Laura, who's a DC, knocking on my slightly open door.

'Yes, Laura? Come in.'

'It's the partial toxicology report on Yolande Calverley. You were right, it was succ—succ—'

'Succinylcholine,' I supply. 'Most people call it Sux.'

'Yes, that. A massive dose. Didn't have a chance to break down and be missed as death by natural causes.'

I take a deep breath in, involuntary but necessary. I do it every time I hear about Sux. If you're injected with it, you don't have the chance to do that.

'It's hideous. I don't know why I haven't heard about it before, but it's basically like drowning in air,' Laura says.

I know, I think.

'It almost immediately paralyses you and stops all the muscles in your body working.'

I know.

'And it stops you from breathing or moving. So you know what's going on, but you can't breathe and you can't do anything about it. So you basically lie there and suffocate.'

I know.

'It's hideous. I can't believe someone would do that to these women. I mean, isn't it enough he brutalised and burned them, does he really have to come back years later, when they think it's all over, and kill them? But not just kill them, suffocate them so they know what's going on while it's happening? It's so nasty. So unnecessary.'

I'm surprised by this outpouring from a police officer. She's youngish, but she hasn't just started. She must know the evil that stalks the corridors of everyday life, why does this bother her?

I mean, it's clear why it bothers me, why does it bother her?

183

'I don't get why anyone would do that. I mean, yeah, people do awful things all the time, and this isn't my first murder investigation. But this feels so *personal*.'

'They all feel personal.' Human pain, human loss, human erasure, it all feels like it happened to you. I just get better at pretending it doesn't damage me as much.

'I suppose. But it's like he's sat back for all those years and waited for her to get all comfortable, start to get her life together and then, *bam!*, he comes back to kill her.' She shrugs. 'It's just wrong. And it's really got to me. Maybe it's because of what you told us about Harlow coming to you all those years ago. I kind of feel like I knew her because you did.'

This was what I wanted. I wanted them to feel like it meant something to them so they would put that bit extra in to the investigation, would go that extra mile to get it solved. But I didn't want it tipping over into being too emotional to stand back and see the bigger picture, to be cynical and critical when necessary.

'I didn't know her, not really. I just saw her, I experienced how brave she was being despite what had been done to her.' I pick up the cup of coffee that sits on my desk. I can't remember when I made it. The mug is still warm, so it wasn't that long ago. I shouldn't drink coffee. It gives me palpitations, triggers hot flushes by switching my adrenals all the way up to eleven. I know my body. When you've tried everything to conceive, you tend to. I shouldn't drink caffeine, shouldn't eat sugar, should cut down on oestrogen-rich foods, eliminate alcohol, cut down stress, meditate, simplify my life. I know that I have to do all of those things to give my body a fair chance at getting pregnant. It's unfortunate that my life, my job, my age are just designed to be unable to do those things.

I put down the cup.

'We should get on with today's briefing,' I say to Laura. 'See what we've turned up today.'

'It's like being buried alive,' Laura replies, completely ignoring what I said. 'That's always been my fear. Being buried alive and no one knowing that you're still awake. I remember seeing this show once where that happened. Except the guy was evil so the mortician knew he was awake and still carried out the autopsy on him. Urgh. I shouldn't watch those things.' She shudders. 'I wonder if it was Sux in that film as well?'

'Possibly. Could you—'

'I really hope that's the only type of drug out there like that.'

'There are loads of them.'

'What?' she almost shrieks, her panicked eyes seeking out mine.

She heard that, of course, any work-related things she's deaf to.

'Sux is a neuromuscular agent, they're used essentially to stop you moving during surgery. They're used to keep a patient still while the other anaesthetic drugs put you to sleep. No one really uses it on its own unless someone is in respiratory distress and they need to get a tube down quickly. No matter what, though, you have to ventilate – breathe for – the person. Otherwise, as you say, you suffocate.'

Laura is eyeing me up suspiciously. 'How do you know so much about it?'

From what Jovie had said, Harlow had said, what Carrie who walked into Lewisham Police Station had said, they were given something fast-acting to knock them out when they were first snatched. Chlorine on a rag doesn't work fast enough. Sux would incapacitate you, but needs something else, like ketamine or potassium chloride, to knock you out. A mix would work like an anaesthetic, much quicker than chlorine on a rag – even if it was injected into the muscle instead of the vein. Which had me checking out doctors who might have been connected to Jovie and then Harlow. Nothing so far.

'This isn't my first complex murder, Laura,' I reply. 'Each murderer has a signature, which is not just about who they kill or the way they kill. There is also how they kill and what they get from the way they kill.'

Laura nods.

'Can you get everyone together, I want to see where we are with everything.'

'Yes, Guv',' she replies.

I like when they call me Guv'. It makes me believe that I can do this. I can find The Blindfolder.

And end him.

Jody

Wednesday, 12 June

Now that Callie has chosen *BN Sussex* as the publication she'll talk to, I need to check out the journalists involved.

If we are going to do this thing, I would have preferred one of the more well-known publications, a national, so we could reach as many people as possible. But I let her choose, so I have to respect that.

It's going to blow up, of course. The other papers would start to run things to spite Callie and dilute the story before it could come out in the other publication; they'd be trying to find someone to leak them information from the official investigation. Then they'd be going back over other cases, anything similar to make links they think we've missed but we've most likely dismissed as irrelevant. All this will do is cause panic. It will empty out clubs, dial up the fear women live with about being out alone, tap into the old stereotype that stranger sexual assault is the only type of sexual assault there is.

Stop it, Jody, I tell myself. *Stop getting distracted.*

I open up the file on Ned Wellst. Crime wise, nothing remarkable except a couple of speeding tickets. The only other interesting thing

187

is how much he has moved around. He rarely stays in any one place for long, doesn't seem keen to put down roots. I flick away from his file but then come back to it.

It's rare for a person who has no family history of it – parents in the army, oil rigs, diplomatic service, etc – to move around so much as an adult. He went to school and sixth form in London, then Leeds to university. After that, he didn't seem to settle anywhere. I stare at the list of addresses for him. Nearly forty of them over a twenty-five-year span. He seems to have moved at least every year, sometimes three times in a year. Constantly moving. No dependents, no wife, no children, just him. Always in motion, gathering no moss, none of the detritus we all pick up along the way.

I frown at the screen. He's forty-five and has never lived in one place for more than a year. Why? And now he's here, a part of this case. Hmm . . .

I bring up the file on Pieta Rawlings. Nothing remarkable, except a missing person's report.

Pieta Rawlings
Thursday 30 April, 2009

```
Thirty-five-year-old Pieta Rawlings was reported
missing by her mother, Mrs Aida Rawlings, on
Saturday 25 April, 2009. Her mother hadn't heard
from her in over forty-eight hours and said
that was extremely unusual. Pieta's father,
Gerrald Rawlings, had been to her property
and she was not there. We initially were not
concerned until a basic PNC showed that her
mobile phone had been handed in at Tower Hill
```

Police Station on the last day anyone had heard
from her.

An initial visit to her property indicated
that she had not been home. Calls to the
numbers in her mobile phone showed no one had
heard from her. After she didn't turn up or
call in sick for work on Monday 27 April, we
visited a Mr Jason Breechner, the number most
called and most calls received. He told us
he had spoken to her on Friday night at about
11 p.m., and had made plans for her to visit
him at his home that Saturday, but she
hadn't shown up, nor had she called to cancel
or rearrange, hence the large number of calls -
she always called to cancel and almost always
answered her phone to him.

When Miss Rawlings failed to call into work
for three days in a row, we visited her
property again on Thursday 30 April with the
intention of gaining entry and searching it for
clues as to where she might have gone. Before
we attempted to gain entry, we knocked on the
door a couple of times while waiting for a
locksmith and Miss Rawlings answered. We spoke
to her in her flat and after a little while,
she told us she was fine and had 'been on a
bender'.

She didn't show signs of suffering the after-
effects of excessive alcohol intake or drug

abuse, but insisted that was what she had been
doing. She seemed nervous and unable to settle.
She kept constantly looking at the other
attending officer, PC Ewan Jerrand.

I questioned Miss Rawlings without PC
Jerrand, a male officer, present in the
hopes Miss Rawlings would be more forthcoming
about what had happened to her in the time
she had disappeared. Although she visibly and
physically relaxed once PC Jerrand had left the
room, she still maintained that nothing had
happened to her and that she hadn't been
sexually assaulted or similar.

Despite what she said, it was quite clear to
me that Miss Rawlings had been quite severely
attacked, most likely raped several times over
a sustained period of time. Possibly by more
than one assailant. She exhibited very overt
and classic signs of extreme post-traumatic
stress consistent with this type of assault and
moved as though in some considerable pain.

I gave her my card, and told her to call into
the station or ring me if she wanted to talk.
I doubt she will.

I know this report goes beyond the usual
scope of a missing person's report, especially
when the subject has been found, but I thought
what I observed should be recorded somewhere in
case Miss Rawlings decides to come forward at a

later date to report her attack. This could
help to back up her claims.
   PC Margie Koit, Thursday 30 April, 2009

I finish the report and stare into space for a while.

I was right about Pieta Rawlings. She was a victim who hadn't dealt with what had happened to her. But there was more to it than that. That's what had been nibbling at the edge of my mind like a caterpillar working its way through a cabbage leaf. I'd been so pissed off with Callie that I hadn't properly registered it at the time: Pieta Rawlings's responses were off.

Yes, she was a rape victim, but . . . I close my eyes so I can better conjure up her face. Ordinary, normal, but guarded, wary. She'd been triggered, as any victim would be, but the way her eyes had stared at Callie's scar . . . It wasn't the shock and horror that the photographer showed, it was different. I'm not sure how to describe it to you. It was like she'd seen it before, but at the same time it was something new to her. It was a brand-new familiar terror.

I open my eyes again.

Am I reading something into this situation that isn't there? Because that's what I do. When I'm in the midst of an investigation, I find ways to link everything – and I mean everything – to what I'm working on. I mean, several times I've had to quietly and discreetly eliminate Winston from my enquiries. (Poor guy has no idea I always check out his alibi for the time of the crime I'm working on because I don't ever want to climb into bed beside him with even the slimmest shadow of doubt that he could be the person I'm looking for.) Am I doing this with Pieta

Rawlings? It'd be a hell of a coincidence if she did know something, was possibly another victim of The Blindfolder.

I close my eyes again.

Her face had contracted in genuine horror when Callie said The Blindfolder's other victims had been killed and that he was clearly hunting down the ones who'd survived the first time around. I can see it now: she looked terrified. None of the other journalists had responded like that to the news of the other murders. It was shocking to them, news that they were going to hook their stories on, but not the panic that Pieta Rawlings showed.

My eyes run over the report again, like fingers seeking out snags in a piece of expensive silk: '. . . *visibly and physically relaxed once PC Jerrand had left the room . . . quite severely attacked . . . raped several times over a sustained period of time . . . moved as though in some considerable pain*' jump out at me.

She disappeared for a weekend, she didn't call work, her boyfriend said she hadn't shown up, she was in pain . . .

She's one of them, isn't she?

Pieta Rawlings is one of the ones who survived a weekend with The Blindfolder.

Jody

Friday, 14 June

Pieta Rawlings isn't very pleased to see me. Her face does that thing where she's trying to decide how she's going to play this – pretend she doesn't know me or act like I'm her new best mate.

'Detective Foster, isn't it?' she says. 'Hello.'

Not so much my new best mate, more someone she knows and would rather meet for a coffee somewhere public to avoid a scene.

'That's right. Detective Inspector Foster, if we want to be accurate and, you being a journalist, I'm sure you want everything correct.'

That niggles her – it subtly changes the look in her eyes. The alteration is almost imperceptible to someone who isn't looking for signs on how to read this woman. Someone who isn't me, basically.

'How can I help you?' she asks and moves to cling on to her front door, bridging the gap between it and the doorpost. If she was previously going to voluntarily invite me in, that isn't going to happen now.

'Is this a good time? I wanted to talk to you.'

'Well, not really. I've only just convinced my son to go to

sleep, any noise will wake him and he'll be up half the night. Which actually means I'll be up half the night.'

She really is not going to give it up easily.

'It won't take long and I promise I won't make any noise.'

With a scant, wispy sigh she steps aside. 'Down the corridor,' she says when I stand looking uncomfortable in the vestibule of this, frankly, ginormous Victorian villa flat. I watch her as she steps back and shuts the door. Her shoulder-length hair is teased back into a ponytail/bun that, I guess, is meant to keep her hair out of her face when she is carrying out her chores. She wears a navy denim skirt, a slash-necked, electric-blue top, and striped rainbow leggings. It's quite the contrast to how she was dressed the other day when she was wearing a grey suit that virtually matched Callie's one. Her feet are bare and she has a blue and white tea towel over her shoulder.

Pieta Rawlings is small but in no way petite. She has curves under her clothes, an undefined waist, and she walks tall, making her seem taller than her five-foot-five maximum frame.

The corridor is long and wide, with pictures and various pieces of art on display along the white walls.

'How old is your son?' I ask as we arrive in the large space of her living room. The view out of the window from behind the television is glorious. I feel jealous all of a sudden; I envy her ability to look out over this part of Hove.

'What did you want to talk about?' she replies, skilfully avoiding the question. This is the sort of thing I've been trying to coach Callie to do – if you don't want to answer a question, ask them something in return or answer the question you want them to ask.

'I, erm, I want to talk to you about The Blindfolder.'

I am facing her full on when I ask this. I want to see her expression, her fright when I bring it up.

Nothing. Not a flicker, not a whimper, not even a barely-too-long blink of the eyes. All she does is fold her arms defensively across her chest. That could be a tell-tale sign, or it could be an act of frustration. 'What about him?' she says.

'Well, you know that Callie has chosen your publication as the people to tell her story.'

'Yes.'

'I wouldn't be doing my job if I didn't check you out. After this, I'll be paying your colleague a visit. Just to chat with him. Lay out some ground rules, etc.'

'That sounds very much like press intimidation,' she says.

'Oh, goodness, no!' I shake my head. I need to start again, get her on side. Clearly I was off-base, obviously she isn't a victim of The Blindfolder. 'Despite what she might think or how she acts, Callie is very vulnerable. I have to do all I can to protect her. I'll admit, I didn't want her to talk to the press, I still don't to a certain extent. But you've met her, you know that she's very determined to do this so all I can do is support her and make sure I check out everyone involved.'

'Right.'

I look around her living room. It's cosy, for want of a better word. Sofa, chairs, a large white unit with equally-sized squares overflowing with books and board games, DVDs and computer games. There's a rug covering the parquet floor at the centre and lots of pottery. Lots and *lots* of pottery. Jugs, cups, mugs, bowls, vases. All of them distinctly handmade. On the glass coffee table in front of me, there is a large fruit bowl, with a sea scene. The top is a chaos of uneven, curled lines that look vaguely like waves. While the inside is painted several shades of sea blue-green, the wavy top is crested with white like the foam, the outside is a sky blue dotted with white clouds. It's rustic, but pretty in a way.

'Do you make pottery?' I ask her, tearing my gaze away from the fruit bowl. It's one of those odd things that you would aesthetically call 'ugly', but actually is intricately, intimately beautiful.

'Yes,' she says, surprised that I've asked. 'I, erm, started when I was pregnant. It was calming and I got to use a different part of my brain.'

'Why did you need calming down when you were pregnant? I always thought it must be the most wonderful experience: the chance to feel in touch with yourself and the universe, the opportunity to be an Earth mother?'

Pieta smirks, not in a nasty way, just incredulous. 'You've obviously never been pregnant,' she says.

Oh, but it stings. It really does. It always does. Look, I'm not some baby-obsessed woman who spends her time looking to be upset by something that's not going to happen, but things like that sting. I want to be. I want to be a mother, I want to experience pregnancy. I get hurt when people unintentionally remind me it's not going to happen. Is there something wrong with that? Is there something I should do to make you feel more comfortable with my hurt?

'No,' I mumble. 'I've never been pregnant.'

Pieta softens before my very eyes – my admission has broken down the wall around her; made her see me as human.

She moves into the room, flicking the tea towel off her shoulder as she goes. 'I had trouble . . . you know . . . with all of that, too. I was told at one point it'd be highly unlikely I would have children. When I was told that, I kind of fantasised about what it'd be like to have a baby. Then I actually got pregnant and it was nothing like I thought it would be – at all. No channelling of Earth motherness was forthcoming. The pottery thing helped. I got to focus on something else and not worry so much about . . . well, all of it.'

Her guard is down, it's now or never. 'Well you certainly seem to be prolific when it comes to pottery.'

'I don't know if that's an insult or not, so I'll take it as not one.'

'It wasn't one, truly. It's really quite impressive how much you've done.'

'Thank you.' She runs her fingers over the ragged edge of her water-inspired fruit bowl.

'Can you tell me this, though?'

'What's that?'

'How did you manage to escape?'

Pieta

Friday, 14 June

'How did you manage to escape?'

My fingers snag on one of the waves of the fruit bowl at her question.

This fruit bowl was one of the first things I made when I took up pottery. The uneven top had caused me anxiety at first. I was someone who liked smooth, clean lines, so the teacher had encouraged me to try to flatten it off, make it the even thing my mind craved. But it didn't work. Nothing I did worked. So I decided to go with it. Let what was inside out. Inside I was still in shock. I was choppy, wild, constantly undulating, for ever unstill. And at the same time, I was numb. Nothing could get through. I couldn't think for all the emotions and feelings rollicking around the ice-cold core of my being. I let go and allowed my fingers to embrace the unevenness of the clay, and then to go further, to mould it – allow what was in me to flow into the shaping of the damp, grey clay. And they came out as waves. Distinct, frozen waves. Before the pottery, I used to stand on the beach, watching the water. Sometimes it was so calm, it was almost glacial, unable to do anything but move in the tiniest of increments.

Other times, it would rage at the sky, hammer at the beach, it would let loose and show the power it held within its depths.

I was like the sea, I was like the clay, moulded to be all these things.

When I made the fruit bowl, it'd been four months since The Before and The During, and I'd had to quit my job.

I couldn't go to that part of London without feeling anxious and agitated, terrorised and terrified. I managed a month of my three-month notice period before I had to beg my doctor to sign me off sick.

I couldn't live in my flat without worrying he would come for me because he'd taken my driving licence, which clearly displayed my name and address. (I'd thought so many times about changing my name, but my work was linked to my name, and since I'd never been tied up in anything controversial, I wouldn't be able to explain to anyone why I'd changed it. And I couldn't tell my parents what had happened so how could I explain a name change without marriage?)

I couldn't leave my flat without wondering who was watching, who was going to grab me, whether I'd disappear again and this time stay disappeared.

At the end of it all, it boiled down to this: I stayed in London or I stayed sane.

My flat sold quickly, and I had enough to buy another place in Hove. I was moving on. I was leaving all of that behind. That was the understanding I had when I swapped the city for the sea. I was moving forward.

I had left it all behind.

But then, had I?

I took up pottery at around the time I discovered I hadn't really left it all behind at all; when I had a decision to make because everything felt like it was at critical mass.

'Pardon?' I ask the police officer.

'How did you manage to escape?' she repeats.

I snatch my fingers away from the bowl, from remembering how I was when my fingers fashioned it. 'Escape what?'

I turn to face her then, because she's trying to find out something. I think she suspects, but I can't give myself away. Not until I've decided whether I'm going to come forward as a victim of The Blindfolder and ask for police protection.

'London,' she says simply.

Her face has changed and her body has relaxed. Her manner was clipped and efficient when she'd crossed my threshold, she was there to put the frighteners on the journalist who was involved in her investigation, and to maybe question my motives. Then she let slip that she obviously struggled with her fertility, and her whole manner had exuded vulnerability, a side to her I guess that few people saw. Her shoulders had hunched a fraction, her fingers had loosely knitted themselves together and her eyes, her beautiful brown eyes, had looked bereft.

I'd felt sorry for her. I'd understood that pain, that hurt, that feeling of having been robbed, that chasm of a life deferred that was always there. Her agony had reached out to me, and I'd responded. I'd shared with her and wanted to be nice to her.

Now I fucking hate her.

How dare she come here, trying to sneak into places that she didn't belong. *How dare she.*

'I'm a Londoner, you're a Londoner,' she says. 'I'm just

wondering how you managed to make that leap to come down here?'

I flick my tea towel back onto my shoulder and move to the other side of the living room. 'I'm busy, Detective Inspector Foster, was there something else you wanted?'

'As I said, I've been doing some background reading on you and your colleague, Ned Wellst. It's a real coincidence that you went to school together and then ended up in the same university. And now you're teamed up to work together on this.'

I should be more disconcerted that she has done so much research on me, but I'm not – it's exactly what I'd do in her position. 'Yes, I suppose it is.'

'What does your partner or husband think of that coincidence? Is he OK with you working with someone so handsome from your past?'

Without thinking, I fold my arms across my chest. 'I don't have a partner. And even if I did have one, he'd understand it was work.'

'All work? Nothing else?'

'Like I said, I don't understand why you're asking these questions.'

'And like I said, I have to check out everything to do with this case.'

'I don't see how who I might or might not be sleeping with would have any influence on this case.'

'Does your son see his father?'

'That's none of your business.'

'Ordinarily, no. But—'

'But *what*?' I ask sternly. I've had enough now. Yes, I'll be checking her out, but I won't be running my mouth off to her – or anyone – about it. And my son is off limits to everyone. 'What is it that you think you want to know?'

'Just curious about whether your child sees his father.'

DI Foster is staring at a picture of Kobi that is standing on the long, low windowsill in the bay window. She is staring at it and staring at it, as though she sees something familiar about him. I move to that part of the room, stand in front of the display of pictures so she can't see him any more. I don't want her here, asking questions, looking at my son like he has anything to do with her.

'That's none of your business.'

'Miss Rawlings, I know Callie has chosen you as the person she wants to speak to, but that's on the understanding that the police approve of you; that you pass the most basic checks. I'll be questioning your colleague in much the same way. This really is nothing personal. I just don't want to have any shocks.

'So, can I ask you again if your son sees his father? I don't want him to come storming in at any point causing problems. If he's on the scene, I'd like his name so I can do a check on him too. The same with Mr Wellst's partner.'

She has me. I need to do this, for more reasons than one. I need to do this so I can keep my job. Beyond that, more importantly than that, though, is the need to speak to Callie. I need to hear her story, see if there are any clues in what she says so I can start to work out who he is. Because I'm coming to the conclusion that I need to find him before he tries to kill me.

I have to speak to Callie and this woman is telling me if I don't cooperate with her, that won't happen.

'No, his father is not on the scene,' I say tartly. 'We never really got together properly and I didn't find out I was pregnant until I moved down here. I didn't tell him. There didn't seem to be any point in prolonging the misery.'

'Is that Jason Breechner?'

My face must contract because all my internal organs do. I haven't heard that name in so long. And it all feels connected. Like the coils you put on your basic shape to build up a clay pot. You place it on top and then blend it in, smooth it down to try to fuse it together until you can barely see where the join is. Jason was like that. I'd never really felt anything for him, but he was fused into that part of the story of my life; into the very edge of the end of The Before. 'You really have been checking up on every aspect of my life,' I state.

'Like I said, it's important for me to know as much as possible.'

'How did you even know about Jason?'

'It was on the missing person's report your mother filed. That time you disappeared for a weekend? The officers went to talk to him, just before you turned up again.'

'I'm sure he was as helpful to them as a chocolate teapot,' I mumble. That report. I should have known it would come back to haunt me eventually.

'Well, I wasn't there so I can't tell you that. But something interesting that I can tell you: did you know that Ned Wellst knows Jason Breechner?'

The raging that is inside me slows ... slows ... stops. The swirling that is around me slows ... slows ... stops. 'What are you talking about?' I can barely get the words out of my mouth.

DI Foster raises her eyebrows in satisfaction now that she has me. She has found the thing that I have no protection against. 'I don't like coincidences, Miss Rawlings. I don't think they happen as often as people seem to believe. So when I saw that Ned had taken the photographs for Jason Breechner's brochure for his warehouse rental business, I became suspicious.'

I glance down at my hands, and they are shaking. 'Are you serious?' I ask.

'Very.'

I move to drop into the seat furthest from the door because my legs can't promise to keep me upright. My back starts to throb. I can feel the skin contract, pulling like it did when I found out Callie was number 26.

What if it *was* Jason? What if he set the whole thing up to punish me for not loving him? He got me out of the club by constantly calling me to talk. He could have been waiting around the corner on his phone, trying to get me into a position to be snatched.

What if it *was* Ned – a sick extension to how he used to treat me? What if he's here now to finish what he started all those years ago? What if he's here now to kill Callie, to kill me, take Kobi?

What if it *was* Ned and Jason? They could have both been there, both done that.

I need to speak to Callie. As soon as possible. Then I can decide.

'I'm sure there's a perfectly reasonable explanation for that,' I say to the policewoman. My words, they're falling flat again.

'I'm sure there is,' she replies. 'I'm sure he'll be able to shed more light on it, in any case.'

'Yes, I'm sure.'

'We're hoping the media appeal and your article will bring more of the victims of this man forward. We need to find them so we can offer them protection. And they may not even realise that they know something that will help us catch him.

'The more survivors we can find, the better it will be for everyone, not least the other women he's going to do it to. Hopefully, once his victims realise how dangerous he is, how he is coming after them, they will come forward and ask for protection from him. We can do that – we *can* protect them.'

'Yes, I'm sure. Do you mind showing yourself out, Detective? I have a few things to do.'

'Oh, yes, of course. Of course. If you can think of anything you want to talk about or tell me, do give me a call. Otherwise, I'll see you next week when you begin to interview Callie?'

'Yes, yes. See you,' I manage before the world descends into the chaos of my sizzling, burning skin and my haunting screams.

Jody

Friday, 14 June

All right, all right, don't hate me.

I didn't enjoy doing that, especially not to someone who seems quite nice, but it was necessary. She was good, better than I expected after the way she reacted the other day in the hotel with the interview. I seriously thought she wasn't going to give it up, that I'd got it wrong about her. So I had to push it, had to see if I was right about her. And I was. She is absolutely someone who has had an encounter with The Blindfolder.

And I wasn't lying when I said I don't like coincidences. I don't. There is something brewing here that I am not seeing. Callie. She is the new player in this. So is Ned Wellst. Both of them have just popped up when the guy starts to hunt down his victims. What if Callie is a decoy? What if he let her go, hoping she would go to the police, which would draw out more victims that he could pick off?

Ned Wellst turning up, finding himself a job as a photographer on a very important assignment when the paper have regular photographers, is a very clever way of inserting himself into the investigation.

I sit in my car and stare at Pieta Rawlings's flat. From here I can see the comforting glow of the light from her living room. On the windowsill is a collection of photoframes. I'd stared at them with a lump in my throat. Her and her son had looked so happy. There was only one of them together, the others were of him on his own and him with, I presume, his cousins and wider family. But the picture of him and her – her in a soft, powder-blue jumper looking at him, him with his arms hooked around her neck, grinning at her like she was his whole world and he was hers . . . that picture had got to me.

It wasn't jealousy, so don't go there. It was knowing that after everything, she had the capacity to be happy again. To laugh in front of the camera, to care for her son.

I was happy, I suppose, that she was happy.

I don't want anything to happen to her. I don't want that photo, that smile, to end up tacked to my board while below it is another photo of her face-down in a park, her number on display. I don't want to tell her son that his mother isn't coming home because I didn't push her when necessary.

And Jovie could have had that. Jovie could have been happy again if I had given her the chance.

So don't hate me, ok? I lied about Ned Wellst and Jason Breechner knowing each other. I'd found one of his photos on a site that featured one of Jason Breechner's warehouses. There were no other connections. No other links. No mutual friends on social media, no business conducted in the same area at the same time.

Oh, don't look like that. I said it because I needed Pieta to come clean and I needed her to do it quickly. It might be Ned.

We have absolutely no idea. It might not, but you have to understand that everything I do, I do to protect *her*. And all the other women out there whose lives are now on the clock.

And don't worry, I'll call her tomorrow and let her know I made a mistake. That Ned and Jason don't know each other after all. I can't do anything about the sleepless night she's going to have tonight, but, you know, it might push her to come to me – come to the police – and tell me everything she knows. And if she does, the end will definitely justify the means.

Pieta

Sunday, 16 June

'Why are we down here so early on a Sunday, Kobster?'

My son, of course, side-eyes me, eviscerates me with his glare for daring to call him Kobster. Only Sazz is allowed to do that. 'Sorry, I mean, Light of my Life, My Illustrious Firstborn, why are we down here so early?'

'You know why,' he replies.

The sea is calm today, it sits out on the horizon like layers of blown glass. The sun has edged itself into the sky and the clouds are hanging low but aren't yet threatening rain. We're treated to interludes of bright yellow sunlight as we walk towards Brighton from the block opposite our road that leads down towards the sea.

Only a couple of dog walkers and joggers are out this early. Everyone else is at home or in bed.

'I do not know why,' I state. Even though I absolutely do.

'Mum, the seagulls are up to something. It's my job to find out what.'

'They're not up to something,' I say quietly.

'They are! They are plotting to take over,' he says. 'The things they do, it's not right. They're up to something.'

It's a good thing Kobi doesn't know about the movie *The Birds* – it would give credence to this theory.

'What do you think they're actually going to do?'

'Take over the world, of course.'

'Of course.'

We pass a dark green bench, one that I regularly used to sit on when it was just me in that house, and it took coming to the seafront and experiencing that expanse to make me appreciate my flat wasn't too big for one, after all.

'Can I borrow your phone, please?' Kobi asks. 'I need to take some photos.'

'Nope.'

'Why not?'

'I'm not encouraging this nonsense, Kobi. Your good buddy Sazz might indulge it, but not me.'

'Fine,' he huffs, sounding exactly like me. 'I'll have to do it myself.'

'What do you mean?'

He marches over to the bench, sheds his rucksack and retrieves his A4 sketchpad and range of B pencils. Indignantly, he flicks a couple of sheets over and starts to sketch. I can see from here the shapes he's making, the basic structure of a bird in flight. I've always been fascinated by how he can do that. Art seems to flow from his fingers – no effort, no worries, he simply renders what he sees onto paper.

I can do that with writing – the words seem to flow from out there into my fingers onto the keyboard – but not with drawing, not with art. The closest I come to it is with my pottery. But that is not in the same league as Kobi's drawing. He's an amazing artist, an excellent mathematician, and has a natural talent for languages.

My son is amazing. He has all these abilities, these gifts, and none of them come from me. Every time we have a moment like this, when he just effortlessly executes something that would anguish me to attempt, I'm sharply reminded who his father is. And if these talents are from him, what else could he have possibly inherited?

'Kobi, you know I love you, right?' I say to him.

'Yes, Mum,' he replies, shading in a seagull's wing.

'Good, because I have to follow that up by telling you there is no way on Earth that the seagulls are planning a takeover.'

My son doesn't dignify my words with a reply. He simply raises his forefinger, taps his nose and then returns to displaying a talent I know he didn't inherit from anyone on my side of the family.

Part 4

Pieta

Monday, 17 June

Callie Beckman has moved from the hotel in Arundel to one of the smaller ones on the seafront in the centre of Brighton. It's an opulent place, everything just-so and clean; the carefully maintained side of shiny.

I'm not sure if this is a logistical thing or if they held the initial interviews out in the middle of nowhere to make it harder for her to get papped, but this one is definitely easier to get to. Ned sent me a message saying he'd meet me at the hotel as he was going to get there early to work out lighting.

I'd been tempted to reply asking Ned if he knew my ex, Jason. Because even though DI Foster had called me Saturday morning and apologised unreservedly for getting it mixed up about Jason and Ned knowing each other, I hadn't known what to think. She didn't seem to be someone who got much wrong, but when I did searches myself, there had been nothing to connect Ned and Jason except they both knew me at different points in time. I'd left it and put it down to DI Foster trying it on for whatever reason.

Today, I am dressed like me. I am wearing my denim skirt

with a three-quarter-sleeved red top, fluorescent tie-dye print tights, my rainbow-striped armwarmers and white trainers that have a red heart stitched on the inside. Lillian had nearly flipped when she saw me this morning, I looked like all her unprofessional woman nightmares come true, but since I'd got her the story, she'd chosen to bite her tongue. Hard.

My love of the restorative nature of colour came from when I painted a plate at the Mirin's Pottery Palace with lots of rainbow colours. When it'd been glazed and fired, a sense of joy diffused through me as I held that plate, and I'd find myself regularly tracing my fingers over the lines of colours, trying to absorb that joy into me. Bright colours, multicolours, make me happy, keep me this side of sane, keep me safe. I don't care, really, if it makes me look ridiculous. It's what I need to keep me grounded and what I need to get through today.

Lillian's last-minute pep talk basically boiled down to: 'Don't mess it up, Pieta.'

Officer Perry from last week is waiting in the foyer when I arrive. He is out of uniform and sitting in one of the foyer's bucket seats, but he looks like he'd be more comfortable in his uniform, standing guard outside the room. He manages to get me from the foyer to Callie's room with three words: 'Hello.' And 'This way.' I, on the other hand, have managed to babble: 'I'm Pieta Rawlings. Remember? From the other day? At the other hotel in Arundel? Not that I expect you to remember my name, just my face. Not that my face is unforgettable or something. But then, you're a police officer, they're expecting me, so I'd guess you'd know my name. And the White Tern wasn't *that* long ago, so you'd probably remember my face. Or at least, think that you'd seen my face somewhere before. Shall I just go up? What room number do I need?'

Callie is in the ominously named Room 101 on the first floor and DI Foster answers the door.

We stare at each other for long seconds. Could we have been friends if we'd met at another time? We're about the same age, we're both Londoners, would we be hanging out right now if we didn't meet under these circumstances? At the moment, it feels like we're fighting over a man – someone we both think is the be-all and end-all, someone we'd willingly lose our best friends over, only to realise in a few years that winning him was the dud prize, and we should have just let our friend have him while keeping our friendship.

Could we have been friends?

I stare into her shiny, fawn-brown eyes, she stares directly back into my mahogany-brown ones.

No.

We wouldn't have been friends. Possibly friends of friends who can get on within a group setting, but not one-to-one. There is a side to her that is too brutal and ruthless for me; there is a secret too deeply twisted around the core of my being to allow me to get close to anyone.

I suppose that's what hurts me most about what happened – it has shut me off from the comfort of other people. I can dress brightly, I can work at my job, I can share in-jokes with my pals at work, I can laugh with Sazz, I can cuddle my son, but I can't get past that barrier with other people. I know, deep down, that I can't trust anyone, and that means every relationship will stay surface, remain safe.

'Pieta,' DI Foster says, finding a smile. It actually seems quite genuine. 'Come on in.'

She leads me down a wide corridor, passing the white-tiled bathroom on our way, and into the main room. The room is an expanse that I wasn't prepared for. The bed is the centrepiece, large and made up with a cream duvet cover adorned with cherry blossoms. Through an archway there is a sofa and the television as well as a coffee table.

Callie is sitting on the sofa while Ned stands in front of her, large camera in hands taking photos. Her head is lowered, clearly uncomfortable with the attention from the lens, so she instead focuses on her hands. Every so often she looks up as he's about to snap a shot and he must capture that vulnerability that was not on display the other day.

'Hi, Ned,' I say brightly. I need Callie to be comfortable, to think I am nice and easy to talk to, not someone harbouring a grudge against the man in the room.

Ned glances away from Callie, blushes when he sees me, then returns to his subject. 'Hi,' he says stiffly. If anyone didn't know better, they'd think we'd had an unsatisfactory one-night stand from his behaviour. 'I'm, erm, I'm just getting some prelim shots of Callie. Lighting and the like.' The pink continues to glow on his cheeks, while the shiftiness settles around his eyes.

'Hi, Callie,' I say, moving into the room.

She's raised her head and now has a smile that is frozen in the direction of the camera. Her eyes keep darting in my direction, unsure if she should look away or not now she's managed to look at the camera. 'Hi,' she pushes out through her rictus smile. 'Hi.'

Ned shoots her a beatific grin when he realises what she's

doing. 'You can move,' he says gently. 'I am going to be taking hundreds of shots of you while you talk, so the more you move, the better it will be for me to get the different light levels.'

She dramatically lowers her shoulders and unhitches her smile from where it was hoisted around her ears. 'Hi, Pieta,' she says. She goes to stand up but then stops, turns to Ned. 'Can I stand up?'

'Yes, yes you can,' he says. 'You can do whatever you like. After a while, you won't even notice I'm here.'

She stops again and then stares right at him, as though startled by that idea. 'I doubt that. Who could not notice you were here?'

Ned blushes even harder and I have to stop myself rolling my eyes. *Can this not happen, please?* I think. *Can Ned Wellst not have a 'thing' with a vulnerable woman, please?*

'Can we establish some ground rules,' Detective Inspector Foster states. It's not a question nor a firm request. It is a straight, unadorned order. 'You can talk about the attack, you can talk about yourself, you can talk about your recovery, but nothing about the police investigation, what little you might know. Nothing to do with the most recent murders, nothing to do with a description of the attacker.'

'But how will any of this help if I can't talk about those things?' Callie asks. Her eyebrows are drawn together, confusion in every crease. 'I'm only doing this to help other women. If they don't know women are being murdered, how will they know to come forward? And what if they come to you with a completely different description?'

'You let me worry about that. I just need you to stick to the stuff about you. And you only.' She grins at us, sitting on opposite ends of the sofa, my silver tape machine between us and my notebook and pen on my lap. It's one of those loaded smiles that manages to be part-way genuine, part-way stern, and all-the-way terrifying. 'Since this is all about to "go on the record", the only thing I'll be able to do if you break any of our conditions is end the interview and find a legal way to stop you talking to anyone else.' Another 'smile'. 'I don't want to do that . . . *please*, don't make me do that.'

If there was ever any doubt in our minds that DI Foster was in charge and in control of this whole thing, that has just been erased.

'OK, go ahead. Don't let me stop you from having the talk you need to have right now.'

She retreats through the archway, retrieves a chair from in front of the desk/dressing table and places it just at the edge of the archway, facing the window and the substantial sea view. She picks up her phone and then sits on the floor, instead of the chair. Her back is resting against the bed. She seems to tune us out, but I know and Callie knows, she is listening to every word.

I need to find a way to take DI Foster off Callie's mind. I need her to focus properly, completely on me and telling me what happened.

'All right, Callie, I'm going to record this, if you don't mind. I will be taking notes as well, but try not to let that put you off. We're essentially just having a chat.'

As I'm about to hit the record button, she reaches out and covers my hand with hers. Automatically, instinctively, I snatch my hand away.

'Sorry, I didn't mean to make you jump,' she says.

'It's fine, I just wasn't expecting it, that's all,' I reply.

'Before we start, I just want to say I'm sorry, about last time. How I was. I'm sorry.'

'Not a problem,' I reply.

'Well, it is, and I'm sorry. I'd been talking to people all day and they seemed, I don't know, they all seemed to be doubting me in some way because I wasn't how they expected a victim to be and I thought you were one of them. I thought you were doubting my story. Sorry.'

'There's no need to apologise.' I click on the recorder, quickly, to not give her a chance to touch me again.

I say the date and time into the recorder, I ask her to say her name and the date into the recorder.

'What star sign are you, Callie?' I ask.

'What?' she replies, her shoulders unknotting at the unexpected question.

'I'm a typical Libran – always on the search for justice and balance and fair play. What about you?'

Her forehead creases, her eyes go up to the right as she considers the question. 'You don't believe in all that stuff, do you?' she replies.

'I'll take that as "Capricorn",' I reply. 'Every single person I know who is a Capricorn says that. Every one.'

She laughs, relaxing her face for a moment, allowing us to see the strong lines, the quiet, understated beauty in the shape of her face, the set of her eyes. Ned has been taking photos the whole time, even when DI Foster was talking. Clicking away so the sound becomes part of the background noise and not something that will distract her from talking, or place her on edge for the pictures.

'Tell me about yourself, Callie. Where were you born?'

'Where was I born? Right here in Brighton. Up at the Royal Sussex. But we moved to the countryside when we were young. Over near Herstmonceaux.'

'I love that word – Herstmonceaux.'

'I do as well!' she says. 'Hurst. Mon. Zoo. It's not at all spelt how you say it.'

'I know. When you say "we", who was it you moved with?'

'My parents – Mum and Dad and my older brother.'

'When did you move to London?'

'That's a bit complicated. My parents split up when I was thirteen. My dad moved to London so my brother and I had to go and visit him sometimes.'

'You don't sound like you enjoyed it much.'

'It was the other side of London so we spent hours travelling up there. The last thing you want to do when you're a kid.'

'Do your family know what happened?'

'No.' She wilts. 'No. I have to tell them.'

'That will be difficult.'

She's silent and I can see her slipping away from me. I shouldn't have gone in so soon, but I was trying to see if she was ready to talk about it yet.

'Do you have a good relationship with your family?' I ask. I'm holding my breath, this will either push her away or draw her back in.

'Do you?'

'Yes. Unless we spend too much time together, then all bets are off and we want to throttle each other.'

She smiles in recognition. 'Same with me. Do you think all families are like that?'

'Yes. Well, no. But a lot of healthy families are like that. What job did you do? I'm just assuming you're not working right now.'

'I worked in publicity and public relations. I worked for lots of companies. I loved my job. I loved being able to make the most mundane thing sound interesting, or being able to put a positive spin on something. I love having the ability to shape and mould something. Do you know what I mean?'

'I do know what you mean. Were you out with work friends when this happened to you?'

Callie sits back against the arm of the sofa and stares down at her hands for long seconds. I try not to breathe too hard, try not to fill the space where words need to go.

She slowly raises her eyes to me, then she looks away, runs her hand through her hair. This is it. The moment she's ready to talk.

Pieta

Monday, 17 June

'Let me take you for a coffee,' Ned says afterwards.

I've helped him carry his stuff outside into the corridor so he can pack up there because Callie is a mess. By the end of our conversation she was shaking, losing words in her sobs, looking closer and closer to tearing at her own flesh. I kept taking deep breaths to stop myself joining her – her distress as infectious as it was affecting. I wasn't sure when Ned had stopped taking photos but he sat quietly in the corner of the room, his camera lowered and his head bowed. DI Foster stopped pretending to ignore us and simply watched as Callie disintegrated.

I shake my head, aware of Officer Perry who is sitting in a chair in the corridor facing the room ignoring us, even though he doesn't seem to have moved for the hours we've been inside.

'Come on, you look done in,' Ned says gently. 'We'll just go and sit downstairs in the café bar, but I don't think either of us wants to be alone right now.'

I glance at Officer Perry, seeking his approval to go for a coffee with a man who made my life hell. I'm sure I notice the corner of his eye twitch for a moment, signalling his not

complete approval at the idea. Ordinarily, this wouldn't be happening, but Ned has it right – I don't want to be alone right now.
If I am, who knows how much of The During will crowd itself
into my mind, growing and consuming, taking over like a deadly
bacteria until there is too much of that for there to be anything
else.

I help Ned with a couple of the easier pieces of equipment and
we descend to the ground floor, find ourselves a spot in the café
bar that has a full-frontal view of the seafront, and drop heavily
into our seats.

I want to order something strong, something that will burn
the lining off my throat, but I have to drive, I have to look
after Kobi, I have to be adult when, right now, I really don't want
to do anything but hide.

We don't speak while we wait for coffee. We sit with our
bucket chairs facing the window, watching the people punctuate
the coastline as they carry on with their lives. A couple, dressed
like tourists, lean against the aquamarine railings opposite the
hotel eating chips, blissfully unaware of the circling seagulls.
I've seen seagulls swoop down and grab food from people's
hands before, I've seen them sit in rows and watch while people
eat, I've seen them front up to cats and dogs twice their size. The
way they're scoping out this unsuspecting couple right now, I
don't blame Kobi for thinking what he does.

'My son thinks that seagulls are plotting to take over the
world,' I say. 'Watching them stalk those poor people over there,
I don't blame him for thinking that.'

It feels good to say something that isn't a part of what Callie
revealed. This feels like normal conversation with a normal

person, not something that exposes the nefarious underbelly of human nature. This brings me back to a normality where I can go home and be a mother to my son.

As I pick up my coffee cup, I see Ned's eyes flick to my left hand. It's bare, of course.

'You have a child?' he says in surprise. 'Really?'

'Why is that such a shock to you?' I reply defensively. 'Staggered that someone would ignore my rolls of fat and piggy face long enough to screw me, possibly with the lights on, let alone knock me up?'

'No! Jeez, no! I didn't mean that. I was just surprised, that's all. I mean you haven't mentioned him, you're not wearing a wedding ring, and you don't look completely knackered like most parents do.'

'Right.' Nothing like being aloof and sanguine in the face of someone who nearly destroyed you years ago and from whom you're keen to hide that damage.

'You're not fat,' he says.

'I know that.'

'And you don't have a piggy face.'

'I know that too.'

'And even if you were big, fat, overweight – which you're not in any way – but if you were, it wouldn't preclude anyone from wanting to make love to you.'

'And I know that.'

'And no matter what you look like, even if you weren't as beautiful as you are, it wouldn't mean no one would want you.'

'Yup, know that.'

'You're not fat, you don't look like a pig and even if you were those things, it wouldn't mean you're not attractive,' he reiterates.

'I know all that, Ned, the question is, do you?'

Saturday, 25 April, 2009

'Why are you doing this, Peter?' I asked.

'Are you going to analyse me, now, Pieta?' He was tracing the tip of the blade over my skin, drawing an intricate, infernal pattern. I wanted it to stop. All of it to stop, but this part, this bit particularly, terrified me. That was why he did it, I was sure. Out of everything, this was the part I couldn't control my breathing for, couldn't slow the thundering of my heart about, couldn't stop myself from leaking tears of fear over. I had to get a handle on it. If I could control myself when he did this, he might stop it. 'Are you trying to get into my head? Find out if I've got "mummy issues"?'

'I just want to know why you're doing this.'

'I do have "mummy issues", Pieta. And "daddy issues". But that's not why.'

'Why then?'

'Because I can. Haven't you worked that out, yet? Because I can.'

He paused his knifepoint, pressing it a fraction deeper into my skin as he moved it. I wanted to scream at him to stop it, but I had to do this. I had to concentrate. 'I . . . I . . .' *Breathe, breathe, breathe; calm, calm, calm.* 'I think there's more to it than that.' I got the words out, forced them to sound normal as they left my mouth. 'I think there's more to you so there's more to why you're doing this.'

Mercifully, the knifepoint paused its journey over my flesh. *Breathe, breathe, breathe. Calm, calm, calm.*

'I . . . I think you feel things so intensely, you think about things so deeply that there is more to this. I . . . I think . . . there's so much to you that the world hasn't seen, and there must be a real, profound reason why you're doing this in this way. And . . . And I'm just asking you what it is.'

I'm just asking so you'll stop doing this to me.

He stood back, took the knife away. I wanted to relax, to collapse in relief, but I couldn't. If he saw that, he would know, and he would do worse to me.

My eyes were burning, I'd been squeezing them so tight because these were the times when I knew I would open my eyes to end this cruel bit. He hurt me constantly, consistently, completely, and this torture with the knife added another layer to it.

I could hear him breathing, inhaling and exhaling heavily, rapidly, as though he'd been running. He was angry. I'd pushed him too far. I felt the rush of air as he brought his arm and the knife up high, really high, from the velocity of it. He paused, his breathing increasing with every passing second.

I forced my eyes shut even tighter, I didn't want to watch when he did it. Didn't want to see it coming.

He growled, loud and angry, the sound sending shockwaves of fear through me, as he slammed the knife down towards me. The wood of the bedframe splintered as he drove the blade deep into it, the force of it violently shaking the bed. I flinched, cowered as I waited for the rest of it, the consequence of pushing him too far.

Then he was gone. Not simply standing to the side, waiting for me to open my eyes, but properly gone. For the first time, he slammed the door behind him.

Monday, 17 June

'Yes, I know that,' Ned says. 'Of course I know that. I was a shit, Pieta. I can't deny that. I haven't tried to deny that. And I am sorry for what I did. But who I was back then is not who I am now. I wouldn't imply, or even think, that you wouldn't manage to get a man or be in a relationship.'

'Fine.'

'Fine?'

'Fine.'

We sip our coffees without speaking, passing the time in a silence that isn't unpleasant but isn't companionable. I understand why he suggested this, why he needed to decompress with someone who was there. I feel a bit sorry for Callie. Not simply for what she went through, but the fact she was left with DI Foster as the only source of comfort after revealing the most traumatic experience of her life.

My skin is tingling. I've been ignoring it, pretending that it isn't, but it's prickling. Like a million biting ants are skittering all over my body. This is probably part of The After, of reliving it with Callie.

I close my eyes for a moment.

This is my fault.

There is a vat of guilt that bubbles like a cauldron at the centre of my being and it is probably guilt that is crawling all over me. Guilt. Culpability. Remorse. Responsibility. I should have told.

When the police came to my flat, I should have told. When I found I couldn't live in London, I should have told. When I came to Brighton and I was still standing on the beach, trying to imagine myself as the raging sea, I should have told. But once I'd made my decision, I knew I could never tell. It was as simple as that. Once I had decided, I was shackled by that choice.

Saturday, 25 April, 2009

'Do you still want to know why I do this, Pieta?'

'Yes. Yes, I do.'

'Do you know what you look like? What you truly look like?'

'Yes.'

'Do you, Pieta, really?'

'Yes, Peter, I know what I really look like.'

'I see you. I see you and what I see is ugliness. For forty-eight hours, I have taken that ugliness away from you. For forty-eight hours, you won't be able to see what the rest of the world sees and I've done that for you.'

'I don't believe you.'

The knife was immediately at my throat, a chance for me to fold, to give in, to say what he wanted both of us to hear. 'Say that again,' he snarled.

'I don't believe you because I'm not ugly. I don't care what you or anyone else says, I am not ugly. So that's not the reason.'

The very tip of his blade pressed harder into the soft flesh at my throat. It was going to go in deeper, slice its way through, then cause my throat to peel back. He was probably going to cut my throat, silence me for saying it, but I had to say it anyway. Like everything else, I had to do it.

'You can lie to me all you want,' I whispered loud enough for him to hear, 'but I don't know why you're lying to yourself.'

'You know nothing,' he whispered right by my ear. 'Nothing.' He pushed the tip even deeper. 'Do you? You know nothing.'

'I know nothing,' I said quickly. 'I know nothing.'

Monday, 17 June

The last few sips of this Americano are circling the bottom of my white cup and we both should be leaving. I glance at Ned. He is slumped in his chair, his coffee cup in his hands, his eyes fixed somewhere out there but not on the sea. He's not ready to leave.

I am sitting in almost exactly the same position as him, holding my cup in almost exactly the same way, but inside I am circling the drain of my memories of The During, doing all I can to stop myself finally going completely down the plughole into that place with no hope of return.

Neither of us is going anywhere soon.

'How did you manage to do that without breaking down?' Ned asks. His voice is so sudden, unexpected, I start a little. 'It was so hard to listen to, but you kept going, you got her to keep opening up even when I thought she might be shutting down. How did you do that?'

To be honest, I don't know. I don't know how I've been able to do this. How I've been able to remove myself enough from this story to listen, question, record. 'It's my job,' I reply.

'Well, you were incredible at it. I mean . . .' He shakes his head. 'That was tough. I hope the pictures will do the story justice.'

'I'm sure they will,' I say reflexively.

'How are you going to cut it all down? Get all that you need to say into it but not make it too long or too salacious?'

'I don't know. I'll have to do it somehow.'

Ned's hand on my bicep causes me almost to leap out of my seat. 'Sorry.' He snatches his hand away. 'I was just . . . I just thought . . . do you want another coffee?' he asks.

'Yes,' I reply with a smile. 'But only if you don't talk any more. I can't take any more talking.'

'No, me neither.'

Saturday, 25 April, 2009

'Girls like you have no time for me.'

No blade, no weapons. He returned a while ago, but stood above me, staring, watching, studying. My throat hurt where he had held the sharp point earlier; he'd obviously nicked the skin and it was sore, stinging every time I swallowed.

'You don't notice me. I am always there but girls like you won't look in my direction. You all think you're so much better than me. You all think I'm not good enough for you. I try to talk to you and you look at me with those sneers on your perfect lips and that condescending disgust in your flawless eyes.' He moved his face even closer to mine and I had to stop myself from shrinking away as all the revulsion I felt gushed to my nerve endings. 'You all think I am beneath you. Until you're here. When you are here, I can do what I want. I can make you do whatever I want you to. I am in control, just like a man should be.'

He nuzzled into the crook of my neck and I stopped my body from recoiling. Inside, though, I screamed; I screamed and screamed and screamed.

'Here, you are all mine.'

Monday, 17 June

'I'll probably need to speak to Callie again,' I tell Ned at the revolving door of the hotel. 'You should probably come and take some photos then, as well.'

'You don't have to sound so happy about it.'

'You don't have to sound like I should be so normal about it.' I'm not good with impressions, but being from the same place as him allows me to harness the Ned inflections when I reply.

He grins. 'Touché.'

'Olé.'

This amuses Ned and he laughs. 'You're funny, has anyone ever told you that?'

I nod thoughtfully. 'Almost no one.'

He laughs again and I can see he's about to reach to touch my arm, to tap it as you would a pal. When I step aside, he changes his mind and lowers his hand. 'I'll see you, then.'

'You certainly will,' I reply. 'Do you want a hand to your car with your stuff?'

He shakes his head. 'No, no, I'll go and bring my car round.'

I reach out for the nearest panel of the revolving door. 'Bye.'

'You know, Pieta, it's been good to see you,' he says. I lower my arm and turn a little towards him. 'I mean, not for you, clearly, but you've obviously done really well for yourself – great career, you're a mother and you live in one of the most amazing places on Earth. It's good to see that things turned out all right for you.'

'Is that your guilt talking, Ned?' I reply.

'Yes.' He exhales deeply. 'Yes, it is.'

'Good. As long as you still feel guilty, we'll continue to get on just fine.'

He laughs again. And I fling another 'bye' at him and push through the doors before he says something else to stop me leaving.

Saturday, 25 April, 2009

'Do you understand now, Pieta? Do you understand how when you're here, you're all mine?'

Couldn't speak.

Couldn't think.

Could barely breathe.

Jody

Monday, 17 June

I want to make love to my fiancé.

It's been one of those days. One of those hard days. It was like being skinned alive listening to Callie talk, knowing that Jovie went through that. All of us were deeply shaken by what she revealed. I'd heard her statement, more than once, but the things that Pieta Rawlings got out of her, the way she managed to slide into spaces I'd never have even thought to explore was incredible. The result, of course, was the type of information that didn't help to capture this man, it just renewed and strengthened my resolve to find him and to make him pay.

But I need comfort now, I need the strong embrace of the man I love. I want to hold him, have him touch me, kiss, explore, screw with the intensity you can only really get from someone you know and trust. I want that so much.

I want to have sex with him, but I can't. This case is messing with my mind. They always do, but this one in particular is battering me.

Work doesn't just distract me and make me emotionally unavailable, it chains me physically, too. Cases like this creep into every avenue of my mind, soak under my skin. I've never been sexually assaulted or raped. Yes, like most women, stuff that is inappropriate has happened to me, but the stories I hear from work tend to stay with me. The stories, the words they use . . .

Winston and I will be together in bed, we'll start to make love, and someone's story will start to flash through my mind. I hear what happened in the broadest terms, and then I learn the detail, the minutiae of the ordeal so that we can build a case, find the unique elements that speak to a wider pattern, that narrow down suspects and possible perpetrators. The interviews are necessary, they're what is needed to help the woman who has come to us; it's an essential part of my job. And these words run like a ticker tape at the bottom of my mind when Winston and I are making love.

My mind, as saturated as it is with other people's traumas, other people's words depicting their pain, will conjure up the terror of having her body being controlled, see the way the pain ripples through her nerves, hear the phrases she says he used. It doesn't happen every time we make love, it doesn't even happen most of the time, but it happens enough to make me pause, think, wonder if having sex is worth taking the chance of having those images play out.

Winston is very good about it. He always stops when I freeze, and he rarely initiates when I'm in the middle of a case because he knows I could stop cold right in the middle of sex and it makes him feel bad.

But right now, I want to have sex with him. I want to do something normal and loving. I want to remind myself that there are

236

good men out there, that sex isn't about power and pain, control and supremacy. Sex is about connection and communication and consideration, and respect and fun and pleasure.

I want to have sex with my fiancé.

'When was the last time you kissed me?' I ask Winston.

He frowns, and then theatrically purses his lips while he thinks about it.

'All right, let me put it this way – why aren't you over here kissing me right now?'

Winston tosses aside the remote control, then comes across the large sofa towards me. 'No, the question is, why didn't I think of kissing you before now?'

He takes me in his arms and we take a moment to look at each other, to see each other. An excited thrill bolts through me and I grin at him. I see it happen to him, too. His smile deepens and his body relaxes against mine.

I slip my hand under his white T-shirt as he lowers his head and kisses me. I place my hand over his heart, feel it beating. Reminding me how connected we are, how alive we are and how much we have together.

When he starts to move his hand under my T-shirt, I press my hand on top of his to stop him. I can't do it. Not like this, not right now. He takes his hand away and carries on kissing me instead.

I want to make love to my fiancé, but I can't.

'Did you know that my sister was actually my twin?' I ask Winston as we're climbing into bed.

I know the answer, but I want to talk about her, my Jovie, after today's remembering. Missing her is a constant ache. And I have space to do it, room to let the memory of who she was expand and fill all the empty spaces in my heart.

Winston is mid-stretch, mid-yawn but stops to turn around and look at me. 'Your twin? I mean, you said you had a sister and she died, but in ten years you never mentioned that she was your twin.'

'I know. It's just that she died a long time ago but it feels like yesterday all the time. It never gets old, or easier, so I don't talk about her much at all. We were identical, but nothing alike. And she killed herself. I haven't told you that, either. She was the victim of a crime and that was too much for her to bear.'

My fiancé scoots across the bed and takes me in his arms.

'I wasn't very nice to her.' This is why I'm talking to him. I need to externalise this stuff inside. I need to tell someone this secret. Well, as much of this secret as I can get away with telling anyone. 'She told me what happened to her and I wasn't very nice to her. I didn't completely believe she didn't bring it on herself.'

'But, you're not like that, Jodes. Everyone always comments how good you are with victims, survivors, whatever you call it.'

'I know.' I blink a few times, try to clear my blurry, teary vision. 'I've always found it easy to put myself in someone else's shoes, say what they need to hear, except with Jovie. When she needed me to just understand her, to be, you know, a sister, just a fucking human being, I let her down.' I rub my hands over my face. 'It haunts me. It constantly haunts me.'

He cuddles me towards his body. Holding me close, protecting me from myself. What if I had held Jovie like this? What if

I'd made her feel loved and protected and safe? Would she still be here? Would I be taking her through an interview now, getting her to help me to find this man?

'I don't know what to say. I'm sorry about your sister, Jodes, that must be rough.'

'What if I do it again? What if I mess up and I end up damaging one of the people in this investigation?'

'You won't, you won't,' he reassures. 'You know as well as I do that we treat those closest to us worse than we treat other people. It's a shit thing to do, and I have to work really hard not to lose patience with my parents or get frustrated with my brothers, but for some reason, that's what we do.'

'Biology has a lot to answer for, eh?' I say.

'Yeah, yeah it does.' He lets me go. 'Turn out your light, babe, and tell me about your sister.'

In the dark, everything feels better. I can hide in the dark, I can control my breathing, there are no shiny surfaces for me to see Jovie's face. In the dark, everything feels much more manageable. She was always telling me to open my eyes, but sometimes, I preferred to keep my eyes closed so I could stay safe and secure in the dark.

I talk to him about my lost twin. I tell him as much as I can without making her sound awful, without making me sound judgemental.

'It's hard, you know, Jodes,' Winston says when I pause to reassess what feelings all the talking about Jovie have loosened. 'I was the bad one in my family. I was the one always in trouble. I got arrested a few times, stopped loads more. Most of it was bull, the police getting an easy mark. But you know, there was stuff that wasn't bull, things that I did that were wrong and illegal. I smoked a bit. Got a bit rowdy. Bit of shoplifting. This was all before I became focused on my football, but you know, Jodes, it was still wrong. I remember a lot of it was about not feeling heard. Wanting, I don't know, to be noticed. My parents didn't do anything wrong, my other siblings weren't anywhere near as much trouble as me. I can't explain it to you, it was just something I did.

'But I turned myself around. Some people don't do that. It wouldn't have been fair to expect everyone to be understanding until I got myself together. Some of them weren't. A couple of my brothers are still . . . I don't know, pissed off with me, I suppose, even now. I don't blame them. I was a nightmare. Doesn't mean I didn't deserve to be loved, but that doesn't mean they weren't allowed to be angry with me, either. And to wash their hands of me if I was causing them too much pain.'

I understand what he's getting at, what he's trying to say about me and how I treated Jovie. He's trying to say it was understand-able. Not right, or good, but understandable. I appreciate it. I appreciate him. He really is the perfect man.

'You won't mess it up, Jodes,' Winston says. 'You're going to do whatever you need to do to solve this. I know you and I know you'll do it. And you'll be doing it with Jovie in mind. That will be good for all those you help, won't it?'

'I suppose,' I reply.

Obviously Winston has no clue that doing whatever I need to do to solve this means I've also been planning a murder for the last thirteen years.

*

'Tea?' Harlow asks.

She's sitting at the table in my South London flat.

She has odd-shaped crockery in front of her. Very rustic and very obviously hand-made. The teapot is large and misshapen, its rotund belly and spout are ringed with rainbow stripes. The bobbly, wobbly cups have blue and white spots, the blue piercing and sharp, and the wave-like saucers are an eye-watering navy green.

'Please excuse the tea set, my sister made them,' Harlow explains as she pours champagne from the teapot.

'Sister?' I reply. 'Who's your sister?'

'You know.'

'I know? I know?'

'Oh, come on, of course you know. Of—'

My eyes jump open in the dark. I have to swallow a few times to moisten my mouth and throat, to calm my racing heart, but I don't need to look at the clock to know where I am – ensconced in the deepest part of the night, as far away from each side as I will get.

The dream with Harlow and tea again. At least this time she didn't bring the others, at least this time they didn't get the chance to tell me what I already knew – I am culpable. But this time, we had the crazy crockery.

Not hard to work out what that was about.

As well as everything else, I have to decide what to do about Pieta Rawlings. I can't storm into her life and accuse her of being The Blindfolder's victim, but can I just leave it? I've been hunting this man for thirteen years. I have a live, recent victim who is willing to talk, and I have many others out there I do not know what has happened to. If Pieta is a victim, then she might hold the vital clue. But if she is a victim, then she clearly will not admit to it easily. At any point since she was assigned this story, she could have come forward. She knows why Callie is doing it, she knows now her life is in danger, but she still hasn't said a word.

It all comes down to that question she asked about whether Callie had told her family. Pieta most likely hasn't told anyone. Why would she? She has a sorted life, a nice home, her son, her job. Why would she drag that into the present?

I don't have children, but I know what mothers are like. How protective they are. Someone like Pieta Rawlings would do anything to protect her son's life – literally and metaphorically.

That picture of them together comes to mind. They looked so happy, like they are each other's world. If I'd got pregnant when Winston and I had first started trying, our child would be about his age. Well, maybe younger. We started trying seven years ago and her son looked a bit older. Maybe around nine, ten?

The air starts to buzz, fizzing with that thought.

Her son is about nine or ten.

I slip out of bed, go to the living room where my computer is still sheathed in my black laptop bag. It takes an age to boot it up. *Her son is about nine or ten*, I keep thinking as I watch the screen light up and the icons pop up one by one.

Her son is about nine or ten.

I open her file and read the missing person's report again.

April 2009.

That means . . .

I know who she said her son's father was. But the way she stood in front of his pictures, hiding him from me; protecting him from scrutiny . . . And actually, she didn't say who her son's father was. She implied it was Jason Breechner but never actually named him as responsible. I can't believe it didn't occur to me before. Maybe I am too close to this. Maybe this is the wrong side of personal. I am missing things, I am missing *huge* things.

Gigantic things like this. If Pieta Rawlings is a victim of the man I am hunting, then it is also quite possible that her child is The Blindfolder's son.

And that means I could get access to the DNA evidence that we desperately need.

Pieta

'When's your baby due?' The woman who asked this had a smiley face, happy eyes and a bonny disposition. We sat in the upstairs part of the doctor's surgery, outside the midwife's room.

'February,' I said.

'Oh, snap!' she said excitedly. 'Your first?'

I nodded. I didn't want to talk, I didn't want to think let alone talk. 'How about you?' I replied when it was obvious she expected me to ask her.

'Yes, my first, too. Can you tell how excited I am? All my friends are sick of me. I can't help it though. We've been trying for so long.' She ran her hands over the swell of her stomach, prominent even under her thick, cream jumper. It was about the same size as my bump. 'This is my miracle baby.'

I smiled at her. I was pleased for her. She was so full of joy, so blissful, it was nice to be around. It was lovely to be reminded that this was what being pregnant was about.

I hadn't known. Not for nearly four months. I thought it was what had happened. I thought it was my on-going problems with endometriosis and other fertility-limiting issues. I thought it was my body playing tricks on me while I recalibrated myself.

But four months. It'd never been four months before. I'd had a period after the last time I had sex with Jason, but nothing since for the following four months.

I knew before I even paid for the test. I was certain before I weed on the stick. I had the answer before the timer sounded.

I had been categorically told that I would have trouble having a baby. That gynaecological issues would always leave me struggling to conceive, and could cause problems with carrying a baby to full term. I looked at the results of the pregnancy test and knew that it shouldn't technically be possible. It shouldn't technically be something I had to worry about or deal with. But neither was what was done to me by that man four months earlier. It was rare, it was not the sort of thing that happened all the time.

'Pieta Rawlings?' the midwife called.

I gathered up my notes, my coat, my bag and stood up. 'Good luck with your baby,' I told the other expectant mother.

'You too!' she trilled. 'I might see you at the hospital!'

'Yes, maybe.'

'How are you, Pieta?' the midwife asked. She hadn't been that friendly the first time I met her. She'd been busy, and was clearly having a bad day. I'd been in shock, still. I hadn't made any real decisions, but thought I should see someone just in case I decided to go ahead with it. I almost didn't go back after the way she was so dismissive of me that first time. Her bad day plus my 'situation' almost added up to me going home and pretending it wasn't happening. I couldn't stand to possibly go through with having a child and have people be dismissive and rude along the way.

I'd braved her offices again, and since then she'd been better, sometimes over-the-top nice as if to make up for it.

Today, she was typing something into her computer, not looking at me, which gave me the opportunity I needed to speak, to say what I needed to before the courage deserted me. 'I was sexually assaulted. A while ago. I'm worried about the birth. I can't have people's hands on me. I'm worried about what will happen.' I didn't sound like me. This was the first time I'd said it out loud and my voice didn't sound like mine. I sounded scared, vulnerable, but also detached and defeated.

I daren't look at her but I could tell she was staring at me.

'Is your baby the result of the assault?'

She'd have to write that down. She'd have to write down everything I said. And I didn't want that to follow me around, follow the baby around, be there for everyone to see and make judgements on. I shook my head. Once, twice, three times. 'I just . . . it's the birth. I don't want people touching me.'

'It's OK, it's OK,' she said kindly. 'We'll make sure you're comfortable, that no one touches you unless they have to. And even then, they will tell you clearly who they are and why they're touching you. Please don't worry, Pieta, we'll do everything we can to make this all right for you so you can focus on your baby.'

'Thank you. Thank you so much.'

She reached out to touch me, but changed her mind halfway through. 'I'm sorry this happened to you,' she said. 'I'm so sorry.'

'Thank you,' I replied. 'Thank you.'

Thursday, 4 February, 2010

He was perfect. Everything about him was perfect. His crinkled fingers that he kept trying to stuff in his mouth, his eyes that were barely open, his slick body that immediately found its place in the crook of my arm. He was so perfect. I stared down at him and saw every incredible thing about him.

I was ignoring how pale my son's skin was, which told me that *he* had been white. I was pretending my child's nose wasn't small and nothing like mine, and therefore probably came from *him*. I was make-believing this baby had come from love, not from hours and hours and hours of terror.

My son was perfect. Absolutely perfect and that was all I was focusing on.

Pieta

Wednesday, 19 June

'Courier package for you, Pieta,' Reggie says.

He places the package on my desk and walks away. It'd been even more awkward since he tried to ask me out again, and we'd been forced to work together quite closely on this article. I pull the headphones out of my ears. I'd been transcribing my interview with Callie. Transcribing is fine, because they are just words and I can transfer the words from my ears to my fingers to the computer without anything sinking in in between. It's a process I've done hundreds of times before.

I pick up the package and watch Reggie return to his desk. Inside the package there are photographs, I can feel their shiny surface as I pull them free. Pinned to the top is a handwritten note:

> For you, of you. This is how the world sees you –
> Beautiful. Ned x

Me. A pile of photos of me. I hadn't realised he was shooting me as well. I would have asked him to stop, I would have told him to focus on Callie.

It's a shock to see myself. They are black and white, so you can't see the vivid stripes of my rainbow armwarmers, you can't see the fluorescent colours of my tights, you can't experience the vivid red of my top. What I do note are the twist-out curls in my hair that are full and framing my face. What I can clearly appreciate is my face, frozen in a thought-filled pose while I'm concentrating on Callie.

'Wow, is that you?' Tiffany asks.

'Erm,' I reply and start to shuffle the photos back together. 'Yeah.'

'Let's see.' Avril is out of her seat and over by my desk in seconds. 'Wow,' she breathes when she sees them. 'He's captured you really, really well. You look incredible.'

'Oh, go on then, let me see,' Connie concedes and she is by my desk. She whistles. 'Bloody hell. I didn't realise you were such a beauty.'

'All right, you lot,' I say as they pass the photos around each other. 'A girl could get offended, you know. You are basically saying in everyday life I'm nothing special. Cut it out.'

'We're not saying that,' Tiffany admonishes. 'It's just, have you seen these? He's got such a great eye. You're only smiling in one of them and you still look . . . I want him to take my photo.'

'Me too,' says Avril.

'Me three,' adds Connie.

They are nice photos, but I'm not sure why he sent them to me.

'Have you seen these, Reggie?' Tiffany calls. I think she secretly wants him and me to get together. 'Pieta is looking pretty gorgeous in these photos, just saying.'

Reggie comes over to our bank of desks. 'They are good

photos,' Reggie agrees. 'May I?' He takes the bundle from me and starts to shuffle through them. I watch his professional, art director's eye look them over, carefully scrutinise each one. 'Is this the guy who came with you to photograph Miss X?'

'Yes,' I mumble. I don't think I've been the centre of so much attention before. Not like this.

'He's good, he's really good. He's completely brought out "you" in these. I look forward to seeing his other photos.' He hands them back to me and smiles.

'Thank you,' I say, completely bashful. 'And thank you every-one for invading my desk. Can I get some space now?'

Ten minutes later my email pings with a message from Reggie:

> That photographer was right in his note –
> you are beautiful. X

Jody

Thursday, 20 June

Nothing. We have nothing.

The team have come up with so much stuff, have worked methodically through these women's lives, and there is nothing to connect them except they were all taken by this man, abused by him, branded by him and eventually, years later, murdered by him.

The records of their phone usage showed nothing out of the ordinary. They all had minimal social media presence. They had jobs, a couple of them had partners. They had ordinary lives that hadn't been disrupted at all in the weeks leading up to their deaths.

Each member of the team takes it in turns to explain what they have found, and we all listen, some ask questions, others make notes. The frantic energy that had started this, had captured them when this was hours old, is waning. Most of them are used to working on more than one case at the same time, most of them are used to us finding something tangible by now. We usually have something to build something else on. The clock is ticking, the sixth Monday is counting down above our heads and we have nothing.

He's good, The Blindfolder, that's what it comes down to, I suppose. The lack of forensic evidence. The branding. The terrifying of the surviving victims so effectively that few of them go to the police for fear of retribution. He is very proficient at what he does.

A profile had been written up about him a few weeks ago, after the second Brighton murder. When I'd first read the report, anger and frustration flamed inside. It spoke in generalities, maybes, possible considerations. Nothing firm, nothing that would help us move forward. We are no closer to finding out who he is now than I was back then.

The conversation in our investigation room moves on to Sux and how difficult it is to get hold of.

'Has anyone thought to trace where he might be getting it from?' Laura asks.

I almost give myself away by saying yes, I'd spent years tracking Sux and ketamine and other anaesthetic drugs, but had got nowhere. 'Not to any great degree,' I reply. 'Can you get on to that? You're looking for any suppliers who have shipped to private individuals, any suppliers who have had shipments going missing or which have been stolen. Not just doctors, vets, too.'

Laura nods as she notes this down. 'Maybe I'll try dentists, as well?'

'Maybe, yes, good idea.' I turn to look at the pictures again. 'Have we been through all their social media profiles with a fine-tooth comb?' I ask no one in particular.

'Yes,' says Ralph, one of the tech guys. He's only here part-time because he has to work with other departments, and does the best he can to give us time. 'I have done all manner of searches and they don't have a connection.'

'Not even the same followers?'

'A couple of them followed The Black Girls' Bookclub on Twitter, but that was it as far as I could see. They had a few similar followers, but I have run checks on all of them and nothing.'

'Tell me about this book club,' I say.

'They have events, get authors in, but as far as I could find from checking the women's bank accounts, credit and debit cards, neither of them went to events. They just followed them.'

'Which two?'

'Freya and Bess.'

'The clock is ticking, counting down to the next murder – we can hear it, but we can't see it to turn it off. There's a woman out there, with a number on her back, who is going to be murdered on 22nd July, the sixth Monday.' Judging from the silence in the room, I've said all that out loud. I probably shouldn't have.

I turn to my team. 'I'm sorry. I sounded bleak then. He seems so meticulous. The way the bodies – both living and dead – are cleaned, the way there's no trace of evidence, the way the victims aren't connected. It shouldn't be technically possible. He should have made a mistake by now. We all make mistakes. That's what makes me worry for the next woman.'

'Maybe they work in forensics or they're a copper?' Laura says.

This silence is so heavy it clunks loudly on the ground.

'Oh, what? Everyone's been thinking it, no one wants to say it. It's true. They could be someone who is right here in this room for all we know.'

'True, Laura,' I say. 'And it could also be the man who makes really delicious coffee near where I'm staying but has watched one too many episodes of *CSI* and thinks he knows how to get away with murder.'

A few people smirk loudly. 'Oh, grow up,' I say with a laugh.

'Maybe I should check the location of most of their followers,' Ralph says. 'See if I can get a more comprehensive geographical profile of the victims going.'

'Yes, that would be helpful,' I say. I tap my pen on my teeth. 'What I'm about to say needs to stay in this room. My problem is this one.' I tap my pen onto Callie's photo. She's smiling, her hair wound up in a chignon. Below that is the image of the scar on her back – the prominent number 26.

'How do you mean?' asks Karin Logan. Detective Constable.

I sigh as I look at Callie. 'She's a wild card. Unpredictable. Prone to temper, which loosens her lips. And . . .' And she's hiding something. I've got this unshakeable feeling that she has something huge that she is not telling us; that if she told me, I'd be able to help her while at the same time helping us. I sigh again. 'I don't especially trust her and, I don't know, there's a piece of her jigsaw missing.'

I can't tell them she's hiding something until I know what that is.

'I think that's a bit out of order, actually,' Karin says, voicing what a lot of them are thinking.

'Why's that? We're always suspicious of people in an investigation.'

'Yeah, but she's been through hell. We've seen the scars, we've heard her story, we've seen the video statements. It's not rehearsed, it's not constantly changing, everything is as it should be with this woman, I feel it.' She looks around at the other people in the room who are carefully avoiding eye contact with me. 'We all feel it.'

'You know what, Karin, you're probably right. What I'm seeing is most likely her survival tactic.' I have to concede here, until I know what it is that Callie is hiding, I have to give in to everyone else's gut instinct. 'But hopefully,' I continue, 'when Pieta Rawlings has written her article, we will have other women coming forward. Hopefully they'll lead us to something.'

And hopefully, I won't need to get the DNA from Pieta Rawlings's son. Because if this carries on, I'll have no other choice.

Part 5

Pieta

Saturday, 22 June

Ned is staying down at Brighton Marina, a twenty-minute drive from my house to the other side of Brighton. There are white cliffs over there, and from the road an amazing view out to sea. Kobi and I often come down here to go to the multiplex cinema, the bowling and crazy golf. When Kobi decided for three months he wanted to be a street dancer back in 2017, this was where I used to bring him.

From the boardwalk where there are several restaurants, I make my way down a metal walkway to the gates to where the moored boats and yachts of different sizes ring the Marina like bared teeth. The thick, mesh-like cladding clangs underneath my feet. It's late, and even though there are people around and the Marina doesn't look like it's anywhere near ready for bed, I've walked here from the car park with my heart in my throat.

The moonlight seems to bounce off the shiny surfaces and the moon's watery reflection shimmers and glitters out in the middle of the water. Ned told me which boat he was on and its whereabouts. I type the code he gave me in to the metal keypad at the gate and the metallic whoosh of the door releasing is magnified in the hush down here at the water's edge.

Lights are on in some of the yachts I pass; laughter and chatter escape from others; and on a few of the upper decks, people sit outside, wrapped in blankets, sipping from mugs and wine glasses.

Ned's boat has a dark-grey bottom, a ring of dark, racing-car green around the middle and a cream top. The boat's name – *The Louis Lynn Evans* – is stencilled in cream handwriting script on the green part of the boat. On the upper deck is a large wooden and glass square with a slightly domed roof. Carefully, I step off the walkway onto the wood-and-tile steps that lead up a small curve onto the upper deck of the boat. I don't get a chance to knock on the wooden door with its huge glass pane because Ned is suddenly on the other side, opening it.

'Hi,' we both say at the same time, awkwardly, shyly. I hadn't known what to say to him about the photos he sent, nor his note, so when I'd arranged to come and pick up pictures of Callie, I didn't mention them.

'Come in, come in,' he welcomes as he steps back into the upper deck.

I'm surprised to be greeted with a built-in terracotta-coloured padded seating area. It is arranged as a square and there's a small, low table there, too.

'The photos are this way,' he replies, nodding towards the large, mottled, wooden steering wheel. I'm confused for a moment then realise he means the full-length wooden swing doors beside the steering wheel. He leads the way down the stairs beyond the doors into the belly of the boat.

As usual, dread, terror, the urge to run away whip through me.

It's fine, you're fine, it'll be fine, I tell myself. *Everything is fine.*

The stairs are steep and I hold on to the handle as I follow him below deck. Behind the white door at the bottom of the stairs, I feel as though I have stepped into a designer's wonderland.

The upper walls are studded with silver portholes. In front of me is a brown leather easy chair, a couple of blankets slung over it. Beyond that is a circular dining table, covered in the photos I've come to collect.

To my right, next to where I stand, is the entrance to the three-sided kitchen area. There's a modern-looking butler's sink, a shiny silver cooker and oven, a microwave on the maple-coloured wooden worktops. A plate and a glass sit unwashed in the sink, but everything else from, I presume, cooking has been washed up and is draining on the metal rack. The walls have shelves where everything is lined up and organised. On the other side of the kitchen area is a large, squashy, terracotta-coloured sofa adorned with several lifeboat-ring-shaped cushions.

Beyond the sofa area and the dining table area is a doorway, which, I'm guessing, leads to the sleeping cabins.

'This is really nice,' I say.

He stops on his way to the dining table, squeezes a quizzical look in my direction. 'You sound surprised. What did you think it'd be like?'

I shrug. 'I've never been on a boat before so I don't know, really, but not this. I wasn't sure if I was meant to ask permission to come aboard or something.'

'Technically, I suppose you should have, but I'll let you off, because I'm nice like that.'

'Have you always lived on boats?'

'No, just when I'm near the water. So while I'm down here.

When I was up near Bath, I lived on a boat then. I like being on the water.'

'I moved to Brighton to be near the water. I didn't know that till I got here, though. I was kind of drawn here and then I realised it was because it's near the sea. I could stand and watch the sea for hours. It changes and changes, but always stays constant. Sometimes I used to stand with my back to the sea so I could just smell it and listen to it, and feel how it displaced the air.' I'm surprised at myself, saying that to him of all people. His face moves as if to speak and continue the conversation, but I interject, 'Sorry, I should get the photos and get going.' No need to start talking to him like we could be anything other than acquaintances.

'OK. I was hoping though . . . I was hoping you could have a look at them. There are so many and I started to choose the best ones, then I realised you need to do it. You're writing the article, you should decide what will go with the words.'

'That's a nice thought, but to be honest, it really doesn't matter what I think. It'll come down to what the art director, picture editor and Lillian want. I'm being nosey, really, asking for them now. I wanted to put them up while I was writing so I could constantly look at her while I hear her voice in my head, if that makes sense?'

'Yes, perfect sense. But have a look anyway, see what you think.'

He wants me to see what he has done, to see if he has captured the essence of Callie, her vulnerability and determination, her anger and sorrow.

They take my breath away. They *are* Callie. Her talking. Her staring into the distance. Her with her head bowed because it's all too much. Tears brimming in dark-green eyes. Short nails on the hand she uses to move her hair from her forehead. Mouth askew as it shapes the words to describe difficult moments.

'These are amazing. I mean, truly incredible.'

'Don't sound so surprised,' he says with a shy laugh, but it's clear that he's pleased I like them.

'I'm not. I mean, I've seen your stuff and the ones you sent me, I know you're good, but wow, I wasn't expecting anything as touching and *honest* as this.'

'I've got some other ones, of her . . . of her scars. But I doubt the police officer will let us use them.'

He starts to put the pictures together like he is restacking a pack of cards.

'I doubt she'll let us use them, either,' I reply. I'm glad he hasn't got the branding scar pictures out, I couldn't stand to look at them. I take the envelope he's put the photos in with two hands. 'Detective Foster will probably have a fit again about Callie being identified when there's . . . when . . .'

'When he's going back and killing his previous victims,' Ned supplies. He shakes his head, scratches his ear. 'I've got to say, I'm struggling with this, Pieta. Kidnapping women, torturing them, branding them, and then coming back years later to kill them. It's all stuff you see on TV, in the movies, not something that happens in my real life. And to be this close to it . . . It's messing with my mind a bit.'

'Yeah,' I reply. I do not want to talk about this. It's taking a lot for me to be able to write this, I can't talk about it, analyse it too. 'I'd better be going.'

'I don't suppose you'd want to stick around for a bit? Sit

upstairs and have a couple of drinks?' He's back in his kitchen area, reaching down into the fridge and retrieving a beer. He twists the cap off, flicks it into a pint glass, half-full with other beer lids that sits beside the draining rack. I head for the stairs, needing to get back to the car park before it gets much later and I start to try to work out how I can get a taxi from here to my car.

'No. Thank you, but no, I've got to drive home. My mother's staying for the next three days so I can pull a couple of all-nighters to write the article. And I don't tend to drink anything when I drive.' I smile but not at him. 'I'll see ya.'

'Do you believe in redemption?' he asks me before my foot makes contact with the bottom step. I lower my foot and turn towards him. He stands in his kitchen, looking smaller than I remember.

'Depends what you mean by redemption. For yourself, yes, I do believe in that. I believe you can become a better version of the person you were when you did whatever it is that needs forgiving.'

'But you don't believe in forgiveness for other people?'

I force myself to look at him, properly, totally. I blink in shock, when I take in the full composition of him. He's not a boy, he's not a young man, he's a fully formed adult. His blond hair is streaked with grey, his skin has been pressed and creased with emotion, his body is neat and strong.

This is what Ned Wellst looks like now. I've not really looked at him since that first day in the office, I've kept him at the periphery of my vision because that's what I do. In The After, I thought I would look at everything, I would want to see as much as I could. But in reality, I can't. I am cautious about what I let in through my eyes, about how I fill my line of sight. And I'm terrified. I'm constantly terrified I'll look at someone, catch their eye, and recognise in them the features my son got from his father.

But I'm doing it now, with Ned. And it's fine. It's truly fine. He doesn't have Kobi's nose, nor the shape of his chin. He is Ned Wellst and it is fine to look at him.

'What's this conversation really about, Ned?' I ask.

He doesn't speak for long seconds and I can tell he's assessing the best thing to say. Eventually he opens his mouth: 'I want to know if there's anything I can do to get you to forgive me for what I did to you. Anything I can say or do? *Anything*.'

I stop looking at him now because what I have to say won't be easy to hear. 'Ned, the thing about seeking forgiveness from someone you've hurt is that you're hurting them again by asking for something else from them. If you're sorry, say you're sorry, apologise, let them know you've realised the enormity of what you've done and won't do it again, but leave it there. Don't expect anything else from them. Don't require them to say they forgive you so you can feel better. Or expect them to move on according to your timetable. Or to even give the whole thing any kind of headspace. Apologise and then leave it. Sit with how you feel about not being forgiven despite how sorry you are. Don't make it worse.

'Leave them to decide if they've forgiven you.' I raise my head to seek out his gaze again. 'Do you understand what I'm saying?'

He nods.

'Good. I'll see you whenever.' I turn to the stairs.

'I'm sorry,' he says.

I lower my raised leg again. And stare at the grey treads that lead out of here while I wait for him to say something else.

'I am so very, very sorry. What I did to you was terrible. You didn't deserve it. And I'm sorry. I'm so, so sorry.'

I am not that person any longer. All those years ago, when I was in The Before, I would have longed to hear him say those words. I would have listened and then I would have thrown that apology back in his face. I would have reminded him that I was an adult now and I didn't need him to say anything to know that I didn't deserve what he did. That I had got there all on my own, by feeling the pain, by learning I didn't deserve it, by realising there was nothing wrong with me and *everything* wrong with him and his acolytes.

In The Before, I found a way to deal with being a bullied child, a tormented young adult; in The After I didn't need to say anything to his apology. I didn't even need to acknowledge it if I didn't want to.

I stare at him across the gap, and despite how sad he looks, how bereft he seems right now, I know that he has had a good life. My bully didn't get his comeuppance, he didn't fail in life and need me to step in and be the bigger person by rescuing him. I think things like that rarely happen. We hear those stories because they're unusual. In reality, I think the bully goes on with their life and never really thinks about the carnage they left behind; in reality, I think the bullied goes on with *their* life, but is regularly reminded of what happened, sometimes being crushed by it, but ultimately getting on with life. I think, in reality, the bullied and the bully just get on with it.

And I have just got on with it.

'I'll see you in a couple of days.' I smile at him. 'All right?'

He nods, his eyes staring intently at me as he raises his beer bottle. I watch the pale gold liquid disappear into his mouth, his throat bulging and contracting as it slides down.

'Do you want to stay?' he asks. My leg is hovering over the bottom step again, and I have to lower it *again*.

'What for?' I say without looking at him.

When he doesn't reply, I rotate again to where he is standing. 'What for?' I repeat.

'I don't want to be alone,' he confesses. 'I want some company.'

'That's not why,' I say. 'Tell me the truth.'

Ned moves nearer.

'All right,' he says after a swallow. 'I want *your* company.' His gaze does not waver from mine. 'I have feelings for you.' He shrugs. 'I didn't expect that to happen. But I'd like you to stick around for a bit. Well, for a lot longer than a bit. I really like you, Pieta, I'm drawn to you, and I'd love to spend some time getting to know you.'

Jody

Saturday, 22 June

We're out, out. Winston and I, we are out, out. Which is rare at this point of an investigation. This type of investigation usually consumes me, prevents me from doing anything other than work, but I am taking a time out, a step back to go on a date. Things almost always come to me better when I'm focusing on other things.

A shortish walk away from the flat is an Italian restaurant called Buon Appetito with red, white and green signage that sits on one of the corners of Western Road, one of the main roads into Brighton from Hove. This whole area where the restaurant is has a villagey feel to it: there are streets with huge regency blocks of flats, there's a lovely green area in the middle of a couple of busy roads, planted with flowers called the floral clock. I'd spotted this area and eatery the other day and had mentioned it to Winston as somewhere to try.

It's a small place with a large spiral staircase that winds downwards out of sight, and it has a nice atmosphere that you can feel the second you cross the threshold. There are several tables placed close together and the lighting is intimate. At the back, there is a small bar in front of a serving hatch. Above the bar hang rows of wine glasses, the shelves behind are lined with spirit bottles, the belly of the bar is filled with wine bottles. 'Mambo Italiano' is playing in the background, and there is a low thrum of chatter from the other couples in here. At the back is a large floor-to-ceiling picture of, I presume, the owners on their opening day. There are six people standing in front of the place, smiling at the camera.

'Welcome, welcome, welcome,' says one of the men in the picture coming towards us. 'Table for two?'

I'm about to say yes, when I spot Karin Logan. Detective Constable. Even from here I can see she's shed the pinch-faced, dour demeanour that she shrugs on when she comes into the incident room every morning – she's let her brown hair down and she's put on lipstick and eyeliner, possibly blusher. I bet she's got heels on, and a nice dress.

'Yes, table for two,' Winston says when I don't reply to the man in front of us.

'Come, come, this is our finest table,' he says and leads us to the table next to Karin and her partner.

I'm now going to be in one of those situations: do I ignore her or do I make fake nicey-nice? And it would be fake. She still doesn't know that I know that she went crying to DCI Nugent about me after that first day. With real tears in her pretty eyes, she'd sobbed her way through her tale of how innocent her was being bullied by evil outsider me, who was giving her too much work. And couldn't she just come back to proper CID? Couldn't she just be allowed to do her normal job with a superior who respected her abilities and trusted her to find her own way? DCI

Nugent had put her straight about a few things – including the fact he thought it was a marvellous idea to link up Disclosure and FLO duties. 'I told her to go cry on the Chief Constable's shoulder if she didn't like my reply,' he'd said to me. 'You want to watch her, though,' he'd added. 'She's as sly as they come.'

And I *had* watched her: coming to work every day with a bad attitude that she flicked about as often as she flicked her ponytail.

She clocks me and her face almost disintegrates under the sourness that takes over her features. That makes me smile, makes my eyes light up. 'Oh, hi!' I say.

She forces her face to put together something approximating a smile – it looks painful. 'Hi,' she says, her voice a forest of icicles.

That just pisses me off, makes me want to be extra nicey-nice just to piss *her* off. 'Karin, this is Winston, my fiancé,' I say.

She looks over the man beside me as a police officer first of all – trying to see if she's ever encountered him, arrested him, cautioned him – then as a woman who is interested in men – is he good-looking, would she make a pass if she was drunk enough, would he respond? After assessing from a woman's perspective, she moistens her lips, sits up a little bit straighter. Yeah, Winston has that effect on women, especially the ones who don't like me – they often fantasise about taking him off me in the ultimate act of revenge.

'Winston, this is Karin, one of the, erm . . .' I'm about to say DCs from work when I realise that she may not have told her companion what she does. (A lot of us keep that quiet for a while because love interests often react badly to finding out you're a police officer.) Hell, she might be undercover on someone else's case for all I know. Shit, she might have told him her name is something other than Karin. 'One of the people I know from around Brighton.'

Winston side-eyes me – hard. Then smiles. 'Nice to meet you.'

'You too,' says Karin. 'Winston, Jody, this is Ross.' The brown-haired man who has, until now, had his back to us, twists in his seat, smiles uncomfortably and then raises a hand in hello. I take it from the look on his face he has heard chapter and verse about evil old me. 'Ross, this is the new person at work, and her other half.'

We all 'hi' each other, then slip into an uncomfortable silence.

'Have you been here before?' Ross asks. 'It's great.'

'No, first time, actually,' Winston replies.

'Try the lamb shank, it's amazing.'

'Will do,' says Winston and we all slip back into that silence.

'You know each other?' the friendly Italian man asks. 'Shall I put your tables together?

'No!' Karin and I say at the same time.

'Actually, can we sit over there? I feel a bit of a chilly breeze here,' I add.

'Of course, of course,' he replies and ushers us to the other side of the restaurant.

'See you later, have a good meal,' I throw in her direction.

For the rest of the evening, I glance over at Karin and Ross – they seem to be having a good time, but it's the kind of good time people post about on social media – designed to show those looking in that they are having so much SUPER FUN, even though the reality doesn't really match up. I'm fascinated by

Karin. She seems so bitter most of the time, no one really seems to be her good friend at work, but clearly Ross likes her. Is that what people think about me? I have no real friends at work and I'm regularly labelled an icicle, but Winston seems to like me. Oh God, I am Karin Logan. Detective Constable. We just look different and have different ranks. How awful is that? I shudder at the thought of it. I don't want to be anything like her. And actually, I'm not. Because, you know what? When people look at me and Winston sitting in this restaurant, chatting and drinking and eating, they'll know we actually *are* having a great time.

Winston switches off the alarm by typing digits into the cream number panel beside the front door and then shuts it behind us. World out there, us in here.

Before I can move away from the door, Winston presses me against the wall. 'We could do this,' he says. 'We could become Brighton people.' He leans his body against mine, moulding himself against me, fitting against me in the way his body does, the way it has done for the ten years we've been together.

'Brighton people, us?' I reply. I love the way Winston smells, it's a sharp, lemony scent with undernotes of the sea.

'I can sell this place and a couple of other properties. We can buy a big place near the front.'

'Sounds like you've thought a lot about this,' I say, and slip my hands under his jacket, pushing it off his shoulders.

He grabs my waist, pulls my hips towards him, his fingers caressing me there. 'I've had a look at some properties,' he says. 'It's what I do.'

I unbutton the pearly white buttons on his shirt, tug it open, immediately place my hands on his chest. I love the feel of his warm skin under my palms, the soft, wiry map of his chest hair. 'What would I do down here?'

He lifts the skirt of my dress, hooks his fingers into the waistband of my knickers and tugs them down until they fall away. I step out of them and open my legs. 'I'm sure the people down here would love to have you.'

I undo his belt, unbutton his trousers, unzip him. I tug the trousers and tight, black underwear over his neat hips, then lick my hand before sliding it over the full length of his now free erection. He groans in response and uses his knee to firmly push my legs further apart. 'But why would I want to leave London?'

He stops for a second to get me to look at him in the dark of the corridor. In heels I'm nearly the same height as him and he doesn't have to dip his head too far to stare into my eyes. His hands are on my thighs, and he pulls me forwards, pushes the tip of his hardness up against me, about to enter me, when he stops. 'Why wouldn't you want to leave London?' His hands are suddenly on my biceps and he drags me towards him, spins me around and then shoves me against the wall, flattening my cheek and pinning my body. In the next instant he's inside me. 'Why wouldn't you want to move here with me?' he whispers in my ear as he plunges deep into me. 'Why wouldn't you want this all the time?' I groan loudly, my knees weaken at his hard and fast thrusts. With a deep, throaty moan, he starts to pound into me, bringing us closer to the delicious, explosive end. Then his fingers are between my legs, seeking out my centre of pleasure, rolling it between his fingers in time with his thrusts until there is nothing else, nothing but the pleasure gushing through me, the ecstasy escaping into my veins, the orgasm screaming out of me. Then he is coming, too, filling me.

Afterwards, Winston pulls me away from the wall, gently turns me to face him and kisses me on the mouth, long and slow. We hadn't kissed before sex and he likes to do that. He likes kissing, he loves cuddling, he favours sessions where we indulge in each other's bodies. He also loves me. And because he loves me, he knows that the sex I prefer is quick and meaningful; maximum pleasure in minimum time. It's the type of sex that gives me no time to think about anything, least of all the brutal things people do to each other.

'Do you really want to move to Brighton?' I call to him as I head towards the bedroom to change into my pyjamas.

'I'm thinking about it,' he replies. He pauses to switch on the coffee grinder. By the time he's finished grinding the beans and is filling the coffee pot to go on the stove, I'm in my pyjamas, having had a quick shower, and carrying my laptop. Something occurred to me during dinner: maybe the person has access to anaesthetic drugs because they're a pharmaceutical rep? They would have to register their supply of drugs because they have to give them out as samples. It'd be very easy to keep a little back from each client.

'Why?' I ask Winston. 'I suppose I mean, why now? You've had this flat for years but you've never once expressed an interest in living here.'

'Yeah, but it's being here for a little bit. It's got a good vibe. We could get married. We could afford a huge house if I got rid of a couple of properties. We could talk about . . .' He stops talking to busy himself with taking his silver coffee pot off the stove and pouring it into a cup.

Adoption. We could talk about adoption. We haven't properly discussed it, we've sort of danced around it as the years stretch behind us and in front of us without me getting pregnant. We've both had every test available, I've had surgery to 'fix' the fibroids and polycystic ovaries and *technically after the operations* it should be possible. We've tried three rounds of IVF and *technically* it should have happened. But it hasn't.

Adoption is there. Adoption has always been there. We've just never really discussed it.

'Would they even take us at our age?' I say.

'Yes.'

'And would they consider it with my job?'

'I don't know, Jodes, I haven't gone that far into it. We can just talk about it. Like we can talk about moving here. Or we can not.'

'Hey, hey, why are you getting snappy with me?'

'Because, Jody, sometimes you don't seem to understand that we get one life. We get one life and we have to make the most of it. We have to try things, we have to take chances and accept what happens if we fail. We don't always need to throw "yes, but" roadblocks in the way of something.'

'I wasn't—'

'You were. You spend all your time hunting things out, investigating stuff, and you mean to tell me you couldn't find out the age limit and occupational limits on adoption if you wanted to?'

He has a point.

'Look, if you don't want to talk about it, if you don't want to do it, no problem. But just be honest with me so I know what the future might possibly look like.'

I get up from my chair and go to him. Slip my arms around his solid torso, gaze up into his big, soppy brown eyes. 'I'm sorry. I do do that. I look for problems before we've even outlined what the plan might possibly be. I'm sorry. We can talk about adoption. We can absolutely talk about adoption. And moving and getting married. We can talk about all of that. I just need to get this case out of the way first. All right? Once this is done, we will absolutely talk about all of that. All right?'

My fiancé nods slowly.

'*All right?*' I repeat.

'All right,' he replies.

Even though he's still a bit narked with me, he lets me kiss him. And pretty soon he's kissing me back.

After this case, of course, I'll have a better idea of whether I'll be on trial for murder or not.

Pieta

'Open your eyes, Pieta.' His voice was softer than normal, gentler. 'It's only a few hours now until you can go back to your life, so open your eyes.'

'No,' I said.

I flinched as he lowered his face until it was touching mine. His skin was warm but clammy against my cheek. Revulsion tremored in my veins like it did every time he came near me.

'Pieta, open your eyes and I won't kill you,' he coaxed.

'No.'

'Open your eyes. I want you to see me. I want you to know what I look like in our last few hours together. Come on, open your eyes, look at me.'

'I can't, Peter.'

'I won't kill you. If I'm telling you to open your eyes, that means it's what I want and it won't count.'

'I can't. I can't open my eyes.'

'I know how much you hate the knife. I know how much it scares you. If you don't open your eyes, I'll have to bring it back. But please, just do this one thing for me. Please.'

'I can't, Peter,' I said in the smooth concave of a sob. 'If I do, you'll have to kill me because that was the deal. And I don't want you to have to do that. I don't want you to have to live with doing that.'

He stopped for a moment and then stepped back away from me. 'What?'

'What will you feel like if you have to end me? It will devastate you, and I don't want you to go through that. I don't want you to suffer like that. So no, I won't, Peter. I won't open my eyes. I won't do that to you.'

He was watching me now because he was confused, because he didn't understand what I was saying, why I was saying it.

'You care what happens to me?' he eventually asked.

Nod, Pieta, nod.

I ordered myself not to flinch this time when he stroked his thumb down my face. I willed my body to relax as he pressed his face against mine. I made myself shut everything out as he started again.

I forced myself not to recoil no matter what he did.

Sunday, 23 June

My body jerks suddenly and snaps my eyes open.

My vision takes a moment to adjust. The walls look like wood and glass, not the buttermilk of my bedroom, there are windows all around instead of just in the bay. Panic lightning bolts through my body. *Kobi. Where's Kobi?*

I'm on Ned's boat, still. My head is resting on his thigh. I roll my head to the left and see he is sitting upright but is fast asleep – his head is thrown back, his mouth is open, and he's gently snoring.

I have no idea what the time is, but I can't see any lights from the windows.

I'd stared at him for a long time after he told me he wanted to get to know me. This wasn't like Reggie asking me out. Reggie I liked and in another life I'd love to be with him. But I couldn't, because I had a son and I had to put him first; *because I had a scar and no one could ever see it.*

I'd almost accepted that I was going to be alone for the rest of my life. That the scar, my exaggerated startle response, never being able to trust anyone would mean a life of solitude. Only almost, though. Sometimes I did crave companionship. Sometimes I did want someone to share a beer with, to talk to, to watch telly with. I could do that with someone like Ned because it wouldn't mean anything. And, most importantly, I knew he didn't really have feelings for me. This wouldn't work if he did have feelings for me, if I had to worry about hurting him by never completely committing to anything beyond surface companionship.

'I'll have a beer,' I'd said to him.

'You're going to stay?' he asked, incredulous.

I shrugged. 'For a bit. I want to see your bedrooms and maybe look at some more of your photos.'

'Really?'

'I'll have to call my mother, though, and tell her I'm going to be a bit later than I said but yes, I'll stay for a bit.'

He'd shown me around the rest of his boat; the cabins were larger than I expected, the shower room and bathrooms were all designed to a high spec. We'd taken our beers and sat upstairs, looking out over the water, not really talking.

'What's the deal with you and your son's father?' Ned asked.

I stared at the beer label, wondering what to say without sounding defensive, without lying. 'So did you never get married or anything like that? Kids?' I decided on.

It was his turn to stare at his beer bottle label. He sighed and eventually said: 'No. I spent my twenties and thirties thinking I could have any woman I wanted and that I'd have plenty of time to settle down. I hit my forties and the shagging around lost its appeal in a big way but the women who I was meant to settle down with had all got on with doing just that with decent men, so potential partners got rather thin on the ground.'

'So that's a no then.'

Ned grinned at me. 'That's a no.' He returned his gaze to his beer bottle. 'I wasn't being nosey when I asked about your son's father. I was trying to find out if you were single or if I had a potential rival.'

I shook my head. 'You don't have feelings for me, Ned. Well, not in the way you think. You feel guilt and remorse. Not any-thing else.'

'I do feel guilt and remorse. I also feel . . . so much more.' He started to pick at the label. 'A whole lot more.'

'You're one of those blokes, aren't you? You don't "get" women so if you spend a bit of time with one and get on with her, you think it must mean something.'

He grinned without looking at me. 'You could be right. But you could also be wrong.' His gaze found mine. 'You could be completely wrong about what I feel for you.'

'Can I see some of your other photos?' I wanted to change the subject. He was ruining it. I didn't want to know if he had feelings for me. If he did, genuinely, then I couldn't spend time with him, I couldn't have him as a surrogate companion. He was ruining it by sounding earnest. 'You know, the photos you take with your mobile or a disposable camera.'

'I don't know what you mean, Miss Rawlings.'

We sat side by side, our arms brushed up against each other, while I went through his photos. At some point he put his arms along the back of the sofa. At another point, I rested my head on his shoulder while I flicked through his albums. When he'd stroked his hand over my hair, I'd looked up at him. He'd gazed down at me, asking if it was OK. It was fine, I realised. It was fine for him to do that. It was safe for him to do that. He'd stroked my hair and I'd closed my eyes, enjoying the sensation of his soothing, rhythmic motion. That's probably when I fell asleep.

I sit up. I hadn't meant to fall asleep like that. And I need to leave now. Get home to my mother and my son, get back to my article, get back to my real life.

'Hello, you,' Ned says, making me start.

'That wasn't meant to happen,' I state as I push myself away from him. He stretches his neck and rolls his shoulders, while I bend down to right my purple and white trainers so I can slip my feet into them. 'I was meant to stay for a bit and then go home.'

'I was meant to wake you up, not fall asleep too.'

I find the clock on the wall near the steering wheel: 3:30 a.m.! 'My mother will have a nervous breakdown. I'd better get going.'

'Do you want me to walk you to your car?'

'No, no, I'll be fine.'

The gentle rocking of the boat, the sound of it lapping against the dock fills the silence between us.

'This is awkward, isn't it?'

'Yes,' I reply.

'Do you think if we kissed it'd stop the awkwardness?'

'Probably not.'

'Can we try anyway?'

'No, Ned, no. This is all a bit too weird for me. Tonight wasn't what I was expecting. And I kind of like you but I'm really wary of you; I kind of don't like you, but I'm curious to see if you've really changed. So let's not rush anything, all right?'

He's disappointed – it's plain on his face, but I can't do anything about that. This is more than I expected to happen. 'All right. At least let me walk you to your car.'

Sunday, 26 April, 2009

He placed the silk scarf across my eyes, then he gently moved my head and tied the scarf around the back of my head. He was blindfolding me again. He was letting me off. He was telling me that I wouldn't have to keep my eyes closed the whole time; giving me a way to relax and keep my eyes closed without all the effort, without taking the risk of being killed.

'Peter?' I called when I heard his footsteps leaving.

He stopped but didn't say anything.

'Thank you,' I said. 'I really appreciate you doing this.'

Sunday, 23 June

It's like a ghost town over here. The ASDA is open twenty-four hours, but there isn't much sign of life. The cinema is shut, the restaurants and bars are all shuttered for the night. The hush of the wind on the water is a constant, undulating backdrop. Off the gangplank and off the gated part of the Marina, we walk towards the car park, our footsteps echoing so loudly I start to feel that we really have wandered into a ghost town where something hideous befell all the previous residents.

I jump when Ned hooks his fingers around mine but I quickly realise I don't mind it actually – it makes me feel safe, even temporarily.

'This is me,' I say to him when we reach level 3 of the car park and arrive at my car.

'I'll see you in a few days,' he replies.

Awkwardness, again. The feeling that we should kiss, again. I take matters into my own hands and step forward, slip my arms around his middle and hug him. It's not a natural hug and he's not sure how to respond at first. Slowly he wraps his arms around me, even more slowly he lowers his head and rests his cheek on my head, even more slowly I feel him inhale, breathing in my scent.

Too much, too much! Too close, too fast!

I immediately step back, busy myself with opening the car door, throwing my bag and the photographs onto the other seat.

'I'll see you, Ned,' I say, again ignoring his disappointment.

'Yeah, yeah.' He steps back as I shut the car door and nods at me as I start the engine. The noise is obscenely loud in the dead of this night, the lights illuminating everything in the flood of their bright, white glare.

I don't know what I'm doing; I can admit that the further away I get from him. I can't be with him, not after what he did. But is he the answer? I'll never be able to completely relax with him, I'll never allow myself to fall completely in love with him, so does it matter what our history is? Because, right now, it's either him or nothing. And tonight has shown me that I'm not as accepting of nothing as I thought I was.

Jody

Monday, 24 June

'I know this isn't ideal, but I'd like you to delay running the interview for a few days,' I say. I'm on speakerphone to Pieta Rawlings and her editor, Lillian Laird.

'Unacceptable!' Lillian immediately replies.

'What's happened?' Pieta asks as though her editor hasn't spoken.

'There's been a development,' I explain. 'I've had to go to London and it could have a bearing on this case and your article. I'm not asking you to pull it, I'm just asking you to delay it by a few days.'

'And as I said, that is unacceptable. The story is already leaking out, those NDAs aren't worth the paper they're printed on. All it will take is one person to leak it on the internet and that's it, our exclusive is gone.' This is Pieta's editor again.

I'd love to say I don't care about her exclusive. That she can stick her exclusive where the sun doesn't shine, but I need to not alienate people who can screw me over. I need to not alienate people full stop. 'OK, we're almost ready to release a proper public appeal for help. I'll let you know when, so at the same time you can say you've got an exclusive story with one of the living victims. I don't know how it works. But wouldn't that be better, to be able to advertise that you've got an angle that no one else has?'

'I think that's a great idea,' Pieta says. 'Everyone else would be doing the advertising for us. People will be gagging to read it. Actually, Detective Foster, I think this would be a brilliant way to get us the traction and national recognition that this story deserves.

'Just think, Lillian, we could devote half the issue to this. Look at these sorts of crimes, make it relevant to Sussex, but also the crime stuff on a national scale. Your editor's letter could be a meditation on whether you think the police are doing enough – no offence, Detective. Everyone would have to take us seriously because we have something they haven't. Yes, I think this could work really well for us. Really well.'

I'm impressed by Pieta's ability to take something I've dropped on them and spin it to her boss.

'I'll leave it with you,' I say. I have to get off the phone. 'I'm not around for the next few days, but if you call the office and ask for Laura Whittaker, she should be able to help.'

'Is it OK if I speak to Callie again in the meantime?' Pieta asks.

'Why?'

'I've written up the story, but there are a few gaps about her background. I won't ask her anything about the case directly and you can listen to the tapes afterwards just to make sure I haven't overstepped the mark.'

I'd rather she didn't, but she's just helped me out with the editor and I can't focus on this right now. I also need to get her onside because at some point, I think I'm going to need her. 'Nothing about the case,' I state sternly.

'Nothing, I swear.'

'All right. I'll talk to you in a couple of days. Bye.'

I ring off the phone and turn to go back into the room I left to make the call. I'm in London.

'I'm sorry about that,' I say to the forensic examiner who had begun to talk me through his findings. 'Can you start again? Where were these remains found again?'

'In East London. There used to be an area of warehouses that were marked for renovation. They ended up being demolished after a series of fires destroyed them. It took a while for them to be rebuilt. We think it was in that time period that these remains were deposited there, sometime before the cement was poured. They could have been stored elsewhere and moved there. I think that's likely given the state of decomposition. Either way, we may never have found them if the contractors hadn't thrown the building up so badly it essentially fell down and needed complete demolition.'

I fold my arms across my chest, hiding the way I dig my fingernails deep into the palms of my hands. 'When were they found?' I ask.

'Around March.'

'So why am I only hearing about it now?'

'You know how slowly these things move. There are quite a few more things that are further up the list. But, having said that, I did my best to make these a priority since we identified three separate bodies, which indicated the work of a serial.'

He spins on his chair away from the photos to his computer.

'Once everything was entered into the system, DNA matches for all three of them came back quite quickly. They were all reported as missing after a night out between twelve and ten years ago. That seemed to fit the MO of who you've been looking for.' He types into his computer, clicking through old images of young women. 'Jolene Benkko, disappeared in 2007.' Click. 'Robyn Kiernan, also disappeared in 2007.' Click. 'Sandy Vainna, disappeared in 2008.'

They must have been the ones who couldn't keep their eyes closed, who didn't manage to escape and make their way home.

'Any chance of a cause of death?'

He shakes his head. 'I've tried. I'm trying, but it's been so long, the bodies exposed to so many different elements. I haven't given up, but don't hold your breath.'

'I know it'll be a long shot to see if there are any metabolites left after all this time, but you could try Succinylcholine. That's how the more recent ones were killed.'

'I'll give it a go.'

'OK, thank you.'

Jolene. Robyn. Sandy.

More names to add to the list. More photos for our wall. More women to come to tea in my dreams, accusing me, reminding me that I could have done more to prevent their deaths.

Pieta

Tuesday, 25 June

Opposite Room 101, Officer Perry seems to be sitting in the same position in the bucket chair as he was the last time I was here, last Monday.

I don't know if he's been here all week, but by the greyish tone of his face, and the slightly weary slump of his shoulders as he sits in his chair, he's definitely been there all night.

I wonder what the other people on this floor think, of a man sitting in the chair in the corridor all night. I wonder who they think is staying on their floor. I nod to him before I move to knock on the door.

He nods very briefly, so briefly I wonder if I'm imagining he did it at all.

My fingers are very loud rapping on the wooden door, and I'm embarrassed – when PC Perry is so still and quiet, I'm disordered and messy creating all that noise, encroaching on the ordered calmness of his world.

'Who is it?' Callie calls.

'Me. Pieta.' I'd messaged her yesterday asking if I could ask her some follow-up questions.

'Oh, hi, Pieta. Is it that time already? Let me just put on some clothes and I'll be right with you.'

After a while, she throws open the door saying, 'Come in, come in.' The last time I saw her, she was falling apart, in the midst of a complete breakdown. She's got herself together now, so much so she seems even better than when we first met. She's wearing a pretty blue-and-white flowered summer dress, her hair is loose around her face, rather than hanging there as something to hide behind. Maybe that's what telling the truth does. Maybe it brings about a cathartic release, brings you a new type of peace.

The police wouldn't have needed to hear everything that Callie told me. They wouldn't require all those intricacies to try to find the man who did it, they'd just need to know all about The During. Maybe a little of The Before, maybe a little of The After. I needed to know all of it to tell her story, and that seems to have freed Callie.

'Sorry to keep you waiting,' she chatters like a bird as she leads me down the corridor past the wardrobe and bathroom. 'I didn't realise the time and we were up a lot of the night, talking.'

I register the 'we' at the exact same time I come into the main room and see, sitting on the edge of the bed looking sheepish and dishevelled and like he's just spent the night, Ned.

Monday, 27 April, 2009

'It's nearly time to let you go, Pieta,' he murmured against my ear. 'But I don't want you to go. I want you to stay with me. Would you like that? Would you like to stay with me.'

I kept myself very still. I couldn't move because I was screaming inside. If I moved, I would start screaming outside, too.

'If you tell me you want to stay, I'll keep you. I will keep looking after you. I will take care of you like I have. I've been good to you, haven't I? *Haven't I?*' he repeated when I didn't reply.

'Yes.'

'Do you want to stay with me? Just a little while longer?'

Tuesday, 25 June

I feel foolish because I *am* foolish.

What on Earth was I thinking? That Ned and I would get together? That what happened between us meant anything? So stupid. *So . . . stupid!* They probably sat and laughed at me, like he used to do with his other little friends. Laughed at poor, fat, pig-faced Pieta, thinking that anyone could be her friend, thinking she could somehow break through her loneliness in even the smallest way.

I shudder, their laughter practically ringing in my ears as I walk around the corner to where I've parked my car, my footsteps quick and determined; I need to get away from here as quickly as possible. I mean, what was I *thinking*? Ned Wellst? *Him?* Well, quite clearly, I wasn't thinking.

Callie talked for about forty minutes but was constantly yawning and shifting in her seat until she said she was too tired to talk any more: talking, remembering, revisiting was exhausting and when you'd been up all night, it just made matters worse. 'Can we call it a day?' she asked at the apex of another yawn. 'I'm too tired to do this. Sorry.'

We were sitting on the sofa, my silver-coloured tape recorder whirling away between us, and my gaze constantly straying to the bed. *How many times did they do it?* I kept wondering. *How many times, how many ways? Or did he just put his arm around her, like he did with me?*

'No worries,' I'd said, packing away my recorder and note-book and pen, glad to be allowed out of there sooner than expected. 'Call me later if you're up to it.' I'd found a smile, right from the bottom of my heart where I stored up the appropriate responses to the things that hurt me, and had beamed it at her.

'You're such a love,' Callie had said.

Ned had been skulking around, first in the shower and then, when he returned, dressed, polished and generally looking refreshed, he'd picked up his camera and started taking her pic-ture again. They'd obviously planned for him to stay the night, since all of his camera equipment was in the corner of her room. Or maybe, urgh, he'd been taking *intimate* pictures of her last night. I shudder again, and move faster.

Underground car parks with no view of daylight or the street, and limited exits are my idea of hell. But the position of her hotel means I have no choice but to park here. At the bottom of a slope down into the car park, I scan my ticket at the entrance and wait for the door to slide back.

I go to the machine and don't bother to search my bag, which is always a graveyard of small change, and simply pay by credit card. I've been just over an hour – literally five minutes over – so the price has shot up. I don't care. I just need to be away from here.

In the car, I'll put on loud music, I'll drive as fast as I can within the speed limit and I'll put all of this behind me – literally and metaphorically.

I hear footsteps and every nerve in my body jangles to attention. *Move*, I tell myself. *Don't freeze, move. Just get going, get to your car, get to safety.*

More footsteps, the squeal of wheels.

The squeal of wheels. My body almost stops. The squeal of wheels, the hand on my mouth, the arm around my waist, the lifting sensation as I'm yanked up and away.

No, I'm not going to stay still, I'm not going to let it happen again. Kobi needs me. I want to live.

I break out into a run, and I hear the footsteps running too, keeping pace, catching up. *No, no, this isn't going to happen.*

'Pieta!' Ned calls. 'Pieta, wait!'

His voice makes me run faster. I weave in and out of cars, desperate to get to mine, which sits like a light-blue beacon, waiting for me to leap in and speed away.

'Pieta!' he shouts.

I make it to the car, but haven't got my keys out. That's how churned up I was, how upset, I didn't even do something I usually do as standard. I didn't even sling my bag across my body. I rip the pink suedette square off my shoulder, stick my hand in and start to feel around for the keys. *Where are you, where are you, where are you?*

'Pieta, look—' Ned says and places a hand on my shoulder.

I quell the scream that rises up through my body, and tear myself away from him. 'Get away from me!' I shout at him. I throw myself back. 'Don't touch me! Get away, get away, get away!'

293

He raises his hands in surrender, his palms as pale as his horrified and confused face, and he does what I need him to do – step back a few paces, put distance between us.

'I need to talk to you,' he says carefully, his face still bathed in bewilderment, his hands still up in peace.

'What do you need to talk about to me of all people?'

'That wasn't what it looked like. Nothing happened.'

'I don't care what you do,' I reply.

'I didn't do anything. Nothing happened.'

'I honestly don't care what you do, but you know, Ned, she's really vulnerable. Really, really vulnerable. She might say she doesn't want to be defined by what happened and she's fine and she's moving on, but talking about all of this has made her even more fragile. And I can't believe you'd take advantage of that.'

'I didn't do anything,' he insists.

'So you didn't spend the night with her?'

'I spent the ni— She called me. Do you hear? She. Called. Me. She asked me to take some photos of her. She just wanted to see herself differently after the intensity of the last few days. After the photos, she said she didn't want to be alone. I know what it's like to not want to be alone. And yes, I could see that despite everything she's said, she is delicate. So when someone's on the edge and they ask you not to leave them alone, what do you do? Walk away? Not me.

'I thought I was helping her. All I did was be there when she asked me not to leave. I slept on the sofa.'

'Yeah, right, a good-looking woman asks you to stay and you slept on the sofa. Look in the dictionary, Ned, my picture's right next to the definition of "gullible".'

'I didn't— I wouldn't, all right? It would have been easy to, she dropped enough hints about wanting us to do it. But I know she's vulnerable. And besides . . .' He shakes his head. 'Besides . . . there's someone else I'm kind of seeing right now. Well, not seeing, that's stretching it. But we're entangled. I like her a hell of a lot. I think she's incredible in so many ways. Beautiful. Funny. Warm. Clever. Insightful. Seeing her is the best part of my day. Not seeing her or hearing from her is like I've missed the sun coming up. Pieta, I've been a lot of terrible things in my time but not a cheat. And I wouldn't do anything with anyone else when I'm involved with her.'

We stare at each other across the distance. I want to believe him. Of course I do. I want to have someone care about me in the way he's just described, to genuinely feel like the sun hasn't come up because he hasn't seen or communicated with me. But he has form for being rotten, and he has that form with me. And I would be silly, no, actually, I would be self-harming, if I didn't feel suspicious about what he did or didn't do with Callie last night.

I watch him bury his hands in his pockets.

I'm never going to know what happened last night. Even if she tells me the same story, I'll never completely know if anything happened between them. If he was tempted, if he made a move, if it was actually *her* who turned *him* down.

This is a warning shot fired across my most exposed side – getting involved with Ned is bad news. Just the hint of him being with someone else is making me ignore my own safety, taking risks I can't afford to right now. A killer could be stalking me and I'm being reckless because the guy I shouldn't even be talking to might be screwing someone else.

295

I'm sure Kobi will understand when someone's sitting him down to tell him his mother isn't coming home because she got emotionally, romantically involved with the man version of the boy who made her life hell.

'Get your head in the game,' a newly qualified teacher once told Kobi. 'Get your head in the game,' my son often parroted to me.

Get your head in the game, Pieta. You have so much at risk.

'Does Detective Foster know you feel like that about her?' I say, and I'm grateful when he treats me to one of his indulgent smiles.

'Can I take you for a coffee?' he asks. 'Spend a little time together?'

'I'd love that,' I say with another of those smiles conjured up from the bottom of my heart. 'But I really need to get back and transcribe today's stuff in case I have to go back to talk to her.'

'OK,' he says.

I don't know what he's thinking as he walks away, but I have well and truly got my head back in the game. And it's one that doesn't involve Ned.

Part 6

Jody

Thursday, 27 June

Callie has come into the office. When they called from the front desk to say she was there (accompanied by PC Perry, I hope) I knew it would not be good.

I stayed in London to revisit the other crime scenes again. I wanted to see them in context now that I have seen Preston Park as well as the other Brighton parks where the other women were left. At each scene I wondered where the others were? What did he do with the others who couldn't keep their eyes closed? Or was it only these three newly found bodies who couldn't manage to keep their eyes closed? I've asked Laura and Karin to go through the missing person reports for 2007, 2008 and 2009 to see if they can find any women who fit this description. It didn't occur to me over all this time to look up missing person reports. It would help to plot which clubs or pubs or bars they were at when they disappeared.

I also went with the officers to make the follow-up FLO calls. That was something I could have done without. Seeing the devastation, hearing their anguish . . . I forced myself to do it so I could steel my resolve. I had to remind myself what I had to do.

And now, back to a visit from Callie.

This cannot be positive.

She sits in my depictured office. I do not want her looking around at the images and putting extra worries into her mind. I've got enough of that for all of us. Laura had been here, but Callie asked if it could be just her and me.

'First of all, I want to say I'm sorry,' she states.

Oh God, I think. *This is going to be terrible.*

Callie Beckman reaches into her bag and retrieves a mobile phone. She slides it and a SIM card across the table to me.

'What's this?'

'He, The Blindfolder, gave it to me.'

'He gave it to you.'

She clasps her hands together and keeps her head lowered. 'He let me go early. He said he wouldn't kill me if I helped him to find more women. I didn't manage it, you see. I didn't manage to keep my eyes closed but I begged him not to kill me. I begged him and begged him, I cried and pleaded and promised to do anything if he wouldn't kill me. In the end he said he would let me go if I helped him.'

I think I'm squeezing up my face like I'm squinting at the sun. Like I'm pained. And I am pained. I am *agonised.*

'I said yes.'

We should be sitting in an interview room right now. Another officer should be here. She should have a solicitor. This is messy and so many lines are being blurred. I don't like this. I like order in my investigations. I like my victims to be victims and everyone else to be a potential suspect. I don't like my victim to be sitting here, telling me that she agreed to help the man who kidnapped and tortured her.

I especially don't like the fact I was right about not trusting her; I particularly don't like the fact she could have a few dozen more related secrets lurking in there and she won't tell me them until she has to.

'I know it sounds bad, but I would have said anything to get out of there. I was going to go straight to the police. You know, tell them everything. And then I realised he could be watching me. I was too scared. I was in pain with my back. I just left it. I thought it'd be all right.' As she talks, she's doing that thing she does where she wrings a tissue. She squeezes it and twists it, turns it and crushes it. 'And then I got angry. I mean, who was he to do that to me? I wasn't going to be a victim so I did go to the police. But I left out the part about him letting me go because I knew they'd think I was in it with him.'

'I don't understand how we get from there to a mobile phone.'

'He started to write to me. He had my address from my driving licence. In the letters he told me what he wanted me to do. How he was looking for someone, one of the other women that he'd, you know, kept, and he needed me to—' The tissue comes apart. 'He needed me to help him. He said it would be easier for him to approach these past women if he had a woman with him. They were nervous around him, he said, so a woman would make it easier.'

I look beyond Callie to the activity outside. All these people working so hard to find Callie's abductor, and here she was, telling me she helped these women to meet their ends. I look at the officers outside my glass box and wonder which one I should get to arrest her.

'I didn't do it,' she says. 'You're looking at me like I'd ever do that. I wouldn't. He sent me these letters and then I get the one I told you about. The one with the picture. But what I didn't tell you, it also had that mobile phone. He said it was clean, that it would be hard to trace. He said to keep it on me at all times, to wait for his call. When he found the woman he was looking for, he'd call me to help him. That's why I panicked and ran. I didn't turn the phone on.'

'Do you have any of these letters?'

'No.' Head shake, tissue twists. 'No. He said to shred and burn them because that way there'd be no trace.'

'But you kept the mobile phone when you left.'

'Because I knew I'd give it to you one day.'

'Callie, I could – in fact *I should*, charge you as an accessory after the fact.'

Her tissue twisting, halts and she draws back in her seat, horrified by this revelation.

'You knew about one of the murders; you might have been able to prevent the subsequent murders if you had come forward at that time. We could have put the appeal out months ago.'

Her hands fly up and knit themselves over her mouth and she sits back in her chair, horrified anew that she has had a part in this. 'Those women died because of me,' she says behind her hands. 'Oh God, I feel sick.'

'You should feel sick, you should feel absolutely sick to your stomach,' I say. 'You didn't kill them. But you didn't help them, either.'

Her face pleats itself with anguish, tears collect on her long eyelashes, her mouth corrugates with a swallowed sob.

'You need to cut this shit out, Callie,' I say, unmoved by her

302

display of emotion. 'If I'm not going to arrest you here and now as an accessory, or charge you with obstructing the course of justice, destroying evidence and perverting the course of justice, you need to tell me everything.'

She nods, tears dripping down onto her cheeks.

'Tell. Me. Everything.'

'I will. I will.'

When she tells me what he wants and what he is doing, I know exactly why he is doing it and who he is searching for.

Pieta

Friday, 28 June

In all my years, all the news stories and features I've written and edited, I've never been in a real life Murder Investigation Office. It's late when I'm shown in and DI Foster meets me at the door. She's asked me to come in for a chat, which I'm guessing translates into me bringing her the recordings from my last Callie meeting. I'd tried to make excuses but she'd gone quiet to everything I said. In the end, I just had to say yes otherwise she was going to come to my house.

It's eerie in here. There are no people, the computer screens are off, the phones aren't ringing. I've always thought these places were on the go 24/7, never stopping in the quest to solve murder. Especially serial murders.

'If you could come this way,' DI Foster says. She takes me past a large, clear board covered with pictures and I don't know if I'm imagining it, but I'm sure she slows down. I'm sure she wants me to see the faces of the women up there, to see smiley photos, the dead photos, the pictures of the numbers on their backs. I whip my gaze away; I can't let them into my head. It's bad enough with Callie, I can't see any more of them.

In her office, which is really a smaller version of Lillian's, she offers me a seat and closes the door while I lower myself into the chair opposite hers at her desk. She has pictures in here, too. My eyes are hitched on them, caught up in them. They look so normal, ordinary and, most heartbreakingly of all, happy. I have to look away. That could have been me. That almost was me. My face could have been up on that wall. My number could have been up there.

'Pieta, look, I don't have time for niceties and to dress things up. Events are spiralling out of control. I'm scared, genuinely scared, that we're going to end up with another murder any day now. Which is why I'm going to go ahead and release a description to the press tomorrow and ask women who have encountered him to come forward. We'll be offering them police protection.'

'Why are you telling me all this?'

'You know why.'

'Well, the story is written, it's been through editing and legal so it's all ready to go.'

'OK. Look, there's something else that we're not going to release to the press but I *am* telling you. We believe he's not simply hunting down the women who survived last time and killing them – we now have reason to believe that he is searching for one particular woman and he is killing to get her attention.'

'What?' I'm trying to swallow but I can't. My throat has closed over. My heart has stopped beating. 'Why?'

This room is too small. The air in here is stale, old, not fit for human consumption. I need to get out of here.

'He left his DNA behind. This is the one and only time, as far as we can tell. He is meticulous, so careful never to leave a trace.

But we think with this one woman, he left his DNA behind, we're not sure why.'

'How do you know he left his DNA behind?' I really need to get out of here. Escape. Go somewhere I can breathe, can get my heart to start beating.

'Because she had his child.'

'He knows that?'

'I think so.'

I lift my hand to run it through my hair, which I'm wearing loose today, and realise I'm shaking, trembling, so I have to lower my arm again.

'I think he's looking for her and his child. And I think he's going to kill as many women as necessary until he finds you.'

My body stills, my mind stills, my blood stills.

'It is you, isn't it, Pieta? You're the woman he's looking for. You're the woman who had his baby.'

My fingers look odd, underlined as they are by the edge of my armwarmers. They peek out from the sleeves of my jacket. I originally started to wear armwarmers for the colours, for the warmth, but very soon, I wore them because they brought me comfort. I stare at my underlined hands, at their creases and bumps and scars. I stare into the chasm of my life, its triumphs and losses and complications.

I don't know what she expects me to say. How I'm supposed to react. Part of me wants to disintegrate into tears. To finally let go of the secret that has kept me frozen for over ten years. Part of me wants to swear at her, lie and tell her to stay away from me. Part of me wants to admit it and ask her how she can help me.

Because things have become all the more terrifying now he is after one person. After me.

'Why do you think it's me?'

'I worked it out. From the missing person's report, the way you interviewed Callie, the way you react as though none of this is new – horrific, yes, but not new. And when I found out you'd had a son nine months after you disappeared for that weekend, I realised I was right. You're one of The Blindfolder's victims and you're the one who had his child.'

'I don't know what you expect me to say,' I reply.

'Tell me I'm wrong.'

'What do you want, Detective?'

'Your son's DNA.'

My laughter is like an explosion – short but loud. 'You are hilarious,' I reply. 'You are absolutely hilarious.'

She slams her hands down on the desk, leans forward in her seat. She is tired, the dark circles under her eyes are pronounced, exaggerated. She is angry, the lines around her mouth are stretched back as they form wrathful words. 'You think murder is funny? You think the deaths of all these women, the brutalisation of more, is hilarious?'

'No, no, of course not.'

'You can stop all this. You can end all of this. You just need to let us DNA test your son.'

My head is shaking and my body is moving, I am standing and I am leaving. 'No. That's all there is to it. No.'

DI Foster darts out of her seat and is standing in front of the door before I have got very far.

'You can stop any more women being killed.' She points to

the wall of faces, of women who I could have been. 'You can get justice for what so many other women went through. For what you went through.'

'Can you move please, Detective? I'd like to leave now.'

'Pieta, Pieta, come on, just think about this,' she says suddenly placatory. 'Just think for a moment. It's a non-invasive test. Really quick, easy. It won't hurt him at all.'

It won't hurt him? Is she joking? 'I'd like to leave now.'

'This is the game-changer we need. We have nothing else. Nothing. He doesn't leave anything behind. I don't know why he didn't use a condom with you. But this is his one mistake. And mistakes are how we catch people. I wouldn't be asking if we weren't desperate. But please. *Please* can you help us?'

If it was anything else, I would. I honestly would. But not this. 'I need to leave. I need to go home now. Can you please move?'

'*WHY WON'T YOU HELP ME?*' she screams at me. She isn't merely angry and shouting, she is hurting, she is expelling all of that pain outwards at me. I can tell by the way every sinew in her neck, her face, her body is stretched to its limit. 'WHY?'

I take a step back. I can't take this. I can't take on this kind of fury. It's more than just frustration, indignation and outrage – it is hurt, a very real, very deep soul wound. I take another step back and butt against the desk. I can't take it and I can't be around it. I need to get out of here.

My sudden panic, my desperate need for flight, must filter through to her because she stops. Her body calms down, her face returns to normal and she puts distance between us, wheeling on her heels and moving to the other side of her small office.

'He's a rapist, he's a murderer, why wouldn't you do every-thing in your power to help us catch him? And it literally is within your power to help us identify him. Why wouldn't you do that?'

'Why?' I reply. I want to scream at her. I want her to see that inside me rages the sea. Inside me is a gulf of confusion and ter-ror and anger and agony and shock and sadness and fear and deep, deep sorrow. I never wanted any of this. I was dealt this hand and I have played it to the best of my abilities. 'Why would I? That is the question you should be asking. If I come forward, if I allow you to do the DNA test and it comes out who he is, my life as I know it is over. Over.

'I'll have to tell my family, my friends, my colleagues before the news leaks out. I have to tell them that . . . tell them what happened to me.' My fingers tremble at the thought of it. 'That I was . . . And then, I know what will happen. I will become the poster child for the anti-choicers. They'll use my story to further their ideas that abortion is wrong under any circumstances. "Look," they'll say, "he was a murderer, a rapist, a torturer and she *still* had his baby." They won't listen or try to understand that I was too terrified to get help. That I didn't even know I was pregnant because my periods have been so messed up pretty much all my life. That I was so scared that if I tried to get an abortion, I'd have to tell someone even a fraction of what had happened, and I couldn't stand to even think the words let alone say them. They'll say that women can't get pregnant from real rape. They'll say – whether I knew it or not – I am one of them. I don't want those people to use me or Kobi to control and dimin-ish other women. I don't even want my name in their mouths.'

'We would protect you, conceal your identity, no one would ever have to know.'

'And how do I protect my identity from my son?'

'What do you mean?'

'I do this, and then it's out there that my son's father is a killer. And he will find that out. I can't stand the thought of him knowing. Of him knowing that half the blood that flows through his veins comes from someone like the man who did that to me.'

'You can't protect him forever.'

'No, I can't. But what about protecting him now?' I point my finger at her. 'Because once you type that DNA into your computer, if it gives you a name, you'll have to tell him how you found him, won't you?'

From the look on her face, I can see that DI Foster has got there. She's finally got there, where I have been for ten years. She steps back and rests lightly against the glass wall, her face haughty and haunted.

'And once you tell him, once he knows, that means he'll have definite proof of paternity. That means he'll be able to demand contact with my son. Because the courts won't care what he did to me, what he did to those other women, they will just say my child has a right to a relationship with his father. And, besides, they'll say, if he's in prison, he won't be able to harm anyone but he *will* be able to get visits from my child. And if the court decrees it, that means the police – *you* – will have to make sure I comply.'

She has deflated a little with every word. This is the bit that she can understand, all the other things that have kept me trapped and frozen don't matter to her, but this, this shows she and the rest of the police will have to side with a murderer so he can get what he wants.

'You don't know he'd want contact,' she eventually mumbles.

'The man tortures, controls and kills people, how else is he going to get his kicks from prison? Legally, too.

'DI Foster, I have thought about it. It's always on my mind. For ten years this has been on my mind – what if he finds out and comes for my baby? I'm not as worried for me as I have always been for Kobi.'

'I can understand all that. I honestly can. But Pieta, he's coming for you, either way. He is looking for you. He's looking for his son.'

'Kobi is *not* his son. He is mine.'

'Yes, yes, sorry, I'm sorry. But you know what I mean. He is coming for you, Pieta. And on the sixth Monday, there will either be another victim of The Blindfolder dead, or he will have you. If you don't help me, I don't know if I'll be able to protect you.'

'I don't need your protection. Not if it comes with conditions.'

'It doesn't, it absolutely doesn't. Look, let me take you both into protective custody—'

'I don't think so. We're fine.' I strengthen my voice. 'I'd like to leave now.'

Reluctantly, she steps aside, allows me access to the only escape route in this room. 'Pieta, I don't want you to end up on my board.'

I turn to her before I completely leave. 'Neither do I, Detective. And I can promise you, there is no one on Earth more focused on making sure that doesn't happen than me.'

Jody

Saturday, 29 June

I've come to apologise. See? I *can* do the right thing.

I knock on her door and wait for her to answer.

'I've come to apologise,' I state before she can speak.

'There's no need,' she replies. Her colours are off the scale today. Most of them fluorescent and not a match. Looking at her for too long could probably cause a headache, it'll definitely make everything swim. It wouldn't surprise me, though, if this was the point of how she's dressed – she wants to deter people from looking at her, become anonymous, hide right before your eyes.

'Yes, there is. I behaved appallingly. Especially since I know what you went through.' I produce the bunch of flowers I bought. I had them specially combined, as many colours as possible. Her face wrinkles into a smile; I did the right thing bringing her a floral rainbow. 'I brought these for you, to apologise.'

'Thank you.'

'I know your editor wants your article to go ASAP, so I'm here to discuss with you the appeal bit. How we can make it more comprehensive than the one we're going to put out tomorrow. I was also hoping you wouldn't mind giving me a sneak peek of your article?'

'I can't do that. You might decide to censor it or pull it.'

'I thought you might say something like that, but I was hoping to win you round. Ho-hum. Can we discuss the appeal bit? We're doing it first thing on Monday morning, and then your article will come out a few days after.'

She is still wary of me, despite taking the flowers. I don't blame her. I did behave appallingly. I couldn't keep it in any longer, though. There is so much inside, so much bubbling and broiling that I couldn't control it.

'It won't take long. And I'm aware I delayed the article last week, so I don't want to hold you up any longer.'

This makes her step aside to allow me to enter. 'I really am sorry,' I say to her as I lead the way down the corridor. 'I was about to say I don't know what came over me, but I do. It's the utter frustration. None of which is your fault or problem.'

She shows me into the living room and says she'll get her laptop. The TV is on mute, and a large, shaded standing lamp in the corner casts an amber glow throughout the room. I stand there, feeling uncomfortable, making the place look messy.

I wonder what she was doing before I knocked. The TV is showing a drama that I had been trying to follow a couple of weeks ago, a half-drunk glass of water sits on the side table by the sofa. I'm purposefully not looking at the photos on the windowsill. I feel wretched that I asked her. I do not need to be reminded that the little boy I was trying to get DNA from is a real person. One whose whole life could be wrecked by me.

'Here we go,' she says on her return. She seems taken aback that I'm still standing. 'You can sit down.'

'I know, but I didn't like to presume.'

'Did you think I'd make you stand while I type or something? Is that how I come off to you?'

I shake my head. 'No. No. I suppose I wouldn't like it if some-one did it to me, so I'm mindful of doing it to other people.'

A look flitters across her face, as though she is taken aback by this. 'I see.' She waves her hand around her seating. 'Well, take a seat. Anywhere you fancy.'

I sit on the part of the sofa furthest from the windowsill of happy memories and she places her laptop on the coffee table. 'Do you want a glass of wine or something?'

'No, no, despite how it might seem, I'm still on duty. I just need to get this done and then I can get off home. Wouldn't say no to a coffee, though.'

'Coffee it is. How do you take it?'

'Black, two sugars.'

'Coming up.'

I sit in this seat for as long as I can. I can't stay here, in her cocoon-like home, which smells and looks and feels like my idea of heaven. This is what I thought Winston and I would have: comfy home, child asleep somewhere in the house. I leave the living room and stand in the corridor. It really is huge. As well as the pictures and artwork on display, there's a bank of cupboards, which houses coats, I assume, and a shoe rack that holds their shoes. I'm guessing, since going right leads to the cupboards and the front door, going left is towards the kitchen. I head back towards the front door and kick off my shoes, which I should have done when I arrived. I expect everyone to do it in my house so I'm not sure why I didn't do it this time.

'Actually,' I say to Pieta in the kitchen, making her jump.

'Don't do that!' she says, clinging on to the worktop.

'Sorry, sorry. I was just coming to say, do you have herbal tea? I shouldn't drink coffee. It's bad for me. I love it, but it's bad for me.'

'Peppermint, OK?'

'Perfect. Well, not perfect. I'd rather the coffee but it'll do in the face of trying to do things that are good for me. For once.'

I sip the tea while I give her the appeal information she needs to add to her article. It doesn't take long, but by the end of it, I feel like staying. I feel like sitting back, curling my feet up under me and asking for that glass of wine.

At the door, I'm about to leave when I stop and say to her, 'I really am sorry for the way I behaved yesterday.'

'Thank you for saying that,' she says. She doesn't say it's OK, I notice that. She doesn't give me a pass, but she is gracious in accepting the apology.

Honestly, I'm sure if the universe hadn't messed up with putting us together in this way we could have been friends. 'I don't suppose we'll have any reason to be in touch after this,' I say. 'Unless, of course, you change your mind about what we were talking about yesterday. I mean, the appeal is for women to come forward.'

'Let me know if you want me to write a follow-up piece after the appeal goes out,' she replies, formal and cold now.

'I will. I will.'

Yes, all right, I shouldn't have done it.

But you know what I went there for. I'm sure she'll have

known, too. I mean, we all know I could have given her the appeal specifics over the phone so we all know I was there to get her son's DNA.

I found a few hairs, a couple with their white bulbs attached, snagged into the shiny black lining of his school hat.

I'm not saying I'm going to get them tested. Yet. I just need to see how this appeal pans out. I'm hoping it will get women who were taken by The Blindfolder to reveal themselves before the next sixth Monday. Before 22nd July. Otherwise, another one of them is going to end up dead in a Brighton park.

But if the appeal and article don't work then I'll *have* to get the DNA tested. I'll *have* to. It could be the only way to save other women's lives. And I know that, deep down, saving lives is what Pieta Rawlings wants, too.

Jody

Serial Rapist & Killer: London and Sussex Police Appeal for Help

By Pieta Rawlings

Sussex Police are appealing for anyone who may have been the victim of a serial rapist who calls himself The Blindfolder to come forward. The detectives in charge of the case say they believe the man has been operating in the London area for over twelve years but has recently moved his focus to Brighton.

The man is known to snatch women from outside late-night bars and clubs in various areas of London, blindfold them and hold them for 48 hours, during which time he sexually assaults and tortures them.

The lead detective in the case, Detective Chief Inspector Nugent, said, 'We know this man has been attacking women since at least 2006, but we have reason to believe

317

he may have started before that. We're appealing for those who think they may have encountered this individual or who were subject to an attempted abduction to contact us as a matter of urgency.'

The police believe that The Blindfolder may have escalated to murdering his past victims in recent months. DCI Nugent added: 'It's imperative that any women who have been abducted and abused by this man contact us. We are prepared to do whatever it takes to protect the women who have fallen victim to him, but we do need them to identify themselves.

'If you recognise any of the details of this crime and believe yourself or someone you know to have been a victim of this man, do contact us.'

The appeal is being made after six women, all believed to be previous victims of The Blindfolder, have been found murdered in London and Brighton.

If you think you might have been a victim of The Blindfolder, contact Sussex Police on the numbers listed below.

To read more about The Blindfolder, pick up a copy of our magazine BN Sussex *this Thursday, where we have an exclusive interview with one of his most recent victims.*

I can tell which bits Pieta Rawlings wrote and which bits were added by an over-zealous editor. But it's of no consequence. It will do the job. Which will, of course, bring me a whole new set of problems. Mainly, of course, too much information.

Some officers like appeals and they go out of their way to

get them done as soon as possible. I hate them. I always prefer to get as much info together as possible before we invite in a lot of leads, most of which will, ultimately, take us nowhere.

I toss the paper onto the table before I grab my notebook and head out into the briefing room. Might as well get this done now before the phones start ringing relentlessly.

Pieta

Monday, 8 July

Today is one of those days.

I guess I was owed. I've had a good run recently, have been so fine and balanced and buoyant for weeks, no, *months*, that I'd almost forgotten what it was like.

I know the moment I open my eyes that the coming hours are going to be the longest – stretched and overextended; the approaching minutes will be overburdened with an oppressive and crushing atmosphere; the impending seconds will be filled by the blinding, stark solitude of bright, white light.

The bright colours won't work; the grasping the strands of who I am and wrenching myself together won't take; the keeping calm and carrying on will bounce off with barely a scratch.

It's Callie.

It's The During.

It's The After.

It's the hormones that are bringing me to menopause or keeping me mired in perimenopause.

It's the endometriosis that physically ravages different parts of my body and has come back twice despite being excised.

It's the article, the response to it, the emails from other women jamming up my inbox wanting to tell their story. I read them all and I am punctured by every one of them. I know how they feel. I know how they cope or they don't cope. And it's too much.

It's Lillian, wanting me to do a follow-up now the story is out there and being syndicated and getting *BN Sussex* the attention Lillian craves.

It's DI Foster asking me for Kobi's DNA. It's knowing that I can't give it to her without her wrecking my life and Kobi's life but at the same time knowing that if I don't, other women could die. I'm already responsible if he really is killing to get my attention; my refusal to help via DNA will just add to my culpability.

It's knowing that it's probably only a matter of time until The Blindfolder finds me. He has my name, it's not that hard to find me in general. I leave work every day checking to see I am not being followed, on edge for every second of every moment.

It's knowing that I will have to leave everything behind and not knowing where Kobi and I will have to go next, not knowing if we'll ever be able to settle again.

It's the perfect storm of my life that brings me here.

For Kobi, I drag my unwilling, uncooperative body out of bed. I shower in water that feels like a hundred thousand spikes brutalising and penetrating my skin. I switch on the radio like normal, even though the sound of it is like sandpaper rasped across each nerve in my head. I flip an egg to make it the ideal combination of cooked and dippy, even though the stench of it keeps me on the very edge of vomiting.

Every sense is heightened, over-sensitised, raw.

For Kobi, I walk him to school, listening to and smiling at his re-enactments of every pass, tackle and goal from last Friday's playground match; I nod and grin and say hi to the parents who are my friends and acquaintances and just familiar faces.

For me, I walk home to pick up my car. I unlock the doors, climb in, then sit because I want to crawl back into bed. I want to hide from the world.

For me, I sit in my car, I stare straight ahead and I claw at my forearms over my sleeves so no marks will show, while trying to swallow the sadness before it engulfs me.

Claw, claw, claw.

Every moment is agony.

Each instant is a glimpse into the horror inside.

Claw, claw, claw.

I need to scream so loudly, so noisily, so piercingly, every millimetre of the world will hear and understand what this is.

I long to curl up so tight, so tiny, that I disappear.

Claw, claw, claw.

I have to go out there and be the Pieta Rawlings everyone knows. I have to smile, I have to talk, I have to appease my boss, excel at my job, I have to come home to my son, I have to take care of my life like normal.

Claw, claw, claw.

It's been deferred for a long time, but today is one of those days.

I guess I was owed.

Jody

Wednesday, 10 July

I have less than two weeks left. I have less than a fortnight until another body turns up in a Brighton park. We could get people to watch the parks, but what about the Downs? The countryside area that is slung around Sussex like a luscious green stole is vast and we don't have enough officers to cover that. We actually don't have enough officers to cover the other parks in Brighton.

I have less than two weeks left, and every day for about a week or so now, I have been getting this little plastic bag out and staring at it. Staring at it, watching it, thinking on it. Ruminating, pondering, vacillating.

The article has been positive, much more than I thought it would be. There have been many phone calls, and some are proper leads, but nothing that has led us right to his door. Nothing that has been forensic enough for us to link to any one individual – which is unusual as we usually have at least one suspect by now. But the reality is, everything is slow. Much slower than anyone wants it to be, but checking properly is always laborious and time-consuming.

But even with the new potential leads and information about a series of break-ins that could point to where the hard-to-source Sux might have come from, there is nothing that will do what this little bag could do. This little bag of five individual hairs. They could be the key to all of this. It's really unlikely such a prolific criminal will not be in the system. It's highly unlikely that entering Kobi Rawlings' genetic code into the national computer will *not* produce the name of The Blindfolder.

I have to do it, don't I?

The clock is ticking, counting down until the sixth Monday when the next woman will be found.

I look up, and catch a glimpse of them reflected in the glass of my office wall. Harlow, Shania, Freya, Bess, Gisele, Robyn, Sandy, Jolene standing together, smiling, laughing, sharing a joke. They could be a group of friends; they should be out there right now doing this with their actual friends. And soon another woman will be added to them.

I don't know what to do.

The old me, the me who has been hunting this man for thirteen years, would have had this analysed and entered into the Police National Computer within hours of leaving Pieta's house, no question. But I have got to know Callie, I have got to know Pieta Rawlings, kind of. And I have remembered the words of Jovie: open your eyes. Open your eyes and see how what you do can devastate another person's life. Open your eyes and see how not doing this could end up killing someone.

Laura comes to my door, knocking briefly before she opens it wider. I hide the bag away under a file. No one knows I have this, no one knows about Pieta Rawlings.

'Come in . . .' My voice dribbles away when I see her face.

She's pale, she's trembling and she looks absolutely terrified. I'm on my feet before I have a chance to think about it. I am on my feet and grabbing my coat, grabbing my bag, ready to dash out. 'What is it?' I ask as I prepare to run out of the door. 'What's happened?'

I know the answer, I know what she's going to say: another body. Another woman found murdered. While I sat around being sensitive and thoughtful, he hasn't stuck to his pattern and another woman has been killed.

'Guv' . . . it's . . .' She stops speaking. Laura can be maddening. Out of everyone out there, I like her the most. She's empathetic and efficient and says the things no else would dare to. But she also favours dramatic pauses and theatrical retellings and letting her words drain away to create tension. 'It's bad. It's really bad.'

I drop my bag when she tells me. I have to sit heavily on my desk when she finally speaks. It's almost as bad as another body. Almost.

Pieta

Friday, 12 July

> Pieta, Hello. Now that I don't have a legitimate reason
> to see you, and you didn't pick up on my other hints,
> can I ask you out officially? N x

The Ned Factor.

I genuinely thought he'd forget all about me once the article was published. He'd come into the office a couple of times before it was released and we'd ended up going around the corner for a coffee. Ashley had raised an eyebrow or two at that, but it was nothing. And I knew I would drop off his radar once he started a new story or assignment with a woman he had to spend time with, which would lead him to believe he had feelings for her. But no, here he is, asking me out officially. He'd hinted at it – asked me if I was around on certain dates, invited me to his boat – all of which I ignored because my head was back in the game of The Blindfolder.

I really hadn't prepared myself for the Ned Factor.

'Pieta, *two* courier packages for you,' Reggie says before I can tip forwards into untangling the Ned Factor mess along with everything else that is racing through my mind.

'How come you always bring my packages up?' I ask before he has a chance to scuttle away to his desk. I like Reggie and I want things to be normal between us again. We went straight back to being awkward with each other after he sent me the email about agreeing with what Ned had said about my photos.

'Do you know how many things I get couriered every day? I'm always down in the post room so if something's there for you, I pick it up.'

'Yeah, but you don't bring anyone else's post up.' I lower my voice to say this because I don't want to alert the others to my preferential treatment, or encourage Tiffany in trying to get us together.

He drops his volume to reply, 'Cos no one else has got Lillian off my back like you have.'

'Fair enough then. Thanks, Reggie.'

He grins at me. 'Not a problem.'

The first package has familiar handwriting and is book-shaped. It's a book from a publicist who always makes sure I'm on her first run list. I add it to the stack of books on the floor beside my chair. *I really need to go through these*, I think as I reach for the second package, a white, padded Jiffy bag. The plain label doesn't have a company logo or anything remarkable to identify it. I almost add it to my to-be-opened pile, but decide against it. Seeing as it was couriered rather than posted, it might have time-sensitive information in it.

I reach inside and I feel silk. I immediately snatch my hand away. Since . . . since *then*, the touch of silk makes me queasy, brings back hideous memories.

Instead, I shake the contents out onto the desk. Out tumble two pieces of paper, and a blue-and-white tie-dyed silk scarf that sits in front of me like a partially coiled deadly snake. I reach first for the small rectangle that is clearly a photograph. I turn it over knowing without knowing who is going to be on the other side: a young boy, about nine or so. He has curly black hair that would be big and wild if his mother didn't regularly use clippers on it; he has large, brown eyes that most likely came from his mother; he has a small nose that doesn't match hers; he has a chin shape that probably came from his father; and pink-red lips that his mother has convinced herself come from her.

I take a deep breath, then another, then another, then another but no air seems to be able to get in; no oxygen seems to be entering my body as I stare at the photo of my son. His hat is askew but his tie is in place, he is staring intently at his mother as she tries to reason with him. Another breath, another breath, trying to get air down past my fast-hurtling heart.

This can't be happening.

Not so soon. I thought I'd have more time, that I'd be able to formulate a plan.

I swallow hard against the boulder of terror that has blocked up my throat, and stare at the silk scarf. The silk *blindfold*.

Slowly, I reach for the thick, white rectangle that also came in the package. I drop it the second after I turn it over, before I even register fully what the four words say:

See you soon, Pieta.

Pieta

Friday, 12 July

The last time I was here, Detective Inspector Foster shouted at me.

She wanted my son's DNA and it enraged her that I wouldn't let her have it. I'm pretty sure on my way out I'd sworn never to return here; I was never going to set foot here, never going to put myself in the situation where I *needed* to speak to her. She embodied – whether she could see it or not – the very reasons why I couldn't tell. I needed to protect Kobi from the world who wouldn't see my son, but what he stood for. He is the product of rape. That is all anyone would see.

Some people would think he was something that I shouldn't have even contemplated giving birth to. *How could you do that?* they'd ask. *When your body was so abused and damaged, how could you consider continuing with the ultimate reminder of that?*

Some would think that they should have the right, the power to stop me aborting and then disappear into thin air while I had to live with the consequences of bringing up a daily reminder that *twice* other people have had dominion over what I did with my body.

Some people would think that I should be willing to do whatever it takes – even using a child – to catch a criminal.

And some people, people like me, knew that one day I'd have to have that conversation about who his father is, and that I'd rather tell him I had an unwise one-night stand with someone whose name I didn't even remember, than admit he shares the same bloodline as someone capable of evil.

I don't know how finding out his father is a criminal will impact Kobi. He used to talk all the time about becoming a police officer. Originally in the fanciful way of a boy who didn't understand what the job might entail, then in the specific style of a child who had a strong sense of right and wrong and justice, who wanted to uphold the fairness he found lacking in society.

When Kobi talked about the punishments the sporty kids were spared at school because their abilities earned them a blind eye being turned, when he saw people parked on double yellows even though it wasn't allowed, when he commented on people throwing recyclable items in the normal bin, it reminded me that he found bad behaviour, criminal activity, intolerable. Yes, he'd probably find as he grew older that things were never as simple as they seemed, but in the present, I can't really imagine what finding out he is only here because of a crime would do to his mental balance. Because I'd have to tell him. If I gave DI Foster, the police, his DNA, other people would know. Other people would find out. *He*, The Blindfolder, would find out. And I would have to have that conversation with my nine-year-old, twenty years before I'd be ready because I couldn't have everyone else know and him not.

How would I find the words to do that to my son? The

age-appropriate words are there to explain an absent father, to elucidate a non-existent one, but not to rationalise a rapist, a killer.

The last time I left here, I swore I would never come here again, and I didn't think I'd need to. I have no choice now, though. I have to be here, I need to be here to protect Kobi and me. I've called the school: Kobi is there, Kobi is safe, they're not going to release him to anyone except me.

After I moved to Hove, I didn't change my name, but I did my best to keep it off everything I could. I told the various people I worked for that I was keeping a low profile from a dangerous ex, so my name was either altered on articles, or listed as 'staff reporter'. I often took my name off mastheads, and I avoided being public on the electoral roll, haven't updated my driving licence address, had no social media presence in my name. I basically became as invisible as possible for many years and it was only really when I was promoted at *BN Sussex* that I allowed them to use my name. Many years had passed and I thought it was over. I thought he wouldn't still be looking for me. But now . . .

The incident room is a frenetic, frantic hub of people when I arrive. There are more people than desks, they are talking loudly at each other, some are standing at desks using the phone while another person works on that desk's computer. I didn't realise it would be like this in here. It was deserted last time, yes, but now it is over-full, rammed. I've been ushered in by a blonde police officer who came out to collect me when the person on reception called her.

The busy-ness of the place does nothing to alleviate the creeps it gives me. It's the whole idea of it, all the information about the end of the lives of a group of women is concentrated in this place. All the clues and hints and truths and theories about the rape and torture of a group of women is here. There is stuff about me here. She hasn't put up my photo or Kobi's photo, but that doesn't mean it's not here somewhere. Once she had that information, I know she would have shared it with these people. She would have made me the victim she believed me to be.

None of this stuff says survivor, it says victim. It says inevitable end.

'Over there,' the officer says and points at the glass box office at the back of the room where DI Foster is on her phone, pacing.

'Can I just—' The officer is gone. Dashing back to her desk, picking up her receiver and punching in digits before my sentence is finished.

I weave my way through the desks. Everyone seems frenzied, almost anxious. *Have they had a breakthrough? Has something happened?*

DI Foster and I lock eyes as I cross the threshold. She hangs up her mobile without saying goodbye.

'What's going on?' I ask her.

She stares at me, her face set in a way that makes me think, for a moment, she's going to be completely honest with me; she's going to tell me everything – not just the stuff she needs to reveal to get me to do what she wants.

DI Foster folds her arms across her chest. 'How can I help you?' she replies. Answering a question with a question, my favourite thing to do when I want to avoid telling someone something.

I reach into my bag and my fingers close around the envelope.

Just before I pull it free, I look around again. There is something unnaturally overwrought about the people in here; panicked, scared. *What is going on?*

'The . . . The Blindfolder,' I say. I hate his name. That he gave me his name and I've used it. That he still gets to define so much of what happened and happens to me.

My saying his name has an odd effect on DI Foster – she becomes immobile while terror bolts across her features.

'Something's happened, hasn't it?' I ask. 'He's done something. Has he killed someone else?'

'What about him?' she says, another question to answer a question.

'He's found me. He's found Kobi. He's going to come after me. Us.' I go to hand her the envelope but she inhales deeply, steps back then falls into her chair. She sits staring into the mid-distance. I've never seen her like this, except when she was talking about her infertility. Other than that, she's always been focused and slightly cold; aloof and professional.

'Detective Foster!' I snap when she doesn't respond or move for long seconds.

She comes out of her reverie and stares at me as though seeing me for the first time. She shakes her head, clearing her mind. She stands up again. 'It's Detective Inspector,' she says. 'I've told you before, it's Detective Inspector Foster.'

'And that's important right now?'

'No, no, it's not. Tell me what makes you think The Blindfolder has found you?' As she speaks, she keeps looking over my shoulder, outside to the office, as though expecting someone to come running in at any second.

I hand over the envelope. 'He sent me this. To my work. I don't know if that's because he doesn't know where I live precisely.'

She doesn't take the envelope. 'Put it on the desk, the less people who touch it the better. Which is probably why he sent it to your work – more people will handle it, skewing the chance to get positive fingerprints or DNA from it.'

She stares at the package as she asks, 'What's in it?'

'A picture of me and Kobi at his school and . . . and a blindfold. And a note about seeing me soon.'

'Where's your son now?'

'At school.'

'OK, I'll have someone go and pick him up, and we'll put you both into witness protection.'

'Just like that?'

'What do you mean?'

'I mean, I show up and tell you that he's sent me a note and you're not even going to investigate, it's straight into witness protection? Since when have the police just acted on the word of someone? You haven't even had a chance to look in the envelope. What's going on? I mean, what's *really* going on?'

She sighs, puts her head on one side, assessing my ability to deal with what she's about to say.

'Try not to panic,' she says, which immediately sets everything on edge. 'He's taken Callie.'

Jody

Friday, 12 July

I knew I shouldn't have told her.

I was trying to avoid it for as long as possible because I knew she would get that exact look of panic and horror on her face, and I knew she'd look around for an exit from my office as well as the situation – and she'd start to back away from me.

'It's not as bad as it sounds,' I say to reassure her. Obviously that might be more effective if I hadn't lost it a minute ago and practically collapsed in my seat like I did. I don't panic – you know I don't panic – but this case has got so far under my skin, I've been feeling far too much and I can't seem to keep myself together sometimes.

And I have been thinking far too much of others before the case. That is near fatal when it comes to police work. You can't be effective if you can't at any given moment step back and see the bigger picture; can't do whatever is needed despite others.

Those other women are here, in the room with me. Watching me, judging me, making sure I don't mess up. Callie's going to be with them soon – she'll take their place beside them to condemn me.

I focus on Pieta Rawlings. 'We're all working flat out to find her and it shouldn't be too long before we do and have her safe again. In the meantime, we'll take care of you and your son.'

'How did he find her?' she asks.

I can't answer that, I just can't. 'Where does your son go to school?'

'You don't know how he found her, do you? You don't know if he's one of your officers, if one of them out there is working with him, if someone is leaking info. Hell, it could be that Callie called him herself.'

'There's no evidence—'

'That's it, isn't it? Whether it's been confirmed or not, you think she called him, told him where she is so he can come get her.'

'I think she got scared and she called someone she knows, despite being told not to, and The Blindfolder has used that information to find her.'

'I don't even want to think what he's doing to her right now,' Pieta Rawlings says dejectedly, voicing my thoughts.

'Look, we can talk more about this once you and your son are safe.'

'Safe? With you? You think I'm going to entrust our lives to you? Are you kidding me?'

'Pieta, we can protect you. Better than anyone else.'

'Tell that to Callie,' she replies.

I don't blame her. If I was her, I wouldn't trust me right now, either. I'd be taking my child and running as far and fast as I can while The Blindfolder is distracted. No, I would not be allowing the people who so catastrophically messed up to do it again with me.

'We will look after you,' I tell her. 'Please, we won't mess up again.'

We won't end up with another officer in the hospital, so badly beaten he's only a little way from being in a coma. We won't misjudge and minimise the obvious Stockholm-type connection Callie has to her former abuser.

'Nope, not going to happen,' Pieta says.

She practically runs out of the incident room. I can't stop her because I don't blame her. I'd be doing exactly the same if I was her. And anyway, the best way to keep her and her son safe is to find The Blindfolder and get Callie back.

Pieta

Friday, 12 July

By the time the taxi pulls up in Chickham, near Chichester, it is nearly dark and Kobi has his head on my shoulder, drifting in and out of sleep. He's been napping on and off for the last leg of the train journey here and I'm struggling to keep my eyes open, too.

The sun is about to disappear over the horizon so it seems a lot later than it is, the air is cooler than it has been most of today. I take our bags from the boot of the car, then pay the taxi driver.

'Are you sure you want to be dropped off here?' he asks. I know what he means: it's mainly grass and greenery around here, the only buildings and houses are out in the distance.

'Yes,' I reply. I suppress my usual urge to explain, to let him know that we'll be all right out here in the almost dark – I have to make sure we leave as obscure a trail as possible. He may be able to tell the police at a later date that yes, he picked up the woman and her child, but he won't be able to tell them where we went to after that.

After his lights have disappeared into the distance, Kobi snuggles into me, using my body to prop himself upright, closes his eyes and tries to sleep again. I take a deep breath in and then hold it, suspend myself in time. We really are out here alone. Anxiety stirs at the bottom of my stomach. *I know what it's like to be around a serial killer, I know what it's like to be his victim,* I remind myself. *It's unlikely one will be lurking out here waiting for hapless prey to pass by. Besides, I would have noticed if someone had followed our convoluted route.*

The lights of an approaching vehicle almost blind me, and Kobi growls a little, turning his face into my side to get away from it.

The car slows down as it nears our position, then comes to a complete stop.

'Are you going to tell me what this is all about?' Ned says when he climbs out of the car. He was the only person I could call, the only person I knew who would help me at short notice.

'Yes, I will,' I say, nodding towards Kobi. 'But later. I think Kobi and I could do with a sit down and something to eat.'

Ned's face softens when he looks at my boy. He does look especially cute with his curly hair squashed under his baseball cap, and his barely open eyes (although he would scowl in the utmost displeasure at being told that). 'Ah, the famous Kobi,' Ned says. 'Cool hat, mate. I have one just like it.'

Kobi's suddenly able to stand upright, open his eyes and speak. 'You support Liverpool?'

'And Arsenal, mate. I am a Londoner after all.'

'Me too! Cos my mum's a Londoner and all my cousins are Arsenal supporters. Apart from the ones in Liverpool.'

'My cousins are in the 'Pool, too,' Ned replies.

'Maaate,' Kobi says, like he and Ned are the same age, have the same life experiences and are regularly going down the pub together.

'Maaate,' Ned replies.

'Can we get in the car before I fall over?' I interject.

'Sure, sure. Mate, are you going to sit up front? You need to tell me your dream team cos I know it's all up there in your brain.'

'Oh yes,' Kobi replies. 'It's all up there.'

I left the police station in a panic. By the time I reached the end of the road, though, I'd formulated a plan. I didn't have time to panic, I had to sort things out or Kobi and I would be dead. It was that simple. I went to the bank and withdrew £1000 in cash, which was the most I could get in one go. Then I stopped off on London Road and bought a pay-as-you-go phone with cash. It was cheap and functional and would do me for the interim.

I then drove home, packed as much as I could fit into two rucksacks, put them in the boot of my car, which I drove to a road parallel to the school. I had to take a few minutes, calm myself down, force myself to focus on behaving normally when I walked into the school to pick up Kobi. I focused on playing the part of Pieta Rawlings, mother. I'd had so much experience of it, so many years of pretending I was like everyone else, so I was able to engage with the other parents, wish people a good weekend, say we'd arrange reciprocal playdates soon. All the while I was saying goodbye to them in my mind. I didn't know when – if – I would see them again. We were leaving and we wouldn't be back until the danger had passed. Whenever that may be.

As we went to collect our rucksacks, I told Kobi we were going to stay with a friend of mine for the night, possibly the weekend. He'd been fine with that until I told him the journey there entailed a train ride to London and then a train ride to Chickham.

When we arrived in Victoria to change trains, I'd made him change his jacket and cap and I did the same, to throw off the CCTV. I also pushed our rucksacks into holdalls I'd brought with me for the same reason.

After I left the police station, I'd also texted Ned and asked him for his help. I said I was in danger because of the story and would he be able to meet me somewhere with his boat as I knew it'd be harder for them to find us on it. He'd called me back a while later and said to meet him near Chickham where he could get moorings at short notice.

Kobi is finally asleep.

He and Ned took to each other as though they had been friends for a lifetime. While Ned baked pizza and put together a salad, they had talked non-stop about football. Their chatter had been a pleasant, soporific backdrop to my racing mind. I was trying to think of what to do next, and trying not to think about what was happening to Callie and trying to stay calm and normal so Kobi wouldn't be any more suspicious than he was.

My child was fizzing with excitement when we rolled up to Chickham Marina. 'You really live on a boat?' he kept asking Ned. 'All the time? That is so cool.'

He'd inspected every part of the boat, and had been impressed with everything, but when he saw his cabin, he'd almost back-flipped with joy. For a child who has a bedroom four times the size of a cabin that is only really big enough for a wooden bed, a flip down table and hanging rail, I was surprised at how happy he was.

He'd saluted Ned before he went to get changed for bed. 'I

don't mind the long journey now, Mum,' he told me in the hollow of a huge yawn. 'It was worth it.'

Ned is outside on the upper deck, leaning over the railings, staring off into the distance when I approach. I bring up the video baby monitor that I packed – I wanted my eyes on Kobi at all times and this was the best way to do it without sitting over him, especially while he slept.

It's dark now but you can still make out the outline of the estuary and the sea beyond. This area is only thirty miles from where we live, I could have driven it in under an hour, but I wanted to make it as difficult as possible for anyone to follow us and for the police to locate us.

Chickham Marina is nothing like Brighton Marina, which seems to keep buzzing late into the night. Here, things are a little more sedate. There is a large brown, wooden-slatted building with an orange tiled roof right on the jetty. The boats are berthed in a trident shape that looks out onto the large estuary where the sea comes in, and we're surrounded on three sides by lush, green countryside.

It's so quiet: as close to silence as I think you can get in a place teeming with people. I make my way across the deck of the boat until I am standing beside Ned. He's holding a beer bottle in his hand and he offers it without looking at me.

Without thinking, I take it. The brown bottle is heavy since it is almost full. I'm tempted to gulp it down in one go, to feel the warm buzz of alcohol as it spreads out through my veins and numbs everything away. I need a clear head, though. I need to be able to think. I swig a couple of times and hand it back.

'I've berthed here a couple of times,' he says. 'It's not really me, though. Plus it's a pain trying to get to London quickly if I've got a job.'

'Well, thank you for coming here at such short notice,' I reply.

I lean beside him and stare at the coastline. Apart from the view, you can hardly tell you're on a boat: it doesn't move much, the water doesn't make that much noise.

'Are you going to tell me what's going on?'

Where do I start? What do I say? How do I explain the inexplicable?

He turns his head to look at me, waiting for an answer.

It's not warm, so I've wrapped my large, grey cardigan around me. I shed it, ignoring the way it pools at my feet. I lift my pink T-shirt and drop that onto my cardigan.

His face asks what I'm doing, but his mouth doesn't. He just watches as though I am speaking. If he suspects, he doesn't show it. I'm not like Callie; I am not defiant and angry and trying to make a point. I am scared and ashamed and using this because it's quicker than words.

I don't take off my vest. I always wear thigh-length vests no matter the weather because I don't want anyone to even accidentally see my scar. I've never done this before. I've never shown someone the way I have been marked; physically as well as mentally altered. Slowly, I lift the vest to my middle and then even slower, because I have to order my legs several times to move, I rotate my body until I have my back to him.

Until I show him.

In that moment, I reveal The Blindfolder's work on the canvas of my skin. What he did to me to make sure I would be for ever his.

'Oh, Pieta,' Ned breathes.

343

Number 25.

My designation, my place in The Blindfolder's story.

I hardly ever look at it, even though I'm always aware that it's there. It is a mottling of light brown and beige against the dark brown of my skin. It is shiny, and uneven and painful-looking. It is clear and defined and I hate it. I hate it more than anything else.

Everything else I can pretend away. But not this. Not this aberration. I have other scars: from my shoulder surgery, from my keyhole surgery, from falling over, from accidentally burning myself. I have other marks and disfigurements and every single one of them is fine – a part of who I am, part of the physical biography of how I relate to the world. This scar, this brand, was done to me. This was forced on me. And whenever it tugs, whenever it twinges, whenever I suddenly remember it's there, it hurts. Not the pain of the metal melting my skin, not the inerasable, pungent smell of my burning flesh, but the unrelenting, searing agony of remembering.

'I'm so sorry,' Ned says, his voice catching on the last word. 'I'm so very, very sorry. I had no idea.'

I pull down my vest, put my T-shirt back on, re-swathe myself in my cardigan. I take the beer out of Ned's hand and put it to my lips. 'So now you know,' I state and gulp down half the bottle in one go.

Ned has got another beer but hasn't drunk from it, even though I can see how shaken he is. I've given him the briefest of rundowns on the situation and what happened today and he has listened without saying much.

Eventually, when the fragmented reality that my words and

344

revelations created have settled around us, Ned starts to drink from his bottle.

It feels very . . . odd, this new reality where someone else knows. When DI Foster told me that she knew about me and knew who Kobi's biological father was, I'd felt under siege rather than exposed. That she was backing me into a corner and I had to come out fighting. Even when she came to my house and apologised, I'd felt defensive rather than unmasked. But that was because of the way she went about it.

With Ned, I feel unsettled. It's been a necessary revelation, but I don't feel defensive or overly uncovered. Maybe those were feelings I'd have the luxury of experiencing if I didn't know that someone is coming to kill me.

'I thought it was me,' Ned says eventually. I notice his hands are trembling, even though he's doing his best to conceal it from me. 'The way you were sometimes, I thought it was because of me.'

'Don't do yourself down, it was to do with you, too.'

He shoots me a vague smile, then glances down at the deck below our feet. He's barefoot and I'm wearing my trainers. When he looks up again, I know what he's going to ask.

'Is—' he begins.

'Yes, yes he is. And no, he doesn't know. No one has ever known until Detective Foster figured it out.'

'This is a huge burden, Pieta. And you've been carrying it all alone.'

I take his new beer bottle from his hand, replace it with the empty one in mine. 'It only feels like a burden when I think about it all,' I say. 'And mostly, I don't think about it.'

Jody

'Laura!' I shout from my office. I don't usually do that, I'm not that much of a terrible boss. I just can't face it out there. Everyone is working so hard to try to correct my mess, and I can't face them.

'Yes, Guv'?' she replies when she appears in my doorway.

'Have you got the results of that DNA back yet?'

'No, because it wasn't officially assigned to any case, I can't mark it as urgent and they said they would have to put it in a queue.'

'Right.'

'Whose DNA are we testing again?' she asks as though I'd told her and she'd forgotten.

'It's better for you and everyone out there who wants to keep their job that only I know,' I reply. 'I thought you got that from the way I said, "Can you get this tested on the quiet and make sure you don't let anyone else on the team know." Ring any bells?'

'Oh, yeah.'

'Any news on PC Perry?'

'He's stable and they think he may wake up today.'

'Poor bloke.' He put up quite a fight to protect Callie, but the

346

beating he took was vicious and unnecessary. 'How's it going out there?'

Laura steps into my office and shuts the door behind her. 'Not the best,' she replies. Long, dramatic pause . . . 'We're doing the best we can but it's like she's literally dropped off the face of the Earth.'

'I know.'

'I don't understand how he found her,' she says.

'Oh, come on, Laura, don't do that, don't pretend.'

She pulls out a seat and sits down. 'Do you think it was Stockholm syndrome?'

I shrug helplessly. I've already taken the dressing-down of all dressing-downs from DCI Nugent and the ACC. I did so many things wrong: didn't put the appeal out early enough, shouldn't have let her talk to the press, should have moved her out of the area to a witness protection house sooner, should have, should have, should have . . . I deserved it all but it still smarted. They were giving me seventy-two hours to find her or find The Blindfolder, or someone else would take over. They meant take over everything, not just finding Callie, but didn't actually say it. 'We should have seen it. *I* should have seen it. She kept lying to us, to me, and we were almost wilful in not seeing it. She almost certainly called him, she must have had another mobile phone. God knows where she hid it since we searched through her things.'

'You know when you said you didn't trust her?'

I nod.

'I thought . . . *everyone* thought you were bang out of order.'

'Yes, I remember Karin Logan, Detective Constable, telling me so.'

'But you were right in the end.'

'Would rather have been wrong and, you know, still have the victim within sight.' I blow out air. 'I should have got her counselling. All that talking to the journalist, all the speculation in the press, the fact she was lying to us . . . I should have insisted on a psychological evaluation before doing the article.

'He was clearly using Callie to talk to the public, to put fear into his past vics and to scare other women. I've basically allowed him to terrify every woman in this country. He has terrorised women for nearly fifteen years and now he's doing it on a national scale. And I let him. I'll be lucky if I keep my job let alone my rank.'

'It won't be that bad, surely,' Laura says. She's a good person, that's what I like about her. Under all the dramatics and theatrics, she's a caring person.

'Maybe not. But I'll do my best to make sure none of you lot are blamed.'

'What was that journalist woman doing here earlier?'

'Checking up on the article, seeing if we have any leads.' It's quite easy to lie to Laura about things like this. I am, in a way, still trying to protect Pieta, although by rights I am hindering the investigation by keeping this from my team. I've already let one victim down, though, I don't want to do that to this one. I know she's gone on the run, and I know she thinks she'll be able to outrun this, but she can't. The Blindfolder is hunting her, seeking her out because she was special in some way. Special enough to leave his DNA behind. And now he knows where she is, it'll only be a matter of time. People who try to hide, try to disappear, always make the same mistake – they contact someone from their former life. Always. They may leave it weeks, months, even years, but they always have to make that connection to their past and that is always when they are sunk. Your past defines you, and it is almost always the instrument of your destruction if you can't let it go.

'She left in a hurry,' Laura comments.

'Yes, I told her about Callie and she freaked out. I think they got quite close.'

'Is that wise, Guv', telling something like that to a journalist?'

'What's she going to do, Laura, write an article that will make people look out for Callie?'

'True.'

'Sorry, I didn't mean to be sarcastic then. I just don't want anything to happen to her. I want us to find her alive.'

'So do I . . . I'll get back to it.'

'Thanks, Laura.'

She shuts the door behind her.

I am not handling this very well. I was up last night going through every file, *every* file, looking for a clue, trying to work out who he is, where he might have taken her. I place my head in my hands, massage my temples.

The problem with Callie going to him is that these situations never end well for the Stockholm victim. Callie said he was looking for someone. Pieta. Pieta said he'd found her, I saw that from the package she left. I did wonder why he didn't just take Pieta and her son when he saw her and instead took the picture of her, but then I realised – like everything he did, he needed to clean up. He needed to erase all the ways we could trace him and that includes eliminating Callie.

Why send Pieta that package, though? Surely he would have thought she would run, she would run straight to us or simply disappear.

He didn't seem like a gambler, someone who would take that risk. But maybe this is far more of a power-play game to him than I realised? Or what if he had no choice? What if he needed to put Pieta on high alert because he wanted to terrify her into making a mistake? No, no, that doesn't chime with everything he's done so far.

And in all of this there is Callie. The woman who has gone to him, not knowing that she is almost certainly going to her death.

But what will he do now that Pieta isn't in easy reach? Will he keep Callie alive? Did he allow her to go into police custody so she could tell him how we do it – what code words and code names we use, which sort of places we have them stay in?

Maybe that was it: maybe he thought killing past victims would trigger Pieta into coming to the police and he could find her that way. Or maybe he thought we would put Pieta and her son in the same place as Callie and he would have easy access to her. Either way, he has been using us.

This is a game to him. And, so far, he has won every round.

I massage my temples even harder, trying to press away the headache that has been blossoming and flowering in my head since we found out Callie was gone.

I can't see how this is going to end. Usually, I can stand back, look at a case and see how it's likely to pan out. I can see if we will get a resolution or if it'll need to be put on the back burner for a while until something else happens. This case, it has all the hallmarks of a back-burner case, something that we will eventually solve – except the sixth Monday deadline has kept it firmly on the front burner.

I am so lost in my thoughts, wandering the labyrinthine paths in my mind that I almost don't hear the phone. From the edge of my desk, my little red and silver mobile that Winston got me for Christmas last year, bleeps. I take my time picking it up because it won't be good news. It won't even be neutral news, it will be something that adds more bad news petrol to the raging inferno of this situation.

I call up the message and then have to carefully place the phone back on my desk. Another moment. Another moment when I am about to be shackled by the choices I make.

He says he wants Pieta. And her son.
He's going to hurt me if he doesn't get her.
Help me.

Part 7

Jody

Friday, 12 July

This place called Seaford is really quite beautiful.

I've driven here along the coast road with the sea as a constant companion telling me I shouldn't do this. I should stop, go back, tell everyone on my team what has transpired: about the DNA, Pieta, her son, the package. The text messages.

I'm not going to do that.

I was never going to do that.

I'm protecting Pieta's son. I'm protecting Pieta. I'm trying to save Callie.

And I need to avenge Jovie.

No, I haven't forgotten that. I haven't let that slip from my mind. All the other stuff might be at the forefront now, but this underpins everything – that man destroyed my sister and I'm going to destroy him in return.

As I come round the A259, the horizon opens up to me. Encountering this seascape with white cliffs, beaches and sea that seems to go out for miles is like coming to the end of the world. It's dark, but that doesn't take away from the sheer beauty of this place. The sick, twisted irony of doing something so ugly in a place this beautiful doesn't surprise me. There is something very wrong in The Blindfolder, something that needs to obliterate beauty whenever he encounters it.

The satnav directs me through the streets, some that are narrow and quaint, others that are wide and modern. I navigate my way, driving slowly as the streets are so alien to me that I'm not sure what I'll encounter around any corner. I eventually come to the pub car park where he told me to park the car and then to walk ten minutes to their location.

I don't know what time it is. I don't wear a watch and I had to leave my mobile phone behind, so to get to their location, I've had to print out a map. No one noticed me doing this. And no one will notice I'm gone for a while. I've left my computer on, my phone on my desk, my bag is there on the floor and my coat is hanging behind the door.

He was very clear: if I didn't come with just Pieta and her son, he was going to kill Callie. I'd tried to negotiate for time but he knew that Pieta wasn't at her house and he wanted her. Now.

He's obviously going to flip when he sees she's not here, but that's a chance I'll have to take. My hope is that I can convince Callie to join me, let her know that she'll always come second to Pieta so if we come together to overpower him, she'll be free.

I wish I was on a beach somewhere.

Any beach.

The one I just saw along the coast from Seaford, that would do. Any of them would do. I wish I was on a beach somewhere, reading a book and debating in my head when I should apply sunblock. I wish I was on a beach somewhere and not walking towards my pretty much certain death.

I arrive at the warehouse where he is holding Callie, where he expects me to deliver Pieta and her son. It is smaller than the word 'warehouse' implies, but still big enough to drive a transit van through its double garage doors. That's how they did it, isn't it? Got themselves a garage – warehouse – where they could drive straight in and unload their cargo – an unconscious woman – out of sight. Same with when they returned them, loaded them out of sight of prying neighbours' eyes.

I doubt they used this place previously, too far from London, too quaint and quiet for people not to notice how much movement there is late at night. No, I reckon they had somewhere near where those remains were found recently. It was deserted out there, no one would know how many times you came and went there.

Why do I keep saying they? Because it's become clear to me that there had to be two of them. You can't snatch someone, keep hold of them, inject them and then speed off within seconds on your own. People would notice a fight, a struggle, a person restraining another person, a van waiting to drive away. No, you can't do things as efficiently as he did alone. The Blindfolder had a partner.

Callie is the most recent one, I'm sure. She has either been broken down and brainwashed to help him, or has negotiated herself into the position to avoid being killed. She probably does have feelings for him, but they have blossomed from being in captivity, from developing an empathy with your captor to save yourself. We all do different things to survive. For example, this mission to end The Blindfolder, not merely bring him to justice, has helped me survive all this time.

Losing Jovie was a defining moment in my life. It twisted itself around my core and for a long time, I was lost. I felt like I was going through the motions. I did not see the point to life, even though I was living. I fooled everyone: I seemed to throw myself into my job, into my relationship, into every single day. But the reality was, until I met Harlow, I was surface living. Skimming on the top layer of life, unable to break through to the real, murky, complicated, incredible, beautiful, ugly layers below. When Harlow showed up, I discovered my purpose, my reason for not joining Jovie days after she left. I had something to focus on, an end goal that would balance the cosmic scales. Someone good had been taken out of the world, now someone evil had to be removed, too.

So it doesn't matter if he has someone with him who helps, if he has a partner, it won't stop me. I've been on this mission for thirteen years, I'm not going to stop now.

The building, at first glance, is dilapidated. The upper levels of its white walls are rough and uneven, the white paint peeling off in patches. The lower level has red-orange brickwork that looks worn and battered. There is a window in the upper level, boarded up, adding to the rundown look of the place. There is another larger window at the front, which is also boarded over. The place appears to be mostly abandoned, but if you look closely, you can see the boards are new, the paint is actually fresh in parts, the peeled back ones are just there to make it look of no real interest. The large, black garage doors are modern and new, electric, I would guess. This place is not what it seems – at all.

I knock on the garage door.

Wait.

A clunk, then a whirr as the doors lift, opening up to let me in.

I am walking towards certain death. I'm fine with that. Truly. Because if there's one thing I know, I am taking him with me.

Pieta

Friday, 12 July

'There is so much I can't tell anyone,' I say. 'Because once it's out there . . .'

'It makes it real?' Ned finishes.

'Not just that. People will use it, twist it, tell me it's not my reality. It shouldn't bother me what other people think and say, but it's so brutal out there sometimes, it's hard to screen it out.'

'I don't know what to say.'

'What is there to say? The truth of it is I wanted to live so I . . .' *So I talked to him, appeased him, made him believe I cared.* It messes with my head, even now.

Years and years ago, I interviewed a prostitute for an article about buying and selling sex. Of course, I did a Pieta and got very much engrossed in hearing her story. One of the things that always stayed with me was that she said if you wanted to make money and get repeat customers, you had to make *every* punter/'client' believe that he was the best. No matter how vile – and all of them *were* vile in different ways – you had to act like that every time. You had to switch off the part of you that felt anything, and get the rest of you to believe, *actually believe* what was a lie was the truth. That was the only way to get through it. You could try to fake it, but if you got one of the punters whose ego wasn't so huge that they managed to notice other people, they would be on the lookout for any signs you were pretending. You had to do everything you could to make you and them believe what you knew to be an absolute lie.

In The During I had to do that. I had to do that to survive.

I woke up and he spoke to me. He told me what was going to happen. And as my limbs came back to life because the knock-out drugs were leaving my body, I realised I would never manage to keep my eyes closed for forty-eight hours. I would never manage to endure it. I had to do something else to stay alive.

I had seen enough, read enough, to know that even murderers struggle to kill people who they think of as human. I had to humanise myself to him. I had to become a real, living, breathing, feeling person to him in a way that would make it difficult for him to dispose of me. And to do that, I had to pretend I was somehow attached to him.

I wanted to live so I had to make him believe that I was his to do whatever he wanted with.

It still messes with my brain on a daily, sometimes hourly basis. I didn't have time to shut off the part of me that feels while I did it, so it became entangled, swirled together with my normal thoughts and feelings. A bit of what I had to make him believe ended up inside me, bleeding into every single part of my being.

I still have to remind myself that I did what I had to do to survive, because a tiny, poisonous part of me judges myself for being able to. For not just giving in and letting him end me rather than going along with it.

And if I, the person who was there, who had to do anything to stay alive, judges me, what will everyone else do? I can't tell anyone about it because my words, my story will be translated in so many different ways and most of them will find the interpretation something completely different to what I experienced.

I keep these words, these realities, these tactics I used to ensure my continued place on Earth locked away inside, even though they tear me apart. I would love to unburden them, share the horror I feel at what I had to do with someone, but I cannot risk it. I could not survive another person telling me what the poisonous voice in my head tells me.

I live in colour, I mould pottery, I focus on my son; I do it all so I do not have to think about what I did, I do not have to think about people blaming me even half as much as I blame myself.

'You can tell me,' Ned says. 'I won't judge you. I won't say anything, I'll just listen.'

I stare at the image of my son on the screen in front of me. He is asleep, not the fake sleep he sometimes tries to get away with, but properly ensconced in dreamland. He is incredible. I could not love him more than I could love anyone else on this Earth. He is my sun rising, my reason for carrying on. And I know every feature that isn't mine came from his father. Came from a certain type of evil.

I cannot say that, either.

No one can ever know that sometimes . . .

I throw my hands over my face, allow the horror of what I feel to explode. I fold in two, broken by the agony of who my son is and what he means to me, about me.

No one can ever know that sometimes . . . just sometimes . . .

Ned's arms slide around me and I don't pull away.

It's something else to feel a man's arms around me, something alien. This hasn't happened in over a decade, for nearly a quarter of my life I haven't properly experienced human, *adult* touch in this way.

No one can ever know that sometimes . . . just sometimes . . . I look at my son and I . . . My crying is silent, an agony that would be ear-shattering if it was ever made sound. I've accepted that when I break down, it has to be hushed, quiet, unheard because once it becomes sound, it's a few short cries away from the words leaving my mouth. They can never enter my mind because I do not ever, ever, EVER want them to exit via my words.

No one can ever know that sometimes . . . just sometimes . . . I look at my son and I h—

The crying becomes more intense, it feels like it will break me apart piece by piece. Ned does the best he can to hold me, probably not knowing that he's actually helping to hold me together.

Jody

Friday, 12 July

In the entrance just beyond the doors of the warehouse, a white transit van sits with its rear to the doors. To the left, there are pallets of animal feed, huge sacks piled on top of each other. The frosted-plastic bags are labelled 'Organic' and look expensive. He's a vet. Or, at least, in the animal business. We were right – that's how he had access to Sux and ketamine and other anaesthetic drugs. He is a vet, not a doctor or pharmaceutical rep.

There is a darkness beyond the van and the pallets of feed. Unless you knew something was being hidden back there, you would think this was it. You would assume that the van and the feed take up all the available space. But beyond is where he is. Where he is keeping her.

'This way, Detective.' His voice floats out from beyond the van, from the sinisterness that lurks back there. I pause for a moment, close my eyes, try to experience his voice like Jovie did, like Pieta did, like Callie did, like Harlow did, like all those other women did. I try to put myself in their shoes for just one moment. His voice is soft, soothing, like hot cocoa after a night out in the cold. How it must have turned the blood in their veins to ice, how it must have turned their stomachs.

Since he doesn't mention Pieta or her son, I'm assuming he has CCTV outside that shows that I am alone. I step towards the unknown, working my way around the obstacles. As well as being a good cover for what goes on in the back, they are an excellent barrier to a quick escape.

I see Callie first of all. She sits on a high-backed chair to the right of where I enter. She has her back to the wall and he has strapped her to the chair: her arms are behind her back, linked; her legs are tied to the front two legs of the chair. Around her eyes is a green silk blindfold.

I hadn't really thought what it would be like seeing her, how he would be treating her. But clearly, he doesn't need her any more so he has relegated her to this. At least she is still alive.

'Are you OK, Callie?' I ask.

She quivers, her face fighting to stay brave as she nods. I go to her, remove the blindfold, untie her hands. I unstrap her legs and use the sound of the tape unsticking to cover my murmuring, 'Run if you get the chance.'

Once I have freed Callie I turn to face the man in the dark-brown leather chair. I can't see him properly because of the way he has placed his chair facing three other similar leather chairs. He really thought I would bring them, one of them a child, because he has decreed it. He really is delusional.

I walk towards him and he, The Blindfolder, comes more into view. More and more until I see him.

'We meet again,' he says.

And we do. We do meet again. He was sitting in a chair the

last time I met him, too. He had his back to me but he did turn around briefly, he did talk to me.

Ross.

The boyfriend of Karin Logan. Detective Constable.

Pieta

Friday, 12 July

We sit on Ned's sofa, below deck, a bottle of beer each on the table in front of us, neither of us drinking or talking.

Everything around us is fragile, friable, ready to shatter at the lightest of touches.

I keep thinking of Callie, what she is going through now he has her back. What he's planning to do to me. What he might do to Kobi. We can't stay on Ned's boat for ever, and I need a way to get our passports sorted. If we can leave the country, we may have a chance – we could possibly make it without him finding us.

'Whatever you had to do.' Ned makes me jump by speaking suddenly. 'Whatever you had to do, I'm glad you did it.'

'What?' I turn to him and find he is staring at me. Openly examining me with dark, hazel eyes.

'I'm glad you did whatever you had to and you got out of there alive. I'm glad you survived and that you're sitting here right now with me. I'm not judging you. We all make choices every day that help us get to the end of that twenty-four hours and sometimes, we can't do that. Sometimes, it's too hard and we can't do

it any more, but I'm glad you said whatever you had to, did whatever you had to, to get through it.'

'You don't know what I did, though,' I reply. I want to look
away, to avoid eye contact like I normally do, but I have to watch
his response, see what he really thinks instead of what he thinks
he thinks.

'I don't c—'

'I talked to him. Despite what he was doing to me, I talked to
him. I asked him questions, I listened to his answers. I kept
engaging with him until I made him believe that I . . . that I cared
about him. That there was something between us. And at the end
of the forty-eight hours . . . he asked me if I wanted to stay with
him. He believed it, you see, he believed that I thought we had
some kind of connection, and he thought he had been taking
care of me, that he'd been good to me. So he didn't want to give
me up, and he asked me if I felt the same.'

'What did you say?'

*'If you tell me you want to stay, I'll keep you. I will keep look-
ing after you. I will take care of you like I have. I've been
good to you, haven't I? Haven't I?' he repeated when I didn't
reply.*

'Yes.'

*'Do you want to stay with me? Just a little while longer? Do
you want to be with me?'*

Ned's question hangs in the air between us, waiting for me to
pluck it down and put it away by answering it.

'He would've known that it'd all been fake if I told him no. He would have realised that I didn't mean any of it and he would have killed me. I truly believed he would have killed me.'

'How much longer did he keep you?'

I hesitate, wait to admit this, this other thing I cannot share. 'Another day. Another twenty-four hours.' I had another twenty-four hours of being there with him, enduring what he put me through, and it's another thing that eats away at my peace of mind, terrorises my thoughts.

'I'm glad, Pieta.' Ned's voice is fierce and certain, his gaze doesn't waver. 'I'm glad you could do that to save yourself. I'm glad you got out of there.'

'You don't have to say that.'

'I do, actually. Because you need to hear it. You need to know that whatever you did, there are so many people who would celebrate you still being here if they knew. And no one, no one knows what they'd do in that situation until they're in it.'

I can't argue with that. If life has shown me anything, it's that you never know how you'll react to anything until you're in it.

'Can I say something about Kobi?' he says, automatically lowering his voice. He's staring at the small screen of the baby monitor with the image of my boy. I stare at the grainy picture as well, counting his breaths as they go in and out.

I don't want to talk about him, not with anyone, especially not with someone who knows about his parentage, but I'm going to be having this conversation with most of my family soon. I will have to tell them what happened, and then I'll have to tell them about how it is connected to how their nephew and grandson came to be here. And I'll have to listen to their judgements on the situation. I don't want to talk about it to anyone, ever, but I will have to so I may as well start with Ned.

'If you want,' I mumble.

'I've only met him for a few short hours, but he is incredible. He's amazing, a really fantastic boy.'

'I can't argue with that.'

'*You* did that. You brought him up to be like that.'

'Ned—'

He ploughs on: 'I suspect I know why you broke down earlier.' He shakes his head. 'I . . . There are so many things I want to say to try to make it better for you but I think they'll come across as trite and condescending. What I can say, though, is that choosing to have Kobi was, hopefully, a way for you to take back some of the choice and control that was ripped away from you.'

I've never thought of it like that. I was so *afraid* and stuck, that I didn't realise that, yes, the bedrock of it all was my choice. Out of everything that happened to me, this was a choice *I* could make. And if I had ended the pregnancy, that would have been my choice, too. My body, my choice.

'It makes me angry that there are people out there who think they can decide what women get to do with their bodies. If you had chosen to abort, that would have been for the best, because it was what you wanted to do. I say that having met and been utterly charmed by the brilliance of Kobi. But the fact you had him is an equally valid choice, and how you might sometimes feel, sometimes wishing . . . *things were different* still makes your decision a valid choice.'

Choice.

Kobi was my choice.

I have always been so trapped in the memory of what happened and my determination to not let it define or break me, I didn't see that I had made the choice to continue the pregnancy. To bring up the child despite where part of his genetic code came from. I made that choice in fear, in pain, in a haze of shock, but it was my choice. And if I went back, I might not make that choice again – I may well have an abortion because that would be my choice.

Kobi has turned over now. The left side of his face is in profile on the pillow. He looks like he does when he's thinking really hard, trying to come up with a theory for how the world works the way it does because what he's been told just doesn't ring true for him. He looks how he does when he's trying to work out what the seagulls are plotting.

'You know the world's completely messed up when Ned Wellst is the voice of reason and comfort,' I say.

When he laughs, quietly, I look at him again. He's staring at me, his face very plainly telling me how he feels while his hazel eyes hold mine.

Eventually, his laughter melts away but the look, infused with so much emotion and longing, doesn't. He wants to say something, do something.

I want him to say something, do something.

I don't know how I'll respond, but I want him to—

'Another beer?' He's on his feet, breaking the moment by moving and reaching for our full beer bottles. 'These are practically warm now, sitting here undrunk as they are.'

'No. Not for me, thank you.'

'Yeah, I'm not feeling the beer tonight, either. A port would go down really well about now, though.'

'Have you got the cheeseboard, cigar and cravat to go with that?'

'I'll have you know I have some of the best cravats this side of the Downs, and my cheeseboards are legendary, so don't be trying to port-shame me. I'm unshamable.'

'Wouldn't dream of it.' I get to my feet, stretch my body; arch my back as far as I can, enjoying the long, deep pull of the muscles in my torso, along my neck, feeling the twinge of where I had surgery on my shoulder. It still hurts sometimes. Years later, it still grumbles and complains and reminds me it's there. Just like the number 25 brand. 'I think I'll head off to bed,' I say. 'Which way is it, again?'

Ned returns from the kitchen area. 'The one next to Kobi's cabin.' He points down the corridor; each room off it is shut, apart from Kobi's, which I left ajar. 'My cabin is opposite yours, in case you need anything.'

I can feel the heat from him, he is that close. I want him nearer, to occupy the same space as me. I glance up and find him staring down at me with the same expression he had a few minutes ago on the sofa.

He snaps out of it again, glances away, takes a step back. 'Goodnight, Pieta. I don't know what tomorrow will bring, but try to get some sleep.'

Without thinking it through properly, I reach out, lightly place my hand on his arm to stop him walking away. I'm not looking at him, I'm pretty sure he's not looking at me. But we are connected now. A small part of each of us is occupying the same space. Slowly, I move my hand down his forearm, until it is resting against the back of his hand.

All I can hear is the sound of the water, the buzz of the electrical lights, the thick rhythm of our breathing.

Carefully, he moves his body to face mine; just as unhurriedly, I move my body to face his. I want to be closer, nearer to him. Gradually, he moves his fingers until they are between mine, intertwining us. Deliberately, I raise my eyes to look at him. He stares down at me, holding my gaze. Tenderly, I raise my hand and stroke across his cheek.

What are you doing? I ask myself. *What the hell do you think you're doing?*

We stare at each other for long seconds, stretched minutes, until time becomes irrelevant, something that doesn't concern us because we're connected, we're close, we're sharing the same space.

Gradually, carefully, Ned lowers his head and, cautiously, gently, as though I may break, he presses his lips onto mine.

What the hell are you doing? I ask myself again, this time louder, more forcefully.

I don't know, I reply as I relax against him, let go of his hand. *I don't know.*

He pulls me closer, kisses me a little harder.

Bad idea! Bad idea! Bad idea! part of me is screaming. *Bad idea! Bad idea! Bad idea!*

I know, I know, I know, another part of me replies.

Ned suddenly pulls away, his breath coming in short bursts. 'This is probably not a good idea,' he says.

'It's definitely not a good idea,' I reply.

He kisses me again, and I don't do anything but kiss him back, unwind into the delicious motion of it.

He pulls away, rests his forehead against mine, our unsynchronised breathing hard and fast. 'This is actually—' he pauses to press his lips against mine '—what they call a bad idea.'

We're kissing again, connecting again, bonding again. 'Oh, it's a terrible idea,' I state when we part again, noses brushing, foreheads touching, bodies panting against each other.

More kissing, more closeness, more connection.

When we finally break apart properly, we both instinctively take a step back, but keep staring at each other, our eyes sizing up the other.

Bad idea! the inside of my head is still screaming at me. *Bad idea! Bad idea! Bad idea!*

'There's a voice in my head telling me this is a bad idea,' he says.

'Snap.'

'Are you going to listen to it?' he asks.

I lean over and pluck the baby monitor screen off the coffee table. I start to move backwards, down the narrow corridor, walking carefully until I'm outside my cabin, opposite his cabin.

This is Ned Wellst, the voice inside reminds me. *This is Ned Wellst who made your life hell. He said you were ugly, he made you feel worthless. Are you really going to do this with him? Of all people, him?*

This is Ned Wellst. The man who grew from the boy who bullied me. The guy who tried to carry it on into college. Who altered the course of my internal life. I had to unlearn everything he and his various acolytes had said; had to learn how to ignore, disbelieve and overcome every word, remark and taunt.

That is who Ned Wellst is.

This is Ned Wellst. The man I've come to when I needed to hide with my son. The only person on Earth I've told my most terrifying secrets. The only man who has been able to explain to me that my son was my choice, and that my fears and worries and shameful thoughts are normal and to be expected.

That is who Ned Wellst is.

Still staring at him, I reach out and open the door to his cabin.

That is the Ned Wellst I want – *need* – to be with right now.

Pieta

Friday, 12 July

My hands tremble as I unbutton then unzip my jeans. My heart throws itself against my ribcage as I tug my jeans down over my hips, revealing my fuchsia-pink knickers. Pink knickers for Fridays. For the start of the weekend, to make sure the last day of the working week is no longer just the day of the week when my nightmare began.

I kick my jeans aside to reveal my odd socks. Yellow and orange. When I'm wearing trousers, I always wear odd socks, to get a double-hit of colour next to my skin. I push off each sock with the opposite foot.

Without me asking him to, Ned stays on the other side of the cabin. This isn't his usual cabin, I realise, he's given that to me. His cabin is large with a bigger bed, more storage. This room is smaller, a double bed, no visible signs of where to store things.

I watch him take off his navy-green jumper and pale-green T-shirt in one go. His body is as firm as I thought it would be, with a slight paunch around the middle that slopes down into his jeans. I observe him unbuckle his belt then unbutton his jeans, and I want to look away, stop myself from watching him become naked in front of me, but I can't. The last time a man undressed in my presence, I had my eyes closed. I had to link the sound to the action in my head from memory without ever being sure which bit was which – I had to prepare myself for what came after the sounds of undressing stopped.

I have to watch Ned, see him, experience it and make it normal. Make it part of what normal sex is about.

I baulk slightly at his penis, now it's uncovered; it stands red, hard, erect between his solid, hairy thighs. I haven't seen one like this for so long.

My eyes sweep over his body, assessing him, reminding myself that this is what men look like when they're naked. And this is what having sex is about – using all of your available senses to enjoy it. This is what I can be a part of, not apart from.

Run away.

Run away.

Runawayrunawayrunawayrunaway. The panic builds in my head, in the well of my chest. *Runawayrunawayrunawayrunaway.*

He comes towards me and the panic continues to build. What is he going to do? Is he going to hurt me? Torture me? Force me?

In front of me, Ned rests his forehead on mine and closes his eyes. 'This is still, officially, not a good idea,' he murmurs.

The panic disintegrates and I can slip my arms around his body. His lips find mine, mine carefully kiss him back. 'Oh, it's the worst idea.' I pull away for a moment and stare into his eyes. 'I can't take my top off because of the . . . becau—' He cuts me short by kissing me, telling me he understands, he doesn't expect me to do anything I'm not ready for.

On the bed, our lips move smoothly and longingly together. His hands move lovingly over my body, stroking and caressing, attentively bringing pleasure to each part he touches.

He rests his fingers on the top of my knickers, then pauses, silently checking it's OK to do this, to remove them, to bring us one step closer together. 'Yes,' I whisper and kiss him. 'Yes,' I say against his lips.

He rolls down and removes my knickers, then positions himself between my legs. Our kissing intensifies and suddenly a flame is lit, and passion, an unexpected craving, ignites.

I want this.

I need this.

My eyes are open, staring into his; his mouth is smiling as he gazes down at me, my hands are on his face, his are in my hair and everything seems to stop for a moment. Just a moment and we connect with the people we are behind our eyes.

I gasp as he pushes into me, brings us even closer, allowing us to occupy the same space.

Our eyes stay linked as he starts to thrust. Deeper, faster.

I cling to him as he moves, my fingers pressing into his skin, my legs wrapped around his body; he stares at me, groaning softly with each push.

'Ohhhh,' I unexpectedly moan. 'Ohhhhhh.'

He grins at me and drives himself further into me.

'Ohhhhhhh,' I moan again and the pleasure pulses and surges through me. His face watches mine and he moves – slows, speeds, intensifies – in response to everything I do.

Another deep groan from us both and he begins to speed up, move faster and harder, our eyes always connected. I feel myself letting go, allowing the orgasm to take on a life of its own as it races up through me, galloping and hurtling through every cell, bounding and sprinting through every blood vessel, every artery, every muscle until it hits the top, crescendos in a mass of cries that escape my lips, and tremors that move my whole body.

Ned keeps going, keeps thrusting and pushing until I sag against the bed, finished, spent. Immediately he pulls out, pushes up the front of my top before loudly moaning my name as his orgasm spills all over my abdomen, my pubic hair, the bed.

'No condom,' he explains between panting breaths and deep swallows. 'No condom.' He flops down onto the bed beside me. 'We really shouldn't have done that without a condom, but definitely couldn't finish without one, much as I wanted to.'

'Told you it was the worst idea,' I reply between my own heavy breaths.

Ned turns his head to look at me, I do the same and we gaze at each other in the half-light of the room, smiling. 'Worst idea or not, that really was most excellent,' he says.

Gingerly, because this is all so new, so surreal, I reach up to touch his face to remind myself that I can do that. I can touch him, I can move away or towards him, I can look at him, I can talk to him without pretending. Carefully he leans in and kisses me.

'Most excellent,' I reply.

His grins changes, becomes almost shy, bashful. I'm not sure why he's smiling at me like that – is he pleased that I agree with him? That I've had sex with him? That we're together like this? I'm not sure.

'I'm sorry about the mess,' he says. 'It's been a while.'

'It's been a while for me, too,' I reply.

I see a question pass over his face that doesn't settle in his eyes: *Is this the first time since what happened? Am I your first since then?*

Yes, is the answer, *absolutely yes*.

'Let me get some tissues to clean you up,' he says, vaulting off the bed and out the door. He returns in seconds, winding the loo roll around his hand, about to reach for me.

'I'll do it,' I say, and hold my hand out for the roll.

'No, no,' he says with a laugh. 'It's my mess, I'll clean it up.'

'No!' I snap. 'I said I'll do it, and I'll do it. It's my body, I'll clean it how I want, when I want.'

Every part of me is on edge because this is what it was like, what *he* would do. He was in control of everything for every second of those seventy-two hours: when I drank, when I ate, when I went to the toilet, how I was cleaned up. Everything was forced on me by him and I never want to be in that position again.

'Please give me the loo roll.' I keep my trembling arm outstretched.

'I'm sorry,' he mumbles and gives it to me. 'I'm sorry, I didn't think.' He shakes his head, unable to meet my eye. 'I just didn't think.'

We're back there. Back to the reality of the situation. What this is all about. Yes, I forgot for those few minutes; yes, I had sex and we enjoyed it; and yes, we didn't either of us try to hide how much we delighted in each other. But the reality is, I'm here because I'm hiding from the man who held me hostage; who is probably this minute torturing Callie. The reality is, this was an unwise interlude from a scary reality.

'I didn't think either,' I say. 'And I should have. I really should have.'

Jody

'Take a seat,' he says pleasantly.

He is normal, a man who would blend into the background in most places. A man who found a way to insert himself into the investigation so he could keep an eye on things, see what we had. He probably thought he was just going to get a vague sense of what was going on by getting close to someone from CID, but he'd still have enough of a connection to it to benefit from it. He obviously couldn't have known that he would hook up with someone who was not only on the investigation, but hated me. What a bonus he got! She wouldn't have been able to help herself – she would have regularly ranted about the decisions I made, the tangents I ordered us to go down, the amount of work she had to do. It's natural to off-load to a partner, after all. How could she know that her sense of being wronged would benefit the man we were looking for?

I sit in the chair directly opposite him.

'You don't seem as surprised as I thought you would be,' he states. 'Were you suspicious of me?'

'I'm suspicious of everyone. I'm sure Karin told you that. As well as everything else.'

381

'She certainly does not like you,' he says.

'I can live with that,' I reply.

He smirks. *You're assuming a lot*, he tells me with that smirk. *You're assuming that you're going to live.* 'I can't help but notice that you're missing two guests,' he says.

'Yes.'

'And you liberated my companion without asking my permission first.'

'I did.'

'A very disappointing start, Detective. A very disappointing start indeed.'

'I'm actually disappointed in you,' I reply. 'I thought you were intelligent. I mean, we've been chasing you and you've eluded us until now so you must be clever – or so I assumed. But no, you actually thought I would bring an innocent woman and her child to you.'

'I thought you would – to save Callie.'

'I don't sacrifice people to save other people.'

'We'll see.'

'When did you find out about Pieta Rawlings?'

'Why would I tell you that, Detective?'

'All right, you don't have to tell me that at all. But I know you like games, so how about this? I tell you something about you that I can't possibly know, and you tell me the answer to my question.'

'Why would I play a game that you've chosen, with your rules?'

'Scared I'll outsmart you?' I sit back in my seat. 'Or scared I'll reveal something you don't want to hear? That you don't want Callie to hear?'

'Nothing you say will turn her against me,' he says with a certainty that chills me. Maybe I was wrong, maybe I won't be able to bring her on to my side.

'So why won't you play?'

'Tell me something that you can't possibly know.'

'Your mother used to take half of your beatings for you.' Shock jerks through his eyes. He hides it quickly, but not before I spot it. 'I'm right, aren't I? Your father used to beat you and your mother could only stop half of them by taking them herself.'

Ross's green eyes run over me again. He assessed me when I got here, but because he'd seen me before he didn't think he needed to look at me properly. He doesn't like this, being on the back foot, not being completely in control, and he's now desperately studying me, trying to play catch up.

'Well, clearly I got that right. So now, fair's fair, you have to answer my question: what was so special about Pieta?'

'I'm not an idiot, Detective,' he replies. 'I know you're probably wearing "a wire" as they say. A dozen other police officers will be sitting outside listening to me right now.'

I stand up, untuck my shirt from my trousers, unbutton my jacket, unbutton my shirt. He doesn't flinch, doesn't react when I show him I'm not wired, not backed up, I really have come here alone. I know I should care that I've just shown a serial killer my body, a body that he would usually prey on, but I have bigger things to worry about.

'I'm curious,' he says while I button myself up again, undo my belt and tuck my shirt back in. 'Why have you come here all alone, Detective? What did you think was going to happen, especially when you didn't bring me what I wanted?'

'No, you're playing the game wrong,' I reply firmly. 'I told you something right about you, so you have to answer my question: what was so special about Pieta?'

'She . . . was different. She cared about me. She wanted to stay with me.' I must look incredulous, because he insists: 'She *wanted* to stay with me. I asked her at the end of the forty-eight hours if she wanted to stay and she did. She stayed with me because she cared about and wanted to be with me. She stayed for seventy-two hours, none of the others did. From the start she was different. I thought some of the others were, too. The ones who didn't cry or scream or beg straight away. But none of them were like her in the end.'

Seventy-two hours. She never told me that. But then, what *has* she told me? Other than she wouldn't let me use her son's DNA, what has she really admitted to? I don't even know the number on her back.

'Why have you waited until now to come for her?'

'No, no, Detective. That's not how the game works. You want me to answer a question, you tell me something about me that you could never know.'

'All right . . . The first girl to break your heart was black. But she didn't dump you, she was your friend. She cared about you, she did her best to make things better when your father hurt you. She just didn't feel "that way" about you. She broke your heart because she didn't love you like you loved her.'

Ross sits back in his chair. *Right again.*

'Why have you waited until now to come for her?' I ask.

'I've been in prison. Involuntary vehicular manslaughter. Nothing I could do.'

'Talk about irony – the one time you didn't mean to kill someone and you went to prison for it. All right, where to next? OK, you were once accused of something that you don't think you did. I mean, you did it, but you didn't think it was "that bad" and you didn't think she was right to tell anyone about it or get you fired. It was just a bit of banter after all, and you just got a bit handsy, what was the big deal?'

His scrunched-up lip tells me that is another correct assessment of him. He is easy. He is a tick-box exercise in dysfunction and perversion. It's not hard to work this stuff out when you look at his victims, his actions. He sees himself as a victim of women. He has been wronged by them, misunderstood by them, sidelined by them, unworshipped by them – and he is paying them back.

'How did you find out about her son?'

That question detonates an anger that twists the lines of his face and evaporates his cool. 'He is *my* son, Detective. Make no mistake about that. He is *my* son. *Mine.*'

'How did you find out about him?'

'I found her, I found him.'

'No, no, you're not playing the game properly. You're lying. If it was that simple you wouldn't have murdered the other women to get her attention and find her.'

His gaze switches from me to Callie, incredulous that she told me this. He is clearly wondering what else she might have given away. 'Who said I murdered the other women?'

'I showed you, I'm not wearing a bug, no one else is listening in. Tell me why you went after those other women?'

'May I remind you that's another question, Detective.'

'No, you lied so that invalidates the other question. This is a new one that you've got a chance not to lie about: why did you murder those other women? After all those years, after they had got their lives together again, you came back and killed them. Why?'

'Because I could.'

'Lie.'

'I'm not quite sure what answer you're expecting, Detective. I did it because I could.'

'LIE!'

'They weren't important—'

'LIE! Why do you keep lying? Why aren't you proud of what you did? Why aren't you just gagging to talk about it? You killed those women, now crow about it. Tell me why. That's what you really want to do, isn't it? Tell me the truth. Tell me why you murdered those women when they had moved on with their lives? Why don't you crow to me about why you were so cruel?'

Again his gaze ricochets from me to Callie, but this time doesn't immediately bounce back. He stays looking at her for long seconds. Long, long seconds.

While he looks at her, I look at him. I didn't do that before. I had seen him in the restaurant, I knew who he was, so I'd decided I knew what he looked like. But that was from only glimpsing him in a low-lit space a couple of weeks ago. And the truth is, I didn't do a police officer's assessment – I didn't look at his face to see if I'd arrested him before, come across him before; I didn't check to see if he had any familiar features or identifying marks; I didn't even properly take him in. This is what I mean about being too close to this, about how it was causing me to mess up. I couldn't step away, though, not when this meant so much to me.

386

But I hadn't been doing my job properly. If I had, I would have noted those green eyes, the shape of them, the depth of them. Their similarity to the woman standing at my shoulder. The same with the contours of his forehead, the sweep of his cheekbones.

If I had done my job correctly I wouldn't have asked him that question, I would have asked the woman standing beside me: 'Why don't you crow to me about why you were so cruel?'

And she would have said: 'The cruelty's the point,' before she hit me across the head with a heavy object.

Pieta

Friday, 12 July

The quiet here is both unnerving and hypnotic. The outside air is thick with pockets of heat; the sounds of this area are a penetrating hum of little insects and water lapping against the boat.

I'm sitting in Ned's living area, drinking the beer that he'd put back into the fridge earlier. Ned went into the shower after me and has been in there a while. I can't sleep. I can't relax. I keep thinking about Callie. How I've abandoned her to her fate, while I sit here, in hiding.

What am I going to do? That is the question that keeps circling my brain like vultures over a rotting carcass, constantly swooping down to grab the entire piece of the solution but only coming away with a bit – the answer to the question seems to present itself but then a roadblock of some kind gets in the way. Everything I think of seems to have a downside that will, in the long-term, negate any short-term gains.

What am I going to do?

'I'm sorry,' Ned says as he enters his living area. His hair is still damp, and his bare torso is glowing slightly from the heat of

388

his shower. 'I'm sorry for ruining it earlier. For making you remember.'

I reach out my arm, beckon him to come towards me, to join me on his sofa. When he sits at the very edge, as far away from me as he can, I beckon to him again. 'Come here, silly,' I say. 'Come where I can cuddle you.'

We manage to squeeze ourselves together onto the terracotta-coloured seat, our bodies finding a way to tessellate like they were designed to fit like this.

'You know what your boat could do with?' I say to him as we look into each other's eyes. It's a revelation being able to look some-one in the eye again because I've told them almost everything.

'No, what could my boat do with?'

'A bit of pottery.'

'OK.'

'I'm serious. Pottery. It'll transform this space. You won't know the place once you've got a few plates and bowls and jugs and vases.'

'I'll, erm, think about it?'

'Oh, you unbeliever. How you'll regret your scorn once you see how they invigorate and enliven my place.'

I see another question pass across his face: *Will I really get to see your place?* I can't answer that question because I don't know if I'll ever get to see my place again.

Carefully, I put my hand on his face and focus on him while I speak. 'It wasn't you, you didn't ruin anything.'

'I should have thought—'

'We're doing the best we can, here. I don't know what to do next. I'm too scared to call Detective Foster in case they haven't

389

found Callie. Or they have and she's dead. I can't go home, I can't stay here for ever. I'm having sex with someone I pretty much hate. I mean, there is not a lot there for you to ruin.'

Ned's face has changed. He's looking at me so curiously, I have to ask: 'What are you looking at me like that for?'

'Do you really hate me?'

'I used to. I don't any more.'

'When did you stop?'

'About three minutes before we had sex.'

'*Really?*' he replies.

'Yes. Why, did you think it was all cool between us or something?'

'Well, yeah. A bit. A lot actually.'

'No, Ned. Doesn't work like that. Well, not with me, anyway. I don't actively hate you, I haven't for years, but you damaged me. If we hadn't been thrown together in this way, there's no way I'd even give you the time of day, let alone go to bed with you.'

He is crestfallen all of a sudden, and it winds me, how I've hurt him. I think I like him more than I'm willing to admit to myself. I think he means more to me than I dare to imagine. He stares at a point over my head for a while, and the sounds of silence and night start to seep in again. 'I hope you know that I really am very sorry. If there was a way I could go back and erase all those years of hurt I would do it in an instant. I don't even properly remember why I did it. I was just a nasty piece of work and you suffered as a result of that. I'm sorry. So very sorry. I'm going to spend every day making it up to you.'

'I know that. I know you're sorry. And I don't hate you any more, I truly don't.'

'But you're wary.'

'I'm wary of most people.'

'D—'

'Ned, either kiss me or help me work out what I'm going to do.'

'B—'

'I'm serious,' I cut in. 'I need to work out what I'm going to do, or I need you to be kissing me. Nothing else. No other chat, no other activities. Except maybe beer drinking. But nothing other than that.'

His eyes explore my face, my eyes, my lips. When he realises I'm serious, he goes for the kissing option.

Part 8

Pieta

Saturday, 13 July

It's not like Kobi to sleep in late, but I've checked on him multiple times now and he is out for the count. Mostly flat on his back, often with his mouth open, eyes firmly shut as he stays in dreamland.

I wish I'd been that free.

I sent Ned to bed when he kept nodding off, and I sat on the sofa in his living area, legs pulled up to my chest, worrying. By the time the light started to seep in through the portholes at the top of the cabin, I was no closer to deciding what to do. Short of taking off with Ned and Kobi and sailing around the country, never staying more than a few hours in any port, I couldn't work out what to do next.

There probably is nothing to do until I get the courage to call Detective Foster and find out what is happening with Callie. I've turned off my phone because I know tracing it is a very simple way for them to find us. I can't stay off-grid forever, though. And what if he's gone after my mum and dad? Or my siblings? What if he's out there now, torturing them, hurting them, branding them to get to me?

'You look like you've not slept a wink all night,' Ned says.

And then there's the Ned Factor. I'd conveniently dropped that out of my thoughts last night.

'Coffee?' I ask, spinning towards the kettle I'm standing in front of so I don't have to face him.

'OK. Yes, coffee. And maybe addressing the awkwardness before it starts to take root?' He stays on the other side of the room, thankfully, as I flick on the kettle. My hands are trembling as I open cupboards looking for mugs. I just got one out for myself, but with all this awkwardness about, I've forgotten pretty much everything.

'I don't even know if you have milk in your coffee,' I say brightly.

'All right, so you regret it. And you're probably back to hating me.'

'I don't hate you, Ned.'

Morning-after pill. I have to add that to my list of things to deal with. Yes, he pulled out at the last minute, but I've known since before I started having sex that withdrawal is one of the least safe methods of contraception and with my luck . . .

'Well, that's something, I suppose. But you do regret it, right?'

'No, I don't regret doing that with you last night.'

'Good. That's good.' He pauses for a long time. 'I really don't regret it. In fact, I'm kind of hoping we'll do it again, sometime soon? How about you?'

I turn to face him at last. His eyes seem a darker hazel this morning. Or maybe it's the way the light comes in through the portholes. He's got on a white T-shirt under a purple-checked shirt, dark-blue jeans, fluffy white slippers. He's pushed his hair back and I can see the road map of his life in his wrinkles. Ned's face tells the world he's been on a journey, that he has seen many things and they have left their imprints on him.

'Maybe, who knows?'

He grins at me and I can't help but grin back. I need to get my head in the game. Pushing myself away from the side and going to meet him in the middle of the room is not having my head in the game. Smiling at him as he puts his hands on my face is not having my head in the game. Practically swooning as we kiss is not having my head in the game. It's the very epitome of not having my head in the game. And I don't care, to be honest. It's nice being here with my head well and truly out of the game; it's so much more liberating being firmly and decisively in this kissing game than it is out there, dealing with real life, adult reality, the things that stalk my world.

Somewhere over his shoulder, Ned's phone starts to ring, peeling into what we're doing like the cry of a baby.

'I thought you turned your phone off, like I did?' I say to him.

'I did, I just turned it on again to check my messages.'

'But people will guess we're together. If they trace your phone, they'll find me and Kobi.'

'Sorry, sorry, I didn't think. It's only been on for a few seconds. I'll turn it off now.'

As he goes to his phone to click it off, 'Muuummmm,' comes from the cabin area.

I bustle past Ned to get to Kobi. He'll be freaked out, wondering why he isn't at martial arts, when we're going to go home and how come I've let him sleep so late.

He looks like he used to when he was small, tucked up in his cotbed, waiting for a story or for me to talk to him until he fell asleep. I used to talk to him all the time. It was such a novelty, having someone there all the time, I couldn't help myself talking to him. And it helped get rid of those other feelings, which were sometimes so strong, so virulent in the first few weeks and months and years of his life. I was so ashamed they happened, so I used to combat them by talking to him, communicating with him, bonding with my son so the other feelings, those sharp, white edges, wouldn't find a space in our lives.

Kobi has the duvet right up to his ears, the smoothness of his almost-shaved head the only thing I can properly see.

'It's all right, Kobi, it's all right,' I hush.

My son pulls down his duvet a little so I can see the crinkle of his frown, the scornful derision in his eyes. 'Of course it's all right, Mum. Why wouldn't it be?' he replies.

'I just thought you might be a little . . . All right, never mind. Why were you calling me?'

'Are we going to live on this boat for ever?'

'No, no. Maybe a few more days, but not for ever.'

'But it's so nice, Mum. Why don't you think about it? You've got your own room and I've got my own room, and Captain Ned has his own room.'

'They're called cabins, as well you know. And he's not Captain Ned, he's just a man called Ned who owns a boat. And we're not living on a boat.'

'We'll see,' he replies.

'Excuse me?'

'You always say that about things that might or might not happen, so I'm saying it about this.'

This stubbornness, this intractable certainty about particular things is all me; every last drop of it comes from my DNA.

'What do you want for breakfast? You can choose from Rice Popperz with milk. Rice Popperz with water. Rice Popperz without any liquid. And . . . no, that's it, those are your three breakfast choices so far. Which would you prefer?'

'I'll take the Rice Popperz, please, Mum.'

'And would sir like to drink either water or the rest of yesterday's juice?'

'I'll have a black coffee please, Mum. Easy on the sugar.'

'Water it is then.'

'Can I have breakfast in bed?' he asks, already sinking back beneath the covers.

'If you want,' I reply. 'I'll bring it to you soon.'

Ned is standing in the corridor outside Kobi's cabin. He is pale, his features set like granite in the stone-greyness of his face. When I leave Kobi, he moves quickly towards the living area.

There is cement lining the bottom of my stomach, where my heart plummeted after seeing his face.

'Is she dead?' I whisper, clamping down my teeth to stop myself from crying. 'Has he killed her?'

His eyes are wide, ringed with red, the whites are bloodshot. He looks terrified, absolutely petrified by what he has seen. But he shakes his head: no, he hasn't killed her; no, she isn't dead.

He holds out his phone. I take the black rectangle from him.

He has a photo up. A woman lies face down on a stone floor. She looks like she's had her head caved in, from the way her thick, black hair is matted with blood. *Why is he looking at this stuff?* I look up at him, confused and disgusted. *Why is he showing me this?*

Hang on, is that . . . ? I look down at the screen again. *It is!*

It's Detective Foster. I almost drop the phone in fright. 'What's going on?' I ask him. Why is someone sending him photos of a beaten-up, possibly dead, Detective Foster?

'Scroll on,' he whispers.

Breathe, breathe, breathe. Calm, calm, calm.

I use my trembling finger to move the message on.

A woman sits on a chair in the next picture. She is average height, average size. Her skin is a warm brown and her mouth, which is used to smiling, is a straight line of fear. Her long, beautiful plaits are pulled back into a ponytail. Around her eyes is wrapped an orange silk blindfold. Her hands are behind her and from the angle of her body, the discomfort apparent in every muscle, I can tell she is tied up.

Sazz.

Sazz has been taken by The Blindfolder.

'Read the message,' Ned murmurs.

I don't want to. I don't want to know what he's done to her, what he's going to do to her. I don't want to know. I don't want any of this. I just don't want to know.

Breathe, breathe, breathe. Calm, calm, calm.

I gather all my strength, force it into every muscle and force myself to read the message.

It's time for you to meet your destiny, Pieta. You always knew this day would come. Bring my nephew with you. If you don't, the delightful Sazzleoj here, dies. It's really that simple. And if you go to the police, she'll be dead before they break down her door. You, me, your son. Be here by noon. Callie

Part 9

Pieta

Saturday, 13 July

'Before we go in there,' Ned says, stopping me from leaving his car. I sit back in my seat and stare out of the front windscreen. 'Let's make plans for afterwards. I was wondering . . . thinking, that we could, possibly, you know, go away together?'

I have to look at him as I ask, 'Pardon?'

'When this is all over, how about you, me and Kobi go sailing around the country? It'd be awesome.'

'It would be totally awesome,' I say, sounding like Kobi. I know why he's suggesting this – to give us something beyond what is coming – but I can't commit to anything. I want to live, and I want to believe that I'll get out of this alive, that Ned will, that Sazz will and that DI Foster will recover in hospital. But I don't know if that will happen. I don't know if I can go into another situation that threatens my life and come out of it alive. That's why I had to take my son and hide him as best I could in the time I had.

Ned grins at me. 'I know it's only been a nanosecond since this began, but I'm falling for you, Miss Rawlings. Really hard.' He reaches out to put his hand on my face. 'I really want you and Kobi to be a big part of my future.'

I lean forward and push my lips onto his instead of saying anything. I can't answer that, I can't say something similar because I don't know what is going to happen. I don't know if I'll be around to be part of anyone's future. I mean, in real terms, this could be the last time I get to kiss anyone. And it wouldn't be so bad if the last man I kissed was Ned, but I don't know how I feel about him, not really. Last night was incredible, and we've come to mean a lot to each other in this briefest of points in our lives. But how would I feel about him if The Blindfolder wasn't breathing down my neck? Would I want me and my son to go into the future with him? I don't know and I don't have time right now to work it out. So kissing him is the best I can do.

We break apart and rest our foreheads against each other, breathing deeply. I'm trying to get strength from this. I have to get strength from anything I can.

'Shall we get on with it?' he eventually says.

Before he can get out, it's my turn to stop him, hold him back. 'Thank you, Ned. For everything.'

'Not a problem.'

Jody

Saturday, 13 July

I feel humiliated.

I should do, as well. I can't believe I've got myself into this mess.

I woke up just as I was being dumped on the floor. I tried to open my eyes but I had something tied around my face. I could tell, though, it was daylight and I had been out for hours. Before I could react, or even move, someone grabbed my wrist and cable-tied it to something. From the faint bubbling sounds, the near-silent shushing, I guessed it was a radiator. They had taken me somewhere, which suggests they drugged me to keep me unconscious. All of this added to the feeling of humiliation. I was suspicious of Callie, but all along I thought she was in his thrall. I never imagined she was a part of it. No, not just a part of it. From the way he kept looking to her, she was clearly the mastermind.

'Are you sure she'll come?' Ross/The Blindfolder asked.

'Yes. For the millionth time, yes,' Callie replied, her frustration not even barely restrained. 'This is her nanny. She will come because she will want to rescue her.'

'That's what you said before about that one. And she didn't bring them.'

'I overestimated how important I was to the police. I thought good old Jody would do anything to get me back. That's not the case here. Pieta has known this woman for years. She *will* do anything to get her back.'

'But do you think she'll bring the boy?'

'Oh, for pity's sake, when did you get so needy, Brett? You're being pathetic.'

Brett, his name was Brett, not Ross.

'I just want to see him. I just want to see my son, hold him.' Brett's voice softened to the point it sounded like he had genuine feelings for the boy. 'I still can't believe it. I've got a son. She had my baby. I told you she cared for me. She cared for me so much, she had my baby.'

He was delusional. That must have helped him to do the things he did. I'd been a bit surprised that they thought I was going to bring Pieta and her son to them, but I was completely taken aback that they thought it would happen today.

It didn't matter who they kidnapped and threatened, there was no way Pieta Rawlings would put her son in harm's way. That pointed very clearly to sociopathic tendencies on Callie's and Brett's parts, even if you ignored the obvious with the murders and torture. Neither of them could put themselves in someone else's shoes enough to realise that Pieta may come herself, but she wouldn't be bringing her son.

'Do you think she'll let me see him?' Brett asked. 'Regularly. Like a proper father? Because I am his father. He's my son. When I make it right with her, do you think that will work?'

'Yes, Brett,' Callie replied. Callie clearly didn't think that was the case, but was humouring him. I could hear the irritation in her voice, the incredulity that he thought it would happen. 'I think she will. But not looking like that. You don't look like dad material right now.'

'You're right, you're right. I need to show her that I can be a father to our son, that I can parent with her, maybe even get together with her properly, so I'd better get cleaned up.'

'And I'll go and get a few more chairs,' Callie replied. 'Be good, ladies.'

Two sets of footsteps left the room and then I heard them going upstairs.

'Hello?' I whispered, 'Is there anyone there?'

'Yes. I'm here,' a young female voice replied. 'What's your name?'

'Detective Inspector Foster,' I said, still whispering. 'What's your name? Are you blindfolded?'

'My name's Sazz, and yes, I'm blindfolded. I don't understand what's going on. This man knocked, said he had a delivery. He had a white van double-parked outside with the side open like a delivery van. I opened the door and he just shoved me in . . . What's going on?' They'd obviously brought me to her house to try to get to Pieta again.

'I was investigating something these people did a while ago. Do you know Pieta Rawlings?'

'Yes, I take care of her son.'

'Right. The woman is the one that Pieta interviewed recently.'

'I read that. Were they talking about Kobi, Pieta's son, just then?'

'Yes.'

'Is that man Kobi's father, then? Did he hurt Pieta? I always thought Kobi's dad was a waste man, that's why she didn't talk about him. I didn't realise he—'

We both stopped talking as we heard footsteps on the stairs.

'Oh, don't mind me, keep chatting,' Callie said, returning to the room. 'I suppose I should have introduced you. Jody meet Sarah, Sarah meet Jody. You both know Pieta Rawlings and she's going to be the reason why you both die.'

Neither of us reacted to her dramatic statement, but I knew she was going to do it. I wasn't sure if Sazz had any real idea.

After Callie returned, we sat in silence, waiting, until now. Until I jump at the loud, unexpected knock on the door.

'They're here!' Callie trills. 'Isn't that great, girls, the gang's all here.'

Pieta

Saturday, 13 July

I've been to Sazz's house three times in all the time she has looked after Kobi. Once to bring her home when she wasn't well, and twice to drop off birthday and Easter presents Kobi insisted that she had to have on the day.

I've only just realised that she has been a huge part of our life, but we've never really been a part of hers. She's had boyfriends over the years, but no one that she wanted to be serious about. She goes on holidays with her sisters, and the pictures of them together are always oozing with happiness. She has many tales to tell, always something funny or silly or just part of who being Sazz is. Kobi once told me that Sazz is his best friend who's an adult.

'And what about me?' I'd replied, completely affronted. I thought I was the most important person in his life, but no, Sazz had apparently beaten me to that particular post.

He'd replied, 'You're my mother, you can't be my best friend.'

Sazz is a huge part of Kobi's world, of my life, I have to do everything I can to save her. *Everything*. Except sacrifice my son.

I pull my stripy armwarmers into place, use them to steel my courage, then knock on the door.

I've had a lot to process in the last few hours and I've had a lot to do, as well, to be able to get here for as close to midday as possible. I'm guessing she gave me all this time because she has had stuff to do, too.

I'm sure, like me, none of her stuff involved the police, either. Obviously I don't know what the situation is with DI Foster, and I never really met any of the other police officers, but I know Callie is serious. I know she will kill Sazz without a second's thought – because anyone who would have herself branded so she can go and lie to the police has proven herself to be someone who does not make idle threats.

I am sure Callie has killed before. I'm sure she was there while I was being held. I'm sure she has done a lot of things to draw me out.

I don't know why, though. In all the processing, I haven't worked out why she would do this. Why she would subject so many women to the abuse and torture? Why she would devise something so difficult for them to do? Why kill them?

Callie opens the door dramatically. 'Hello, Pieta,' she says with a warm, genuine smile. 'So good of you to come.'

My original plan had been to rush her, punch her out and go to find Sazz. We were about the same height, I'm slightly larger than her, I reckon I could take her in a fight. Or, at least, overpower her. But I have to ditch that plan, and instead try to make up a new one as I go along because Callie Beckman has a gun pointed directly at me.

Pieta

Saturday, 13 July

Callie's smile, which is all the more menacing for how warm it appears to be, dims a little when she sees Ned standing behind me.

'I said to bring the child, not *him*,' she snarls at Ned.

'He got the text before me, so he came with.'

'Where is the boy? I told you to bring him.'

'You knew that I was never going to bring my child here, didn't you,' I state. Although, from the look on her face, it's clear she did think I would. She actually thought I would do as she ordered because she had ordered it. Callie is used to people doing as she wants. It's not surprising since she has managed to manipulate us all over the last few weeks. Rather expertly, too. She played on every single prejudice we have about who would be a worthy victim, and she told me so. She constantly told me: *'I'm not a proper victim'*.

'Not even for dear old Sarah?' she sneers.

Like her brother, I have had to work out how to handle her, especially now that overpowering her isn't an option. I'm pretty sure she doesn't respect weakness. She will expect me to be weak now, suppliant. She will expect the begging to start and that will only lead to her killing me, killing Sazz and killing Ned because we would not be worth her time. But at the same time, I can't be defiant. Defiance suggests I am in fear of her, that I need to stand up to her because she thinks she is somehow above me.

In the processing I have done, I have put together in my head as much stuff about her as I can and I have worked out that to deal with Callie, I have to be me. I have to be the me that Lillian sometimes sees and backs away from because she knows she's crossed a line that will make me bite back.

'Are we doing this on the doorstep?' I reply.

'Oh, goodness me! Where are my manners? Come in, come in.' She steps back, keeping her gun trained on me the whole time.

I've only seen guns on television and in the movies. I've always been against Kobi playing with them. I've 'disappeared' them if he gets them as presents and I've talked to him long and hard about making the right choices when he goes to friends' houses. I've turned a disapproving eye to nerf gun parties, to laser gun parties, to water guns he gets on the front of magazines and I've tried to speak to him about how, in the real world, guns hurt people, damage people, result in the most awful acts of fatal violence.

All the while, I've never actually seen one up close. This one isn't an old-fashioned grey metal pistol with a spherical barrel, this one is matt black, the barrel is square and the handle has a hatching pattern. It could be fake, but Callie isn't the type to have a fake gun.

'How have you got a gun?' I ask when we are inside the front door.

She scoffs at me. 'I arranged the abduction and murder or release of twenty-eight women without leaving any forensic trace, do you really think getting a gun would be difficult for me?'

Twenty-eight?

Twenty-eight women. *She* arranged that. *She* did that.

'Oh, look at your face. That bothers you, doesn't it? Because there were so many before you? If it makes you feel any better, we only started branding them with number three, when I realised we had to keep track of them.'

Stop, stop, I tell myself. I mustn't get distracted. I can't think about this. I can't think about her doing that to all those other women and keep going.

'There were no others after you, if that makes you feel any better, Pieta.'

'What?' I say.

'Oh, my manners again . . . Please hand me your mobile phones.'

Reluctantly, I take out my mobile and hand it to her. Ned does the same.

'Really, Pieta, this is your phone?' I got the cheapest pay-as-you-go I could get and it is hard to believe that it is all I have in this day and age.

'I don't like to be tracked,' I reply. 'And since someone started tracking me, I had to ditch the other one and this is all I'm left with.' I raise my arms. 'You can search me if you want.'

She grudgingly accepts this and indicates to put them on the floor. She immediately smashes them with her heel, making sure if we were being tracked or were going to call for help at some point, it won't now happen.

'This way, come on.' She moves back through the small, terraced house that Sazz lives in. I've been trying to work out how she found out about Sazz, where she lived. I can only guess that she had her followed.

My heart turns over when we enter the living room. Sazz is in the middle of the room, tied to a kitchen chair. Her arms are cable-tied behind her, her ankles are cable-tied to the front legs of the chair. She has a blindfold around her eyes and she looks exhausted. Her checked shirt is hanging off her left shoulder, exposing the strap of the white vest she has on underneath. Her whole body is slumped. I don't know what Callie has done to her, but she looks like she has been through a lot.

My instinct is to run to her, untie her, hug her, try to save her, but that will not help. It's much more likely to encourage Callie to harm her.

Please forgive me, I say in my head as I turn away from her. My heart flips over again when I see DI Foster. She is on the other side of the room, cable-tied to the radiator. Her usually neat black hair is messy, a part of it is a mass of congealed blood. Her dark suit is dishevelled, her white shirt is flecked with blood and her body is slumped against the wall underneath the window. She looks dreadful, as though she can't move, as though she has been through an ordeal as well and is teetering on the edge of not surviving it. She is also blindfolded, so I can't tell if she's awake or not.

I say nothing to either of them, although everything in me is crying out to. I can feel Ned close to me, but he is silent, too. Probably taking his cues from me, probably trying to work out what he can do without getting himself or one of us shot. Because that's what I'm doing; I am running through scenarios that do not end up with one of us seriously injured or dead.

I have to take on Callie. That's the immediate task. I have to engage her, to keep her focused on me and on not harming anyone else.

I turn my attention to her, my gaze sweeping over her – I note the colour sitting high on her cheekbones, the wildness of her dark-green eyes and the deliberately combed and styled nature of her hair. In the midst of all of this she has paused, more than once I'd guess, to fix her hair.

'What do you mean I was the last?' I ask Callie.

'I have a seat over there for you, please take it.' She uses her weapon to point to it. 'And you, take the other one,' she says to Ned. 'It was meant for the boy, but never mind. You'll do, I suppose. God knows how many times I've seen you making puppy-dog eyes at her.'

Instead of arguing, Ned and I do as we're told. But I sit in the seat intended for Kobi and now Ned, instead of my designated one. It's on the left of Sazz, and nearest the door.

I glare at Callie. The atmosphere in the room is heavy, over-burdened with the responsibility that I have right now. Everyone's lives are rested on my shoulders, on my ability to deal with Callie like I deal with other difficult people. 'How could you do that?' I say to her. I'm not playing her, I'm genuinely stumped about this. 'How could you do that to all those women? To have them abused, tortured and murdered? How could you do that to another woman? Let alone twenty-eight of them?' I shake my head. 'Just how could you?'

'Why does it surprise you?'

'Because you're a woman! How could you do that?'

'Because I'm a woman.' She twists her lips into a bitter little smile. 'Ah, the refrain I've been hearing all my life. Because of the sisterhood? Female solidarity? We're fed all that from such a young age and it's all such bollocks, isn't it? Where is the female solidarity when a woman starts fucking her best friend's husband? Where is the female solidarity when a woman screws over a work colleague by wanting to "see both sides" with a man accused of assaulting someone because she likes him? Where is the female solidarity when it comes to voting for someone who will damage the lives of women in general but will help you personally? Where is the female solidarity when supporting a "sister" doesn't fit in neatly and completely with something that's going on in your life?'

She moves to stand in a part of the room where she can see everyone, can protect herself from any sudden moves.

'Besides, aren't I the ultimate feminist? Anything a man can do, I can do too?' She shrugs happily. 'I proved that. Women are equal to men.'

You're sick, I want to say. 'Why? You've explained how you can do it, tell me *why* you did it?'

'My brother turned off the video after the first couple of hours with you,' she says, ignoring my question. Ignoring my question and trying to distract me by distressing me. 'Too special, apparently. I wonder, though, if it's because he did things to you that even he knew would be too sick to be seen by anyone else?'

I can feel myself slipping. I'm about to slide back into remembering.

'Why don't you tell your friends here what he did to you? How

416

he kept doing it for the whole weekend and then, at the end of it, you asked for more. How you begged him to let you stay for another twenty-four hours because you couldn't get enough of it.'

She's not going to win, I decide. When I was with him, I wanted to live and I wasn't going to let him take my life away. With her, I want everyone to live and I'm not going to let her take them away by doing and saying things like this. I have to ignore it. I can feel and collapse and hurt later. Right now, I have to stay focused. 'Why did you do it? What was the reason for you killing and abusing all those women?'

Callie grinds her teeth; the action ripples her displeasure across her cheeks. She doesn't like this. She wanted to get to me and it hasn't worked. 'I forgot, you love a good story, don't you?' she says, trying to recover her position. 'You love to listen and investigate and empathise.' She rolls her eyes. 'You're so fucking worthy, I could puke.'

'I was only able to listen because you were so willing to talk. I think there was some truth to what you told me. That's why I want to know why you did it.'

'You really want to know?' she asks with a smirk on her face.

'I think you really want to tell me, actually.'

Callie

Saturday, 13 July

You want to know why? Here is why: because I am not a victim.

I keep telling you people that, and you keep not listening. I am not a victim and whenever someone tries to make me one, I come back fighting.

I had the best life. I was so loved. *So* loved. My father, he gave us everything. We moved to the countryside and we got a big house. Our lives were perfect. If you talked to my brother, Brett, he wouldn't say the same. But he was always so much fucking bother. He was constantly in trouble, always making our father put him in his place. It was what it was. None of us is perfect.

What I'm trying to tell you is that life was good. For me, life was perfect.

Then it started to change. Slowly at first, in such tiny increments that it took me a while to notice. Daddy was out later and later, he came home less and less. He started travelling more and more 'for business'. He started shouting at my mother, he started disciplining my brother more often. He was cold to me. He didn't seem to love me as much.

Have you ever had that? Someone withdrawing from you? They pull away, little by little. They stop listening, their eyes stop lighting up when you share your news, their eyes glaze over when you want them to look at what you've done. And in the end, they pull away so far they disappear.

I was twelve when I realised my father had a new life that didn't involve me. He had a separate space and time and a place that made him smile, put a spring in his step and made his already perfect world complete. That's what he said about the whore he hooked up with: 'She makes my life complete.'

And then he left. I thought my mother would stop it. I thought she might change, that she would do everything in her power to keep him. You know, dress up for him, cook his dinner better, have more sex with him. Anything. *Anything* that would mean he would stay. But no, she couldn't do that, could she? She couldn't put up a proper fight for the man I loved. If she couldn't do it for her, why not do it for me?

He left on a Friday night. He packed his bags right in front of us, in front of me. I was his little girl, his princess, he called me, and he just put his stuff into expensive, matching suitcases, got in his car and drove away. No, that's not right. Before he left he told my mother she was useless, he told my brother he was worthless and he told me I wasn't enough to keep him. He loved me, I was the best of them, but I wasn't enough for him to live this life any more.

My mother. She cried. She cried those awful tears that make a woman ugly, show her to be weak.

Despite that, I wanted my mother to hold me, to hug me and tell me it was all right. We'd never been that close, she was always trying to control what I wore, where I went; she was always telling me that girls are difficult, girls can be so bitchy, girls cause so much trouble. But I needed her. I needed her to hug me and tell me it was going to be all right.

And do you know what my mother did? She took a bottle of wine from the wine cellar and then she went to bed. It was Friday evening. My father had left, my brother was kicking a ball against the garden shed and my mother took to her bed.

I went after her, begging her to love me, to hug me, to acknowledge I existed. My father had just proved I didn't exist, so I wanted her to do it instead. She pulled back the covers and then got in and closed her eyes just before she pulled her silk sleep mask down into place.

And she didn't open her eyes again until Monday morning.

She didn't drink the wine, she didn't get up to go to the toilet, she didn't do anything but lie in bed with her eyes closed.

She messed herself, but she didn't care.

I begged with her to talk to me and she didn't listen.

I cried for her to hold me and her arms stayed where they were.

I even got Brett – her favourite – to talk to her and she wouldn't budge. She just lay there, a woman displaced.

I needed my mother, the first time I had ever really needed her and she wasn't there for me.

That's when I started to hate her.

Really hate her.

She tried to make up for it afterwards, of course. Couldn't be more sorry, crept around me begging for forgiveness, trying to buy my affection, but it was too late. TOO LATE.

I NEVER forgive.

But, you know, my mother was weak. Her crying told me that. Her inability to keep my father told me that.

Do you know who I couldn't forgive? Who I *wouldn't* forgive? The woman who stole my father.

People always say that he was an adult, a human, that you can't steal someone who isn't willing. But I knew, even then, it was the other woman's fault.

And she was going to pay.

She was going to go through all that I went through. She was going to know what it was to put on a blindfold and hide.

I couldn't get her, of course, she never left my father's side. But I would get stand-ins. They were two-a-penny. And every time it would be like the day my father left.

Except this time, the other woman was going to spend forty-eight hours like my mother did, while I watched.

Pieta

Saturday, 13 July

'I can't believe that's the reason you did all this. You killed people, you tortured people and then you compound it all by publicly lying about being raped.'

'*I didn't lie!*' she screeches. 'Who do you think my brother started on first? He was always this weird kid that only one person in the whole school liked. He followed her around like a lapdog but she wasn't interested. She just wanted to be friends. And when his "friend" rejected him, who do you think he forced himself on? *Me*. That's right, me.' She is wild-eyed, furious. 'If my father had been home like he should have been, he would have stopped him. He would have beaten him to within an inch of his life, kept him in line like he used to. But no, he was off playing happy families with *her*. And my mother . . . how about this for female solidarity? I told my mother what he was doing to me, and she told me to stop tempting him. Her little boy couldn't ever do anything wrong, he was far too perfect. It had to be my fault, somehow, it always had to be my fault.

'And before you start to dismiss it as a bad childhood habit – he still did it to me. When we were adults, between hunts, he would . . .' She bares her teeth in anger, in possible agony.

422

'You know how awful it is, so how could you do that to someone else? Let alone all those someone elses.'

'Have you ever sat beside a woman who won't communicate with you for forty-eight hours? Who just climbs into bed on the worst day of your life and doesn't want anything to do with you again? I sat there beside her, talking to her, crying for her, begging her to let me know she was coming back to me. But no, she wouldn't. She "couldn't". And all because one of your lot decided she wanted a status upgrade.'

'One of my lot?'

'One of your lot.'

It's becoming clearer, everything is joining up. 'You mean your father left your mother for a black woman so in your mind all black women need to suffer? Is that what you're saying?'

She realises, despite wallowing in the depths of her righteous indignation, when I put it like that, it sounds a ridiculous reason to do it. She says nothing.

I start to laugh, mirthlessly, at her. 'Really? *Really?* There was I thinking you were a proper, real-life psychopath, with real, deep-seated reasons to do this, and really, *really* you're just a run-of-the-mill racist misogynist.'

'No I'm not.'

'Yes, you are. You hate women, you particularly hate black women. I bet you've always felt superior to black girls, and when your father chose someone you thought was inferior to you over you, it was the pathetic excuse you needed to get back at them. And that makes you a racist misogynist.'

'You don't know what you're talking about.'

'Of course I do. Your father, who I bet was Mr Respectability to the outside world, was an abusive arsehole behind closed doors but treated you like a little princess. You think that was a good thing, but actually it means he taught you from an early age that you should do everything you can to appease men, use your looks and a sweet nature to be more appealing. And to always see other girls as rivals. So you're always looking for a way to give yourself an advantage over other girls.

'I bet you idolised your father for the attention he gave you, never realising he was actually abusing you and controlling you to become his perverted idea of what a girl should be. But, boo, your perfect father also turns out to be a dirty skank who cheated on your mother. And then chose another woman over you – not your mother, *you*, his little princess, and that made you so mad. It must have been hell, going up to spend time with his other family, knowing he preferred them.'

'You know nothing of my life,' she snarls dangerously.

'Don't I? What you've been doing clearly shows me what your life was like and who you are. I mean, OK, like a lot of people, you feel wronged, so you seek revenge. But let's look at your payback, shall we? Do you decide to get revenge on men like your dad, you know, the person who caused the actual damage in the first place? No. Do you decide to hurt and humiliate women like your mother, who actually inflicted the emotional pain of shutting you out for forty-eight hours when you needed her most? No. Or, do you go after people who look like someone right on the periphery of your story? You know, the black woman who happened to shack up with your worthless father? Yes.

'Let's examine for a minute why that might be . . . Could it possibly be because, to you, women like her – like me – are not

424

human, not women like you so the insult of being left for her was too great to ignore? That's how you can get your brother to do that to them, to me, it doesn't count in your mind because black girls don't count.'

Callie listens to me with the kind of look that broadcasts how desperately she would like to kill me. I have exposed her for the basic, simplistic person that she is. She isn't complex and clever, she is just an everyday person who expresses her prejudices in a deadly way. And for showing how unremarkable she really is – she would *love* to kill me right now. She even raises the gun more decisively as she points it at my head. I remember during the interview she said that she had grown up around horses, around hunts, and she had learnt to use a gun. She won't miss from this distance, I won't be walking away with just a flesh wound.

My mind flashes back to The Blindfolder's knife, the patterns it traced on my skin, the nicks and cuts I sustained when he liked to play that 'game', and with that flash comes the wave of terror from knowing one move could finish me.

'I would love to kill you right now,' she says. 'But I haven't finished with you yet. You haven't suffered enough. You took everything from me and I need you to pay for that.'

You took everything from me! EVERYTHING! I want to scream, but I control myself to spit instead, 'I haven't taken anything from you.'

'*You took everything from me! EVERYTHING!*' she roars, mirroring what I was thinking. 'After you, he wouldn't do it again. The one thing that gave me satisfaction, that made me feel alive, and you robbed me of that. It was so simple. You had forty-eight hours to keep your eyes closed and you lived, or you opened

425

your eyes and you didn't live. Simple. All so simple. And it worked for years before you. We did it all over the country, and no one could touch us. No one could even begin to identify us. And then you. *You!*

'Because *you* couldn't play your part and be happy with it; *you* had to get ideas and talk to him, pretend to care about him. And after that, he didn't want to do it any more. He wanted you back or he wanted to find someone who cared for him.

'Can you believe that? He wanted someone who cared for him. Like I didn't take care of his every need. Even after everything he did to me, I fed him, I gave him a place to live, got him jobs working with animals, I found him an outlet for his sick fantasises and he tells me that he wants someone who cares for him "like Pieta", "like Pieta", "like Pieta." If I had to hear that *one more time*, I was going to kill someone. Else. I was going to kill someone else.'

She shoves the gun even closer to me, giving me a chance to look into the abyss of the barrel. 'You ruined everything. He felt so close to you, he didn't use condoms. Years and years of our good work and he just decides to go off-plan.

'Do you know how painstakingly I used to go over everything? How much time I would spend cleaning them, washing their clothes, clipping nails, combing hair, wiping and cleansing to make sure not one trace was left on them and he goes and does that? I could have killed him!' Her rage pulses through every word, every syllable.

'But that was all fine. You didn't go to the police, you didn't give them Brett's DNA and then here he comes, out of prison a reformed soul who wants to go to the police and confess. *Confess!*

'Thankfully my brother has always been spineless, he couldn't

426

do that without checking with me first. So, what was I to do? I had to promise him the one thing I knew he wanted more than anything – you.

'I explained to him at length it had to be carefully orchestrated, carefully planned. I had to find you, then find those other women, kill them, to get you to realise you were in danger, to draw you out. I had it all planned. If I did it slowly, it would hopefully give him a taste for it again without ever having to worry about you. But no, Pieta, Pieta, Pieta. That was all he wanted. That was all he would do it for.'

She shrugs. 'Fine, I thought, I will actually get you. I will properly search for you and then kill you. Simple. I will end you and then he'll have no choice but to start hunting again. But then, not so simple. You have a child. You have *his* child.

'And when he found that out . . .' She stamps her foot like a tantruming child, like a thwarted murderer. 'I knew I shouldn't have told him. But I thought he'd just want to steal the child. I thought that would be enough leverage over him so he'd do what I wanted again. But no, he wants to see you, talk to you, *be* with you. Be with you! He was even going to offer to turn himself in so he could have cosy little prison visits with his son. CAN YOU BELIEVE IT?

'What about me? Hmmm? In all of that, WHAT ABOUT ME?'

She gathers herself together, stops herself shaking with anger. The gun is so near, her finger so close to the trigger, it's likely that any more raging and she is going to take my head off without meaning to.

'The only thing I could do was put an end to his nonsense – permanently.'

427

Sazz gasps and DI Foster, who has been on the periphery of my vision, freezes. Callie must have done it here, if they both know about him. He must be in this house and he must be dead. 'He's dead?' I say through numb lips.

He's dead? The man who did this to me is really dead? He's not out there in the world any more, he's gone? I don't have to worry about looking a stranger in the eye and maybe seeing my son's features. I don't have to worry about Kobi meeting him. I don't have to worry about every little thing in case he comes back for me. He's gone. This is too much. I can't process that. Not right now. When there is so much to focus on, I can't take the time to process this information. I have to put this out of my head. Focus on the here and now. On surviving this. On making sure all of us survive this.

'Yes, he's dead. He's in the bathroom. Went up there to smarten himself up for your arrival. Have you ever heard anything like it? I came up behind him, stuck a needle in his neck.'

'You killed your own brother?' I say.

'No, Pieta, *you* killed my brother. *You* made me do it. *You* took him away from me, *again*.' Callie pauses for a moment to run her hand through her hair, to flatten her blonde strands. 'That's why I'm going to do my best to avoid killing you. I'm going to really, *really* hurt you instead.'

She leaves my side and moves to stand in front of Sazz and Ned. 'Which brings me to you two.' She puts her head to one side, staring at them both.

Apart from the gasp when she found out The Blindfolder was dead, Sazz hasn't moved, hasn't whimpered, hasn't even acknowledged that she is aware of anything that is happening. Ned is

staring at Callie and he doesn't look scared, or concerned . . . fascinated is the best way to describe it.

'If you'd done what I asked and brought your brat, things would be far simpler. It'd be a no-brainer who to kill.' She shrugs. 'So, I'm obviously going to have to track him down after this. And obviously I'm going to shoot her,' she says about DI Foster. 'But, before that, you're going to choose which one of these two dies.'

'Not going to happen,' I reply.

'Awww, are you having trouble choosing between the nanny and the school bully?'

My head snaps to look at Ned. Why would he tell her that?

'Oh, look at you, heartbroken because your buddy couldn't keep his mouth shut. What do you think we did that night? I tried everything I knew to get him to fuck me, and he wouldn't. What did he do instead? Talk about you.

'Although, your face was hilarious when you saw he was there that morning. Priceless. Almost as priceless as when I showed you the branding. I thought you were going to have a heart attack.'

I say nothing, just stare at her.

'Don't look at me like that, Pieta. All of this could be over in an instant if you choose. Nanny or bully? Bully or nanny?'

I know what she'll do, if I give even the slightest hint of engaging – she'll kill them both. Or kill the other person if I do choose. She's intent on making them suffer to make me suffer.

'You're spectacular,' Ned suddenly declares. 'I think you're spectacular.'

'Oh, here we go, he's going to beg for his life by telling you how much he loves you.'

'Not her,' Ned says, his gaze never leaving Callie, 'you. You're spectacular.'

Callie double-takes then smirks. 'Oh yeah, of course I am.' She rolls her eyes. 'You honestly think I'm going to fall for that?'

'It's true,' he says. 'I wouldn't sleep with you that night because you were vulnerable, you were a victim. I had no idea who the real you is. The real you . . . this you . . . you're spectacular. I've never met a woman like you.'

She falters, her eyes narrowing – she's not sure what to make of what he has said. *I'm* not sure, either. Because the way he is looking at her, the awe in his voice . . . No, no, he's faking it. He has to be. He can't mean that, not about her. Not when he knows what she's done.

'Callie,' he breathes. 'You are . . . I can't use any other word than spectacular. You've *killed* people. You've evaded the police for years. People only know now because *you* told them. Every part of you is special, and superior, and . . . you're spectacular. I've never met anyone like you.' As he speaks, his face softens, changes, alters. He looks at her like he looked at me when we were in bed together. He's looking at her like he's already, in his mind, making love to her.

This can't be real.

She is wary, unsure, as she listens to him. 'You know, I almost believed that, *almost*. But I'm not easily wooed like some.'

'I don't care what you do to me,' Ned says, sitting back. 'I know now that I could have been with you. You're something unique and I could have been with you because *you* chose *me*.'

I don't believe him and neither does Callie. 'OK, Nanny, your turn. You get to bid for your life, too.'

Sazz takes a deep breath in like she is going to speak, then relaxes out. Nothing more. She's not going to engage. I wonder what is going through her mind, what she thinks is going to happen next.

'Nothing? That *is* a disappointment. Especially when your rival here made such an impassioned plea.' Callie frowns. 'You're so young. You have so much to live for. Maybe you should tell me that you've secretly hated working for Pieta all this time and her son's a real brat, and you would mind very much dying for her. Because that's what your rival has done.'

'I didn't do that,' Ned says. 'I was . . . I want . . . never mind. I wasn't doing what you said.'

'Come on, Ned, tell me what you want.'

'I take photos because I'm always looking for perfection. I took so many photos of you, so many. Ask Pieta. I have hundreds, possibly a thousand or so, of you, because you are so close to perfect. And then I find out that beneath how you look, you've wielded so much power. It's intoxicating. It's like the final piece of your picture has slotted into place and I can see you are complete perfection.' He stares right at Callie. 'I want to be a part of that.'

Sazz gasps again. I think I do, too. DI Foster doesn't gasp, but from the way she holds her body, I can tell she is alarmed. Not because of what he says, but the way he says it. He means it. He's not playing, he's not messing about. He wants this.

Callie, despite her inability to feel empathy, hears it too. She is very still for a moment.

'What are you saying?'

'I want . . . I want in. I want to take your brother's place.'

Pieta

Saturday, 13 July

Callie laughs, the sound is loud and harsh as it hits the air. 'You want in? You want to take Brett's place?'

'You're not taking me seriously,' he says. 'Fine. Forget I mentioned it.' He sits back in his seat and stares desolately at the ground.

'I'm supposed to believe a goody two shoes like you has suddenly decided to come along and join my world? I don't think so.'

'Like I said, forget I mentioned it.'

Doubt flitters across Callie's face. She's not sure now if he's serious or not. I'm not sure, either, and I've spent more time with him than Callie has; I've been intimate with him.

'All right, if you're in, you have to prove to me that you'll do anything I want.'

Ned sighs before he lifts his upset, hurt and angry face to look at her. 'How?'

She and I are thrown again by his sudden change in demeanour and attitude – both of us are starting to think maybe he does want to join her after all.

'You have to kill the nanny.'

'No,' I say. 'No. No. He can't do that.' I lean forward to get a better look at Ned. 'You can't do that.'

Ned doesn't even glance in my direction. 'Why should I?' he says to Callie, ignoring me.

'It's something my brother would never do. I had to kill them. He would do all of those sick, depraved things to them, he would brand them, but he would never end them. That was always my job, something he called me to do. If you want to join me, if you really want to join me, you have to kill, too.'

'Ned, you can't do that. You can't,' I implore. There is real panic in my voice and I don't care if Callie hears it and knows she's won.

He holds out his hand. 'Give me the gun and I'll do it.'

'Ha-ha-ha!' Callie replies. 'You think I'm just going to hand you the gun? You think I'm *that* stupid? No. You have to do it another way.'

'Name it.'

'Succinylcholine. Sux. My drug of choice. It's far less messy. One injection and we're done.'

'Just tell me where it is.'

She marches over to me, places the barrel of the gun against my left temple. It is disconcertingly cold and heavy sitting against my head. 'Over there on the coffee table, in that black foldout bag, there is one syringe left. Go and get it. And just so you know, if you're faking and try something, I'll pull the trigger so fast your little girlfriend won't know what went through her brain. You break the syringe, I pull the trigger. You squeeze it all out, I pull the trigger. Try *anything* and I pull the trigger.'

'You can't do this, Ned. Just tell her you were messing with her. Trying to get into her head.' I watch him walk across Sazz's living room. It is calm, serene in here, everything placed and decorated to be very much Sazz. It feels like it was her sanctuary, her escape from the outside world. And we're violating, ruining it.

'Ned, please,' I say. 'Don't do this.'

He examines the syringe, which has a band of black around the top of its bright-red label. Then he begins the journey back across the room.

'Ned. Ned, listen to me. We've shared so much over the last couple of days. I don't believe it was fake. I don't believe the man who said all those things to me, who made me feel better, would do this.'

He stops then. And I sigh in relief. He turns to me with eyes that are flat, cold, lifeless. 'You don't know me, Pieta. You only got to know what I wanted you to see.'

I have to do something. I have to stop this. But I am frozen, frightened still by the gun to my head, terrified of never seeing my son again. How will I face him knowing I let his friend die because I was too scared to do anything? I want to run at him and knock the needle away, but my body will not move despite how much I command it to. I am literally petrified.

'I'm sorry, Sazz. I'm so sorry,' I say.

'I do this and we get to be together, right?' Ned says to Callie.

'You're really going to do it, aren't you?' she says, suddenly seeming to catch on that Ned isn't trying to trick her, he isn't simulating an interest in joining her. He wants to do this. He *is* going to do this.

434

'Yes, I'm going to do it. But how do I know you won't shoot me afterwards?'

'What?'

'You've killed before, what's to stop you watching me kill her and then killing me to double *Pieta*'s pain?'

'Oh no, only one of you has to die. In fact, only one of you *can* die. I need her to watch and experience that pain, and then I need the other person to be a permanent reminder. I need seeing the other person die to be so painful, she won't want to be around the survivor.' She shrugs happily. 'It's win–win for me. One of you has to end up dead. And it's looking like her long-serving, loyal nanny is the one who gets it today.'

'And we get to be together afterwards, right?'

'Yes, Ned. If you actually do it, then we get to be together.'

Happy now that he's been reassured that a psychopath will keep her word, he returns to Sazz. He roughly moves her plaits aside, exposing the soft brown skin of her neck.

Sazz begins to struggle, now that he's touched her and she knows what he's going to do. I remember that feeling of horror so well. At the end of the seventy-two hours, *he* injected me again. I remember in the seconds when his fingers brushed my neck, clearing a space to put the needle in – a savage terror spiked in my stomach. I'd cried out when he stuck the needle in. I thought that was it, that it was over and I wouldn't wake up again.

Sazz struggles, but her legs are tied to the chair, secured so tightly she can't do anything to stop Ned as he pushes her head to one side and raises the syringe.

Tears are leaking down my face, but I still can't move, my body will not do as I tell it and let me run across to save her.

435

Ned turns to me. 'Say goodbye,' he says before he brings the syringe down and fully depresses the plunger in one move.

'No!' I scream. 'No!'

Ned drops the syringe, takes a step back in shock at what he's done, how it will change everything. He manages to turn his head, to grin affectionately at me before he collapses.

'No,' Callie whispers, horrified, completely blindsided by what he has done. The gun slackens against my head, then falls away as she lowers her hand in shock.

I can move now. I can whip back my left armwarmer and take out the sharp little potter's scalpel I hid in there earlier, then I can jam it as hard as I can into her thigh, aiming for where the femoral artery is. Straight away I follow that with a punch to her stomach, driving my fist so far into her, she doubles over. She loses her grip on the gun, it clatters to the floor while she falls to the ground.

Callie moves to try to get her gun but I manage to kick it away, out of reach and towards DI Foster. Instead, Callie grabs my ankle and yanks me down with her. I fall hard, the impact winding me. She pounces on me, even though the scalpel is still in her thigh. Her punch is powerful, hard, and it knocks stars behind my eyes. I reel for a second, but block her follow-up punch and instead manage to grab the scalpel, dig it further in then pull it out.

She howls in pain, then rolls off me onto the floor, blood spurting out as the artery is uncorked. I scrabble to get up, and then go for her. I punch her once, twice, three times. Each blow finds its spot, splitting the skin on my knuckles.

We roll around, grappling with each other, trying to gain the upper hand, trying to hurt the other one enough for them to stop.

'Untie me!' DI Foster barks suddenly. 'Pieta! Untie me!'

I glance in her direction and Callie uses the distraction to hit me, push me off, then start to crawl away.

DI Foster has the gun. I want to go to Ned, to take him in my arms and cradle him, but instead I pick up the bloodied scalpel and crawl over to where the policewoman is tied up. It takes a few attempts to cut through the cable tie, but finally she's free.

'Where is she?' DI Foster asks once she has ripped off her blindfold.

Breathing heavily, on the verge of screaming and crying, I shake my head. I don't know, I don't care. Ned is dead. Ned is gone.

'Call the police. Call 999, but say officer needs assistance, OK? Tell them it's Detective Inspector Jody Foster, call sign number BNAI125.' She stops, grabs me by the shoulders. 'Pieta!' she shouts. 'Did you hear me? Call sign BNAI125, it'll get a quicker response.'

'I, erm, I don't have a phone. She broke it.'

'Stay here!' she orders and takes off running.

I sit heavily, staring at Ned. I can't comprehend that he is gone.

'Pi-R, Pi-R, what's happened?' Sazz says.

'The policewoman has gone after her. But Ned . . . Ned killed himself.' The last man I was with lies motionless on the floor, his hazel eyes wide open, not moving. 'He killed himself instead of you.'

'He's not dead,' she says. 'Listen to me very clearly, if it really is Sux she used, then he's not dead yet. Untie me and I can help him.' She speaks so calmly, so reasonably, as though the whole world hasn't recently exploded around her. 'Come on, Pi-R, untie me so I can help him.'

I go to her, use the bloody scalpel to cut the cable ties around her ankles and her wrists. She takes the blindfold off herself. She drops to her knees by Ned and looks him over, checks the syringe, then runs out of the room without saying another word.

She returns seconds later with a black medical bag. She throws herself on the ground again. I've never seen her like this. She's always animated, fun, ready with a joke and a laugh. But now she is serious, authoritative.

'It was a massive dose,' she says while rolling Ned fully onto his back. 'He's a big bloke, that will help mitigate it, but that was a huge dose . . .' She gently tips his head back, then covers his face with a green-tinged plastic breathing mask. Expertly and quickly, she attaches a large balloon-like airbag to it and starts to pump at it. 'You're going to have to take over, Pi-R,' she says to me. 'I need to check his heart rate.'

I skittle over, grab the bag and start to pump. 'Slowly,' she says. 'Rest your hand lightly on his cheek, so your hand doesn't get tired, and then pump like I was doing.' I do as she tells me and she reaches for her stethoscope. 'What we're trying to do is breathe for him until the drug wears off. If we don't, he'll suffocate.'

'Is he going to be OK?'

'He can hear you,' she says pointedly. 'He can hear everything you say.' *So don't ask again if he's going to be OK*, she adds silently. 'I need to call an ambulance. Do you have your phone?'

'She smashed it. And his.'

'And mine. Broke the house phone, too. I need you to keep breathing for him while I run to my neighbour's house, OK?'

I nod.

'Talk to him. Let him know everything's going to be OK. And keep pumping.' Sazz dashes from the room before I can remind her to call the police.

After the violence and the shouting, the blood and the threats, it's quiet, it's nearly silent. And it's just Ned and me.

Like last night. When we got together.

I don't know how I feel about him, but I know I don't want to live without him. I don't want it to be like this.

'Ned, it's me. Pieta. I need you to hang on, OK? You are not going anywhere until we've sailed round the UK. Erm, about that, by the way, I don't think I mentioned I get seasick, did I? I'm sure it'll be fine though. Of course it will. Yes, that's the sound of a woman trying to convince herself, isn't it? I obviously haven't told you . . .'

There's a clock in here, ticking. It turns my stomach, but I have to keep going, I have to keep talking and breathing for him, I have to keep trying to keep Ned alive.

Jody

Saturday, 13 July

I tear out of the house, run to the end of the front garden path and stop, searching this way and that for her and trying to get my bearings at the same time. I was unconscious when they brought me here, and I'm not from round here anyway so it's no use trying to work out where I am in relation to the police station, the flat or the centre of Brighton.

We're on a crescent-shaped road, near the apex of the curve so I can see quite far in both directions, but the right turn disappears out of sight first. I can't see her, there's nobody on the road. She's not getting away from me. I heard her say she killed her brother, so he's taken care of, but she is the brains behind it all and she does not get to escape this.

Blood. There was so much blood on the living room floor and the corridor. I look down, and there's a small pool of fresh blood at my feet. She probably stopped here, deciding what to do. The white van is nowhere to be seen, but there aren't any empty spots on this densely populated road so I don't think she's driven off.

Spots of red go off to the right, and that's the direction I take off in. The blood is quite bright, the spots quite large. Pieta

440

Rawlings must have injured her in a serious way. As I run, the spots turn into splatters, turn into pools, showing she's losing more blood. It doesn't seem to be slowing her down, though. At the curve of the road I can see further down the rows of large, semi-detached and detached houses but nothing – there's no one on the street at all, let alone her.

The parking is just as densely packed at this point of the road, and I can't see her. I can see her blood, though. Bright red, splashed on to the pavement at regular intervals. She must be bleeding heavily, but she seems to be able to carry on.

My head is still fuzzy from where she hit me. I don't know what she bashed me with, but it knocked me out in one go. I always thought that was a bit of an urban myth – something off the telly – because I've been hit plenty of times before, very hard and on the head, but I've never been knocked out.

Suddenly, a wave of nausea rises up from the pit of my stomach at the same time the Earth seems to stop spinning and I have to stop to violently sway. Concussion, probably. The pounding I can take, the nausea I can handle, the wooziness, I can't.

I have to stay still, hold my eyes shut for a few moments to steady myself. When I open them again, things are still blurry, still listing from side to side. But I look up and there she is.

She's limping, clutching her left leg as she moves. Is that a real image or a fantasy conjured up by my damaged brain? I shake my head, blink, shake my head again. It's still there, she's still there, running away. Thinking she can leave all of this behind.

I force aside the swimming sensation and take off again. This time knowing I'll catch her. She has to pay for what she's done. I have to get revenge on her for what she did to Jovie, what she did to all those other women. Harlow, Shania, Gisele, Freya, Bess, Yolande, Sandy, Robyn, Ioana, Carrie, Tonya, Jolene. And the others, the ones we don't know about. From all over the country, she'd said. I hadn't found any when I searched, but they may be dead, they may never have reported.

She doesn't get away with this. Any of it.

She's in sight, I'm getting closer and closer. She hears me, realises she's being chased and tries to speed up. But her leg seems to be getting worse, leaking more blood that drains away onto the street.

I stop a few feet away from her, plant my feet in the ground and raise the gun, holding it in two hands. 'ARMED POLICE! STOP RIGHT THERE!' I bellow at her.

My voice shatters the peace of the road, and will have several people running to twitch their net curtains. Hopefully one or more of them will call the police. We are on a flat, wide section of the road and Callie stops. She doesn't raise her arms, she just stops after trying to limp on a bit longer.

'Turn around,' I order.

She doesn't move. Her hands are still out of sight and it occurs to me that she might have another gun. I could shoot her right now. Say I thought she had a gun. But I won't do that. I won't shoot her in the back. I want to see the whites of her eyes, the twist of her mouth when I put a bullet or two in her.

That's shocking, isn't it? That makes you baulk, but this is where I am. This is where all of this has been leading to. Revenge, true revenge, means being willing to take that killing blow if you can.

'I SAID, TURN AROUND!' I shout.

Trembling, still clutching her leg, Callie rotates on the spot.

The wound in her leg is gushing blood, Pieta Rawlings must have nicked an artery, but the fact Callie is still going after such blood loss tells me a lot about her will to survive.

'Are you going to shoot me, Jody?' she says. 'Me? Can you really do that?' Her tone is soft, gentle. She talks like a victim; she speaks like a normal person.

Pain crescendos in my head and nausea swirls through my whole body, both things making me sway again.

'Are you all right?' she asks. 'I'm sorry I hit you. I . . . I panicked. Are you all right? You don't look all right.'

Her form becomes blurry in front of my eyes and I have to shake my head to clear my vision.

She points to a nearby house. 'Shall I go to this house? Call an ambulance? For both of us?' It's her turn to swoon, to violently sway. 'I'm losing so much blood. I need medical help.'

'Stop talking.'

'But Jody—'

'Harlow Gravett. Gisele Monte-Brown. Shania Devenish. Freya Occhino. Bess Straker. Yolande Calverley. Jolene Benkko. Sandy Vainna. Robyn Kiernan.' *Jovie Foster*, I add silently. 'Those are the names of the women you killed. Not your brother. You. Remember those names as you die.'

She puts out her hand to stop me. 'What about the others?' she says quickly. 'What about the other women whose bodies you haven't found? I know where they all are. I can take you to them.'

'I don't care where they are. You don't get to walk away from this. You just don't.'

'You might not care, but their families will. Their families will want something to bury.'

'I'll just have to tell them you said you didn't remember where they were,' I reply.

'You can't just shoot me,' she says. 'I'm not armed.'

'And I'll tell them you came at me, despite the gun. And even if they don't believe me, I don't care. I'm more than ready to do my time. With the number of women you brutalised and murdered – I'll be a hero behind bars.'

I can see it dawning on her that I've thought about this. I'm prepared to do this. 'You can't just shoot me!' she cries.

'Actually, I can,' I reply.

And pull the trigger.

Once.

Twice.

Just to be sure.

Part 10

Pieta

Saturday, 13 July

Earlier

'Oh for the love of . . .' Lillian rolled her eyes when she opened her front door. 'It's the weekend, Pieta, I do not have to deal with you or any of the others who plague my weekday existence. It's completely inappropriate for you to be here.'

She lived out in Ringmer, which was proper countryside – it always seemed to me more green than buildings. Her house was low and wide, with a vast amount of land around it. She had out-buildings and space for horses. She used to keep them but got rid of them recently. I only knew that because of the conversations I overheard; Lillian wasn't one for over-sharing apart from about her sex life. About that, no one could shut her up.

'Can I speak to you inside?' I asked her calmly.

She gritted her teeth and stepped back to let me in. I shut the door behind me.

'I'll get straight to the point: you're a fucking bitch, Lillian.'

She had so little self-awareness that she actually looked

447

shocked at that. Or maybe it was because those words were leaving my mouth.

'Oh come on, let's not pretend you're not. You play up to that role. But I also know, you're a good person deep down. Deep, deep down.'

'And?'

'And I want you to take care of my son for me.'

She started to laugh. 'You are funny, Pieta Rawlings.'

'Someone is trying to kill me. I was kidnapped from outside a London nightclub ten years ago. I was held for a weekend and told not to open my eyes for the entire time.'

'That's Callie's story.'

'It's my story, too. The person who did that is after me. And they want my son. I need to hide him with someone I know will look after him but no one would even think I would go to. That's you, Lillian.'

'Is this a joke?'

'I've never given my son to someone I haven't completely vetted before, Lillian. But I need you to believe me and I need you to look after my son.' I shed my jacket.

I'm doing this for Kobi, I reminded myself as I pulled my T-shirt out of my denim skirt waistband, untucked my vest. I took a couple of deep breaths, gathered the folds of my tops in my hands and then lifted them. Another couple of deep breaths before I turned and showed her.

Lillian, I'd always thought, was unshockable but she gasped when she saw my scars. 'Oh my God,' she whispered. 'Oh my God, I had no idea, Pieta.'

I covered myself up again. 'It's not something I talk about. But

I need your help. I need you to take care of Kobi for the next few hours. If I'm not back in twenty-four hours, I need you to call the police and my parents. Their number is in Kobi's bag. You mustn't give him to anyone except me or my parents. Not even the police.'

'This is serious, isn't it?' she said.

'Yes, Lillian. I wouldn't be here if it wasn't. I have to trust you. I have to trust that your reputation would stop anyone looking for him here.' I stared straight into her eyes. 'Can I trust you, Lillian?'

'Yes,' she replied without hesitation. 'Absolutely yes.'

On the drive over there, Kobi asked me more than once why he had to stay with Lillian. He'd met her a couple of times when he came into the office, and she'd let him sit in her chair and watch internet videos on her computer. He'd liked her, but had wanted to have more than simply, 'Because I have to do some-thing' as an answer. 'What about Sazz?' he kept asking. 'She's not available,' I repeatedly replied. He'd never been a child to accept a non-explanatory reply to a question.

I fetched Kobi from Ned's car, which was parked on the gravel drive, and brought him to her door. 'Can you write code?' Lillian asked instead of saying hello.

'Yes, of course,' Kobi replied, completely nonplussed by her lack of greeting.

'Right, well, that's good. I'm missing my coding lesson right now because your mum wants me to look after you. I think it's only fair you teach me some stuff in return.'

'OK.' Kobi shrugged. 'But I hope you can keep up.'

'Keep up, you cheeky blighter! I'll show you keep up!'

I got down on my knees and took Kobi into my arms. I held

449

him like it was the last time I was going to see him. Because, as far as I was concerned, it could very well be. I'd scrawled down a letter to my parents and one to Kobi. I couldn't explain everything to Mum and Dad, but I managed to get just enough in to let them know I loved them, and I knew Kobi would have a good life with them. To Kobi, I just told him I loved him, I was proud of him and he was the best thing in my life.

'All right, Mum!' Kobi had said, completely mortified that I was doing this in front of another human being. 'I'll see you soon.'

'See you soon, Kobi. I'll see you very soon.'

The police car pulls up outside Lillian's house and it takes me a while to get out because my whole body aches from the way I've been beaten up. My face is a sight to behold: my lip is split in three different places, the left corner of my mouth is puffy and sore every time I move, there is a gash above my left eye that is held together by five white strips, and there are scratches and cuts that extend down across my neck and chest. My split knuckles have been dressed to keep them clean.

I don't feel any of this. I'm aware of it, but I'm numb to everything. The world is going on around me, and I can't feel it. I just want to get to my son. I want to hold him in my arms and pretend that everything is normal.

Kobi shoots out of the house when Lillian opens her white front door.

'What's going on?' he asks as he runs into my arms. 'Why are you in a police car? Did you do something bad? What happened to your face? What happened to your hands? Were you in a fight?

Did the police arrest you because you were fighting? What's happened? Where's Captain Ned?'

Even though they're coming at me at a thousand miles an hour, the last question doesn't simply sail past, it rips me apart inside, opens up an earthquake that feels like it will never stop tearing itself asunder.

Ned.

I can't think about it, let alone talk about it.

'So many questions, Kobi,' I say. 'Can I get a hug before I even attempt to answer them?'

For the first time in what feels like a for ever, Kobi throws his arms around me without rolling his eyes or sighing first. For the first time in a for ever, I can hug my son, knowing I have nothing else to fear from his father.

Jody

Saturday, 13 July

'Guv', you are in so much trouble.' Laura tells me this.

It's like she thinks I haven't noticed the uniformed officer standing outside my room, and the handcuffs that keep me chained to the metal arm of the bed. But why would any of that get in the way of a moment of drama from Laura. I wish I'd known her at school. She would have been so much fun.

'I know, Laura,' I reply. 'It's nice of you to visit, though.'

'How could I not? I was told to stay away, we all were, but fuck it. If you can go off-grid, why shouldn't I?'

'Because you could lose your job, be accused of collusion, get arrested . . . ? Any of these things sound familiar?'

'Fuck it, you only live once. You know who *has* lost her job, though?'

'Who?'

'Karin Logan. Detective Constable.'

I laugh when Laura says it like that. 'I'm not laughing at her losing her job, by the way, just the way you imitated her. It was spot on. Why has she lost her job?'

'Only letting her boyfriend see the files, wasn't she? She was so pissed off with you, she showed him the files to let him see how much work you'd saddled her with. Instant dismissal. The Federation rep said he'll do his best to get her to keep her pension but given she was giving a serial rapist access to the case on him, it's not likely.' She wheels her seat nearer to my bed. 'He told us that. Think he was so shocked at what she'd done and didn't want to represent her.'

'Please apologise to everyone for me. Tell them I'm sorry, and that I'm so proud of the work they did. I hope it doesn't follow them around and I hope they can forgive me some day.'

Laura gives me a funny look, as though I'm being overdramatic. 'Forgive you for what? Everyone's totally behind you. You went off to face him down. Yeah, you went on your own and didn't tell us, but everyone thinks you're really brave. Even braver for not killing that psychopathic bitch.'

No, I didn't do it. I didn't shoot her. I was going to. Honest to goodness I was going to. I was going to avenge all those women they took. I could ignore the rights and wrongs of the situation, the fact we don't have a death sentence in this country; I could square in my mind the fact that Winston would have to find someone else because I was going to spend the rest of my life in prison. I could even balance in my head that I'd be taking a life.

And then . . . then it was like Jovie was at my side. I sensed her at my shoulder, I felt her so very near. 'Open your eyes, Jodes,' she whispered. 'Open your eyes, see who you really are. This isn't you. You don't want those families to suffer, for them to never know what happened to their loved ones. You don't want the story to become about you instead of them. The ones who were lost. Open your eyes, Jodes. Be the person I know you are.'

453

She was right. I couldn't let this become about me, the crazed police officer with the terrible secrets. It had to be about the victims. Everything had to be about the victims. If I hadn't made what happened to Jovie about me, she might still be here.

I discharged the gun into the ground near Callie's feet. To frighten her. And to pull the trigger because I didn't think my fingers would release themselves without yanking it. And then I did it again, just to be sure I didn't want to kill her.

By the time I'd made a tourniquet out of the belt from my trousers to stop Callie's bleeding – she had to live to face the charges – the other police arrived and I had to get down on my knees, put my hands behind my head and wait for them to secure the weapon.

I did everyone a favour by passing out just as a poor, unsuspecting uniform PC put on the handcuffs.

'Is my other half here yet?' I ask Laura to change the subject. I'm still not completely convinced I shouldn't have killed Callie. She is poison. She is manipulative poison. She will make people feel sorry for her, she will find a way to become a victim, too. And because her brother is dead, he can't refute any of her claims.

I've told an open-mouthed Detective Chief Inspector Nugent everything, handcuffed to this bed. He was a lot less angry than I thought he would be. Especially when I explained about Jovie. And, I suppose, I didn't actually kill anyone. 'You'll be on suspension for a while and you'll also be facing all sorts of charges,' DCI Nugent said.

'Not a lot I can do about that,' I said, trying to sound flippant. It bugged me, of course it did. It more than bugged me. I loved my job, I was good at it without letting it consume me, or change me. With my eyes open and my mouth even more open when necessary, I could be a police officer. All of that was gone.

He'd reluctantly smiled at me. 'It's a shame you went rogue, I would have liked you to transfer down to us. You've got an interesting way of doing things.'

'Don't worry,' I replied, 'I'm thinking of becoming a private detective. We'll still see each other.'

That made the smile drain away from his face. 'Don't even joke about it.'

'When you didn't come back, Guv', and all your stuff was there, I thought you'd gone off to . . . Let's just say I thought the pressure had got too much,' Laura says.

'You mean to tell me you didn't go through my mobile or the package I left on my desk?' I ask her.

Shifty-eyed, she shakes her head. 'Was I meant to?'

'I was told not to tell anyone where I was going, but I left my mobile unlocked with the text messages up so I wasn't technically telling anyone. I left the package The Blindfolder sent Pieta Rawlings on my desk. I left an extra copy of the map I printed out right next to my mobile. Are you seriously telling me you saw none of it?'

Laura looks embarrassed as she shakes her head.

'Some detective you are!' I say.

'Thing is, Guv', your desk is an absolute midden,' she replies.

We both crease up in laughter until a knock at the door forces us to tuck away the levity and remember the seriousness of the situation. I could be charged with attempted murder. There is nothing funny about that.

I tell whoever knocked to enter and the door swings open. Winston. Seeing him breaks something inside. I've been stoic, accepting and occasionally funny so far. Nothing has penetrated my exterior. But seeing him, standing there in all his normalness, crushes me.

'Babe, I was so worried,' he says as he rushes to my bedside. 'I called your mobile a million times. And your landline. I thought I'd be getting a death notification visit from your colleagues.' He takes me in his arms and I clutch at him, crush him to me. Then I cry. Properly cry. Like I should have for Jovie. Like I should have for Harlow, Bess, Shania, Gisele, Freya, Robyn, Jolene, Sandy and Yolande.

All their stories, all their ends, all their pain comes rushing towards me like an out-of-control wave. Winston holds on to me while I cry and weep and sob. All of it. He doesn't let go for even the briefest of seconds while I finally face all the secret truths and pain and horrors I've been hiding from.

At some point Laura leaves, but I don't notice. All I notice is Winston's voice saying over and over, 'It's OK, babe, it's OK. I've got you, I've got you.'

Part 11

Pieta

Thursday, 14 November

'Hi, Ned. Hi.'

I leave it long enough for him to reply. For him to open his eyes, and smile and speak to me. He doesn't, of course. He stays very still, in his bed, floating somewhere else away from this world. Away from me.

I can't believe he's gone and I can't believe I'll never get to speak to him again. I can't believe that and stay sane. No matter what, though, I've been forced to accept, to believe, that the longer he is in this coma, the less likely he is to wake up from it. I don't *want* to believe it, but that's what the nurses and the doctors tell me every time I come here. It's what they tell his parents and what Sazz has gently intimated more than once.

He was without oxygen for a bit too long, they've explained, his brain and vital organs were so deprived they may never recover.

Sazz visits him as well. We don't talk about it much, but she mentions if there's been any change (there rarely is). Sazz told me that while Callie had been ranting at me, oblivious to everything except herself, Ned had been whispering to her it would be

459

OK. That I'd make sure she was all right. That we'd all get out of there alive and in one piece.

'Lillian was off on one today. As I said before, she managed to keep her "fucking bitch-ness" in check for, what, all of two weeks? If that. Today's tantrum took all my strength not to let rip. But you know, I managed to keep it in. Thought of colours, thought of the very nice thing she did for me that time I needed her and let it go.'

This all still feels surreal. Four months later and everything is still quite surreal, mainly because of how easy it has been to slip back into normal life. Lillian reverting to type, *BN Sussex* still ticking over, me embarrassing Kobi in front of his friends, Sazz looking after him a bit more now because she has moved in. She couldn't stay in her house after what happened there and I begged her to stay with us until she had sold her place and bought somewhere else. It's almost as if a massive rock was chucked into the lake of my life – it made a huge splash and displaced so many things, but over time, everything has settled again, gone back to how it was with barely a trace of what happened.

'I know I say this almost every time, but I miss you. Which is the craziest thing because you were in my life in a positive way for a microsecond. I suppose you did make good use of that time, though.'

As well as Sazz moving in, Ned is the snag that stops life going completely back to normal. Coming to see him, talking to him, those are things that are out of the ordinary and make my days different to how they were before. I'm not sure if it's helping, or if it makes no difference, but I do it anyway. I have to see him. It's probably guilt, but it doesn't sit like an anvil in the cavity of my chest like guilt usually does, it doesn't scrape over my skin like the roughest edge of a grater, like self-blame usually does. Is it guilt? Is it affection? I don't know, but something keeps me coming back, still connected to him.

'I didn't want to say anything before, but my period started this morning. I decided not to get the morning-after pill after we had sex. I could pretend that I'd forgotten, but I didn't. You were in a coma and I thought . . . oh, I don't know, I left the choice up to Fate. And for a while there, I thought . . . I don't think I hoped I was, no, I definitely didn't hope, I just thought I might be pregnant. But I'm not.'

Ned's hand is heavy in mine when I pick it up, and cool. Not cold, because cold means something else. Something I'm not ready for.

'Now that would have been a thing, eh? Me and you, having a baby after everything. I'd have fun explaining that to Kobi. Oh yes, Captain Ned is the baby's father – after one night we both described as being "a very bad idea" and yet "most excellent". I could see how that would play out.'

I suppose it's the surface or the appearance of my life that hasn't changed, because underneath, everything has been stirred up, churned and agitated, and even though it's settled, nothing has quite gone back to where it was before. For example, Lillian has reverted to type – but she treats me badly like I'm an equal, like I am worthy of my title, position and wage. She has seen who I am and she has reassessed me, I suppose.

Another example is my social life, which has bloomed. No, no wild nights on the town, but no sitting in staring at the television while constantly waiting for my attack to catch up with me. No more hiding my trauma from the people who love me the most. My family know about what happened, about Kobi, and they are supportive.

Yes, on the surface everything is the same, unruffled and unscarred by the rock aimed in its direction, but nothing is truly an exact copy of what it was before.

I don't know what will happen when they formally charge that woman with everything that she's done and we have to go to trial. I have given several statements and I know that it is not over, not by a long shot, but I don't think about that for now. I'll deal with that when it happens.

'Look, I really wish you'd wake up. I don't know what for, other than I wish you were here and not where you are. I want to say take as long as you need, but the doctors tell me that's not good. They say that you need to wake up sooner rather than later. I'd prefer that, too. But, you know, if you're not ready, then you're not ready. I remember you said that we all do the best we can to get from one end of the day to the other. Maybe it's the same for you wherever you are. Maybe you're not ready to come back. Maybe you can't get to the end of where you are, yet. But I . . . I wish you would. I will be waiting for you when you do come back.'

I squeeze his hand, try to pass on with that touch all the affection I feel for him, all the gratitude for what he sacrificed for me.

'I'd better go. I've got a pottery class tonight. I'm making you some of that stuff I said would transform your boat. I can't wait for you to see it. You're going to love it. Talking of your boat, your parents have finally moved it into long-term storage. They didn't want to, I didn't want them to, but it's for the best. Their faces when I suggested they live on it instead. Not got much of a sense of humour, have they? But anyway, it'll be there, waiting for us to take our round-the-UK trip.

'Kobi sends his love, as always. I will let him come to see you sometime soon, but at the moment, I don't think either of us could handle his shock.'

I get to my feet, slowly.

'I'll see you tomorrow, OK? Bye, Ned. Bye.'

'How was your friend?' Reggie asks when I get down to the Eastern Road entrance to the Royal Sussex County Hospital. It's dark, but I can still see the sea from here, I can definitely hear the sound of the waves, I can still breathe in the salt and ozone rolling in from the water.

'No change.'

'Sorry to hear that,' he says.

'Thank you.' We stand awkwardly, both of us still unsure what is going on. He asked me out and I said yes as friends. We've been out doing stuff together as pals. A couple of times we've hugged for too long, we've stared into each other's eyes for too long, we've been a bit too near for too long. But mainly, truly, we're friends. Good friends. Close *friends*.

'Shall we?' He indicates to the direction of Brighton, to Mirin's place where we're going to paint a cup-and-saucer set.

I nod. 'Yes, let's.'

He holds out the loop of his arm and I slip mine through it. We're honestly just friends.

Because I can do that now. I can spend time with people, I can spend time with men, I can act like danger doesn't lurk around

463

every corner. And on the days when I don't quite feel safe, I don't quite feel able to connect with others, I can take my time. That's what I like about the way that the world has been altered after the boulder was lobbed into it – with everything, I can take it one day at a time, I can take it one minute at a time, if I want to.

In fact, I can take all the time in the world.

Jody

Thursday, 14 November

At the back of Mirin's Pottery Palace, Pieta Rawlings is concentrating on painting a cup. She has a sponge brush in her hand and is peering very hard at it while she applies turquoise to its round body.

It's her fault Winston and I are here. I discussed with my therapist that beyond work and television I didn't have any way to relax. I then mentioned that Pieta Rawlings told me how therapeutic pottery could be. I made a throwaway comment to Winston about it and next thing I knew we were booked in. I almost did a 'yeah, but' about it – *almost*. Instead I bit my thoughtless tongue and remembered his words about having one life to live and not giving up on things before I'd even tried. This is our fourth time. Last time we actually made fruit bowls on the wheel. This time we're painting our creations. Mine is so much better than Winston's but don't tell him I said that.

I suppose you want an update? I don't have a job and I don't not have a job, either. I'm on suspension pending review of all my cases. All of them. They're having fun doing that, especially as I know everything I've ever done has always been by the book. I'm not one of those people who cuts corners or omits things. So

465

far, I think, a couple of IOPC (Independent Office for Police Conduct) people have been disconcerted that they've found literally nothing out of place.

Technically, I haven't done anything wrong. I've never used any of the resources for personal gain or to fulfil a personal vendetta, it's always been to try to catch The Blindfolder (both of them as it turns out). Professionally, they're going to do everything they can to get rid of me. I doubt I'll keep my job, but that's all right at the moment.

We've moved to Brighton for now. It makes the investigation easier and I like it here. I love it here. Winston has to travel to London for work still, but being here on suspension is just as easy as being there on suspension. We're looking into buying a place, a big house by the sea so we can start the adoption discussion for real. At the moment there is too much up in the air to start thinking of bringing a child into it.

And what of the living half of The Blindfolder? She is, so far, playing to type: she acts like the pretty, beleaguered victim of circumstance, not the mastermind behind it all; she manipulates as she cooperates, teasing out deals and privileges whenever she can. But she is slowly, tortuously, revealing the burial places of the women who didn't survive forty-eight hours with them. She has shown them where she used to hold the women. It was a warehouse in East London. They told the people they hired it from it was a film set. They had done it up like their parents' bedroom so they could recreate that weekend when their mother took to her bed and wouldn't engage with her children for forty-eight hours.

DCI Nugent showed me the pictures as part of the investigation and me being a key witness. It was the creepiest thing I've ever seen. Even though it hasn't been properly used in ten years, it's still there. It'll be torn down once all the bodies have been found, I hope.

Of course, a trial date won't be able to be set until the investigation is complete and for now, *she* is controlling everyone by setting the pace of when that happens. Sometimes I regret not shooting her. (Oh, what? I'm not perfect.)

Winston and I have hustled through the door of the Pottery Palace, late and a little stressed. His train was late back, I didn't have dinner ready, we both faffed for far longer than necessary. We take our seats near the door, shed our jackets and get out the wine, which is when I spot Pieta Rawlings.

I have to admit that I do feel rudderless, like I am without direction and purpose, but then I no longer have the thing that has driven me for the last thirteen years, so that was bound to happen, suspension or not. But, in some ways, I think I was due a checking-out time, a reassessing period, an acknowledging losing Jovie interlude. That's what the therapy is all about.

'Hello, Pieta,' I say. I have to speak to her. It'd be stupid to sit in this small space and not do so, especially when I quite like her.

She glances up from her painting and does a double-take when she sees it's me. 'Detective Foster. Sorry, Detective Inspector Foster.'

'I don't have that title any more. I'm on long-term suspension. Just call me Jody.'

'You're called Jody Foster?' the man sitting with Pieta says. 'That is so cool.'

Both Pieta and I treat him to the same 'get over it' look and he mumbles, 'Or maybe not,' before returning to his painting.

467

'How are you?' she asks, now a bit softer since she knows I'm no longer officially police.

'I am good. I am trying pottery, thanks to you.'

'So you saying I was prolific wasn't an insult after all,' she says.

'It wasn't. Listen, Winston – that's my fiancé over there – and I are getting married in about three months, do you want to come? Can I send you an invite?'

A frown wrinkles her face. 'You're inviting me to your wedding?'

'Yes.'

'You don't do things by halves, do you, Detective? I mean, Jody? Most normal people would have asked a person out for a coffee or something, not *boom*, come to my wedding.'

'Is that a yes or a no?'

'It's a "coffee next week would be lovely, thank you". I've got your number, I'll call you.'

I can't help but grin. I need people in my life. This is what therapy has shown, living down here has shown – I need to, *want* to make more connections. I need to open my eyes, my life, my self to the world around me. I have Laura, who is my wonderfully dramatic friend, and I'll hopefully have Pieta, who I think has got the measure of me. I'm probably not meant to be in touch with either of them since they are part of an active investigation, but there you go.

'Happy painting, Pieta Rawlings,' I say before I walk away.

'Happy painting, Jody Foster,' she replies. She has definitely got the measure of me.

Callie

Wednesday, 25 December

'Thank you,' I say to the prison guard who clatters my meal tray onto the desk in my room. 'Thank you so much.'

He grunts at me. He always does.

'And Merry Christmas,' I say from my position on the bed with my knees pulled up to my chest. I try to smile at him but can't manage it without tears filling my eyes. I snatch my head downwards, hide my face from him.

'Yeah, Merry Christmas,' he replies gruffly.

'Thank you . . . thank you for being so kind to me.'

He grunts at me and moves to leave.

'I feel sorry for you having to work on Christmas Day,' I say. 'It must be such a strain on your marriage.'

He snorts. 'Yeah. Yeah.'

'Sorry, I didn't mean to upset you. I'm actually grateful it's you today. Makes Christmas feel a bit more like Christmas when I get to see a friendly face.' When I wipe at my eyes, smile at him, he reaches up and strokes his beard with his nicotine-yellowed fingers, offers me a small grin with his tea-drinker, chain-smoker teeth.

He's nothing approximating a challenge, but he'll do.

He'll have to. Because this current situation is not going to stay like this.

'Look, I'll see if I can get you some of the guards' Christmas pudding,' he says quietly. 'It's nicer than that slop.'

I'm going to get out of this. I promise.

'Oh, thank you. Thank you so much.'

And when I do get out of this, watch out, Pieta Rawlings. Watch out, Jody Foster. I am going to make all of them regret Jody Foster sparing my life.

I'm going to make all of them regret the day they were born.

Kobi

Thursday, 26 December

'Are you all right, Mum?' I ask her.

She doesn't say anything for a while. She just stands there, with her back to the sea and her hands up. She looks a bit shocked. Actually, she looks very, very shocked. A bit like 'Huh?'

'But . . .' she says.

I shrug. 'I said we should have stayed at home with Grandma and Grandpa,' I tell her.

'But . . .' she says.

'I said I wanted to stay home and play with my toys.'

'But . . .'

'I said Boxing Day wasn't the day to go to the beach.'

'But . . . Kobi, that seagull just took my pastry,' she says.

'I know.' I shrug again.

'And then his mates came and took my coffee. Two of them. Working together, they stole my favourite coffee mug.'

'I know.'

'But . . .'

She looks at me for the first time since it happened. I tried to help. I ran at the seagulls, shouting, 'Stop! Stop! Thief! Thief!

Stop!' I did my best but it didn't work. They took her stuff anyway. I didn't even care that everyone stopped and stared. I think some of the people thought I was shouting at a human thief.

'Oh, Kobi, this is just . . .'

I was going to draw those seagulls, to try to get a picture of them in case I see them again. But I won't now. She looks far too shocked. This is all going in my book, though. Every minute of it.

I take Mum's hand, she looks like she needs me to. Sometimes, my mum needs me to hold her hand or tell her how much I love her. I think this is one of those times.

'Do you know what the worst part of this is?' Mum asks as I start to take her home to Grandma and Grandpa.

'That I was right all along and the seagulls are plotting to take over the world?'

'Yes,' Mum says. 'That's exactly the worst part of it.'

I smile at my mum. 'Told you so.'

'Yes, Kobster, you really did.'

Normally, she's not allowed to call me that, but since the seagulls took her stuff, I'll let her off. This one time.

Acknowledgements

It takes a small village to create a single book, it honestly does. Here are some of the people in my village I need to thank:

My wonderful editor: Jennifer Doyle
The cover genius: Yeti Lamberts
My brilliant copy-editor: Gillian Holmes
Expert editorial co-ordinator: Katie Sunley
Proof-reader: Rachel Malig
Production: Tina Paul
Expert research help: Graham Bartlett and Vanessa Smith (who gave me the basics and I 'tweaked' to fit my purposes)
Additional research help: Katie Fforde, who so kindly let me spend time on her fabulous boat.
Marketing and sales: Vicky Abbott and Becky Bader
Publicity: Emma Draude and Annabelle Wright

And, thank you to:
My lovely family, who are my support system and without whom the books wouldn't be written; my cheerleader friends, who always have my back; and my splendiferous agents: Ant and James.

And, of course, thank you to you, the reader, for buying this book. I hope you enjoy it.